Praise for Reavis Z. Wortham and His Novels

"Reavis Z. Wortham is the real thing."
—**C. J. Box**

"The most riveting thriller all year!"
—**John Gilstrap**

"A masterful and entertaining storyteller."
—*Ellery Queen's Mystery Magazine*

"Entertaining and emotionally engaging."
—**T. Jefferson Parker**

"Wortham combines the gonzo sensibility of
Joe R. Lansdale and the elegiac mood of *To Kill a
Mockingbird* to strike just the right balance between
childhood innocence and adult horror."
—*Publishers Weekly*

"Populated with richly drawn characters, good
and (deliciously) evil, and propelled by some of
the best dialog you'll find in thriller writing today.
A true winner!"
—**Jeffrey Deaver**

"Reavis Z. Wortham doubles down. Aces high."
—**Craig Johnson**

"A hidden gem of a book that reads like Craig Johnson's Longmire mysteries on steroids."
—**Jon Land**

"Reavis Z. Wortham has once more made this literary (Texas) terrain all his own . . . This is a ripping good tale."
—**Jan Reid**

"Not just scary but funny too, as Wortham nails time and place in a sure-handed, captivating way. There's a lot of good stuff in this unpretentious gem. Don't miss it."
—*Kirkus Reviews*

"A gritty, dark, and suspenseful Western with a final explosive showdown that kept me turning the pages late into the night to see who would survive."
—**Jamie Freveletti**

HAWKE'S PREY

A SONNY HAWKE THRILLER

REAVIS Z. WORTHAM

PINNACLE BOOKS
Kensington Publishing Corp.
www.kensingtonbooks.com

PINNACLE BOOKS are published by

Kensington Publishing Corp.
119 West 40th Street
New York, NY 10018

All Kensington titles, imprints, and distributed lines are available at special quantity discounts for bulk purchases for sales promotions, premiums, fund-raising, educational, or institutional use. Special book excerpts or customized printings can also be created to fit specific needs. For details, write or phone the office of the Kensington sales manager: Kensington Publishing Corp., 119 West 40th Street, New York, NY 10018, attn: Sales Department; phone 1-800-221-2647.

ISBN-13: 978-0-7860-4176-3
ISBN-10: 0-7860-4176-5

First printing: July 2017

10 9 8 7 6 5 4 3 2 1

Printed in the United States of America

First electronic edition: July 2017

ISBN-13: 978-0-7860-4177-0
ISBN-10: 0-7860-4177-3

To the love of my life, Shana Kay.

Chapter 1

A low-pressure front pulled a cold white blanket across the West Texas high-desert landscape. The mercury dropped in a way the residents hadn't seen in over a hundred years.

Heavy snow falling on a thick glaze of black ice almost obscured the temporary Border Patrol check station on U.S. 90. It sat astride the smothered two-lane road running between Ballard and Marathon, funneling the westbound lane to the wide, flat shoulder. The most recent tracks through the station were almost covered by fresh snow.

"Asi, mierda!"

Mean as a rattlesnake and twice as likely to strike, the dark-complected driver slowed the dull white Ford conversion van. He straightened from his slump in the captain's chair as they approached the checkpoint. The weather at first surprised, then pleased him, though it made driving treacherous. The snow covering the slick surface gave them enough traction to reach Ballard. Had it been nothing but freezing rain, they might have wound up sliding into a ditch.

An attractive young woman with silky black hair rode in the other captain's chair. Both wore untucked and oversized Pendleton shirts.

The woman hadn't taken her eyes off the road since the black ice first appeared back in Ft. Stockton. She tensed at the sight of the check station and leaned forward. "I can't believe they're out here in this."

The driver stole a quick peek at the dimple in the corner of her mouth and turned his attention back to the road. "Me neither. This is the one reason we didn't come in from the south." Their plan was to avoid the permanent Border Patrol stations between the Texas border and the towns of Alpine and Marathon. "There's no telling when and where those bastards are going to show up."

She glanced over her shoulder at the passengers in the rear, then faced forward and spoke with a soft Spanish accent. "Stay quiet and follow our lead."

The tips of orange cones protruding from deepening drifts of white choked the van off the highway and into a narrow lane manned by five Border Patrol agents. A sandwich sign marked an open area on the wide, flat shoulder as the "Secondary Inspection." Beyond that, a five-strand barbed-wire fence separated the highway property from a ranch.

Agents in bulky green clothing warmed themselves in a tight group in front of a roaring portable heater that melted a wide semicircle in the fluff. The only tracks beyond that were foot trails around two white Border Patrol Tahoes parked parallel to the highway.

The television blared to life behind the couple, filling the van's interior with the deafening sound of an animated kid's movie. The woman's smooth face twisted in anger and she jabbed her forefinger at the driver's face. "I've had it with this trip! As soon as we get home, I'm filing for divorce. It'll be just you and these kids back there when I'm gone, *then* what are you gonna do?"

He steered into the funnel of orange cones. An agent stepped forward and held up a hand. Four others closed in and took up positions around the vehicle. The driver slammed the transmission into park. "I *told* you a vacation down here was a stupid idea!"

The woman glared across the van, thumbed the switch to lower the electric window. "They're *your* relatives! I don't want to stay with them!"

Her shrill voice boiled out in a rush of warm air and reached the reluctant backup agents who waited with their hands buried deep in the pockets of their parkas. Well-trained and hard-eyed, they were nevertheless victims of boredom and repetition, the same creeping malady known to lawmen and soldiers throughout the world. An uneventful month and the intense cold were the final ingredients to make the team complacent.

The driver lowered his own window, hung an elbow out the side, and rolled his eyes at the agent closest to the door. He spoke without an accent. "Want to trade places?"

The young commanding officer glanced at the driver, keeping one eye on the Belgian Malinois German shepherd at the end of the leash in Agent Baker's hand. The three-year-old canine sniffed the undercarriage.

"Good morning! I am Lieutenant Burke, United States

Border Patrol," the lieutenant recited. "You'll only be here for a moment. How many people are in the van?"

"Two adults and two kids."

As Lieutenant Burke spoke, three other men in crisp green winter gear converged on the vehicle, at the ready but listening to the conversation through the now-open windows. "Of what country are you a citizen?"

DeVaca ran fingers through black hair combed straight back. He adjusted the horn-rimmed glasses on his nose with one finger. "We're Americans, at least I am. My name's Lorenzo DeVaca, but I think she's from some other *goddamn* planet!"

The senior agent, Agent Carlos Flores, stepped up to the passenger door and forced a grin off his face.

Agent Stone stopped where he could see both the passenger side and the rear of the van, narrowing his eyes at the drawn shades behind dark, tinted windows. Taking up a position at the left rear, Agent Rivera glanced at Baker's dog sniffing the driver's side.

"Y'all on vacation?" Lieutenant Burke's questions delivered in a mild tone weren't casual conversation. They were designed to elicit a specific response.

"Yeah. Some *vacation*."

If the travelers stumbled, looked away, or gave any of the signals the agents were trained to look for, the lieutenant would ask them to proceed to the parking area for an inspection. "Where do you folks call home?"

DeVaca turned his full attention toward Burke. "Dallas, Texas, and this . . . this wife of mine is from Ft. Worth." He adjusted the glasses again. At the same time, his eyes flicked to the rearview mirror toward the darkness behind him.

The woman unsnapped her seat belt and twisted toward the rear and into a wall of sound from the television blaring *Finding Dory*. "You kids turn that shit down right now! No! I got a better idea. Get out. All y'all get out!"

She yanked at the door handle as DeVaca unsnapped his own seat belt. He grabbed for her arm and missed. "Dorothy! If you get out of this van, don't think you're getting back in!"

Burke's smile disappeared and he held out a hand. The fun was over. "Passenger! Ma'am, please stay in your vehicle!" His eyes returned to the dog sniffing without interest at the van's undercarriage.

Dorothy kicked her door open. "Kids, get out. Your father can go on ahead without us. We'll be safe here with these nice men."

The situation was spinning out of control. Burke pointed a finger at Flores. "Stop her."

Flores put his hand on the door, preventing it from opening all the way. "Ma'am, y'all need to stay inside."

The agents who'd been lounging near the big heater drifted toward the van to see the show, snickering and elbowing each other like junior high school kids watching the class cutup work his magic.

The van's side cargo door slid back, startling Agent Flores. He stepped forward to catch the handle. "Hey kids, y'all don't get out."

Lieutenant Burke reacted to DeVaca's partially open door and backpedaled from the argument unraveling right before his very eyes. "Driver, I said, do not—"

In seconds, a dozen things happened. Sharp cracks bit off the order as DeVaca produced a pistol from underneath his shirttail and fired. The 9mm rounds from a Glock 17 cut through Burke's jacket, but most were stopped by the agent's tactical vest underneath. He grunted, fumbling for his weapon with a broken right arm that refused to cooperate.

Dorothy produced a similar Glock from under her shirt and pulled the trigger. The first rounds slammed Flores in the chest, but as he fell back, the soft-nosed bullets stitched up his neck and face, blowing great gouts of blood across the white carpet behind him.

DeVaca dropped the pistol into the seat beside his leg and snatched up a CZ EVO 3A Scorpion from the floorboard. He twisted, planted his right foot against the front of the well-step, and spun to his left. Using the van's body as cover from the men behind him, he squeezed the trigger. The machine pistol awoke with the sound of a manic sewing machine.

The dog handler fumbled with the leash and his weapon. The vest under his parka absorbed several of DeVaca's rounds, but one struck Baker in the side of his throat. Blood from the mangled artery fountained against the van's large window like red water spurting from a hose. Ignoring the agent sliding down the vehicle's side, the killer lowered the muzzle and shot the dog.

The sliding door on the passenger side opened and a man called Lion hosed the stunned officers with a fully automatic H&K MP5. They dropped where they stood.

The van rocked on its springs, and the rear doors flew open. Two men dressed in ballistic vests squirted out. Nicknamed Scarecrow and the Tin Man, they poured it on agents Rivera and Stone at point-blank range with similar automatic MP5s, mowing them down from the sheer volume of firepower.

The coordinated attack came so fast Rivera had difficulty removing both hands from his coat pockets. He barely had time to grasp the battle-slung M4 hanging on his chest before Tin Man's bullets slammed him to the ground.

Agent Stone fired three times, one round punching a hole in the rear bumper as he raised his weapon. Scarecrow's stream of ball ammo ended the young man's life.

Gasping, Lieutenant Burke struggled to unholster a pistol with his left arm. DeVaca swiveled and squeezed the Scorpion's trigger again. Burke soaked up half the magazine. As he stilled, Tin Man, Scarecrow, and Lion combined to form a frontal assault and cut down three more stunned agents.

Dorothy grabbed the MP5 from the step-well on her side and added the contents of a slender thirty-round mag to the withering hail of lead. The two remaining agents dove behind the nearest Border Patrol truck, scrambling to bring their rifles into service. The terrified agents' experience was no match for the battle-hardened mercenaries.

Lion and Tin Man split up to flank the agents' position while Scarecrow kept pressure on the official vehicles parked twenty yards away. A pistol popped up over the hood, fired toward Scarecrow, and swept back toward the van, driving Dorothy to cover. By that time,

Lion had the angle and dropped the two men into the snow.

The quiet after the attack was surreal. Weapon still at his shoulder, Scarecrow swept the area for other threats.

DeVaca's voice was calm. "*Informe!*"

None of the mercenaries replied in English, though all three understood the language. Lion changed magazines. "*Claro.*"

Clear.

The Tin Man reloaded. "*Claro!*"

Scarecrow didn't take his eyes off the parked vehicles. "*Claro!*"

The Tin Man noticed a movement in one of the downed agents near their conversion van. He crossed the space in half a dozen steps and finished the wounded man.

DeVaca pulled himself back behind the wheel. "Excellent coordination, people. Everyone back aboard, and would someone please turn that *ruido* down on the television?"

He noticed a drop of blood on the back of his right hand as Dorothy reached through the open sliding door. The noise ended. Studying Burke's body lying in the splattered snow, DeVaca licked the blood off as the others climbed back inside the still running van.

Pleased that ten of the closest trained responders in the area were out of action, DeVaca slid back into his seat and turned on the radio as doors slammed around him. The weather report was on.

"This tropical system coming out of Mexico is

pumping enormous amounts of moisture into West Texas and will meet an abnormally strong Canadian Arctic front. It looks like this historic system will produce the heaviest snow we've seen in our area for over a hundred years. Blizzard conditions have already closed much of Interstate 40 from Amarillo to Albuquerque, and heavy snow is now falling from El Paso and the Big Bend region of the Texas/Mexico border along Interstate 20 as far east as Weatherford, Texas. The National Weather Service is predicting as much as fifteen to twenty inches of accumulation in the Ballard/Alpine/Ft. Stockton areas with drifts as high as four to five *feet*. Folks, hunker down where you are and avoid all travel as this storm moves to the northeast."

Dorothy ejected the magazine from her pistol and dug into a canvas bag on the floorboard. She slapped a fresh mag into the butt, registering the bright red sprays in the snow outside her window. "I thought you said we'd avoid this."

DeVaca shrugged. "It is one of those things. Every military plan becomes moot when the enemy is met."

"This *shouldn't* have happened."

"A lot of things *should not* happen, but they do." He steered over Burke's body as if it were nothing but a soft speed bump and accelerated onto the smooth, unmarked highway disappearing into the bleak and windy expanse of West Texas.

Visibility was worse than when they'd arrived only minutes before, and when DeVaca glanced into the side mirror, the swath they plowed was wide and deep. Huge snowflakes swept up and over the windshield.

"We came this way instead of from El Paso or the border to miss the permanent stations, but there is no way to anticipate these mobile checkpoints."

Dorothy holstered the weapon under her shirt. "I don't like surprises."

DeVaca ignored her and turned up the radio's volume. ". . . most roads are already closed, or will be closed soon. Driving is treacherous out here in the Big Bend, folks, so stay home where it's *safe and warm*. I'll be back with the full forecast after this message from Ballard Plumbing."

DeVaca's stomach fluttered in anticipation. *Safe and warm.* That would soon change. A grin tugged at his mouth.

They were fortunate with the storm. His commander back in Houston, Marc Chavez, couldn't have scheduled it any better. The weather had paralyzed the region, giving them more than enough time to complete their mission and escape. He clicked his teeth together, as if chewing, and fantasized about what his team might encounter next.

DeVaca, a U.S. citizen, had joined Dorothy, Lion, Tin Man, and Scarecrow days earlier after the group had slipped into the U.S. across Lake Amistad, a reservoir straddling the border of Texas and Mexico. They came in with help from a human trafficker who provided a safe house in Comstock, Texas, where DeVaca picked them up in the van two days later.

Dorothy was there with counterfeit documents provided by DeVaca, because he was intrigued by the attractive Mexican national months earlier while visiting a whorehouse in Nuevo Laredo. Dorothy's smooth face and flawless skin made her look naive and delicious. He was pleased to find that she was almost as emotionless as he. It didn't take long to bring her into his cause. For her, his plans were exciting and dangerous, and the promised money didn't hurt, either.

Having her around soon fanned a fire he'd banked years earlier. Cutting his eyes across the van, he saw her nipples were hard against her shirt. Sometimes Dorothy made it difficult to concentrate.

Her appearance of innocence sparked DeVaca's amusing idea of nicknaming his team after characters in *The Wizard of Oz*, a distinctly American movie. The nicknames also kept their dispensable association impersonal, as were the other three components of his army converging on the Ballard Courthouse.

He passed the still-hot Scorpion to her. Dorothy ejected the magazine without a word and reloaded the stubby machine pistol with a fresh thirty-round stick. She watched her side mirror as the checkpoint receded into the falling snow. "With those *migras* out of the way, our chances have increased."

"Yes." DeVaca dragged his eyes back to the road before they flicked to his rearview mirror. "You gentlemen were magnificent." To throw them a bone, he said it again in Spanish. "*Ustedes, señores eran magníficos!*"

The mercenaries gave him a thumbs-up as they passed a snow-covered sign that announced their destination was two miles away. They reloaded their weapons with fresh magazines from the pockets on their vests.

Dorothy handed the Scorpion back to DeVaca. As they punched through the storm, she covered her head and face with an adapted version of hijab, not for religious reasons, but to keep from getting shot in the back by the radical Muslim team coming in from the west.

She'd learned to play all the angles during her short, turbulent life.

DeVaca took his eyes off the road for another look at Dorothy's delicious dimples before she covered them up. "You were wonderful, too."

Chapter 2

The heaviest snow I'd ever seen was falling on my little West Texas town. Thick freezing fog and a patch of black ice covering the sidewalk damn near took me down when I stepped up on the curb. It wasn't really black, but clear and dangerous as hell.

Snow followed the predawn burst of sleet and freezing rain to accumulate on muddy pickups angled in against the sidewalk curb like horses waiting at a hitching post. In fact, iron posts with tether rings still stuck out from the concrete sidewalks. The Chamber of Commerce liked having the hitching posts out front because the tourists thought it made Ballard seem more like the Old West.

An antiques shop and an art gallery bracketed the Chat 'N Chew. Water droplets from snowflakes blowing against the café's eighty-year-old windows melted and ran in rivulets to the sill, where they refroze.

I pushed open the door and stepped inside, pausing to stomp the snow off my feet. The smell of coffee, spices, and frying bacon made my stomach growl.

Sheriff Ethan Armstrong had his back to me at the

counter, working his way through a Western Plate. I kept trying to get Dolores to rename it Heart Attack on a Plate because the *chili relleno* wrapped in an omelet and topped with cheese, bacon, sausage, pancakes, biscuits, and gravy just *had* to be bad for you.

The air was filled with conversation from locals and tourists. Most of the locals gathered on the café's right side, where they had long ago abandoned all pretense of private dining by shifting chairs between tables in ever evolving conversational groups. As soon as one group disbanded, the others adjusted their positions around the tables with the jarring, stuttering sounds of dragging chairs. That chaos, clutter, and our small-town familiarity pushed most tourists to the left side.

Traditional country music from the jukebox backfilled the customer's voices. Dolores won't allow any of what she calls rock-and-roll bubblegum country on *her* machine. Dwight Yoakum filled her bill that morning, and when he finished, George Strait took over.

I unbuttoned my ranch coat, hung it on the rack by the door, and threw up a hand in greeting toward the regulars as I headed for the counter. Most didn't stop talking, but everyone waved back. West Texas folks are courteous, and we always wave when we pass each other on the highway. It seems like most of us drive with one wrist hanging over the top of the steering wheel to make it easy to raise a hand in greeting or to flick an index finger.

You'd always get an answering wave or flick, unless some old sorehead passed, and we had a few of those, like anywhere else.

The tourists were more interested in me than my

friends. Heads swiveled around like radar dishes. It's not my blue shirt and khakis they were interested in, though that's a dead giveaway. It's the Silverbelly hat made by the O'Farrell Hat Company, the Colt 1911 .45 in a hand-tooled holster, and the Ranger badge stamped from a Mexican peso on my shirt. I'm proud to wear that badge, both for the job, and for the history.

Most of the regulars wore sweat-stained Stetsons and Resistols, drooping from hard use in the Texas sun. The hats in our part of the country were tools as useful as a mechanic's wrench or a doctor's stethoscope. The rest wore gimme caps.

Some folks might say it's rude to wear hats and caps in the café, but we didn't see it that way. In Dolores's café and public buildings, most everybody kept their hats on, because hat hair isn't something you want to see while you're eating.

A round stool sat vacant beside Sheriff Armstrong. I've known him since the ninth grade when the Old Man moved us from East Texas to Ballard. We'd been running buddies from the first time we laid eyes on each other and managed to survive most of our high school scrapes with nothing more than bruises and the occasional community-service assignment from Chalk Ferguson, who was sheriff at that time. I straddled the red vinyl, on the opposite side of the Beretta M-9 automatic in his hand-tooled holster.

Ethan cut his eyes toward me, and the crows-feet at the corners deepened when he smiled. He tilted his hat back with a free thumb. "Well, look what the cat drug in, a real-live Texas Ranger. How you doin', Sonny?"

Dolores thumped a thick white mug on the counter

in front of me and filled it with steaming coffee. She knows everybody who lives in Ballard. Her soft voice, light Spanish accent, and strong personality draw people to that woman like a magnet. "Mornin', hon."

I once heard Dolores referred to as "that big-boned gal," and I reckon that's what she is. She's as solid as a tree trunk and don't jiggle at all, well, maybe in a couple of places you'd expect.

Before I could answer, she topped off Ethan's coffee. "Here you go, baby." She was off with the pot.

Ethan swept a forefinger under his brush-pile mustache and pushed the mug away to make more room to work with his fork. "It's a good day to stay inside."

"I would if I could."

"You ain't a-woofin'. You back on the job?"

"Next week."

He knew my desk time on administrative leave was nothing more than a formality after I came up on the attempted murder of a highway patrol officer a few weeks earlier and had to use my weapon. I learned a long time ago to use enough gun, and even though I missed what I was aiming at because of the distance, the heavy slug from my .45 hit the assailant's boot heel, knocking his feet out from under him. The guy went down hard, cracking his head on the concrete. He died from a subdural hematoma, and his death had me riding a desk for a while. We were confident that the routine investigation would prove that I was justified in taking lethal action to stop the murder of Ian Frazier.

Ethan chewed his eggs and the crow's-feet returned. "Been meaning to ask you, did you *intend* to shoot that guy in the heel?"

I leaned in. "You know how I am. I was aiming at his head." I'd never killed anyone before, and it bothered me late at night when the house was quiet and I was laying in bed waiting to go to sleep.

He swallowed. "I never heard of such a thing, a guy getting shot in the boot heel and falling hard enough to hit his head and die."

"It stopped him."

"That it did. That's why I—"

His eyes flicked to my holster and I finished the old saying "—use enough gun."

He laughed and I jerked a thumb toward his plate when Dolores came by. "How about some *huevos rancheros*?"

I was always partial to eggs, beans, and tomato-chili sauce. I learned to like them when I was kid, sweating beside the Mexican hands when Dad went out to help work their cattle. If they had time in the mornings, the ranchers fed us a full breakfast, and that often meant their own version of *huevos rancheros*.

Dolores swung around the counter "Sure thing, baby."

My Old Man was once a Ranger in East Texas, but gave it up after Mama was murdered and he couldn't solve the case, no matter how hard he tried. He lost his taste for that part of the country, and sold most of the family land, but kept some acreage north of Paris. He used that money and a little savings to buy four sections of ranchland on the opposite side of the state, southwest of Ballard.

We lived on beans and potatoes for several years as he worked to make a go of the little ranch, little in the sense that some of the *old* ranches in the Big Bend region are hundreds of sections in size.

My first years growing up on the eastern side of the state is why I speak a little different than the folks in Ballard. I always stuck out like a sore thumb with my way of phrasing things. Most people who've never been to Texas have no idea the state's so big there are five different geographical regions, each with a different way of talking and phrasing things.

"Scrambled, not fried."

"Gringo! But I still love ya, Sonny." She still had the most beautiful eyes in town, despite five husbands, three kids, and a hard life of café work.

Ethan grinned again. "She never called you baby when we were kids."

"She never called me much of nothing." The crowd behind us laughed, and I jerked my head in their direction. "Looks like ever'body decided to stay in out of the weather."

"Smart thing to do. So why're *you* out so early this morning if you don't have to report in?"

"Didn't say that. Right now, I'm an errand boy, but I'd rather do that than sit around twiddling my thumbs. Kelly's taking her students on a field trip to the courthouse, so I'll visit with them for a while. She has this kid I'm mentoring and she wants me to spend a little more time with him."

"Someone I know?"

"You might. Name's Arturo."

Ethan pushed his empty plate back and slipped his finger into the handle of the thick white mug. "Arturo Alonzo."

I was surprised. "That's right. How you know him?"

He blew and sipped. "Picked him up a couple of times, running the streets. He's hanging with some Mexican kids that live in a dirt floor shack about a mile out of town. Those little turds are mean as snakes. I'm afraid he's going to get in trouble with 'em, and they won't give a flip if he goes to jail. They'll wind up hanging something on that boy before it's all said and done."

"Maybe double-teaming him might help."

"Might do it, now that his old man's been deported. I picked him up the other night for fighting and called ICE to come get him."

Dolores slid my breakfast across the counter. "Let me know when that runs out, and I'll fill 'er up again."

I dug in, and our section of the counter quieted for a while. I came up for air when Ethan jerked his thumb toward the flat-panel television on the wall. A weatherman was pointing toward a front coming in our direction.

He cut his eyes at me. "I'm afraid this is gonna be a long day. Dolores, can you turn that up?"

She kept the remote on a long jute cord attached to a horseshoe nailed to a wall stud behind the counter because she got tired of losing it, and really tired of the sports channels. "I will in a minute."

"He's giving the forecast right *now*. It'll be over by the time you get back."

"It's the Weather Channel, you knothead. They say the same thing all day long." She stopped and well-roped the cord with both hands, dragging the device across the counter. She turned the volume up and left the remote beside Ethan and muttered to herself. "That is, if they aren't showing those stupid reality shows of theirs. I swear, the Weather Channel should stick to the weather."

The crowd shifted to make room for newcomers, and chairs squalled on the linoleum. A George Jones song came on the jukebox. Dolores rang up a sale and traded four tourists for six.

"So Kelly roped you into helping her out again?" Ethan kept one eye on the TV screen. The weatherman stood in front of a map of the United States and northern Mexico. A thick blue line bowed southward, indicating a strong cold front dropping down from Canada was already on top of Ballard. From the southwest, the spiral of a hurricane near Acapulco, Mexico, followed a skirmish line of arrows sweeping in a wide semi-circle to the north toward the Big Bend.

They looked to overlap right on top of us.

"Yep. Like I don't have my hands full with her, the twins, and the job. She says it's my mission to help, and she don't mind pushing me toward it, neither."

My wife teaches at Big Bend High, and every time she talks me into helping with some of her students, I say it's the last time, but it never is.

"Glad I didn't marry her when *I* had the chance."

It tickled me to think of her and Ethan as a couple. "Y'all were boyfriend and girlfriend in the third grade, thirty-nine years ago."

"Yep, and that was enough for me. She was too bossy."

"There ain't no other name for it."

Ethan picked up the cup of to-go coffee Dolores brought without being asked. "I got to git. It's gonna be a long day. Tell her to put both of these on my tab. I'll see you after a while."

Ethan left and I went back to frowning at the weather forecast of what they were calling the West Texas Storm of the Century. It *was* going to be a long day.

I didn't know the half of it when I paid anyway and followed him a few minutes later.

Chapter 3

All five members of Lorenzo DeVaca's Syrian team had been in the country for months on student visas, there to study at the Holy Church of the Trinity in Berkeley.

None of them ever stepped on the campus grounds.

Joining the ranks of more than one million foreign nationals who entered the United States on student visas, the radical Muslims vanished as soon as they walked out of customs. Mohammad Hani Kahn and the other Syrians met their contact in the parking lot of the Ground Zero coffee shop not far from campus. They'd holed up in a house in a suburban neighborhood until De-Vaca contacted them with a special code phrase that wouldn't trigger alarms if their cell phones had been hacked by Homeland Security.

In a text suggesting titles to study at the academy, DeVaca listed several classic American novels including *Alas Babylon* by Pat Frank, *To Kill a Mockingbird* by Harper Lee, and *Where the Red Fern Grows* by Wilson Rawls. For extra credit, he suggested *Some-*

thing Wicked This Way Comes, a popular Ray Bradbury novel.

Kahn had no interest in the other titles. The "Wicked" reference told him everything he needed to know. The operation was a go. To avoid suspicion, each man bought his own ticket, boarded at the Greyhound station in Oakland, and scattered throughout the bus headed east.

The ride to El Paso was uneventful. The future terrorists separated at their destination and later met at a *mercado*, or Mexican market a couple of blocks from the station. A Cadillac sedan was waiting. It didn't matter the driver's name was one word, Owaiss.

He was proud to consider himself a homegrown warrior and ready to do his part after declaring *jihad* following 9/11. The radicalized American's instructions were simple. Pick up five Syrian students and drop them off at a rest stop on the outskirts of Ballard.

Three hours later, they stepped out of the warm, comfortable car in the early morning darkness. The night was freezing and the only thing waiting for them was a dented and dirty slant-load four-horse trailer. His job done, Owaiss pulled back onto the highway. His lights disappeared in the falling snow.

Burt Bowden opened the trailer's back doors. Kahn flicked on a tactical flashlight and lit the disillusioned rancher's unshaven face. Noting his scowl, he snorted and scanned the trailer. The solid sides and closed windows broke the wind, making the interior feel warm. The beam lit dozens of boxes and cases stacked against the front end.

The others surrounded him as Kahn leaned in. "I know what pig shit looks like, you know. What animals do you carry in here?"

Bowden was paid a lot of money to pick up the Syrian students and drive them into Ballard, but it hadn't been enough to take any guff off a raghead with a scraggly beard, wannabe mustache, and bad breath. "Hey, we don't raise pork out here. I haul horses in this, and get that damned light out of my eyes. There's enough room for all y'all, and the rest when we pick 'em up."

Kahn skipped his light around the interior as if he'd missed something on the first pass. He longed to get inside and out of the frigid wind, but he still didn't trust the rancher whose mouth was hidden by a thick mustache. "How long will we be in there?"

"Not long enough to freeze to death, if that's what you're worried about. There's all the gear you need, compliments of your boss." He slapped the side of the trailer. "I'm making a loop around town here, to get the rest of y'all. An hour at the most. You'll be fine with the windows closed."

"I ride in front with you."

"No way. You get in the back. Ever'body knows me in this one-horse town."

Kahn maintained eye contact with Bowden while his men examined military cargo boxes and crates. He repeated the emotionless statement. "I'm riding in the front with you."

Bowden's gaze slipped away. "Fine, then."

Chapter 4

Most of the traffic in our little West Texas town was tourists and local pickups, with a Cadillac or two driven by some of the community bluehairs. We recognized the strangers in Ballard by their unfamiliar cars, and a lot of those folks stayed at the art deco 1930s Posada Real Hotel, a hundred yards down Charles Street from the courthouse.

I parked my Dodge dually in an angled slot on that same street in front of the Palace Theater where there's more room for her big hips. The other parking spaces were empty, so it didn't make any difference, because snow covered the lines. I would have walked up from the café, but decided to drive because of the falling weather.

A gaudy movie poster for a high school angst movie curled under the cracked glass beside the ticket booth. I knew the twins would be worrying at me to give 'em money to see it.

Even though the Palace still looked like it did when I first came to Ballard as a high school freshman, the theater seemed tired and aged in the gloomy light, without any of the glamour that appeared when darkness fell and the lights came on over the ticket booth and entrance. I'd crossed the black-and-white penny tiles on the floor a hundred times with buddies and girlfriends, and liked the theater more for the memories than anything else.

"Sonny!"

I turned to see Andy Clark across the street. The skinny little owner of the Posada who always reminded me of Barney Fife without the twitches was standing beside a wooden stepladder. Though Thanksgiving wasn't far away, he was untangling one end of a plastic holiday garland that was half hanging from the awnings jutting out between alternating Mexican palms and tall Italian cypress trees growing in the narrow strip of grass separating the sidewalk and the street.

Andy always tended to lose his direction in a conversation and never learned how to end a sentence or wait for a response. Instead, he'd yap along just fine before drifting off to an odd stop like he just ran out of steam. More sentences than not ended with "and ever'thing."

My curiosity nearly got the better of me because I really wanted to know why he was standing there like he had good sense, staring upward at the building with that garland in his hand. Folks stop and visit when they can, but I was late to the courthouse to see Judge Dollins. I gave him a quick wave across the street. "I'll see you in a little while!"

He waved in return and went back to studying on his decorations. The wind whipped down the alley between the theater and a realty office, blowing snow down my collar. I set the hat tighter on my head and buttoned my coat higher, wishing I had a scarf around my neck. I keep a silk wild rag in the truck, but I'd forgotten to dig the colorful scarf out of the console.

Pressed for time, I wouldn't go back and hunt for it Instead I hurried down the street toward the three-story county courthouse to meet the judge and my wife's high school civics class.

Built in 1886, the Renaissance Revival courthouse with its peach-colored stucco exterior was a long rectangular cracker box with entrances on all four sides. A short hallway across the width of the building intersected with a grand rotunda stretching three stories overhead. Above that, an ornate central dome reached two stories higher.

Dormers jutting out on all four sides, and Roman towers high above the roofline on each corner of the building, made it resemble a medieval castle. My seventeen-year-old twins, Mary and Jerry, said it looked like a fort to them when they were little, but that's because they knew the history of our area. They were convinced that Apaches raided the town even when I was in high school.

But they refused to believe that a band of Geronimo's descendants invaded the U.S. from their hideout in Mexico as late as 1924. Go figure. I always expected kids to be the death of me.

Our Texas landmark housed everything from historical documents, to 100-year-old minutes of city council meetings, tax rolls, land records, and criminal records. The second-floor courtroom handled most of the minor legal infractions through the years. In the third-floor Grand Jury room built on the same footprint directly above the municipal courtroom, tough judges with huge white beards and mustaches once sentenced rustlers, horse thieves, and murderers to the gallows.

On the ground floor, the County Court, Commissioners Court, District Clerk, Tax Assessor-Collector, Justice of the Peace, County Judge, County Treasurer, Game Warden, and County Surveyor all did a brisk business each week.

The second floor housed the District Attorney's offices and the district court, plus Licensing.

Judge Arthur Dollins occupied the county bench and fined the folks my friend Sheriff Ethan Armstrong brought in. Most were for speeding and such, but we got a fair amount of business from the Border Patrol stations.

Those agents were always on the lookout for drugs and illegal immigrants that a lot of folks still called wetbacks. Whenever the Border Patrol found someone with, say, an ounce or two of marijuana, they'd call Ethan to come take the prisoners off their hands.

Judge Dollins fined 'em two hundred and fifty or so, to make it sting a little, plus twenty-seven bucks in court costs. I never did figure out why the odd amount.

Snow squeaked under my feet as a long, mournful whistle filled the air. The Union Pacific rail lines ran past or through every town in West Texas, carrying coal, automobiles, or manifest cargo, double-stack containers, tankers, coal, gondolas, and boxcars. Amtrak passenger trains shared those same rails, hauling folks from one end of the country to the other and stopping on the shoofly to let an express pass.

They clattered past all times of the day, slowing down to about forty miles an hour in town before accelerating to their usual sixty once they got past the city limits. They'd been part of life since the 1850s.

The wind threatened to snatch the hat off my head again. I picked up my pace down the sidewalk, glad I'd fed our lab, Buster, and put him inside with Willie. The twins had rescued the little Shih Tzu two years before, but the cute little mutt decided he liked me best. I figured he was curled up with Buster on my bed, all nice and warm.

Chapter 5

Team Three crossed from Mexico into Texas the day before Burt Bowden was supposed to pick them up. Aided by other illegals who had entered months, sometimes years earlier, they established a GPS system of water and supply caches across the dry desert to ensure the health and well-being of those who crossed.

The first members of the *Bloque de Celda 10* gang waited in the storm just out of sight from Highway 90 until a late-model four-door Dodge pickup pulled onto the shoulder near a wire gate leading into the Hawke Ranch. A blond-haired, meth-depleted skeleton of a woman named Melanie Cooper jumped out of the cab without a coat. She shuddered as snow caught in her greasy hair.

She checked the right front tire as if it were going flat.

The team's tattooed leader, Enrique Rivas, had been waiting for that incident. He worked for *La Serpiente*, a rising cartel flexing its muscles south of the border in Chihuahua. He and his men rose like ghosts from the desert scrub, startling Melanie. She tumbled into the side of the truck.

"You're late. We're freezing to death." Angry, Rivas glanced up and down the snowy highway. "Are you drunk?"

Shivering, she crossed both arms under her almost nonexistent breasts and took an immediate dislike to the man with the sparse whiskers and bad skin. The woman twitched with the constant hyperactivity of a tweaker jonesing for the next hit.

Her broken and rotting teeth chattered. She smoothed stringy hair off her forehead with a shaking hand. "I'm fine. You just scared me."

"No reason to be scared." Rivas checked the highway again.

"Fine. You guys get in."

"*Uno momento.*" Rivas waved his snow-covered men forward from behind a low wave of rocks hidden by a thick stand of prickly pear cactus several yards away. Shivering in cast-off second- and thirdhand clothes, they hurried toward the inviting warmth of the truck cab.

As they passed, Rivas gave Melanie a grin. "Come with me."

She planted her feet, refusing to take her eyes off the tattoos up the side of the man's neck and onto his cheek. "No."

"*Bien entonces.* Fuentes."

Fine, then.

The whipcord-thin Mexican's fist lashed out, catching the tweaker flush on the jaw with a crack of broken bones and teeth. Rafael Fuentes, the shortest and stock-

iest man of their group, caught her before she fell and
heaved her on his shoulder.

"Volver allí." Rivas jerked a thumb over his shoulder toward where they'd been hiding.

Without responding, Fuentes jogged toward the ridge
as if Melanie's limp body was weightless. He returned
moments later, shoving a long knife back into its sheath
on his belt. He climbed into the front passenger seat
and slammed the door against the blowing snow.

The truck pulled back on the highway with Rivas
behind the wheel, but the meth-head from Dallas didn't
care. She lay beside a barbed-wire fence, and snowflakes melted on her open eyes.

Rivas glanced into the mirror at his tatted, scarred,
and dangerous C-10 gang riding in the back. Cell Block
10 had been the Mexican government's experiment in
sociology and the American way of humane incarcera-
tion that went totally wrong. Anyone with any sense
knows that even though a lake is calm on the surface,
that doesn't mean something deadly isn't waiting in
the depths.

He and his men were the only survivors of one dis-
astrous day when the guards in the test block had become to lax. They escaped after dozens died on both
sides. Once free, C-10 became a dangerous ring of
butchers on the Mexican side of the Rio Grande.

They parked the Dodge an hour later in front of a
closed taco shop on the outskirts of Ballard and waited
with the engine and lights off, hoping the meth-head's
tardiness hadn't caused them to miss their connection.

The truck and horse trailer made a second pass minutes later.

Chapter 6

The heavy snow was such a distraction that I wasn't paying attention to what I was doing. I stepped off the icy curb without looking both ways like my mama taught me. A white conversion van nearly ran me down.

I gave a little "feel good" jump onto the sidewalk and waved, trying to be courteous. The driver and his sullen female passenger didn't even lift a finger. Tourists frustrated by the snow, maybe. They followed the one-way street around the corner, past the sheriff's office and out of my sight.

With both hands in the deep pockets of my ranch coat, I felt the leather work gloves I'd put in there a week earlier. I thought about pulling them on, but it was too much trouble for such a quick walk. I ducked my felt hat brim to block the falling weather and turned back to the courthouse.

The walk was a short distance across the street that circles the square. The closest door was the east entrance that most tourists used. Law enforcement tended to use the north entrance, across the street from the sheriff's office.

A feller as old as the hills intersected my path from the sidewalk that circled the building. Mr. Beck Terrill gave me a grin and a wave. "Well dog my cats. If it ain't Sonny Hawke."

He hadn't been around for a while, and it tickled me to see him. The gang over at the café said he'd been down in his back for almost a month. "Mr. Beck." I hunched my shoulders against the wind. "Ain't this somethin'?"

Instead of shaking hands, we bobbed our heads at one another. "It sure is, but we need the moisture." He paced me down the sidewalk, rocking back and forth with an odd duck walk caused by the lack of both big toes he left behind in the Chosin Reservoir back in 1950. Despite the storm, I slowed down to match the Korean War vet's pace.

He cut his eyes at me from under his Stetson's three-inch brim that did little to block the snow catching in his gray mustache. "I been meanin' to ask you about that little scrape with a bad guy."

My stomach flipped again. I'd known Mr. Beck since the Old Man moved us to Ballard. I usually took his good-natured ribbing. This time, though, I cut him off. I'd heard enough about it for one day. "I'm not a great shot at long distance. He was a ways off and I didn't account for the bullet drop."

"I never heard of such a thing."

"Whatever works."

"I reckon. Some folks just need killin' anyway, especially if they're shootin' at the laws. Heard you're straddlin' a desk these days?"

"Yep, they call it administrative leave. It's just a formality until they get finished with the investigation."

We weren't moving fast, and the conversation slowed us even more. "Hell, I'd be inside by the fire, then, if I's you. It's too cold a day to be out."

"Yep. Wouldn't be here, but I'm running errands for my boss. I need to drop off a check for Judge Dollins, too. He's gonna need some help come election time."

Mr. Beck had always been involved in local government. He was proud of the opportunity, because his parents emigrated from Ireland through Ellis Island when he was barely two.

The leather sole of his boot slipped on the snow. I steadied him by grabbing one arm. "Haven't seen it like this here since I was a pup." He kept talking as if he hadn't noticed. "Can't stand the cold since I lost them toes in Korea. I'd just as soon never see a winter storm again."

"At least it's not supposed to last long."

"I hope, but the TV weatherman says thissun's gonna be a booger."

A dull roar came through the brass and glass doors as we neared the building. I answered his question before it came out of his mouth. "Kelly brought her civics class today, and I'm gonna help her out while I'm here."

"Lordy."

"Yep."

Chapter 7

The team of disgruntled Americans intended to change their country through revolution. Such an uprising worked in 1776, and they could see no reason why it couldn't happen again.

Richard Carver was their self-proclaimed "captain." In between drinking beer and watching movies like the original *Red Dawn*, and *Black Hawk Down*, he'd trained the weekend warriors on his farm near Elgin, Texas, two weekends a month for the past five years. They called themselves Texas Regulars, and the tatted, rawboned men with military "high and tight" cuts had met in Valentine the day before.

He had more than seventy-five believers in his "company," but the three in the cab of his truck were the ones he trusted with his life. They were the cream of his crop and had pledged to give their lives for the Cause.

Richard was anxious to get going, but they waited for half an hour before a fifth man joined them. They killed time talking about the upcoming mission in the warmth of Richard's thirdhand H2 idling outside a local café when an elderly man tapped on the window.

Richard's right-hand man, Tom Jordan, rolled the passenger window down. "You looking for us?"

"Wicked sent me. I'm Reddy Freddy."

"How old are you, Pops?"

The man hadn't shaved his gray beard in over a week. "Old enough to know better."

Richard jerked a thumb over his shoulder. "Get in the back."

He opened the back door to find two others already occupying the window seats and waited in uncomfortable silence until a wiry man stepped out. "You get in the middle, old man."

He slid across, sat with both knees together to keep from touching the others, and stared straight ahead. He knew what *their* jobs were, but he had a different role in the revolution.

One that didn't require a gun.

They were out of town minutes later. No one said a word until they met Burt Bowden at a scenic pullout not far from Ballard.

Chapter 8

I gave Mr. Beck a grin and a slap on his bony shoulder as a gust of wind plucked at my clothes. Not even the heavy material of his jacket could put any semblance of meat on his bones.

The pop of metal and a soft crunch stopped us before we could get inside. We turned to see Burt Bowden's truck and trailer headed in our direction. South Charles dead-ended at the courthouse and he must have been going too fast through town before hitting his brakes. The trailer started to jackknife at the turn and he came close to sliding up on the sidewalk before getting her reined in at the curb.

We were close enough to see one another, but Burt turned his head so he wouldn't have to make eye contact. He had a history of run-ins with the local law over the past several years after losing part of the family ranch to back taxes. Instead of letting the county auction his whole place, he sold off half his property for the funds, reducing his income but keeping the home place. Since then, Burt was angry with anyone who was part of the "government." That included me, the school board, and the highway patrol, just to name a few.

I didn't recognize the bearded guy in a sock cap riding shotgun. That wasn't a surprise. The new beard craze was making friends and family unrecognizable. I couldn't wait for that one to pass, along with sagging pants and bubblegum country music.

Without acknowledging us, Burt steered right and made an immediate left to loop around the square, skidding toward the sheriff's car parked on the street. He let off the gas and made another left behind the courthouse.

"Well, if that don't beat all." Mr. Beck kept a close eye on the icy steps. I matched his slow pace up the courthouse steps. "Burt knows better'n that."

I put my hand on Mr. Beck's back, just to make sure he didn't slip. He didn't say anything, probably because he knew what a broken hip would cost him.

The chattering of my wife's class filtered through the closed doors, and Mr. Beck laughed at the sound. "I swear. If I knew then what I know now . . ."

Chapter 9

The mid-century modern sheriff's office across the street looked as out of place in the historic town as a cat in a doghouse. A good man in all ways, Sheriff Ethan Armstrong sipped at the foam cup full of coffee he picked up at the Chat 'N Chew and watched Sonny Hawke and Mr. Beck making their slow way through the storm. The falling snow made it difficult to see much farther than the Texas Ranger and the rancher he'd known all his life.

Ethan knew Sonny wanted nothing more than to be back on the job. He smoothed his brush-pile mustache and took another sip of the strong but lukewarm coffee. Burt Bowden's pickup and horse trailer almost jackknifed at the dead-end in front of the courthouse before sliding to a stop against the curb. It looked like he'd picked a bad time to move stock. Ethan relaxed when Burt straightened the heavy rig and crept to the corner.

"Roads are gettin' bad." Deputy Frank Malone tore his attention from the tube TV mounted high on the wall and joined Ethan at the window, finger through the handle of his own coffee cup. Ten years younger than the sheriff, he was growing his own thin and listless mustache.

Ethan grunted. "Most lawmen get their information from the DOT, not the local weatherman."

Frank took a sip. "Us younger folks use everything available to us, including Facebook and Twitter. We need to get one of those flat-panel TVs and throw that antique in the ditch."

Ethan didn't take his eyes off the Ranger. "Young people have given up on Facebook. They're into other things now."

"Dayum. You know more than you let on."

"Um humm. And I know Burt's driving like he had a stroke or something. He oughta at least kick them wipers to a higher speed."

Burt turned left and gave it too much gas again. The trailer's tires broke free, and Ethan was sure the rear end was going to hit his cruiser. He hunched his shoulders. Deputy Malone hissed through his teeth. They waited for the impact, but Burt regained control and the trailer came back into line, missing Ethan's car by a hair.

He took the next left much slower and stopped at the curb on the "back," or the west side of the building.

"He knows better'n that." Ethan switched his gaze back to Sonny and Mr. Beck Terrill, indistinct behind the white lace of falling snow. "Burt's been driving longer than I've been kicking up grasshoppers."

"Snow makes people act funny." Deputy Malone's attention turned back to the television mounted high on the wall. "The TV says some of the roads were already closed because of the ice, and the rest of the highway'll shut down pretty soon. Checked in on the radio, too, boss, just to make you feel better. Both TexDot and the highway patrol says it's worse in El Paso, Midland, and even over in Ft. Stockton. We're in kind of a belly here right now that's gonna fill in pretty quick 'cause it's snowing heavy over in Alpine. They say it's a hurricane meeting a blue norther. It'll be bad for a *while*."

Ethan considered the day. "You prob'ly need to let the Mayo brothers out, then."

Wild and free as old-time cowhands, Danny and Luke Mayo were single, middle-aged, hard-working brothers who lived to ranch, but when the weather went bad, they headed for town. The boys dropped by the Chat 'N Chew café if they hit town before noon. After dinner, they made a beeline for the Sagebrush Bar, the local watering hole, where they stayed until their pocket money ran out or the weather cleared.

"You gonna charge them with anything?"

"Naw, Danny was asleep in the backseat of their truck when I found 'em parked in front of the Posada, and Luke was sawing logs on the passenger side. We'll do 'em a favor this time, since neither one was behind the wheel. Besides, they need to get gone. If this is as bad as they say it's gonna be, they'll need to tend to their cows. We'll charge 'em next time."

"I hope they won't be too late getting back."

"Well, they never drove slow in their lives." Ethan realized the snow was getting heavier. He turned away from the window.

Chapter 10

held the metal-and-glass door for Mr. Beck and followed him into warmth and a wall of noise. He flinched. "I need to go wet. I'll see you d'rectly." He threw me a wave and headed for the ground-floor restroom.

My little brunette wife, who weighs a hundred pounds soaking wet and full of bananas, was square in the middle of the hallway intersection under the rotunda. Yapping schoolkids surrounded her, every one of them talking a mile a minute and more thrilled about the snow than the tour of the building. Overhead, half a dozen renegades on the second floor leaned over the circular railing, testing the strength of the pecan banister and railing, I guessed.

Kelly caught my eye, waved, and mouthed one word. "Help." One of the girls whispered in her ear and her distinctive laugh mixed with the rest of the excited voices.

I flashed back to the first time I really paid attention to her. She was sitting in her daddy's truck when we were in high school, a cigarette in one hand and a cold

Coors between her legs. Her daddy didn't know she smoked or drank, and we kept that little teenage rebellion to ourselves. They'd just moved from Houston, and she was the most exotic thing I'd ever seen.

Lordy, even after all those years of marriage, that gal's smile made me want to take her in my arms right then and there.

Her students were running around like chickens with their heads cut off. She rolled her eyes. I gave her a wink and thought about wrestling with her later that night after the kids went to bed, with a fire in the master-bedroom fireplace and the snow piling up outside.

"One second." I knew she couldn't hear me, but I held up an index finger and ducked into the first office on the right to pick up an envelope for my superior, Major Chase Parker. Captains used to run the Ranger companies, and mine was Company E, but they changed things here awhile back and put us under majors.

The wooden door was open and a little round secretary was at her desk, talking into a desk phone. Carlita hadn't changed a bit in all the years I'd known her. She built a smile bookended by two deep dimples and palmed the phone's mouthpiece. "Hang on a minute, Joy. Hey, Sonny. It isn't ready yet. Mr. Calvert's on his way in but the snow slowed him up. He said to give him about half an hour."

"Morning, girl. I need to drop something off upstairs anyway. I'll be with Kelly and her class. I bet Dollins won't be hard to find."

Carlita jerked a thumb over her shoulder. "He's in that satellite office of his back here."

"He offices down here now?"

"Since about a year ago. His knees are bad and he

was tired of that creaky elevator. He still uses the second-floor office when court's in session, but his new schedule pushes appearances back to three times a week. Hang on and I'll tell him you're here in a sec."

She went back to her conversation. "No, Joy, it isn't scheduled until January sixth, and then I don't know if the judge will grant an extension . . ."

Katie Bright slipped past me, cradling two cups of coffee with one hand and talking on her cell phone. "Hey Ranger." A little bundle of energy, she shared secretarial duties in the tax office with Sally Gordon. She puckered up and gave me a Betty Boop air-kiss.

"Behave, my wife's around the corner."

Katie raised her eyebrows twice. She put one of the cups on Carlita's desk, leaned a hip against it, and continued her conversation as if we weren't even there. "Daddy, you never answer your phone. Anyway, it's snowing like we live in Colorado. They're talking *feet* of the stuff before it's over with. There's kids here on a field trip, but I bet they'll shut the schools down by dinner. We'll probably all go home, too, about then . . ."

The kids weren't the only ones excited about the snow. I doubted there'd be much work done by anyone after noon. Not interested in settling in for the day, Sally Gordon, the redheaded firecracker from across the hall, inclined her head toward Katie. "She's right, Sonny. Did you hear about how deep it's supposed to get?"

"The snow, or the bullshit from Judge Dollins?" He'd been around for years and liked to tell stories. The storm would impact the day, and I knew the Judge'd wind up holding his own personal court in there with the girls when everything slowed down.

Sally laughed. "The snow, silly."

"More'n we've ever seen." I handed Carlita an envelope and pointed toward the back. I turned back to Sally. "Tell the old fart to shut it all down and y'all go home. See ya later."

"I wish."

I gave Katie a good-bye wink. She returned it and kept on leaving her message to her dad in Washington.

Bracing myself, I stepped back into the short hallway that led to the noisy rotunda full of high school juniors. The smell of the courthouse reminded me of my college library, old books and Pine-Sol. I took a deep breath and grinned at the animated kids.

Kelly clapped her hands until the chattering tapered off. "Quiet down, everyone. You'll all get the chance to tour the building in a little while, but right now we're going upstairs to the Grand Jury room. Remember, the Grand Jury's responsible for reviewing all criminal cases filed by any law-enforcement agencies, including federal authorities, where the crime occurred in Presidio County . . . *what*, Christie?"

"Are they going to cancel school because of the snow?"

"Not until we finish here. Everyone! Off your phones. Put 'em on silent and in your pockets or purses or they're *mine* until Christmas."

Groans and snickers filled the air, but after one last peek at their screens, they put away their devices. I knew her rules on phones in class and it was a surefire bet that she'd be collecting them if she caught anyone, but the losing battle against the technological tide showed no signs of ebbing.

I made a note to bring up phones with Mary and Jerry over the supper table that night.

I caught my son's eye from across the room. Jerry's a lot like me, with a head full of wavy red hair and an impulsive nature. His brief smile said he saw me but didn't want to take it much further. I didn't respond, remembering when I was his age. Peer pressure was strong, even among juniors.

His twin, Mary, was with a gaggle of girls. She'd straightened her wavy strawberry-blonde hair that morning.

A student tapped me on the shoulder and I looked down at the dark-haired girl who called Sheriff Ethan Armstrong Dad. She pointed up and at an angle in the general direction of the courtroom. "Mr. Sonny, will you have to appear up there over that shooting you were in?"

I wondered if her interest was because of the careers in law enforcement her dad and I had chosen, or for other reasons. "Hey, Gillian. Yep, I'll be up there pretty soon."

"I wish I could watch. I love field trips like this. I've decided I'm gonna make an attorney someday."

"I'm sure you will."

"Mr. Hawke?"

The young lady beside her couldn't have been any more different. With her blue-black hair and a darker complexion, Evangelina Nakai caught the eye of every boy in her class. Her dad was Gabriel Nakai, the Old Man's hired hand on our family ranch that dated back to the 1880s.

We were interrupted when Matt Burke hugged me

around the waist. I grinned and hugged him back, because no one could ever be around Matt without getting some love from the happy little guy with Down syndrome.

He pushed back and rubbed the badge on my shirt with a soft, chubby hand. "I'm gonna be a Ranger someday." His speech sometimes made it hard for others to understand, but in our town, we'd all been around Matt enough to figure out what he said, even if his comments *were* sometimes confusing. "Can I come to work with you?"

"You'd be bored, hoss. I'm on the desk right now, so all you'd see is a lot of paperwork."

"Don't you have a TV there?"

"Sure do, but we don't get to watch it for fun. It stays on the news all the time."

His eyes still on my badge, he said, "No, we'd watch *movies*. Do you have *Finding Dory*?"

"Not at the office."

"*Finding Nemo*? That's the first one."

"Sorry, buddy. Hey, did you know you have your shoes on the wrong feet?"

He glanced down. "Yeah, I do, don't I?"

Kelly clapped again and pointed up. "All right, gang. Let's go."

"We won't all fit in the elevator."

"Kerry, we're not riding it, because there's too many of us and besides, we're *walking* up those stairs. We all need the exercise." Her voice went up a singsong lilt. "You people are *lazzzyyyy*! Please do not leave those empty water bottles sitting around. There's a recycle bin beside each exit and I expect you to use them."

Exaggerated groans again filled the rotunda as the kids split up and flowed in opposite directions toward the north and south staircases. Gillian put her arm around Matt. "C'mon. Let's see what's upstairs."

Matt started to pull back, but Mary put her hand on his cheek and turned his head. "C'mon, boyfriend. It'll be fun."

He gave her a sincere look. "You're very kind, but no thank you. We're *talking*."

Mary hugged him, and he leaned into her arms. "We'll talk to Mr. Sonny later."

He gave in. "Okay. I'm gonna be a Ranger someday."

Gillian linked his other arm. "You'll have to work hard." She gave me a look that was years beyond her age, and they led Matt toward the stairs. I made a note to tell her daddy how good she was with him and caught Arturo's eye.

The short, skinny little junior was the smallest kid in high school. He had olive skin, combed and gelled hair, and looked more like a little package of trouble from Brooklyn than West Texas. He was still on the fence and could go either way, depending on what happened in the next year or two. I intended to do my part to try and steer him in the right direction.

The building was warm. I unzipped my ranch coat. "Did you finish the assignment I gave you?"

He toed the tile floor with a worn-out boot. "I guess."

"Where is it?"

He pulled a handful of folded papers from his back pocket and handed them over. I didn't say anything about the condition of his work. Getting him to do it at all was a success. While I untangled the crumpled and dog-eared pages, we drifted along behind the herd of juniors charging up the wooden stairs in a thunder of footsteps. "Good."

We reached the second floor, and the chattering class swarmed to the round banister overlooking the rotunda floor to stare down at where we'd just come from. The joists creaked underfoot, noticeable even over the noisy chatter.

"This way." Kelly pointed toward the open set of double doors leading into the municipal courtroom on the northwest corner. "This is our first stop before we go upstairs to the Grand Jury room."

I caught her eye and tilted my head toward Arturo. She agreed with an eyebrow without breaking her patter.

You don't need a lot of words after twenty years of marriage.

Chapter 11

In the back of the horse trailer, Kahn's men opened wooden boxes labeled "fragile." Excited as kids, they withdrew automatic rifles packed in foam peanuts. The interior smelled of fresh oil as they passed M4 carbines toward the back.

Other boxes yielded tactical vests, ammo, and an assortment of supplies.

Two of the youngest Syrians, Usman Muhammed Al-Zahwi and Muhammad Qambrani, slapped in magazines and brandished the weapons, dancing and waving them around. Though he was smiling and laughing, the taller Al-Zahwi's eyes were dead pools of darkness. The short and skinny Qambrani looked like a young college student, as his papers stated.

Finally dressed in warm clothing, the Mexican team unloaded full magazines and whispered among themselves as their breath fogged in the icy air. They inserted the magazines into the M4s and passed the weapons to anyone who hadn't yet picked one up.

Two of those who spoke only Spanish watched the Syrians clown around. Gerardo Torres and his friend Rafael Fuentes were usually the ones making the rest of their team laugh, but they held back, glaring at the Syrians' strange dress and antics.

Richard Carver and the American team were at the front of the trailer, leaning against the metal and watching the others. They had their own weapons. Carver noted that whoever had planned and funded the operation had provided the same rifles as those he and his men carried, a suggestion he'd offered months earlier when a man calling himself DeVaca made contact. Their conversation had been brief and to the point, and when he agreed to be part of the takeover, DeVaca told him he would provide all that they needed.

Carver said they preferred to use their own Colt M4s, and urged DeVaca to provide the same weapons so they could all be familiar with the rifles, and the necessary 5.56 ammunition.

As the others slapped magazines and charged the bolts, his finger slipped down to the safety and flicked it off. All of those foreigners with automatic weapons made him nervous.

The trailer slewed, throwing those standing off balance. Qambrani and Al-Zahwi grabbed for purchase and fell against the hard aluminum wall. Qambrani dropped his weapon and Torres grabbed it up. He jammed it back into the Syrian's arms and pointed at the floor.

Al-Zahwi's eyebrows became one and he started forward just as the trailer slewed again. He grabbed a bar over the nearest window to hold himself upright. The truck accelerated and stabilized before taking the next turn much slower. It stopped.

Their silent argument over, the terrorists stood. Facing the rear, they waited for the doors to open.

Chapter 12

Arturo started after his class, but I pulled at the sleeve of his jacket. "C'mon. I want to show you something."

Kelly returned to her urchins. "All inside, and keep your hands to yourselves. I . . . said . . . hands to your-*selves* there, Sister Sue. Take a seat when you get in . . . and not out here *on the railing, mister*! Good lord. Y'all are gonna send me to an early grave. You get off of there right now . . ."

We left them behind and scaled the next rise of stairs to the third floor, but I wanted to take Arturo even higher. We stopped at a narrow set of painted wooden steps dead-ending at an odd access in the ceiling. I figured someone closed it to keep the heat downstairs.

Arturo frowned.

"Wait a second."

I climbed the pale green steps that were barely shoulder wide. A simple sliding lock was set into the standard-size door fitted into the ceiling. I slid the latch with my thumb, put my shoulder against the door, and pushed upward. It opened without a squeak into a round, unheated room. I climbed higher and used an old-fashioned hook and eye to secure it to the wall. The whole thing reminded me of a trapdoor in the floor of a kid's tree house.

"C'mon up, hoss."

He followed me into a large, round chamber illuminated by two feeble lights and a dim glow coming from above. More bare wooden stairs wound upward against the outside wall like those in a lighthouse. Simple wooden frames on the whitewashed clapboard walls held a black-and-white pictorial history of Ballard and the Big Bend region from the horse-and-buggy days to the 1950s.

Arturo circled the room that echoed with his footsteps. "These pictures are *cool*." His accent was not as heavy as those of some of the kids who'd immigrated to our town.

"Yep, they are, but they're not why we're up here. You'll ruin your eyes looking at 'em in this light. You can come back some other time." I pointed at the ceiling. "We're going higher."

Some of the steps creaked as we climbed the curved stairs to the next level and into the frigid observation deck some folks call the lantern room. I made a fish-hook turn on the bare floor and waited beside the pony wall surrounding the stairway's opening. I could tell Arturo was impressed when he emerged to find a 360-degree bank of candlestick windows.

He spun in a slow circle staring at the dome and tall windows far overhead. Most kids do the same thing the first time they get up there. Any other time we could see the entire town and the highways radiating away from the courthouse all the way to the Davis Mountains, but our fourteen-square-block burg was completely obscured by the raging storm.

Wind moaned around the cupola, and snow piled on the sills.

"Whaddaya think?"

Arturo put his fingers against the cold, wavy glass. "It's amazing. What are we doing up here?"

"I wanted you to get this chance before the weather gets worse. I thought we'd be able to see the town, but the snow's so heavy I can't see the water tower over there. Try using some other word besides 'amazing,' by the way. It'll improve your vocabulary."

His forehead wrinkled, as he missed the point. "The other kids would love this."

"They won't have time to see it today. I 'magine they're gonna shut school down in an hour or so, which makes you the lucky one."

Not much of a reward on my part for him doing his homework, it beat listening to a dry lecture about Grand Juries, even if it came from my wife. When I was a kid, little things that didn't hold much meaning for adults made a huge impact on me. I hoped these few moments away would do the same thing for him. A shiver ran up my spine, and I slipped my hands in my coat pockets. I think he was glad that I was chilly, because it gave him an excuse to zip up his own thin jacket.

At least he'd brought one. I knew for a fact that half a dozen of those knotheads down there weren't wearing anything but what they call hoodies. Most of them would be freezing to death on the way home, but they'd rather shiver and complain all the way instead of lugging jackets around.

When I was a kid, I loved coats, but as the Old Man always told me, "The times, they are a'changin'." I've been thinking for a long time they're changing for the worse.

"Thanks for finishing your assignment."

He made a noise that I took for "you're welcome." "It was kinda fun."

"You like history?"

"Yeah."

"Yessir?"

"Yessir."

"History was always my favorite, too."

"Do I need it to be a Texas Ranger?"

"No, but you need it to graduate. You want to be a Ranger?"

He bent his knees, swayed, and did that annoying thing young people do with their hands and fingers, thinking it looks cool. "Yessir. There's a lot of criminals that need killin', *ese*."

I didn't like where the conversation was headed. "Number one, do *not* use that gangbanger crap around me."

He lowered his eyes, realizing he'd crossed an invisible line. "Sorry."

My voice softened. "And second, that's not why we go into law work. It ain't to kill people. A Ranger's job's to keep the public safe and to work with other agencies to solve crimes." I wanted him off the track he was following. "Besides, you don't get out of high school and go straight into this branch. You have to be in another division of law enforcement first."

"That's how you started out?"

"Yep, as a highway patrol officer with the DPS. You can do the same thing."

He stared out the wavy windows, shivered, and mimicked me by stuffing both hands in the pockets of his jeans. "But I have to graduate first?"

"Right. You don't graduate high school, you can't go to college, and without college these days, you can't get into any aspect of law work."

"*Vato!* I'd like to skin out of this one-horse town and get a job somewhere to make some money."

I frowned at him and he realized what he'd said. Instead of calling me "dude" again, he plowed on. "I hear they're hiring pretty good out in the oil fields. If I had fare to Midland, I'd head out as soon as this weather clears."

The kid had no idea what he said sounded like "fair to middlin'," a phrase the old-timers used to describe the grade of cotton bought at the gin. It evolved to mean they were feeling good, but not great.

"Well, staying in school's best, and I doubt they're hiring high school kids to do anything right now."

"I could get a job at a gas station."

"There ain't no money in pumping gasoline. You'd be wasting the years you should be getting an education. Get a job around here and work on your lessons at the same time."

"Oh my God, bro." He saw my eyebrow. "Sorry. Who's gonna hire *me*? Every kid in town wants a job, and kids only get shit jobs anyway."

"I don't see many of the other kids out working too hard to find one this time of the year." I thought about Andy at the Posada and his holiday decorations. "I saw a feller fifteen minutes ago that'll probably hire you. You do good and he might hire you to sweep his sidewalk."

"I don't want to sweep sidewalks, that's sh—."

"Shit work." I leaned forward, pleased at the surprised expression on his face. I usually don't talk like that around kids, but I needed to get his attention. "You don't want a job. You want to get gone out of town, and you're just looking for an excuse."

Arturo stared at the painted floorboards. "I want to get away from my old man. He's mean, and the farther away I can get from him, the better."

"That's more like it. Now you're telling the truth. I believe he'll be away for a while."

He ran fingers through the long hair hanging in his eyes. "INS get him? They send him back across?"

He meant the Rio Grande. "Soon if he's not there already."

"Good. He ain't my real dad anyway. Mama, she don't think much of him, either. Calls him a *fronchi,* even though he don't have his card."

I bit back a grin at the derogatory word native-born Mexican Americans use to describe legal immigrants from Chihuahua, Mexico, who bear the U.S. green card that reads, *Fronterizo Chihuahua* or Chihuahua Frontier.

"Don't let any of them hear you say that, or you'll likely get your butt handed to you."

Like any kid I've ever been around, Arturo changed conversations on a dime when something caught his attention. He pointed to the badge on my chest. "Those are way more cool than regular cop badges."

The distinctive star cut from a real silver Mexican

cinco peso fascinated most boys. Granddad was a Ranger in 1962 and wore one of the badges based on the style from the 1800s. The one on my shirt was his.

"There were sixty-two of these give out back in Granddad's day. The new ones are different. You can earn one, but it'll be tough. Right now there are only two hundred and fourteen of us."

"I can do it."

"You need to keep your nose clean. One juvie violation, one serious mark on your record, and you've blown your chance. Your record has to be spotless."

A faint wrinkle appeared in the smooth skin between his eyes. "Do they take someone who's *mano izquierda*?" He flexed the fingers on his left hand.

I wasn't sure what Arturo meant. My Spanish wasn't bad, but I had to think about it for a minute. "You mean lefties? I thought that was *zurdo*."

"It depends on who's talking Spanish to you, but yeah."

"Why wouldn't they? There's nothin' wrong with being left-handed."

"Where my people come from, a *mano izquierda* is evil." When I raised my eyebrow, he explained. "When the old people see someone use this hand, you can see it in their eyes. Mano . . . left-handed people . . . are witches, maybe, and they don't like it. They cut their eyes and sometimes make the sign." He crossed himself and waved at his eyes with two fingers in a way I'd never seen before. "I think that's what my stepdad didn't like about me. I didn't want to be left-handed. I'm not evil."

I felt sorry for the kid. I never did like superstitions, or the dusty old church ideas of sin and sinning. "Kid, there's nothing evil about it. The Rangers don't care about which hand you scratch your butt with. They care about what kind of person you are. Act right, and you'll be just fine."

He laughed and started to answer, but was interrupted by a familiar sound that I never thought I'd hear in my courthouse, the hard, staccato pounding of automatic weapons.

Chapter 13

Because of the snow and Bowden's questionable driving skills, Kahn made an executive decision. "Stop here."

"Wicked said for me to circle the block and park in front of that last house over yonder." Despite his argument, Burt Bowden was grateful to let off the gas and pull to the curb. He was nervous and having second thoughts in his involvement with the takeover.

"I am in charge here. Do as I say. Shut off the engine."

"I'll let y'all out and pull around. I don't want to make Wicked mad."

"You shut off the motor and give me the keys."

The cab was filled with the big diesel's growl as Bowden glanced at the courthouse through the frosty drivers' window. He was in a pissing contest with a man with death in his eyes. "This is my damn truck."

"Give them to me."

Bowden killed the engine, rolled down the window, and dangled the keys outside as if he were arguing with a juvenile. His voice trembled. "I'll do what I want."

"You shouldn't have angered me." Kahn pointed at the courthouse. "They see us."

Bowden turned his head. The Syrian drew a long knife from his belt at the same time and plunged it into the rancher's throat, then slashed outward with the keen edge, cutting through cartilage, tendons, and arteries that spouted a fountain of blood. The keys flew into the storm as Bowden slapped both hands to his neck in a vain effort to close the huge wound.

Kahn wiped the blade on the cloth seat as the man gurgled and thrashed his life away behind the steering wheel. He opened the passenger door. "Your vehicle smells of cow shit. I like the odor of infidel blood much better."

Kahn left the warm cab and slammed the door. He kicked through the accumulating fluff and unlocked the metal doors to release the now heavily armed mixed bag of terrorists.

Richard Carver stepped down and took in his surroundings. His men had trained for a different arrival scenario. "What happened? We were supposed to launch from the other side of those houses."

Kahn watched him, hands full of a nasty-looking H&K MP5. He seemed disinterested and answered in a soft, accented voice. "Change in plans."

Despite the Beretta M9 in the thigh holster near his hand and the battle-slung Colt M4, Carver avoided the jihadist's dead gaze. From the shape of the stubby weapon, Kahn could bring it to bear in an instant. "It don't make *me* no never mind. Let's go, boys." No longer in charge, Carver joined the flow of terrorists who took the most direct route to the courthouse and stormed into the west entrance.

Kahn watched the rest of the men pour from the trailer and charge the courthouse.

DeVaca, aka Wicked, backed his van across the southern lawn and slammed on the brakes, skidding to a stop just short of the entrance. Brandishing automatic weapons, Tin Man, Scarecrow, and Lion squirted through the doors and rushed inside to fan out through the historic building.

Watching his men peel off to complete their assignments, DeVaca tugged a ballistic vest over his Pendleton shirt and smoothed it closed with the Velcro on the sides. He tugged a black cap down over his dark hair. With everything but her eyes hidden by the hijab, Dorothy handed his weapon back and followed him toward the tax office to pick up his first target.

Each team had specific instructions and targets.

Richard Carver and Tom Jordan met Kahn in the rotunda.

The California team listened for instructions from Wicked. DeVaca pointed upward. "Shut it down."

The tallest member, Usman Muhammed Al-Zahwi, shot up the stairway, followed by short and skinny Muhammad Qambrani.

Shouts of fear rose throughout the first floor as Scarecrow dropped his pack and slung a heavy satchel over his shoulder. He fell in behind the Syrians.

Three of the homegrown terrorists, Billy Koval, Milton Jordan, and Danny Woods, shouldered through the congested rotunda and rushed down the hallway to secure the north entrance overlooking the sheriff's office. Their faces were concealed by ski masks that looked like skulls.

The remaining attackers dumped their first load of equipment in the middle of the rotunda floor and charged back outside, knowing they had but a few minutes to unload as much as possible from the horse trailer before first responders could mount a defense.

Mr. Beck Terrill heard a commotion in the hallway as he stepped out of the restroom, a place he needed more and more as the years passed. He found himself staring down the muzzle of a dangerous-looking firearm and his mouth went dry.

The man threatening him with an M4 issued orders in Spanish. "*Manos arribas!*"

The old veteran raised his hands as other armed men rushed past. "I'm a-doin' it."

"*Síguelos. Muévete!*"

Terrill remained where he was, his hands in the air.

The lower half of the man's face was hidden by a bright blue bandana. He jerked his head toward the men dressed in tactical clothing of various styles, some with faces hidden by bandanas and ski masks. Four of them wore headgear that Terrill recognized as wrappings favored by Muslim terrorists.

Shemagh popped into his head and he grunted in disgust. "Can't remember the name of my favorite brand of sausage, but I know what them damned rags are called."

Bandana grabbed his shoulder. "*Síguelos!*"

"All right. I don't follow the lingo. Simmer down. You speak English? *Hablas Inglés?*"

"No. *Muévete!*"

Terrill realized he couldn't hesitate any longer. "Good. You oughta file the front sight off that rifle when you get a chance, 'cause it won't hurt as bad when I shove it up your ass later."

He fell in behind other stunned hostages herded by their disguised captors.

Chapter 14

"No one's answering nine one one!" The woman's shrill, terror-filled voice stopped when DeVaca kicked open the wood and glass door to the tax office. He paused in front of a plump secretary, who glanced up from her phone with wide eyes.

DeVaca glanced down at a photo in his hand and spoke first. "You're not Katie Bright."

Terrified, she held the phone to her ear. Gunshots echoed in the hall, and she yelped. "No." Her eyes flicked to Dorothy, whose face was obscured by the hijab.

He noted the nameplate on her desk. "Carlita, that's too bad."

He drew the Glock and shot her in the forehead.

The report slapped the walls as a fine red mist splattered the shelves behind her. Carlita's arms flapped in a bizarre backstroke and one leg pushed hard, rolling her chair back as if she wanted to stand.

On the other side of the office, a young woman shrieked and did the smart thing. She raised her hands. DeVaca dropped the photo on the floor. "Katie Bright?"

Both her hands and voice trembled. "Yes."

He pointed. "That one."

Dorothy started forward at the same instant a door at the rear of the office slammed open.

Judge Dollins was in what he considered his "satellite" office where he could work without climbing up and down the stairs all day. He sometimes rode the ancient elevator but conceded that he needed the exercise, so he used the stairs despite his knees to quiet his wife and the girls in the office. Sometimes, though, he couldn't bear to do either, so he used the tiny room in back of the tax office.

He dropped his Montblanc at the report of automatic weapon fire somewhere in the building and listened, making sure he wasn't hearing things. Frightened voices coming from the tax office confirmed his mental faculties were intact. Yanking off his reading glasses, the judge jerked open the top right-hand drawer of his borrowed desk and grabbed a Taurus Ultralite revolver he kept there for just such an incident.

He'd dealt with plenty of angry citizens through the years, and had always expected some nut to do more than shout and make threats. Even though the sheriff's office was right across the street, he knew it'd be up to him and the .38 to protect himself and his girls until someone with a badge arrived.

Another slap of a gunshot told him the Crazy Person was in his outer office. Overweight and out of shape, Dollins didn't feel his knees pop when he rose and rushed through the door, intending to shoot the Crazy Person as soon as he saw him.

He yanked the wooden door open and pushed through to find his fury vanish at the sight of Carlita sprawled in her chair, the back of her head destroyed by a massive exit wound. The judge's mouth went coppery at the sight of four terrorists with automatic weapons.

He knew he was outgunned, but surprise was on his side.

Out of practice and frightened, he shot one-handed and too fast with his little snub-nosed revolver. The round passed between the terrorists and buried itself in the door facing.

He jerked the trigger again.

Wicked and Dorothy were caught unawares when the imposing figure of a large man appeared in the doorway of his office and started blazing away with a pistol. Two of the shots missed.

The big man fired a third time and behind DeVaca, Tom Jordan *ooofed*, stumbling backward.

DeVaca glanced around to see one of his home-grown terrorists slam against a filing cabinet. Of course, bullets would find someone else, because he was destined to live and do great things.

Dorothy pointed her H&K and fired at the same time DeVaca opened up with the Scorpion. The swarm of bullets ended the big man's response. He fell back into his office and lay still in a growing pool of blood.

Shaking, Richard Carver knelt beside Jordan. "Tom, you hit bad?"

The white-faced American-born terrorist took a deep, shuddering breath. "Vest. He hit me in the vest and that saved me."

"Come on!" Carver helped him up and they bracketed Katie Bright. Angry and scared, Carver leaned in to the crying woman. "Don't fight, and you'll be fine. We have this planned down to a T."

Disgusted that they were talking and not acting, Dorothy elbowed Jordan out of the way, pushed between them, and grabbed a handful of Katie's blond hair. She jerked the young woman off balance. "Come on, *bitch*!"

A shrill voice down the hall screamed and screamed and screamed. The shriek that could have been male or female ended with the flat report of a single gunshot that sounded like a firecracker. Several more in quick succession told even the most clueless that something more serious than fireworks was making that noise.

The Ballard courthouse drew up a crisis plan after 9/11, but it was only a dim memory of a one-sheet handout distributed two days after the towers fell in New York. However, it never addressed the first critical moments of an assault other than to "shelter in place."

In other offices throughout the building, a few quick-thinking workers attempted to do just that by barricading themselves in a workroom. Had the takeover been orchestrated by a single active shooter, the shelter-in-place concept might have been successful, or at least bought them some time.

The attack wasn't a lone gunman wandering through a building after targets of opportunity, though. The authors of the shelter-in-place plan never expected twenty armed professionals operating under a strategic plan.

Chapter 15

Dorothy yanked Katie along, still bracketed by Carver and Jordan. Jordan's mouth was twisted into a painful grimace as he applied more pressure than necessary on Katie's arms. Instead of shoving her into the growing crowd of frightened hostages on the rotunda floor, Dorothy led the trio toward the open elevator.

The corner of DeVaca's mouth rose, and he shifted the short Scorpion in his arms as he watched Katie stumble between the men, bent almost double by the pressure on her arms. He preferred the stubby little machine gun for close-quarter work, but had provided the others with Colt M4s he'd bought from a man who worked with the CIA.

The twist was beautiful and ironic.

DeVaca adjusted the glasses on his nose. His people were still herding the last of the hostages toward the two staircases on either side of the rotunda. "This is taking too long! I need *this* floor clear right now!"

The rotunda cleared and the southern doors slammed open once again. DeVaca's people lined up, passing metal cases from the rear of the open van backed as close as possible against the double doors. Icy wind sucked through the opening, dropping the interior temperature.

District Attorney Todd Calvert trudged through the snow toward the courthouse, late for work because of the falling weather. For once his titanium legs were coming in handy. Diabetes had taken them from the knees down six years earlier and he'd learned to walk again with a slow, deliberate gait.

At least my feet aren't cold.

Living with his disability was better than bitching and moaning about it for the rest of his life. Tieless for the first time in months, he wasn't in any hurry, confident Judge Dollins would shut the building down by noon. He was looking forward to settling into his chair in the den after dinner, sipping Glenlivet and enjoying a rare afternoon off.

Calvert remembered his son Mark was inside with his class and he grinned at the idea of the stodgy courthouse coming to life with young energy for a couple of hours. Because of the snow, the kids would be bouncing off the walls with excitement.

The smile disappeared at the sight of the conversion van backed up to the door. He wondered if someone might be servicing the heating system, but *damn* they'd pulled up close, and besides, it wasn't a panel van. He was relieved to see he had enough room to squeeze past. Had it been blocked, he'd have been forced to walk around the corner and into the teeth of the steady north wind.

The muffled sound of gunfire rolled through the open doors, and he stopped.

"Shit!"

His son. The kids.

Calvert assumed a lone gunman was inside. His instinct was to drop to one knee, forgetting that those days were long gone. Instead, he balanced his briefcase in the palm of his left hand, using it as a rickety platform. Fingers trembling, he snapped the latches open and withdrew a Glock 19. Calvert pitched the briefcase aside, not caring about the papers that scattered in the snow. He sidled to the right, trying to see around the van. His stiff foot caught and he stumbled.

Recovering his balance, he braced his legs and readied the weapon. He'd practiced on a homemade range in the desert dozens of times, but no amount of conventional shooting prepared him for the man that appeared with a firearm pointed in his direction.

Unlike the times Calvert popped away at paper targets, adrenaline flooded his system. The sights that were steady on the zombie target shook like a leaf. Calvert shot first, but missed. The +P bullet punched a hole in the van's side with a hollow, metallic chink. He side-stepped, lost his balance, and shot too fast, missing again.

That's when *two* streams of automatic weapons fire answered. Hot lances of pain exploded in his chest and torso. A round slapped his titanium shin and knocked him down, whining away as he fell, landing hard on his face.

He didn't feel the icy crystals against his cheek. Calvert blinked a couple of times to clear his vision. Still game, and with the genetic programming of all humans to protect their children, he struggled to raise his pistol. Bullets stitched the ground around him, sending bursts of black dirt and dead grass into the air.

Several of the rounds found flesh and the DA stilled.

Chapter 16

The sheriff's office on the east side of the courthouse was much too modern for most people's taste even when they put it up in 1950. Opposite in style from the magnificent courthouse a hundred yards away, the uninspiring glass and brick monstrosity didn't belong in West Texas.

The central reception area was the first thing a visitor or prisoner encountered. Past the waist-high Formica counter, the sheriff's office was to the left, and a cluster of other offices took up the right. A plain door at the back led to six cells stretched the width of the building, three on each side of the rear exit.

Sheriff Ethan Armstrong hooked the handle of his stained cup with an index finger and drug it off the shelf above the ancient Mr. Coffee the deputies referred to as the Johnny Holmes edition. The coffee-maker earned its nickname from the moans and groans that accompanied a string of obscene gurgling noises during the entire drip process that ended with a drawn out *ahhhhhhh* as the reservoir boiled dry.

No one ever used Ethan's cup from Bubba's Bar-B-

Que in Jackson Hole because it had never been washed with soap. In Ethan's opinion, the dark glaze improved the coffee's flavor.

He filled it from the steaming pot and took a sip, catching the unfamiliar aroma. He grimaced and sniffed the brew again. "What'n hell's this?"

Deputy Frank Malone followed Armstrong into the sheriff's office. He tilted his hat back. "Emily said she wanted to celebrate the snow with something different." He saluted with his own mug. "She calls it 'snicker-doodle.'"

Ethan thumped the cup atop a pile of papers on his desk. "Y'all can drink that crap if you want to, but not me. Tell her to go buy one of those fancy one-cup coffeepots if she wants to celebrate with this foo-foo stuff and leave mine alone. If there's not a fresh pot on there in ten minutes, I'm gonna pour it in the commode, make my own, and find a new secretary."

Frank took a sip and winced. "Don't worry. I'll do it right now."

"Have *Emily* make some more."

"She ran over to the courthouse."

Ethan unzipped his coat just as the reverberation of gunfire reached them. "What'n hell was *that*?"

"Sounds like somebody's shooting." Frank smacked his cup down on Ethan's desk, splashing snicker-doodle on a stack of manila file folders. Separating the venetian blinds on the front window, he peered into the snowstorm. "What fool would be cranking off rounds *in* town in *this* weather?"

* * *

Two long bursts of fire erupted at the south entrance. DeVaca pressed the communication button on his chest. "Team Two. What was that?"

A second exchange swelled and stopped. There were no more answering shots.

Muhammad Qambrani came on the radio. "A suit tried to be a hero." He might have wanted to say more, but his voice was drowned out by another volley of fire. "That one was someone in a uniform."

"Is this Qambrani?"

"Yes."

DeVaca's face flushed. "Why are you at the south entrance?"

"They needed my help unloading your gear."

A voice in the back of DeVaca's mind growled in a high, irritated voice. He was familiar with the Demon. It had been part of his life since he was a child. "Hurry up and finish, then get back to your assignment."

He watched Dorothy step out of the disabled elevator where they'd tied Katie Bright into a chair. "What use is it to make assignments if these fools refuse to listen?"

She knew better than to answer.

Sheriff Armstrong's radio came to life.

"Sheriff, this' Eric!" Deputy Goodlett was breathless, running. "There's shootin' coming from the courthouse, but it's snowing so hard I can't tell for sure what's going on! Aw shit! There's a van and somebody shot Todd Calvert! They shot the DA! I see two men! Put the gun down! Show me your hands! Show me your—"

Deputy Goodlett's transmission ended with a long burst of automatic gunfire.

"Aw hell." Ethan rushed past Deputy Frank Malone and into the reception area. "Who's here?"

"Just us!"

Ethan snatched the radio off his belt and yanked the front door open. "All units! All—"

A wave of snow-filled air swirled around Deputy Tommy Pelham, who was reaching for the handle when Ethan jerked the front door open. The deputy's eyes were wide in shock. "Sheriff, you hear that?"

The whip-crack of bullets slamming into the bricks and glass cut off Armstrong's response. Pelham absorbed several rounds with a gasp, falling over the threshold and into the sheriff's arms. Ethan threw himself backward, pulling the limp deputy inside as the windows and doorframe exploded under a volley of fire.

"Get down! Get down!" Ethan twisted out from under Deputy Pelham's body and crabbed through splintered glass and wood, dragging him to cover behind the counter.

In the dispatch office, Karen Anderson crawled through the door. Deputy Malone pointed toward the rear exit. "Go! Get out now!"

Incoming fire raked the building as Deputy Malone grabbed Pelham's belt and helped Ethan pull. Behind the counter, Ethan was surprised to see the radio still in his now-blood-splattered hand. "All units! All units! This is Sheriff Armstrong. Officer down! Officers under fire at the courthouse! We're taking automatic weapons fire at the station!"

Ethan pointed at the shattered door. "Stay down and keep that door covered!"

"I see armed men at the courthouse door!" On his stomach and shooting around the built-in reception desk, Deputy Malone returned fire with his Glock 21, with the deliberation he used at the shooting range.

Ethan keyed his radio. "Officers down at both the north and south ends of the courthouse! Do not approach the courthouse. The sheriff's department's also under heavy fire! Repeat, we are under automatic weapons fire by multiple individuals in the courthouse!"

Ethan left Pelham and scooted across the linoleum floor to the gun safe. Bullets punched through the walls, spraying dust and splinters. The safe was unlocked, and Ethan didn't need to fumble with the combination. A round slammed through the counter and ricocheted off the floor, barely missing the sheriff's boot.

Staying low as possible, he reached inside, withdrew an AR-15, and slapped in a full magazine. "Frank." He slid the rifle across the floor.

Deputy Malone ejected an empty mag from his pistol and reloaded. Muscle memory took over as he released the slide with his thumb and jammed the hot weapon back into his holster. He grabbed the automatic rifle, charged the bolt, and snugged the synthetic stock against his shoulder. Bullets raked the building as he cranked off half the magazine, hoping to slow their rate of fire. Ethan took down another rifle, repeated the loading process and slid three full magazines to Malone.

Now they were both at least as well armed as their opponents. Ethan keyed the radio again. "All units.

The command center will be at the Posada Hotel." The words came fast and breathless. "Use the hotel's east entrance. Repeat. Use the *east* entrance of the Posada. Charles Street may be under fire. Be careful getting over there, boys, I don't know what the hell's going on." Several rounds shredded the Johnny Holmes coffeepot, putting an end to its obscene gurgling. Hot coffee showered the floor. "But right now stay away from the courthouse. Frank, creepy-crawl out the back."

"That sounds like a good idea."

"Help me with Pelham."

"He's dead, boss."

"We take him with us anyway."

Dragging the body, they crawled between the empty cells where the Mayo brothers had spent the night and through the back door. Out of the line of fire, they rose and hoisted Pelham's body on Deputy Malone's shoulder.

Using the building and snowstorm for cover, they ran through the alley and across the empty street to the Palace Theater. Malone ran panting along behind Ethan as he cut between the buildings to South Charles Street. Heavy snow cloaked the courthouse in a dancing veil of white, preventing those inside from seeing farther than the theater on the corner.

A covey of Red Hat women were huddled in the Posada Hotel's lobby, not far from the roaring fireplace. One of the younger members of the over-fifty fun-society group screamed when the snow-covered lawmen burst through the door with weapons in hand.

Andy Clark was on the phone behind the registration counter. At the sight of the two lawmen and the limp deputy, he trailed off with the receiver in hand.

"Something's going on all right, but I don't . . . an ever'thing—" He hung up without taking his eyes off Malone and the rifle in his hand.

Ethan swept a vase of flowers off a long table and they replaced it with Pelham's body. "No one go outside. Andy, I'm commandeering the building. Frank, cover that door until we get some help. Andy, clear the banquet room, I'm using it as a command post. You have a pistol back there with you?"

The white-faced hotel owner reached under the counter and produced a Judge, a revolver chambered for both .45 and .410 shotgun shells.

Despite what they'd just been through, Ethan's eyes widened at the sight of the large bore in the big revolver that judges have been known to carry into courtrooms for protection. "That'll do. Watch that other door until my men arrive."

Andy faced the doors coming off the patio.

Outside, the snowstorm ramped up.

Chapter 17

The steady chatter of automatic gunfire rolled down the hallway from the northern entrance. Return fire shattered the glass doors and whined overhead. DeVaca regarded the hallway without blinking. "Team Four, report."

An American voice came into his ear. He thought it sounded like the dumpy guy named Danny. "We were about to get company from across the street when some lawmen came out. Ol' Billy and Milton changed their minds for 'em. They're back inside now."

The transmission stopped when the rate of fire escalated at that same end of the building. DeVaca remained rooted to his spot, listening to return fire from outside. He keyed the transmit button when the volume died down.

"Update."

"*Dayum!*" This time Danny Woods's voice was shrill with adrenaline. "They *unloaded* on us, I think they have a mini-gun over there! Do you think that was a mini-gun, Milton?"

Milton's voice shook. "Hell no. There ain't no mini-gun in any sheriff's department in West Texas."

"It don't matter. We pushed 'em back. I don't expect they'll be shooting any more for a while."

Two light pops sounding like a handgun came from the second floor, the echoes reverberating in the rotunda. A torrent of automatic fire cut off a scream. The burst was followed by silence.

DeVaca glanced upward. "Tin Man?"

"Light contact. We missed some secretary who wanted to fight."

"Texans." DeVaca's voice was full of disgust. He pressed the button again. "Do you have the second floor secure?"

The response was immediate. "Yes."

DeVaca grinned. "Excellent. Is the courtroom cleared?"

"Yes. Bring the rest of them up."

"Dorothy! Move them now."

Fahio Muhammed Ally Mslam knelt, placed his weapon on the ground, and opened a black plastic case with a recognizable shape. He withdrew a chainsaw, primed it by pushing the rubber bulb, and gave the starter rope a tug. The engine coughed, sputtered, and died. He tugged again, then again, with the same frustrating result.

Frightened, the Syrian met DeVaca's gaze. This was his one single most important duty. Sweat beaded on his forehead. He knew DeVaca's finger was twitching.

He yanked again, then again, before remembering he hadn't choked the engine. He flipped the switch and heaved on the rope once, then twice, before the engine roared to life.

DeVaca watched the last captives straggle up the stairs, pushed like cattle by the invaders. Behind him, the Muslim terrorist thanked Allah aloud for sparing him and went to work with the saw. He revved it twice and the engine changed pitch as the tip cut through the polished 140-year-old oak floor.

Chapter 18

At the sound of gunfire, Arturo whipped around to charge down the narrow stairs along the curved wall. I reached for his arm and missed.

"Arturo, wait!"

I didn't yell, because the gunshots came from multiple weapons. I had no idea how many people were downstairs, but it wasn't just one or two. Every nerve in my body jangled like an old-fashioned telephone.

I snagged the collar of his jacket, yanking him toward me. "Where are you going?"

"Somebody's shooting!" His eyes were glassy with excitement.

I took a better grip and gave him a shake. "Kid!" His eyes darted in all directions like those of a caged animal looking for escape, the tension and dread between us thick and heavy. "The smart thing to do is to stay right here and not go running toward trouble."

He was like a frightened horse in a barn fire. His eyes rolled and he pulled away. With my nose inches from his, I spoke in a voice that even *I* didn't recognize. It came from deep in the back of my throat and was born of terror for my family and us. "*Listen*! I don't know what's going on down *there*, but you're staying *here*."

The sheer violence I radiated burned through his adolescent hysteria. He held my gaze and settled down. "I hear you."

"Fine then." I drew the Colt from the hand-tooled Brill holster hanging from the Ranger rig on my hips and did my best to tamp down the fear burning like acid. A quick glance through the clear left-hand side of my pistol's grip reassured me it was loaded, with brass peeking through the small holes in the magazine. The other side of the Sweetheart grips held a photo of my grandmother under Lucite. The pistol my grandfather carried in World War II, and on duty as a Ranger, had been my primary weapon for years.

I pulled him to the opposite side of the round room, away from the open stairway, which amounted to about ten feet. "Listen, kid, and be quiet. Something bad's happening down there. People could be dying, so you're gonna do what I say, do . . . you . . . understand?"

He seemed to shrink in his jacket. "Yes."

"Good. We're lucky we're up here." I glanced toward the stairwell to make sure we were still alone and lowered my voice in case someone was sneaking up on us. "You're gonna wait right here while I go down and make sure the room below is empty. Then I'll call you down and show you where to hole up until somebody comes to get you."

Two more shots barked up the staircase.

A woman's shriek came from below and I prayed it wasn't my wife. It was all I could do not to go charging downstairs like Arturo. "There's a door at the bottom of these stairs. Did you see it when we came up?"

He shook his head.

"No matter. It leads into the attic. I'm fixin' to go down first to check things out. Listen, and when I tell you, come down as quiet as possible. I'll have the door open. You duck inside without a word, get it?"

"Yessir." He watched the balustrade beside the floor access.

I hoped the attic door wasn't locked. I couldn't re-member if the long-shanked padlock was hanging open on the hasp when we passed earlier. "Once you're there, stay inside until someone official shows up. Got it?"

A short burst of gunfire resulted in a shriek that faded into a wail. Adults screamed and children screamed, and I knew in my heart that Kelly's students were among them, but I also knew that rushing down right then would help no one. My heart hammered.

Please God, I thought, *give me the strength not to be stupid*.

More pops resulted in another shriek that found its way into our enclosure.

An angry male voice. "No! Get your hands off me you son of a bitch, who the hell are you? I'm—"

Two flat gunshots ignited more chaos. A war ex-ploded somewhere down below, and I made out auto-matic weapons in use both inside and out. I saw a flicker of fear in Arturo's face. "Kid, we have to move! Give me twenty seconds to clear the floor below us and be ready to come when I say. Start counting to twenty, and do it slow. One Mississippi, two Mississippi."

Chapter 19

The chainsaw reverberated throughout the rotunda, making conversation almost impossible. Dorothy stepped close to DeVaca and cocked her head toward the short hallway leading to the west entrance. "Wicked? *Malvado, un momento, por favor?*"

His skin prickled at the musical sound of Dorothy's soft voice pronouncing his mission name. The dusky-skinned woman was fast becoming an impossible obsession.

"What is it?"

She pulled him toward the wall, taking care not to stand in front of the translucent doors. "The trailer is parked across the street."

"You're sure."

"Yes. I was told and confirmed it myself."

His eyes widened in fury. He slapped the comm button attached to his vest. "Kahn!"

Mohammad Hani Kahn was in the tax office when he heard the shout and joined them without hurrying. His lack of immediate response infuriated DeVaca. "Yes?"

"Why is the trailer here, instead of one block over?"

"The snow forced a change in plans. As you said, we must be able to adapt, and I did."

In a red rage, DeVaca thought about swiveling the stubby Scorpion and emptying an entire thirty-round magazine into the radical terrorist. Kahn had no idea that he'd compromised what DeVaca considered the most important part of the mission.

The enclosed horse trailer was a primary tool in transporting what was under their feet if they found what he hoped was there, and the number of items was as described. DeVaca needed the large carrying space to haul everything away, while at the same time becoming a dispersal tool of unimaginable consequences. He'd fantasized about its implementation for months.

But if his goal wasn't met, if the building was sitting on a solid, undisturbed foundation, the trailer was to be a decoy full of escaping terrorists that would draw all the attention from the responders as he alone fled on foot.

Now both plans were compromised.

DeVaca's expression told Kahn that he was about to die. The silence that swept in when the chainsaw went silent saved the man's life. DeVaca relaxed. Killing the radical might lead to more deaths among his men, and he needed everyone until the end.

He remembered a cautionary tale written by an Anglican priest in the 1600s. *For the want of a nail, a shoe was lost. For the want of a shoe, a horse was lost. For the want of a horse, a knight was lost. For the want of a knight, a battle was lost. For the want of a battle, a kingdom was lost—all for the want of a nail.*

DeVaca might need the simple nail staring back with

an insolent expression. "You don't know what you've done."

"I've adapted and improvised, according to my training."

"You have altered my plan."

"Allah will provide the way out."

"He already has, but now I can't—never mind."

DeVaca shoved past Kahn, maintaining eye contact and dismissing the man as if he were nothing, daring him to try and shoot him in the back.

Kahn wouldn't shoot, because no man could kill Wicked.

Chapter 20

Gunfire rose and fell. Something bad was going down, but I knew better than to rush into the middle of things without knowing what was happening.

The Lucite semiautomatic pistol grips were sweaty in my palm, and I took a deep breath to settle my nerves. All was silent. Trembling, I started downstairs one slow step at a time. One. Two. Three. Four.

Boots thumped up the stairs below. A male voice challenged me with a strong Spanish accent. "Hands over your head and come down!"

He couldn't see the upper half of my body, but I was compromised. I gave Arturo a quick headshake and held a hand out to make him stand still. Any shift in weight would give him away if the floor creaked.

I couldn't go back up. If he *was* a bad guy, he'd shoot me full of holes before I could take two steps. I couldn't bring the pistol to bear for the same reason. My hope was that the guy was a law-enforcement officer. I held my hands high, though the upper part of my body was still hidden from the man's view.

My voice shook, and it wasn't an act. I was as scared of that feller as I was of a bear. I bent to see a man with a nasty-looking machine pistol pointed at my chest. I'm not enough of a weapon guy to recognize the gun from that angle, but none of that mattered. The muzzle looked as wide as a culvert.

He wore a black watch cap with one of those tube scarves pulled up over his mouth and nose so I could only see his eyes. Mixed camo patterns covered by a tactical vest and worn military-style boots told me everything I needed to know.

Goosebumps rose on the back of my neck as I stared down the barrel of that killing machine. "You're a cop?"

"That is correct. Hurry."

"Okie dokey. What's going on? Is everything all right?" I took another step down. I was between a rock and a hard place.

"Everything is fine. I am a state policeman. There is a problem downstairs, and I am making sure we are safe. You come down with your hands high until I find out who you are."

State police, my ass. His formal speech was unfamiliar to our part of the world, where we cut words down as short as possible and contracted the rest.

Still bent to see below the floor, I took another cautious step down the narrow stairs. It was impossible to survive a gunfight under those circumstances. I needed to bide my time. While my hands were still out of his sight, I laid the .45 on top of the pony wall around the staircase, hoping my Wyoming Traders coat hid the badge, holster, and gun belt.

I figured the ranch coat would give him the idea that I was one of the local cowboys. Now, why a rancher or ranch hand would be in the courthouse observation deck in the middle of the worst snowstorm in years would be anybody's guess, but I knew criminals were seldom the valedictorians of their class.

Then I remembered the tie around my neck with a feeling of dread. Ranchers don't wear 'em. I hoped this guy wasn't the salutatorian, either. "Easy, hoss. Don't shoot me."

His eyes were hard on me as I reached the bottom step. "*Manos* . . . hands up. Come to me! Who is up there?"

"Easy," I repeated. My mouth went dry as dust. "It's just me. Nobody else. Are you with the sheriff's department?"

Shrieks and cries of frightened people rose from below.

The gunman breathed hard through his nose, as if he'd found himself at a high altitude. "Yes. Come at me and get on the floor and spread your arms and legs. Put your face down!"

"Did Sheriff Hawke send you, Herman Hawke?"

He hesitated. "Yes. The Sheriff Hawke sent me. Are there others?"

The guy was a complete fraud, but he was the one calling the shots. I saw the communication button on the center of his chest and a pouch hanging over his shoulder.

"Like I just said, I'm by myself."

"Get down!"

That wasn't gonna happen. I hoped he hadn't pushed that transmit button to say I was up there, and I didn't think he had, yet. My boot finally touched the bottom step.

"Hey! It's all right." I took two steps forward, frowning like people do when I question them. I waved, lowering my hands a bit. I needed to get closer. "I live on a ranch outside of town. I just came in to pay my taxes and wanted to see the snow from the dome. What's going on down there? Are we safe?"

"*Abajo*! Down!" He poked the stubby muzzle at me as if he was trying to back up an unwanted dog with a stick. He helped my position by stepping forward, probably thinking he could get in my space and intimidate me into shutting up. The knuckles on his right hand were white on the pistol grip. "On the ground!"

"Okay. Okay." I took another step and bent my knees as he ordered. "Jeez. Am I under arrest or something, because I haven't done—"

A voice and a heavy footfall on the first step startled us both. "Mr. Sonny?"

The man jerked the muzzle toward the new threat and gave me the opening I'd been looking for. I charged into him with everything I had and grabbed the weapon's forend with my left hand to drive the stubby barrel upward, away from Arturo. I wrapped my hand over his on the pistol grip and twisted the gun back over his right forearm.

Arms aren't meant to bend that way. He went with it to escape the pressure. I kept pushing and twisting, driving him back. He lunged sideways, to get a better angle and twist the short gun back into my gut. His feet tangled with mine like we were a couple of first-time two-steppers, and he stumbled back to gain some distance.

That was a bad move, because I've always preached attack when in a conflict. Most bad guys waving guns around expect folks to do whatever they say, and un-trained civilians do just that.

I'll never know why he didn't pull the trigger, but I kept the pressure on and it became a struggle for pos-session of the weapon. I stomped his foot with the heel of my boot, and he grunted in pain, giving just enough for me to plant both feet and twist the weapon again, using it and my momentum to sling him off balance.

I felt him relax enough for me to let go of his gun hand and slam him with an uppercut. Adrenaline charged by fear and worry put everything I had behind it. The man's jaw shattered under my fist like glass, snapping his face toward the ceiling. I was surprised at how eas-ily I could cause so much damage.

I still had hold of the machine pistol's forend and wouldn't let go. My granddad used to say snapping tur-tles bite and hold on until it thunders, and that's how I felt right then. I wasn't turning loose, but neither was he.

We struggled for a few more seconds until I got a foot behind him. He went over backwards with me on top and we hit the floor hard, knocking the air out of him in a whoosh. His body armor under my chest was like falling on a boulder.

Despite a broken face, bad foot, and no air, the guy wasn't giving up. He kneed me hard in the thigh. It hurt like the devil, and he tried again. I drove my own knee into his nuts. You want to take the wind out of a guy, you hurt him there, but he was a tough bastard. Bracing myself upright with my other knee, I pushed hard on the gun, pinning the muzzle against the floor.

I'll be damned if he didn't keep fighting. He let go of the weapon and grabbed for the pistol strapped to his thigh in one of those military gunslinger rigs. I threw my weight to the left, pinning his arm, but the guy *still* wouldn't quit. I felt like I was in one of those nightmares when you're hitting someone and they won't stop what they're doing and none of the strikes seem to faze them.

A separate part of me saw our little rasslin' match going on for days. I didn't have that kind of time or stamina, so I did something I never thought would work. I head-butted his nose. Any other time it might have split my own forehead, but my hat acted as a cushion. It didn't work both ways, though. The force was enough to pop his nose like a rotten tomato. I've known that feeling, and it should have taken him out of the fight, but he was tough as boot leather.

He grabbed the tie around my neck with his left hand to choke me as the slipknot tightened. Red pressure built in my face and sparks flickered in front of my eyes. I kept hearing a strange, high-pitched sound in that offstage kind of way where you see and hear things without thinking about them, and realized the sound was coming from *me*.

There was nothin' else to do but let go and drive my fist into his Adam's apple as fast and hard as I could, doing my level best to punch through the man's neck and into the floor. I both felt and heard the cartilage shatter in his throat. He filled the room with a horrible gargle, legs drumming on the wooden floor.

I hit him a second time in the same place, just to be sure.

Then again for good measure.

Chapter 21

The storm dropped the temperature at an astounding rate. North winds drove the heavy snow sideways, reminding the old-timers of what it was like when they were kids.

Finished with checking his cows, Sonny Hawke's daddy steered his truck through the pasture along what he hoped was still the snow-covered two-track road as the storm raged over the peaceful ranch country north of the Big Bend. Herman grinned at a memory of his own dad, gone many years, who always said every time it came a blue norther there was nothing between Texas and Canada to stop the wind except for a couple of bob-wire fences.

Gabriel Nakai grabbed the dash as they drifted off the twin tracks and scraped over a greasewood bush. "Damn. Ass."

Herman was used to Gabe's odd speech. Despite his years in Texas, Gabe still had a few difficulties with the English language and never learned to cuss right, no matter how hard he tried.

Herman rubbed the gray stubble on his chin. "Turn the defroster up, Gabe. The windshield's icin' up."

Gabe came from a dusty little town outside of Parral, Mexico. After his wife died in childbirth, he towed his infant daughter across the Rio Grande and into the United States, hoping for a better life. Since then, he'd seen a lot of weather in his time in the U.S., but Gabriel had never seen so much snow fall at one time.

"It's doing the best, *jefe*. The *limpiaparabrisas* are coming apart, too. The rubber's too old, I think. You should have bought new ones the last time it rain."

"Wiper blades cost money, and 'sides, this drought hasn't called for new ones."

At seventy, Herman's vision was still as sharp as it always was, but he was squinting through the foggy glass into the thick curtain of flakes ahead of them. Each time they dipped into a swag, Herman squeezed the steering wheel of his battered 1985 Ford pickup in a death grip, leaning forward as if a couple more inches made a difference.

One of the brittle rubber blades separated from the wiper, guaranteed to disintegrate long before they got to town.

The narrow path winding through the brushy, cactus-filled pasture was the only way to know they were on the track. The storm was a full-blown blizzard by the time they neared the two-lane highway. The snow was already so deep the oil pan left a furrow behind the truck.

The snowdrift caught against cactus beside the wire gate was knee deep when they arrived. Wire gaps, floppy gates made of bob-wire and cedar posts, caused more than one preacher or ranch wife to backslide and use bad language through the years.

Gabe rested his callused hand on the door lever and sighed. "We need a *protector de ganado* here."

"Costs money. I don't believe I'm gonna pay for a cattle guard when I have a sturdy hand to get the gate."

"Not much of a gate, either." Gabe left the moist warmth of the cab, talking to himself. "Tighter'n a tick about a *protector de ganado* and won't put out money for new *limpiaparabrisas. Madre de Dios.*"

Gabe set his battered felt hat and waded through the snow to pull the aggravating barrier out of the way. Herman drove through and used the mirrors to watch Gabe wrestle the floppy gate back into position against the thick post and reset it in the bottom loop of wire.

Instead of hurrying back to the truck, Gabe disappeared into the storm. He returned less than a minute later and slammed the door. "*Hijo de puta!*" Snow sticking to his hat melted, filling the cab with the smell of wet dust and musk. He took it off and slapped it at the snow on his jeans. "There's a *cuerpo* between the fence and the road!"

Herman tightened. "You sure it's a body?"

"*Sí.* Frozen and almost covered. *Creo que es una mujer.*"

Herman smoothed his thick gray mustache. "What would a woman be doing out here?"

"*No se.* Her throat is cut."

"Good God." Herman's eyes flicked past Gabe and into the storm, as if he could see the extent of the woman's damage. "Well, we better tell somebody."

Gabe plucked his phone from a jean pocket. "I have *dos bares.*"

"Try mine." Herman unsnapped his shirt pocket and passed a scarred flip phone across. Gabe gave it a try while Herman pushed the foot-feed with a gentle touch to keep the back tires from spinning. They did anyway. He let off the gas, shoved the stubby gearshift lever in the floorboard, and felt the four-wheel drive catch. He accelerated again with the same careful nudge and steered onto the snow-covered highway. The tires held. "Sure wish I had my bag phone back. That thing would reach all across the country without a problem. I knew they were making a mistake when they went to these new digital phones. Any more bars on that one?"

"*No 'ueno.*"

"Must be the storm. We'll have to tell Ethan. We can stop in the Posada and call from there. He'll want us to stay close until he checks that body out, and besides, I don't think we're goin' no further'n Ballard today nohow."

The truck slid toward the shoulder, and Gabe grabbed the dash. "Shit! Shit . . . from a cow's ass."

Herman let off the gas and steered into the skid, getting them back onto the pavement. The motion caused the brim of his Stetson to bump the lever-action Winchester hanging in the gun rack in the back glass. Annoyed, he reset the hat farther back on his forehead and concentrated on his driving.

Chapter 22

I crept across the floor and, getting a good grip, unhooked the latch and lowered the trapdoor into the round room's floor. Without any other exit or entrance, our floor was the perfect place to defend, but that was the last thing on my mind.

I always thought that room was a helluva fire hazard, because there were no fire escapes on the outside. We used to laugh over at the café, thinking that if the building ever caught fire, the people in the upper floors would have to jump onto one of those round Browder Life Nets the Three Stooges always used in their movies. We thought it'd be funny to see our out-of-shape volunteer firefighters run around with one of those canvas antiques in their hands, yelling for people to jump.

It wasn't funny anymore.

We weren't safe with the door down, but it made me feel better. "Boy, what part of stay up there and keep quiet did you not understand?"

My voice was low. Still on the steps, Arturo bent to better hear what I was saying. I yanked off my tie and stripped the corpse of weapons, wishing I had time to strap on his body armor. The idea sounded good, but rolling a body around on the floor was out of the question. The vest was secured with wide belts of Velcro, and I didn't need those loud ripping sounds without knowing who was close and how many of them there were.

My one pistol and two spare magazines were no match for all the firepower I expected to find below. I struggled to yank the machine gun's strap free and saw it was an H&K MP5 machine pistol. The three-point sling was a pain in the ass to get off, but leaving the ugly little gun behind was a bad idea.

I never did like weapons like that, though a number of military and law-enforcement agencies once thought they were great. The sub guns fell from favor when those guys went to M4 rifles that fired heavier rounds. The selection switch was set on top of a string of bulletlike icons, automatic fire.

I took his Glock 17 and pulled the slide back. Seeing the brass casing, I released it and slipped the pistol inside the waistband at the small of my back, thankful for the extra seventeen rounds. "Hand me my pistol but be careful." I turned to see Arturo with my .45 in his hand.

Someone had taught him about firearms, because he handed it to me butt-first with Granddad's sepia-toned photo in the grip angled so I could see it. "Whose picture is that?"

In World War II, my granddaddy found some time on his hands and replaced the original grips on the 1911 with pieces of what then was a new material from airplane canopies, Lucite. Prior to putting the grips on, he placed a picture of us under the clear material. A lot of soldiers were doing that, and the replacements became known as Sweetheart grips.

"Grandma holding my dad when he was a baby. We don't have time to talk about it right now." I stuffed the Colt back in its holster.

In all the fighting, rolling, and tugging, the dead guy's headset came loose and dangled from its cord. I traced it to a pocket-sized radio unlike anything I'd ever seen. It was damaged in the fight, and I didn't have time to fiddle-fart around with it.

I scooped my hat up and slapped it back on my head. "Get that satchel and follow me." Arturo slung it over his shoulder and we heard the snarl of a two-cycle engine.

What'n hell are they doing down there. Weed eater? Limb trimmer?

Motioning to Arturo, I pointed at the troll-sized door beside the stairs leading to the dome. I was right, the open lock hung on the hasp. I pulled it free and twisted the knob. An electric hum filled the dark void.

Without heat, the uninsulated attic was like a refrigerator. I flicked the light switch and the fluorescent tubes flickered and buzzed to life. "Inside."

Arturo stepped through and onto a wooden platform. Glad to see he was functioning, I followed and closed the door. If nothing else, the kid was resilient. Most teenagers would have already been catatonic after what he'd just seen. I relaxed for the first time since we heard the gunshots.

Arturo vibrated in the cold air like a Chihuahua. "Are you all right??

My hands were shaking, too, but for a different reason. "Fine. Hang on." I took the iPhone from my pocket and dialed 9-1-1. The infuriating sound of a busy signal filled my ear before the words Call Failed appeared. I hung up and dialed again with the same results.

He leaned into me to see my screen. "You got bars?"

I checked the screen. "Full bars. Everybody with a cell phone's calling nine one one."

I scrolled through my list of contacts and hit an unlisted number for the sheriff's office. I hung up after Call Failed popped up again. I tried Ethan's private number. It rang half a dozen times. Grinding my teeth, I was about to punch the disconnect button when Ethan's voice came through.

"Sonny? Where are you? We're in a situation here . . ."

His voice was so loud and clear I put my hand over the little microphone and pushed the button to lower the volume. I spoke softly, cracking the door to peek out and praying the trapdoor didn't rise. "It's a little tense in the courthouse, too."

"You're *inside*?" His voice pulled away from the phone. "Y'all shut the hell up! Sonny Hawke's on the phone, and he's in the courthouse. What's going on in there?"

"I'd like to know that myself." I told him everything that had happened, and what I suspected.

His voice faded and I thought I'd lost him. He came back with an echo. "Those guys have already killed at least three people that we know of. We're pulling a response team together, what there is of it, but this storm's playing hell with everything we do.

"Most of the guys are out right now, so there's only a handful of us here. It's already paralyzed El Paso.

Midland and Odessa are socked in. I got through to Ft. Stockton, but they say the roads are already so bad they can't move."

"Did you talk to Major Spence?" He was my immediate supervisor in El Paso.

"Yep, and he's cussin' a blue streak, but he's not sure when they can get through. Everything that flies is grounded, and the weather service says it'll stay that way through tonight. Hell, even the media can't get here, and if *they* can't make it, no one can."

"All right. We're one up on these guys, because they don't know I'm here, but that won't last long. I killed one of 'em who came too close." My stomach flipped when it soaked in that I'd killed another man. It should have bothered me more, but he intended to kill me first, and that changed things.

"Jesus. Didn't they hear the shots?"

"No shots, but I was lucky because these guys are pros. They're dressed for war and armed to the teeth. Fully automatic weapons. This guy had an H&K MP5."

"Jesus. You ain't-a kiddin'. They shredded the sheriff's office with something bigger'n that, and we barely got out of there alive. Well, not all of us made it. Todd Calvert and Tommy Pelham's dead, and Eric Goodlett's down and probably dead, too. A couple of the boys tried to get to him and Todd, but they couldn't get close without getting shot themselves. Them boys are still laying out there in the snow."

The phone went haywire, and Ethan's voice sounded like a robot. A stutter of electronic sounds took over before he came back on, weaker, but still talking.

". . . we're setting up a command center here at the

Posada, and I had the courthouse sealed off—Hey, you said we?"

"Yeah. I'm in the attic with one of Kelly's students." My voice broke. The mental image of her and the twins was all it took to bring my emotions to the surface.

I pushed ahead. "She's downstairs with her class. From what I heard, I think they've rounded everyone up. I have a kid named Arturo with me right now."

"Gillian's in there."

Ethan's daughter. The flat statement carried a lot of the weight that rested on his shoulders, and mine, too.

"I saw her with the twins and Kelly."

"Hell." His voice broke, too, and I knew what he was feeling. "Hang on. We'll get 'em out."

A trickle of sweat rolled down my cheek despite the cold. My breath fogged when I exhaled. "Hey, you have any idea why they'd take over the courthouse?"

"Nary one, but this's been coming for years. I've expected them radicals to take over a *school* somewhere first. The whole world's a target for these Muslim terrorists."

"I got news for you, bub. I don't think *all* these old boys are that kind of terrorists. Especially the one that tangled with me."

"You get anything out of him?"

"Well, he had a Mexican accent, but it wasn't much of an extended conversation. He wanted to order me around, but that didn't last long."

"I bet. Is this some kind of gang stuff that's come up over the border?"

"Can't say, but I doubt it. He looked too military."

"All right. Stay put right where you are and wait for me to call back, if I can get through. The phone lines are already jammed. The kids got some calls out at the outset and then the parents went to dialing.

"We'll get something together here, and I'll let you know what. They've already sealed the building off, and with their firepower, there's no way I can get in right now with a handful of men. They'll probably call pretty soon with their demands, so hang tight until I find out what they want."

"Right." I mashed the icon that looked like a receiver, ending the call.

Chapter 23

At the sound of the first gunshot, one of Kelly Hawke's girls screamed, and a couple of the boys started toward the municipal courtroom door.

"No!" Kelly's voice rang out as sharp as the crack of a whip. The boys froze in place. None of them had ever heard their teacher speak in such a tone. "Everyone shut up and listen."

Shrieks, screams, and gunshots echoed through the building, washing over the students in the cavernous room.

Kelly remembered her shelter-in-place training. The alternative was to run if possible, but that wouldn't happen from the second floor. "Someone lock those doors. The rest of you find somewhere for us to hide." She snapped her fingers. "Now, and do it quietly! No talking." She hoped the courthouse had a response plan. Her district had developed one after 9/11, and they had drilled a few times, but never for a situation *outside* of the school building.

Not all of the kids responded as she'd hoped. Some were terrorized to the point of immobility. Over half of them pulled out their phones and their thumbs flew over the screens. She figured they were texting their moms or dads.

Kelly pulled Matt close to her side and led him away from the courtroom's entry doors. Her son Jerry joined three other boys as they searched for something heavy to block the shooters' access. Mary, Evangelina Nakai, and Gillian Armstrong rushed to the opposite side of the room and disappeared through a door in the back corner.

Brian Cartwright's face was pale. His voice quavered. "Miss Hawke, it won't work."

"What won't?"

"We can't barricade from this side. The doors open out, not in."

Behind him, Jerry flipped a thumb lock. "That's all we can do." He glanced downward and gripped both knobs. Pushing the doors, they gave. "I have to open this side and slide the lock on the other one into the floor. That'll make them stronger."

"No time!" Kelly spun on her heel. Four students were manhandling one of the large attorney's tables over the thigh-high bar, the divider between the gallery seats and the rest of the room. "That won't do any good. Put it down."

Dale Haskins gave one of the spectator seats a shake. "These're all bolted to the floor."

Jerry pulled off his belt. "You guys give me yours. We'll strap them through the handles. That'll slow 'em down."

Evangelina ran back. "This is a conference room, but there's no way out."

"It'll have to do," Kelly said. "All right. Everyone

inside. That door opens inward. We'll block it with whatever's in there." She examined the courtroom, desperate for a plan. "Boys, put everything back where you found it. Jerry, y'all come on."

He held up the belt in his hand. "Let us try this."

"Do what I said!"

Voices rose as some of the student's calls connected.

"Mom! Someone's shooting!"

"No, the courthouse! People are screaming!"

"I'm scared. Can you do something?"

"Dad. Come get me!"

Kelly felt like pulling her hair out. "Kids!" Her voice wasn't much more than a hiss. "Be quiet! Text if you have to, but *for God's sake keep your voices down*."

The class packed into the room, barely keeping it together. Despite their low voices, the sheer number of students on the phone was enough to hear through the door.

Gillian Armstrong held her phone out as if offering it for examination. "Miss Hawke, how come I can't get a call through but they can?"

Kelly patted the air with both hands. "Kids, we have to be *quiet*!"

She heard the courtroom doors slam against the wall.

Chapter 24

Arturo was watching my every move. I scanned the dusty attic. "Listen, there's no way to know how many are down there, but by the comm gear that guy was wearing, and the way he's dressed, you can bet it's more than a couple."

"Let's get out of here."

"I'd run if I could, but the only way out is right down through the middle of 'em, and that ain't happenin'."

"You can lower me down outside on a rope, then climb down yourself."

I did my best to be gentle with the kid. "Think about it, hoss. There's nothing but a big empty floor out there. There aren't any windows at this level either, and if there were, we don't have any rope. All I see is insulation, bricks, and a lot of electric and computer panels."

He tried again. "We cut some wire and use that."

"This ain't television."

"What are we gonna do?"

"Here's what *you're* gonna do. You plant yourself right here." I stepped back to see around the structural supports in the harsh fluorescent lights that failed to reach the farthest corners of the attic. The platform made of raw, splintered boards measured about fifteen feet square, and a good chunk of that was taken up with the electrical panel.

The rest of the attic was full of rafters, braces, HVAC ducts, and wires. A singletree and a cracked saddle gathered dust on a platform made of rough-sawn 2x4s. A horse harness was an odd thing to find up there, but then again, the attic was a great place to store things.

A strip of rough plank flooring maybe six feet wide led around the panel to a desk and chair resting on another platform suspended in a cloud of pink insulation. A folded cot behind a wide brick chimney said we'd found the maintenance man's fair-weather hideout in the unventilated attic.

"This's the safest place for you, especially with the lights out. If anyone comes through the door, you can quick like a squirrel work your way over yonder." I pointed. "You get behind that stack of bricks and hide."

"Where are you gonna be?"

I thought about Kelly and the twins and a lump rose in my throat. "I have to see what's happening, and check on the rest of those kids down there."

I couldn't count how many times I'd hammered the twins on what to do if strangers approached, if someone grabbed them, or if a shooter showed up at school.

My entire family knew what to do and how to fight dirty when necessary. I'd taught them there's no such thing as a fair fight, and to go for the bad guy's eyeballs if he laid hands on them, reactions that are shocking to civilized people, but effective. They also knew what to do in an active-shooter situation, to run if possible, and if not, hide. Fighting came last. I prayed my training had taken root.

Arturo wasn't acting like all the kids that hung around my house. He should have already been on his phone and squalling for someone to come get him. "Where's your phone? I need to give you my number if you can get through."

"We barely have money to eat. Mama has a flip phone, but that's all."

Dammit.

"All right. You stay here and I'll be back in a little bit, then we'll decide what to do."

"Aren't you scared?"

"Spitless." I wasn't about to lie to the kid. Fear was a live, twisting thing in my gut. "But I'll push through it. You can be scared too. It's all right, but you have to control it."

He shivered, and this time not from nervousness. The temperature in the uninsulated attic was dropping, which meant the blue norther was settling in.

I stopped to think. "Oh hell."

"What?"

I pointed at the communications panel. "Now I know why that guy was up here so quick. His job had to do with the computers and phones. Hand me that pack of his."

He shrugged the strap off his shoulder and passed over a desert tan 5.11 tactical backpack. I sat it on the floor and peered inside to find a laptop computer, tools, wires, and a black box the size of a loaf of bread.

We bumped heads as Arturo stuck his head in my way. "What does all that mean?"

"I don't understand all I know about this. They have a plan, though, and that means I stopped him from doing whatever he was sent up here to do."

"So?"

"Somebody's gonna call pretty quick and wonder why he isn't finished. When they don't get an answer, they'll be up here to check it out." I felt a sinking spell coming on and knew I had to get after it before I ran out of steam and started second-guessing myself. "Come on, kid. We have to drag that dead bastard in here with us, before his friends show up."

Chapter 25

The landmark Posada Hotel built during the Great Depression buzzed with activity. The steamy lobby was filling fast with anxious patrons full of questions. Hard-eyed men rushed in, their jaws set and ready to do whatever it took to deal with the situation at hand.

Ethan and Deputy Frank Malone took over the banquet room on the far side of the lounge just off the lobby. Andy Clark abandoned his post behind the registration desk and had his staff hopping. A steady stream of employees and guests hauled tables, chairs, office equipment, and televisions through the lounge and into the large room.

Ethan surveyed a table filling with hand-drawn maps, laptop computers, and firearms, glad there were glass doors between him and the noisy lobby. He'd already ordered the lounge to be cleared, and from where he stood, the extra insulation would be invaluable.

"Frank, what are you hearing from the rest of the guys?"

Deputy Malone looked sick. "I don't have a radio. It took a round in the station. They missed me by that much." He held up a thumb and forefinger about two inches apart.

Ethan gave him a pat on the shoulder. "We were both lucky. Take mine and find out where the guys are. See when they'll get here, and tell 'em to come loaded for bear."

Sweating in their worn Carhartt coveralls, Grady Spears, the maintenance man at the courthouse, and his buddy Ricky Grubbs, who worked for the Posada, wrestled a heavy tube television into the banquet room and hooked it up.

Grady commented as he passed the sheriff, "Man, if I hadn't stopped by to visit with Ricky, I'da been right in there with 'em." He plugged the television into the wall and attached a cable to the outlet. The trusty old TV fired right up and they brought up CNN before heading back to the storeroom for more chairs. "Y'all let me know what else you need."

Ethan turned down the volume. "You're lucky. At least we won't have to get *you* out."

The tension in the hotel was thick as jungle humidity. Law-enforcement officers mixed with volunteers who'd in past years worked incidents such as fires, or tourists lost in Big Bend or on the huge ranches surrounding Ballard. The number of conversations raised in a steady volume as they prepared for the worst.

Ethan's phone rang and he stood in the middle of the swirl, one ear plugged with a forefinger. "I can't hear you, Nancy. Hello? Hello? Are you there?" He punched the screen. "She's gone. Frank, these cell phones are going to hell. The lines are getting so clogged that they're failing."

Deputy Malone snorted. "That's what people do

these days every time something bad happens. I'm way ahead of the curve. Andy's bringing some phones in. This room's still hardwired with jacks, so we'll be on landlines . . . if they still work."

"You're a good man. We need some guys outside."

"We set up a perimeter around the courthouse, best we can. No one's getting in or out."

Ethan was glad to see his deputy on the ball. "I doubt those guys want to get out right now, anyway."

Andy hurried through the lounge with two black desk phones in his hands, followed by Ricky, who was loaded down with extension cords, power strips, and a tangle of more phones. "Here you go. Ricky, start plugging these in."

Ricky dumped the cords, stretched a telephone line across the floor, and clicked it into the wall outlet.

Andy lifted the receiver, hearing the dial tone. "You're in business. We can get you more phones if you need 'em, but the lines will probably go down pretty soon anyway, an' we moved Deputy Pelham's body into one of the rooms . . . an' ever'thing."

"Thanks for thinking of it for me." Ethan pointed at the phones. "How many more of these do you have?"

"A bunch, but not as many outlets. You can use all the ones on the desk, and there's one over there in the bar and kitchen. They all work, 'less the lines ice up and . . . an ever'thing."

Ethan slapped Andy on the shoulder as he passed. "All right, Frank, get these guys in here and let's get this show on the road. We've lost too much time as it is."

Chapter 26

Kelly Hawke's attempt at shelter in place didn't work. The terrorists' raid was well planned. She and her students huddled in the semidarkness, the cramped office lit by filtered light through the window, listening to the sounds of people moving through the courtroom.

Footsteps stopped outside the locked door. Holding her breath, Kelly watched the knob turn until the individual on the other side encountered resistance. Her students rippled like a room full of frightened puppies, whimpering and whispering to each other.

Shadows darkened the crack under the door as a Middle Eastern–accented male voice addressed those inside. "I know you are hiding in there. I am going to fire if you don't come out. You will do that now! Come out!"

Kelly realized all was lost. "All right. Don't shoot. Class, do what he says." She rose and unlocked the door.

She opened it to reveal a tall, dark-skinned man with a scraggly beard. Assault rifle popped into her head when she recognized the weapon pointed at her chest. Sonny taught her and the twins how to use his

AR-15, and they shot them often, but the gun in his hands reminded her of a movie prop.

She dubbed the terrorist Stretch. He stared at her with the coldest, most unfeeling eyes she'd ever seen. They roamed over her body before his attention flicked over her shoulder to the class huddled on the floor.

He stepped back and jerked the rifle toward the judge's bench. "Out. Everyone."

"Students. Do as he says." Kelly led and they trooped out behind her, some weeping, others trembling, even more terrified than before at the sight of the terrorist aiming a weapon at them.

Stretch pointed. "You will sit here and do not move!"

They settled onto the floor near the judge's bench. A second, shorter terrorist picked up a wastebasket and waded into the sprawl of students. He spoke with the same accent. "Phones. If you try and keep one back, I will kill you."

Kelly held her own phone aloft. "Kids, do as he says. All of them."

Sobbing and sniffling, they dropped their devices into the wastebasket as the man Kelly dubbed Shorty moved through. A button lit up on the desk phone sitting on a narrow table. She counted thirty silent blinks before it stopped.

The double doors opened, and a group of subdued adult hostages trooped inside, followed by a female terrorist with a compact machine pistol. She spoke through the wrapping covering her face with an unexpected *Spanish* accent.

Confused, Kelly searched for features that might indicate kindness, hoping to establish a bond with the other woman, but found nothing but dark eyebrows and even darker eyes.

"Do not talk. Do not sit with the children." The woman addressed the adults and jerked her weapon toward the opposite corner behind the bench. "You will sit there."

Kelly wondered at the mix of Spanish and Middle Eastern accents. The only sound from the hostages was the rustle of clothing and a few popping knees as the adults grunted, knelt, and sat on the floor. The woman scanned the room, taking note of the students. Satisfied, she spoke to the short man beside the door. "This is all of them. Keep them quiet. If anyone gives you any trouble, kill them."

She moved like a jaguar. Kelly saw Stretch lick his lips as he watched the female terrorist take up a position under the tall windows. The Adam's apple under his beard bobbed. She shivered.

Beside her, Matt had taken all he could stand. "I want to go home."

She put her arm around the Down's boy in an effort to keep him calm. He wiped at his cheeks with a soft hand and refused to look at the men with automatic weapons as they paced in front of the double doors.

"Matt honey, it's all right," She spoke in a whisper. "But we need to be quiet now, baby."

"I'm not a baby." His voice was loud with agitation. Matt set his jaw, rocking as he always did when he was angry or nervous.

She gave him a pat on the shoulder and shifted her gaze over the students. "Shhh. That's right, honey. You're not a baby, and you're doing just fine."

Several of the girls and more than a couple of the boys were also wiping tears. Within arm's reach, Kelly's twins, Mary and Jerry, sat shoulder to shoulder, drawing comfort from each other in the way of all twins.

"I want to go *home*."

Kelly watched Stretch from the corners of her eyes. He was taut, knuckles white on the gun's pistol grip. "I know." She rubbed her fingers through Matt's hair, an unconscious habit she had when she soothed her own kids since they were toddlers. "Shhh."

Stretch launched himself away from the wall and stalked toward her with his weapon at port arms. "No *talking*!" His accent was thicker with anger. He stopped at the bar and glared at Kelly.

She composed herself, but her voice broke. "He's scared and doesn't react the same way as the rest of the kids."

She had a sick feeling that Matt's stubbornness was going to be their downfall. Down syndrome children were known for digging in their heels at the slightest provocation.

The terrorist kicked the top rail that cracked with a loud report. Spindles came loose and leaned outward like jagged teeth. "Shut him up!" Stretch stepped beside the twins and jabbed the muzzle at Kelly and Matt like a spear. "You shut up you!"

The black muzzle was inches from Jerry's head, and she saw his eyes flick toward the terrorist. An icy ball of fear clenched her chest. She knew her son very, very well. "Jerry, no."

Stretch jabbed again. "That is not the name you used earlier!"

Relieved to see the set of Jerry's jaw relax, she hugged Matt closer. "You're right. I'm scared and used the wrong name. I meant Matt."

Jerry met his mother's gaze. He blinked first and scowled at the polished hardwood floor. Kelly knew he wasn't shaking in fear, but in constrained fury, a trait he'd inherited from his father. She worried that her son might not be able to restrain himself as his anger rose in intensity.

Working himself into a frenzy, Stretch stood taller. Spit flew from his lips as he shouted. "You will all be *silent*!"

She held Matt's head against her chest, but he resisted. Gillian slid close, wrapped her arms around him, and whispered in his ear. Matt relaxed and turned his head away from the terrorist, refusing to look at him.

Stretch stayed beside them, pleased by Kelly's admission of fear and the boy's similar response. The bearded man stared at her breasts.

Refusing to lock onto his gaze, she nevertheless couldn't help noticing a mole underneath his right nostril that she hadn't noticed before. For some reason, the blemish identified him as even more sinister than before.

Pretending to get comfortable, Kelly adjusted Matt to help cover her chest while at the same time tugging her skirt over her knees, thankful she'd worn tall boots and heavy tights in the cold weather.

She held the youngster close, still scratching his scalp. Glancing up to see Stretch watching her, she attempted to reason with him. "Buddy, we're doing the best we can, but these kids are scared and I am, too.

We'll do what you say. These are kids. Can't you release a few of them?"

Stretch licked his lips again, his tongue protruding for far too long. It was a disgusting habit that was fast becoming repulsive. "You will do as I say, no matter what. You will go free when my commander says, you American *bitch*. Sit here and be silent."

"Watch your mouth, buddy."

Kelly's stomach hit rock bottom at the sound of her son's voice. Stretch spun toward the other students at the sound of a male voice. "Who said that?"

None of the kids raised their heads.

"It was me." The new voice came from Mr. Beck Terrill, the elderly rancher who'd done his time in hell back in Korea. Kelly swelled with love for the old man she'd known since they moved to Ballard.

The woman terrorist rushed toward the adults on the opposite side of the room. "You will be silent!" She kicked between the barrister posts, striking Terrill hard in the thigh. "You shut up or I'll kill you!"

Mr. Beck grunted and grabbed his leg, fire flashing from his eyes.

Another student voice rose from the opposite side of the room. "No, it was me."

"That's enough!" Kelly's voice was sharp. She knew what they were doing and wanted to stop the dangerous game before Stretch or the woman torqued off. Kelly held up her free hand. "Please, mister. These are *kids*. This is what I have to do every day, listen to them talk without engaging their brains." She was talking more to the students than to Stretch.

The air crackled with tension. "You listen, *woman*." He spat the word, as if it left a bitter taste in his mouth.

"I shoot you if you cause trouble. You hear? Anyone. Your lives belong to me and Allah!"

Kelly lowered her head in submission. "Students, you heard the man. Silence, please."

"Do as he says." Shorty was still beside the door. He had a wispy beard and appeared to be much younger. His voice seemed lighter, even nervous.

Kelly thought he looked like a very young college student. She met his gaze, but found it as empty as the woman's. The sounds of sobbing were low as Stretch turned away.

A soft, quavering voice stopped him. "It'll be me and you one of these days, buddy."

The room went silent enough to hear the muffled vibrating and ringing of phones under thick coats stuffed in the wastebasket. Some of the students had neglected to turn them off. Like a mad dog slipping its leash, Stretch charged the hostages in a rage.

He jabbed at Mr. Terrill with his rifle, hitting his forehead with the muzzle and opening a gash. "You will be quiet!" Spittle flew from his lips. "No more talking or I will kill you all!"

The rancher met his gaze without flinching as blood ran down his face.

"Not one more sound!"

Matt leaned harder against Kelly, spoke in a normal tone of voice, and crossed his legs in that limber fashion of all children with Down syndrome. "I'm getting thirsty."

"Ahhhhhh!" Stretch spun. His finger was tight on the trigger.

"Shhh. Me, too." Her eyes pleading, Kelly held her hand toward the raging terrorist, hoping her voice was soft enough that Stretch would understand that she was doing her best. "*Please*, everyone."

She rubbed Matt's back. He squirmed. "I want to go home."

Kelly wanted to scream, but bit it back. "Me, too, baby." She caught Jerry's attention and gave her head a shake. The white skin at the corners of his mouth told her that his temper was still up.

The female terrorist made a noise of disgust. "Forget him." She pressed her earbud and listened. "I have to go. Watch them." She stalked out of the room.

Stretch collected himself and gave Kelly another long look before taking up the woman's position against the tall windows.

She prayed her son would maintain control and that her husband had made it out of the building. At least one of her family would be safe.

Chapter 27

"Sir." Lorenzo DeVaca stared downward into the ragged hole chainsawed into the main rotunda floor and pressed the transmit button on his chest. Musty, sour dampness rose like steam from a fumarole. All he could see was dirt and rock in the crawlspace below, illuminated by his LED flashlight. "It's ours."

He wasn't talking about the hole at his feet.

The voice in his ear came from Houston, Texas, and belonged to Marc Chavez, the OCD-driven leader of their operation. "I haven't seen much of anything on television, and it's been over an hour. They're giving sketchy updates that are wrong. Where's my media coverage?"

DeVaca pushed the horn-rim glasses higher on his nose and pressed the button again to speak. "It's the weather. It's a total whiteout here, and there's no way the news media can come out until this lets up. This is perfect. We couldn't have planned it any better."

"All right." Chavez sounded disappointed that the takeover wasn't already the lead story on all news outlets. "Fine then . . . fine . . . fine . . . fine. They keep talking about how the roads are closed and they're getting unformed reports of gunfire there, but little else. Make sure you stick to the schedule. Do you have the hostages secure, secure, secure?"

"Yes. There were casualties, but they rolled over as I expected."

An edge crept into Chavez's voice. "Anyone killed?"

"A couple of sheep." DeVaca loved to think of common citizens as sheep, and himself a wolf.

The voice in his ear rang sharp, something DeVaca wasn't expecting. "Don't give me your political views. Tell me how many you have killed and their gender, their gender, I need their gender."

The Demon inside DeVaca's head shrieked like a human being skinned alive. That disembodied *thing* that escaped from the cage in the dark recesses of his mind was everything that drove him, and when it screamed, people died, or worse. DeVaca flinched like an electric shock was running through his body.

He wondered if anyone else could hear it and expected Chavez to shout back. His unlined brow puckered, the rare frown of a toddler and the only surface reaction he ever allowed. "My men reported at least two deputies and a civilian outside, an old man that I think was a judge, two civilians, and three secretaries inside. One had a gun in her desk drawer. *Texans.*"

"The women. What were their names?"

"I have the one you wanted."

"Are you sure? Are you sure, are you—"

DeVaca interrupted, breaking Chavez's obsessive-compulsive habit of repeating things three times. The disorder infested everything he did, from verbal communication to physical actions. "I have the one you want."

"I still need the names of the dead women. What are they? Tell me tell me tell me."

"How the hell do I know?"

"Find out. Now."

Another silent scream lanced his skull. DeVaca closed his eyes to wrest control from the Demon. "Now? I have the one you wanted. You want names for the *hombres*, too?"

"No."

DeVaca caught Dorothy's attention. "Do you have a name on those women Carrera shot?"

"*Un momento,* and I will tell you." She spun and trotted away.

Chavez was silent as DeVaca stared down into the hole and waited for her to return. The mastermind of the Ballard takeover had no idea that DeVaca had uncovered a secondary goal during the months of planning and rehearsal for the mission, a prize that lay somewhere under his feet.

Dorothy came back and read off a scrap of paper. "Henrietta Merriweather, Sally Gordon, and Carlita Mendoza."

DeVaca repeated the names to Chavez.

Chavez grunted. "Good. Get back to me as soon as anything changes. I'll have further instructions. Hold as long as you can."

"That won't be a problem. Doing it now. Out." DeVaca released the comm button and again aimed the beam of his high-intensity flashlight into the hole in the floor.

"Tin Man."

DeVaca's right-hand man joined him. "*Sí.*"

"I need to know what's down there." DeVaca picked up a SCBA mask and tank and passed it over. The self-contained breathing apparatus probably wouldn't protect Tin Man from what DeVaca hoped he would find, if it was leaking, but then again, it wouldn't hurt.

"*Jefe seguro.*" Tin Man shrugged the straps over his shoulder with a worried look and adjusted the face-mask over his head before crawling over the edge and lowering himself down. He squatted and flicked on a Maglite to survey the pier-and-beam foundation.

"Nothing but posts."

DeVaca bit back his frustration. "Substructure. Look harder."

"*Bueno.*"

A gust of foul air from below brought the smell of decayed rats to the courthouse rotunda. DeVaca turned his blank gaze onto Reddy Freddy, the old man who arrived with the Texas team, who raised both hands to the level of his potbelly in an "I don't know" motion. "Hey, You didn't expect that shit to be laying on top of the ground down there, did you? I done told you there's a basement."

The hair growing from the man's ears disgusted De-Vaca. "Tin Man. What do you see?"

"Mortared rock and concrete."

"Keep going down. I want to know what's underneath."

Tin Man climbed out. "I need a hole in that ground."

DeVaca's number-one man from the American team, Richard Carver, took his place, ready to use his military training for the first time since leaving the army three years earlier. He surveyed the area and rose. "You got it. Billy, hand me some bang."

Freddy held up a hand to caution him. "Don't hit it too hard. Those tanks down there are old. If I remember right, they're stacked on the south side somewhere over thataway." He pointed.

Fresh inside from the northern entrance and radiating cold, Billy Koval opened a backpack and handed down a roll of thin explosive compound called det cord. Carver secured it to the rock foundation that resembled a patio floor. "I need some weight."

The terrorists formed a fire-brigade line and passed down cases of paper and heavy files. When Carver was finished packing the det cord for optimum effectiveness, the large oval outline was the size of a bathtub. He attached a detonator and scrambled out.

"Back." They retreated to the far end of the longest hallways. When he was sure the area was clear, Carver shouted. "Fire in the hole fire in the hole fire in the hole!"

He thumbed the detonator. Despite being directed downward, the explosion rattled the courthouse. Dust and dirt filled the air from hundreds of cracks and seams through the building. It combined with an interior snowstorm of paper fragments and whole pages blasted upward before drifting to the floor.

Screams from the hostages upstairs were followed by shouts from their captors.

Tin Man returned to the edge and directed his beam downward through the dust and settling shreds. A darker void gaped through the new cavity in the stone foundation. He flashed DeVaca a huge smile.

"Go!"

"*Bien.*" Tin Man squinted into the drop. He pointed at Carver and struggled for the right word. "Need that *aprovechar.*"

Even through Carver didn't understand the word, he knew what Tin Man wanted.

While he waited for Tin Man to rig up, DeVaca checked on his prisoners. "California leader, report."

Kahn's accented voice came strong into DeVaca's earpiece. "Prisoners all secure."

Satisfied with the answer, DeVaca contacted the rest of those manning the perimeter and fulfilling their assignments. "Texas team."

"North entrance secure. No movement, except for snow."

"Don't get cute."

As the others reported in one by one, Tin Man settled the SCBA gear onto his shoulders and put the mask back into place. He walked to the edge of the hole and leaned back to put tension on the rope anchored to the thick post on the ornate staircase. He fed rope through the harness until he was parallel to the floor, then pushed off. The tension released seconds later.

One person failed to report in. His attention divided, DeVaca peered into the cavity and watched Tin Man flick on his flashlight. He pressed the transmit button. "Scarecrow?"

Scarecrow was assigned to access and disable the communications panel and all computer service before setting up a jamming device that would reach out for a radius of two hundred yards.

The fact he was still hearing the ring of office

phones and abandoned cell phones told DeVaca something was wrong. "Scarecrow, report."

Tin Man stepped back into view and gave DeVaca a
thumbs-up. His smile through the mask was bright as
his flashlight, and he pointed at Freddy. "It's all there.
Just like he said."

The usually emotionless DeVaca felt joy. He would
have danced a little jig had he been alone. Instead, he
adjusted his glasses and spread his arms wide, forgetting that Scarecrow still hadn't answered.

He swallowed the excitement. He'd achieved his assignment, and his own personal quest. It felt like an
early Christmas present.

He couldn't wait to use it, and to hell with the rest of
those around him. Their plans weren't his, but they would
serve him well when the time came.

Chapter 28

Congressman Don Bright glowered at his desk phone when it emitted a soft beep. Ignoring it, he checked the iPhone lying at hand and went back to his laptop. Two sentences later, it beeped again.

He minimized the screen, and picked up the receiver. "What?"

"Are you in one of your moods?"

Willa Mae Dalyrumple was the only person who could talk to him like that. She'd been Congressman Bright's secretary since he was a law clerk to Ralph Davidson of the United States Court of Appeals for the Fifth Circuit. She started out with him in the Dallas law office long before that.

Unlike most rising stars, Don Bright didn't want to "break in" a new secretary every time he climbed the next political rung. Willa Mae went with him whenever he moved. On occasion, gossips and cynics suggested there was something going on between the middle-aged widower and his stern-faced, sensibly dressed secretary, other than professional achievement.

He often laughed at the accusations, explaining that

his taste in women didn't include hooked noses, East Texas "helmet hair," and an inexplicable lack of humor.

"There's a Mr. Desi Arnaz on the line." He didn't pay any attention to her soft Texas accent that was natural to his ear, but most people inside the Washington beltway smiled the first time they heard it. "He says y'all are friends, and he needs to visit for a minute."

The congressman frowned. "Desi Arnaz played Ricky Ricardo on *I Love Lucy*. He's been under the ground a long time."

"That's what I thought. I know you're busy, and I told him so, but when he called your mama's name, I figured he was all right."

He checked the paper calendar on his desk and noted his mother's birthday was in two days. "That reminds me. Don't let me forget to call Florence. I haven't talked to her in over a week."

"I have it down."

"All right, put him through."

"Don't forget you have a meeting in an hour."

"That's what I'm *trying* to work on." He hung up and waited for the other line to light up, checking his cell to see how many emails and calls he'd missed while working on the details of his upcoming meeting.

There were thirty-two "Notifications" on his Facebook icon.

He thumbed through dozens of emails until the desk phone blinked as Willa Mae put the call through. He snatched up the receiver and kept scrolling with the other hand. "Don Bright."

"Hey, hoss!"

"Hey . . . Desi?"

"*Lucy*, you got some 'splainin' to do."

The congressman winced at the painful impersonation. "Funny. Desi, or Ricky." Still not interested, he checked a second, private email inbox. "If this is some kind of joke, then I don't have time."

The Desi Arnaz accent vanished. "This is not joke, *amigo*, and you'll *make* time to talk with me."

Don's face reddened. He learned long ago not to get into arguments with strangers on the phone, political or otherwise. "All right. Good-bye."

"I wouldn't hang up, if I were you, *Congressman*. Katie wouldn't like it."

Don stopped when he heard his daughter's name. "What about Katie?"

"I understand she really wants to talk to you." He switched back to the Ricky Ricardo accent. " 'Cause you're in *trouble*." He ended with a singsong voice.

"Knock it off. It's not funny."

"Aw, ma-un!" The inflection changed, this time to a pure East Texas redneck drawl. "I been workin' on that 'un for a good long while . . . maybe five minutes, I reckon. A-ite, see, little Katie is with some friends of mine, and you're fixin' to do something for me."

The Texas congressman knew the regional accents of his home state, and this one was close, but he recognized it as fake. He moved the receiver from his ear and put the desk phone on speaker. Both hands free, he scrolled through the text messages on his cell phone, looking for her name. Like most young people, Katie often preferred texts to *speaking* with someone.

The last text that morning was about the unusual weather back home. She'd been as excited as a kid. It reminded him of when she was little and wanted to stay home even after a *dusting* of snow.

"What do you want? Is she all right?" He thumbed a quick email to Willa Mae. *Come here now!* He hoped her cell phone was near, and not on silent, or that she had the office email up on her computer.

"I 'magine she's all right at the *moment*."

Just in case, Bright threw a book at his office door. It hit with a bang.

"Now don't get all het up there, Congressman, and start kicking things around. Don't think about trying any electronic magic, either, because you won't have time to do anything about this call. It ain't gonna last much longer, and besides, this is a drop phone, so trying to capture this number won't do you no good neither. I'm 'bout to throw it in the burn barrel and 'at'll be the end of that, that, that."

"I'm listening." Bright snatched a pen off his desk and scribbled a quick note, "OCD?" on the cover sheet of his report on illegal immigration. He penned, *possibly real Texan* under that.

"Good." The faint hint of a Spanish accent took over and sounded genuine. "Here's the deal."

Another written note, *not East Texas. South?*

"My people have the Ballard courthouse and Katie, along with a number of others who happened to be in the wrong place at the wrong time. To the best of my knowledge, everyone is all right, aw, I take that back, there's a few dead folks, but they're nothing to you. The rest are fine, Katie, too, though I hear it's a little cold down there. I'll continue to maintain control over that facility and the people within until you cooperate with my demands."

Willa Mae opened the door, stuck her head inside. "Everything okay?"

Bright shook his head and waved her over. The new accent was real with a soft Texas inflection that could have come from any of the five regions. "Fine. Tell me what you want." He wrote on his notepad. Willa Mae twisted her head to read it.

Guy on the line says he's taken over the Ballard courthouse. They have Katie. Demands are coming.

Willa Mae drew a shocked breath and mouthed, *What do you want me to do?*

"I know you sit on the Homeland Security Committee."

"Yes."

Bright wrote: *Contact the FBI.*

"Hey, you sound distracted. I suggest you stop what you're doing for a second. Everything I say from now on is in your daughter's best interest."

Bright stopped writing and hit the button again. "All right. You're off speaker. You have my full attention."

"Good. I am going to maintain control of the courthouse and everyone inside for the next several hours while you put together a plan to stop the National Guard from going to the border. Then you are going to stop the movement of any *additional* security to the border, and that includes state troopers and that company of Texas Regulars you're putting together."

"What do you know about—?"

"I know a lot of things. The buildup you're sending down to the river is going to stop, and to make that happen, I have your daughter's life in my hands."

"You hurt her and I'll kill you."

Desi snapped back "What are you going to do, huh?

You have no idea where I am or about the situation. I suggest you forgo the TV drama and listen. Understood?"

Bright swallowed the truth. "Yes."

"When we are finished in the courthouse, my people will leave and take Katie with them. You'll get her back once the following demands are met. Are we clear?"

"Yes." Bright's pen moved again. *Texan for sure. Called it the river.*

"You will destroy everything you have on the project and tell them it was funded with dirty money or something, I don't care. Then you will commit political suicide and bow out of the picture. You'll like that part best, I imagine, because when I first came up with the idea, I was going to have you shoot yourself on camera, but I decided that might be a little extreme."

The man calling himself Desi gave a little half bark, half laugh.

"It still sounds like a good idea though, all that blood and brain tissue in HD. Instead, you're going to find some way to leave politics forever. You can say anything you want . . . you've been taking bribes, you're in bed with the cartels and can't live with yourself anymore, you're having an affair with a subordinate . . . ahhh, wait, you've been having a sexual relationship with a male intern. I like that one. But no matter, you will call a press conference and confess your sins on the six o'clock news."

"Why?"

Bright knew why. He was the hardest working, most charismatic congressman in the nation and was pushing for increased border control along the Rio Grande to shut down illegal immigration. His rising star was headed for the White House.

With Congressman Don Bright out of the way, the people massed on the other side of the international border could cross. They were held up for the time being by the increased presence of the National Guard and Bright's Texas Regulars, a shadow company of well-trained military and law-enforcement veterans poised to saturate the Texas side of the border with unimaginable technology and techniques.

With those obstacles removed, the flood of illegals would once again overwhelm the understaffed and under-funded Border Patrol. Thousands of minors, a signifi-cant number of them hardened gangsters, were waiting to cross into Texas and join the ranks of the first tsu-namis of illegal youngsters, setting the stage for future political change.

Bright stared out his window at the bare trees and the leaden Washington sky. "And if I do all that, do you think it will make any difference? Someone else will take my place."

"I don't care."

"If I do what you ask, you'll release Katie, and the others?"

"Sure 'nough!"

"How can I believe you?"

"Why hoss, you cain't, but the truth be known, you ain't got no other choice. Oh, by the way, you don't contact anyone in law enforcement about this little talk we're having. You understand? No Homeland Secu-rity, now that's funny, no FBI, no Special Ops . . . no one, no one, no one. I have people watching you. We're a big organization, and we know what you're doing every minute. No phone calls, no messages, no nothing."

The man's voice rose. "If I see that you've talked about this, I'll kill every person in that courthouse. I'll. Kill. Them. All of them. All of them. All of them. And that's after I torture them, starting with your daughter. Do you understand? Do you understa—."

"I understand." Bright swallowed, his mouth dry. "I'll do what you want. Do I have your word?"

"Yes." Desi chuckled. "You have my word. I'll call you back soon to touch base. I'll be on a different phone, so be careful about screening your calls." He was back to his friendly voice. "Oh, and thanks for your cooperation. I'm sure we're going to have a short, but productive, association. Hey, wait, I forgot something."

Bright's breath caught. What else could this lunatic want?

A new, shrill voice came through the phone, what the guy on the other end probably thought was his best British accent. "I want . . . a *shrubbery*."

"*What*?"

The voice was high and scratchy. Bright realized the man was impersonating the "Knights who say Ni" scene from movie, *Monty Python and the Holy Grail*. "I've changed my mind. I want five five five million dollars." The piercing shriek came again. "At once!"

"What?"

The voice returned to normal, or what was the most normal of all this lunatic's personalities. "Five of the eight million you have in that little offshore account of yours."

"I don't—"

"Shut up! I know all about it. You can't collect that much dirty money without someone talking, and I know, knew, *that* someone *intimately* for a few hours. You'll key in this code within the next thirty minutes to transfer five million that we won't ever discuss again. I won't tell anyone about it." The redneck voice came back. "How 'bout t'at?"

There was no use arguing. "But it can be traced."

"Naw, it cain't. The funds'll hit that account and bounce around like a pinball for a while, at least till it lands in my pocket. Now you're gonna do it, right?"

"I don't know—"

"Fine. Six million. Going up?"

Bright clamped his jaw. "Fine."

The voice was cheery once again. "Excellent. Here's that number, and you better write it down, but don't worry none about chasing after it later, that account'll be gone before you can whistle Dixie." He recited a long line of numbers and letters. "Didja get it?"

"I got it."

"Good. Read it back."

"I said, I got—"

The tone in his real voice was chilling. "Read the damn thing back, friend."

Bright read aloud.

"Good. Bye bye bye now."

Shaking, Congressman Bright hung up and loosened his tie.

Willa Mae reached across the desk and picked up the receiver. Bright put his hand on hers. "No."

"We have to call Homeland Security, or the FBI, or the CIA, or someone, for God's sake."

"You didn't hear all that he said. They have Katie,

and I can't call any law enforcement or they'll kill her. If the courthouse really *is* in the hands of terrorists, Homeland Security'll already be on the way. This part's between us."

Willa Mae's expression hardened. She was from tough stock raised in the rough, hardscrabble mountains of southeast Oklahoma. "We'll do *something*."

He rose and closed the door. Wiping his tears, Bright told her what the man on the other end of the line said. Willa Mae stood rooted to the carpet, a hand over her mouth. When he relayed the part about the Ballard courthouse, Bright picked up the remote from his desk and switched on the wall-mounted television. CNN was all over the takeover, with nothing from Ballard other than file footage. Congressman Bright and Willa Mae learned even more about the massive West Texas snowstorm and its impact on the situation.

After the report, a former Special Forces colonel told the newscaster his opinion of what Ballard's first responders needed to do.

While they listened and Bright sailed through his limited options, he checked his cell and saw that in his haste to scroll through the many calls that morning he had missed a second call from Katie that came through minutes after they had hung up. He put it on speaker and pushed the arrow to play the message.

The terror in the young woman's voice was sharp and painful with a little-girl quality that he knew so well. "Daddy! There's men with guns—" The phone went silent except for a male voice in the distance. The words weren't clear, but a gunshot was. Screaming. Crying. Katie brushed the phone against something with a loud clack that was followed by more gunshots. The staccato sound of automatic weapons filled the background before the recording ended.

Bright and Willa Mae stared at the silent phone in his hand.

"What do we do?"

He met Willa Mae's gaze. "What they told me to do."

Chapter 29

Arturo and I hauled the terrorist's heavy dead ass across the floor and into the frigid attic where we rassled him around behind the brick chimney. The kid did good, even though he looked kinda sick when he first took the guy's ankles.

We were breathing hard by the time we had the limp body tucked away on the maintenance man's cot. I covered him with a blanket and shucked my coat when we returned to the door. "Here, put this on."

"I already have this."

"I know, but it's gonna get cold while I'm gone and it'll be in my way."

The ranch coat was way too big for him, but layers are effective. He pulled the zipper up to his neck and shivered. "Do you have to go?"

I could feel the chill, standing there in my shirt-sleeves. "Yep, I do, but you need to lay low up here. It's the safest place for you."

I slipped into the H&K's sling, adjusted it across my chest, and dropped the spare magazines into the terrorist's tactical bag. I'd dumped the electronic gear beside the body. His 9mm Glock was still in the small of my back. With my Colt 1911 and two extra magazines in their pouches on the other side of the belt, I had plenty of firepower.

I felt like a pack mule with all that hardware hanging on me. I didn't have a military background and had never carried so much lethal gear at one time, other than to and from the shooting range. I hoped that all that practice would come in handy if the time came, while at the same time praying I wouldn't have to use the weapons at all.

The skinny little undersized kid who acted like he was tough dropped his attitude and stepped close. Without a word, he wrapped his arms around my waist, trembling. I hugged him. "I'll be back in a little bit. Stay inside and keep this door closed."

I cracked the door and peeked out. The trapdoor in the floor was closed, the round room empty. I stepped out.

The lock hanging open on the latch was an invitation for someone to come inside. I pushed the shackle until it snicked into the mechanism. The kid would throw a fit if he knew he was locked in, but I hoped that if the terrorists saw it, they'd bypass the attic.

Chapter 30

Three months earlier, a mixed group of intense men and women sat spellbound in the plush living room of a sprawling 15,000-square-foot house in the upscale River Oaks section of Houston, Texas. Instead of the razor-sharp picture on the sixty-inch HD television, raw, fuzzy images captured from online security cameras provided graphic images of the bloody 2004 Beslan massacre in Russia.

The volume on the grainy video was so low they could hear the tinkling of ice in expensive crystal glasses.

Marc Chavez scanned the faces of his crowd instead of watching the video. Some were smiling, despite the horrific scene unfolding on the screen.

Different angles from outside surveillance cameras interspersed with news footage of better quality gave viewers the sense they were watching a movie. The media reports weren't as graphic, but the aftermath and blood-soaked bodies stood out in HD clarity.

When the video ended, a collective, almost sexual sigh filled the room. Marc Chavez, who often liked to impersonate Desi Arnaz, pointed the remote toward the television and the screen went dark. Shuffles filled the room as his guests focused their attention on him.

Well-dressed and ordinary-looking men and women sat on the sofa, love seat, and soft chairs. A few tardies perched on dining-room chairs, like guests at a cocktail party.

Chavez held a crystal tumbler in his palm and gave it three spins with his manicured fingers before taking a sip of the twenty-one-year-old scotch.

Those fingers had been washed three times before he left the restroom. He checked door locks three times, adjusted place settings three times, and even though he was aware of it, he often repeated words or phrases three times. The repetition was the hardest of the many idiosyncrasies he exhibited, because strangers often snickered or projected their discomfort in a number of ways.

He observed the group's body language and expressions. No one spoke. "Y'all are pretty tough. All that blood didn't seem to faze you one bit."

The group snickered, waiting to hear from the man who'd called them together. His dark hair and olive complexion revealed a South American heritage. His parents migrated to the Texas Rio Grande Valley long before Chavez was born.

He took another sip, feeling the warmth of the single-malt Scotch light a pleasant heat all the way down. "Eleven hundred people were taken hostage in a Beslan school and over the course of three days, nearly four hundred lives were lost. This was an *awesome* event that was heard around the world, the world, the wo—" He caught himself and scanned the audience for reaction.

Faces composed, his audience waited for him to continue. They were looking forward to hearing his plan before donating large sums of money to whatever idea he had in mind.

Each person in the room was convinced that the United States teetered on the brink of change, and was willing to help push it over the edge.

"The plan, solid. The results were stunning and far reaching. Make no mistake, this mission was a feint, a trial run . . . a dress rehearsal for things to come. That's why we're here tonight. Our first operation I'm asking you to fund isn't a school takeover like I explained last year. You were generous in your donations, and we've embargoed that money for this event that will build fear in the heart of the American sheep."

He didn't care for that phrase, but the man he was about to put in charge of the first phase of the operation had used it in conversation the week before. Chavez felt those in the room would find a certain appeal to the reference.

He met Lorenzo DeVaca's gaze and held it. DeVaca sat behind the group in the most uncomfortable chair in the room. Balancing a delicate china plate on the knees of his creased khakis, DeVaca's posture was impeccable. Expressionless, he pushed a pair of horn-rimmed glasses up on his nose. Chavez knew that inside that meek exterior, the man was a bloodthirsty monster.

Chavez released the gaze and addressed the group. "We'll do that somewhere down the road." He gave them a brilliant smile, and most smiled back. "And *that* campaign will be splendid. When we do, this country will fall like a house of cards. But first, I want to start with an operation to plant a seed of fear in the people and the government. What I propose is the takeover of a courthouse. I've chosen the one in Ballard, in far West Texas."

Several eyebrows rose. One gray-haired man who looked every bit the part of a television evangelist cocked his head. Chavez answered the unspoken question.

"Because, Mr. Wicker, to date, to date . . . to *date*," he tightened his jaw, "there hasn't been an extended takeover of any kind in this country, and that single event will stun this nation into immobility."

Chavez sipped his scotch. "Our goal will be to inflict as much damage as possible, but not necessarily human, though I expect some to die. This damage will be *psychological*, and it's our strongest weapon, the weapon of terrorism, because we'll be striking at the heart of America.

"Terrorism is such a disgusting word, but all the same, it works. We'll build on the fears already in place courtesy of ISIS. My team . . . your team, will *own* the courthouse and the people, because though we aren't taking a school, they have provided us with an opportunity."

A woman raised a tentative hand. Her face was stretched tight from many plastic surgeries. The false facade of youth was grotesque, cartoonish. Her mottled hands and wrinkled neck hidden by a scarf wrapped to her chin told the real story. She waited for Chavez to pause. "That's no big deal. A courthouse?"

The man sitting beside her agreed. "If you want an historical icon, why don't we occupy something of state or national significance . . . like the Alamo, or a building at the Smithsonian Institution?"

Chavez smiled, but his eyes failed to match the expression. "Eleanor, Alfred, those are good suggestions, but give me a moment and you'll understand."

Chavez continued with the memorized presentation he'd practiced in front of a mirror. He concentrated hard to prevent repetition. "It isn't the significance of the target. It's the vulnerability of something so simple that will shock this country to the core. It's the vulnerability of Main Street America. It's the vulnerability of common, familiar areas.

"Their electronic security hasn't yet joined the twenty-first century. Much of their *electronic* data is backed up on-site and they haven't yet moved it to a secure location, so property and tax records, and all city and county information will be deleted. Despite the fact that many of these documents have been placed on microfilm, computers and film burn well, so arrest records, fingerprint data, marriage, wills, probate, land records, and everything else will be lost forever. It's nothing more than a single bite of a big apple, but that's what it takes. My mother once told me the way to eat an elephant is one bite at a time, and that's how we'll do this. Of course, we sell what electronic data we download to as many people as possible both here and abroad. I don't care if they speak English or not."

More chuckles from throughout the living room.

"You think that's funny?" Chavez's expression was chilly. He spun the glass in the palm of his hand three times to calm himself. "That is minor. What will be most horrific is the class of students who have scheduled a visit to this location on the date I selected. In fact, it is that field trip they posted on their website that gave me the idea.

"Children are this country's Achilles' heel. This will bring the county's weaknesses to the forefront when they realize how easy it is to destroy what is precious and invaluable. The entire United States will realize *nothing* is safe on U.S. soil, and *that* frightens everyone.

"Of course, we'll reference Beslan in our demands. That singular noun will drive the media into a frenzy. They'll fall on it like wolves. They want shock and attention, and they'll get it."

A woman dripping with diamonds waved a hand full of big knuckles. "Why Ballard? Why not the courthouse in Dallas, or Austin?"

Chavez bristled. He'd expected questions, but hated them just the same. His experience with fund-raising kicked in, and he flashed them a brilliant smile.

Chavez worked the room like a cocaine dealer in a house full of rich teenagers. "Lucille, Ballard's remote, close to the border, and miles from help. Hear me. *Miles* from help. They have a sheriff's department like the one in Mayberry with the same kind of sheriff. I don't expect much more defense than the shotguns in their cars."

Some cackled at the recollection.

"Their fire department is manned by volunteers. Response will not be quick, and that's what we want . . . the time to wreak as much havoc as possible, and to instill terror throughout this country. Other than Laredo, which is isolated but with a much larger law-enforcement presence, there's no better location."

"Why not Laredo, then?"

Chavez's smile slipped. "I have my reasons."

They didn't need to know the reasons included another branch of the operation in Ballard that would remain between him and DeVaca, specifically a young woman named Katie Bright. Holding her hostage would put pressure on her dad, Congressman Don Bright, who chaired the House Committee on Homeland Security that was a thorn in Chavez's side.

With the congressman in Chavez's pocket or out of play, the military presence along the river would relax until the government could muster a response plan. During that time, thousands of adults could cross en masse, creating confusion and distraction.

Chavez and his supporters already had a political chess piece in place, funded by millions of dollars from the cartels, and ready for his appointment. *That* congressman, Calixto Diaz, was already the president's next golden boy, and wanted nothing more than to relax Texas's efforts at damming the tide of immigrants.

"Will it be difficult for your team to get inside and take over?"

Chavez snorted. "You've never been to that region of the state. They're what my parents used to call sitting ducks. There are no metal detectors on this courthouse. The sheriff and a couple of deputies are in the station across the street. The highway patrol officers are far away, writing tickets, and the Border Patrol agents are manning the check stations. I'm surprised they have doors at all in this backwater place."

The group exchanged glances. Chavez was a regular Red Skelton, but the time had come to get back to the plan. "Have I answered your question, Lucille?"

"Yes."

"Thank you." Chavez adjusted his tie. "It will be a piece of cake for our people to take control of the Ballard courthouse. When there's nothing else on the news channels, and while the live cameras roll outside, this event will explode into public consciousness. We'll announce our intentions to take over governmental buildings and entire *schools* in more populated areas and much closer to people's homes. By then, parents won't let their children leave the house. No one will go to work. Bill, tell them what happens after that."

They waited as the wiry man cleared his throat.

Chapter 31

I dropped to the floor and raised the trapdoor about an inch, half expecting to get shot as soon I did. The steps were as steep as those from the round room to the dome, but this time the wooden balusters were ornate instead of solid and I could see through them. A man sat on the bottom step, having a smoke.

The heat kicked on with a rusty squeak and warm air rushed through the ducts. A ton of noise came up through the rotunda from people working, talking, and of all things, running a chainsaw. I identified the snarl as the operator revved the engine a couple of times. It changed pitch when he put it to use for the second time that day. It sounded to me like he was cutting cordwood. The smell of exhaust was strong.

The chainsaw died and the man on smoke break sounded like he was right there with me. I angled my head to see he was talking through a comm unit in Spanish.

"Todo seguro."

My Spanish was good enough to know he was telling someone his floor or post was secure.

"*Sí, fuera de la gran sala del jurado en el tercer piso*."

That one gave me a little trouble, but I for sure picked out, *sala del jurado*, Grand Jury, and that was on his floor. Boots thundered and two more guys with what looked like AR-15s came up the staircase. They jabbered at each other while I lowered the trapdoor, careful not to let it make any noise.

In an odd way, their activity seemed ordinary, as if they had real business in our courthouse. Had they not been dressed in assault gear and carrying guns, the ringing phones, talking, and activity would have appeared normal.

It sounded like they had my family and the hostages in the Grand Jury room on the third floor. I could see no way down without getting shot. I needed another way, but not the steps.

Think out of the box, is what the Old Man used to say.

Shoot my way down, or find a back door.

An idea popped into my head, and it scared the daylights out of me. I slipped past the attic access and up the staircase and into the lantern dome. The room was even darker than before. The storm had intensified. Snow piled against the uninsulated glass.

I wouldn't have been able to see the Roman towers at the corners if the sensors hadn't activated the floodlights that lit all four turrets with a soft, cotton glow.

I tried to call Ethan again to let him know what I'd found out, but the phone made an irritating noise, telling me the lines were jammed. I stood there, indecisive. One solution would have been to get back into the attic and wait to hear from Ethan, but I'd eliminated that idea when I locked Arturo in.

I couldn't stay where I was for very long. Someone was bound to come up looking for the terrorist I'd killed, or at least they'd send another man up to the tower at some point. I was surprised they hadn't done so already.

That dumb idea surfaced again, itching like a fireant bite. I stared into the snow, trying not to be as impulsive as my son . . . who took after me.

The layout of the building was the same on all floors, and I'd been in it enough to remember that there were conference rooms at every level in each of the four towers. If I could get into the one off the courtroom, I could come up behind the guards who would be watching the outside doors.

Warm weather would've made it a simple matter to open the wooden casement window, lower myself to the roof's ridgeline, work my way outward to a short intersecting ridge, then slide down the steep pitch to the turret's window twenty feet away.

But the weather was far from warm.

Taking a deep breath, I put both hands on the window frame and pushed up.

The intense cold poured inside like I'd opened a deep freeze. I stuck one leg outside and the frigid wind burned my exposed skin. I hoped the window on the turret above the Grand Jury room was unlocked.

I'd been thinking about it long enough to change my mind.

But I didn't.

"Well, hell."

The truth was that I didn't know what I was doing, but at least I was doing something.

Chapter 32

Dale Marshall, a former college professor with a Ph.D. in Economics, addressed the assemblage in Chavez's expansive living room. "This country operates on a tiny margin. Food stocks were once delivered every day to grocery stores, markets, and the big-box stores. Today, cutbacks due to roller-coastering gas prices have forced most carriers down to two deliveries per week in many cases. Some only once a week, excluding perishables.

"Within days after the Ballard takeover, Mr. Chavez will announce the next target, which will be schools across the United States. Parents will panic at the threat of coordinated attacks on schools. They'll pull their kids out and stay home.

"People won't go to work, and businesses will struggle to stay afloat. Planes won't fly, product deliveries won't be made, and that will include medicines. The American machine will grind to a halt. The stock market will reflect the fear, and the results will be total economic collapse. With that, the country'll turn on those who are in charge."

"Thank you, Dale." Marc Chavez set the empty glass on a napkin, being sure to square it with the edge of the table. "The first part of our plan was implemented when thousands of children and adults crossed the Rio Grande. That brought a great number of other . . . supporters . . . into this country, prepared to act when the time comes to wrest control from those who are failing us. It was because of your generosity that this has occurred."

Everyone in the room understood the reference. The first part of the plan was brilliant, because a bloodless invasion was happening right under the noses of the American public.

Chavez sent people to Guatemala and El Salvador to pass the word that the United States would give amnesty to anyone under eighteen years of age. *Amnistía* became the key to admission, and soon thousands of young people materialized on the banks of the Rio Grande and crossed, seeking out and surrendering to Border Patrol agents using the magic word they'd been taught.

"Amnistía!"

The numbers soon overwhelmed the limited resources along the U.S.–Mexico border. While the agents were busy collecting and housing the children ranging in age from infants to nineteen-year-old gangsters, thousands of adults slipped through the net and into the country.

As many as 10 percent were terrorists. Some of those "teenagers" were in fact hardened criminals who looked young, but were much, much older. "Relatives" picked them up, and they soon disappeared into the

American fabric, formed into teams, and waited for orders.

Chavez resisted the urge to spin his glass three more times. "Then, the people will be in charge, as outlined by our Constitution. We will return to a government led by the people and for the people, the people, the people . . ."

Carlton Hayes, electrician by trade and the owner of the massive Hayes Electric Company, held up his Coors Light. "Casualties?" He was a strong believer in the Cause.

"There will be casualties on both sides." Chavez shrugged and with an effort, restrained himself from repeating the action twice more. "Collateral damage is always a price to be paid. The teams I have assembled are highly trained, but plans always change after the outset of an operation. Unforeseen circumstances might result in casualties, and we can't help that. If you're talking about our people, they are prepared to sacrifice themselves, if necessary, for the Cause."

Chavez had no intention of telling them the plan in its entirety. His hand-chosen leader's sanity was questionable at best. Chavez suspected that Lorenzo De-Vaca was a sociopathic serial killer looking for a unique opportunity to satisfy his needs. Chavez planned to fund DeVaca's bloodlust with a guarantee that the next assignment would have a wider sweep with deadlier results.

He watched DeVaca, knees together to support the plate, wipe his mouth with a linen napkin. Their eyes met, and DeVaca gave an infinitesimal nod.

Chapter 33

My breath fogged as the heavy snow stuck to my clothes. I straddled the windowsill above the ridge on the mansard-style pitched roof several feet below. If I lost my balance and fell the wrong direction, the sharp slant would result in a long, long drop with a very sudden stop. There weren't even any shrubs along the foundation to break my fall.

I'm gonna be white-headed before this is over.

There wasn't much choice. I adjusted the H&K under my arm and the strap on the pack full of ammo. Swallowing the lump in my throat, I wriggled outside. The ridge was farther than I imagined, so I shortened the distance by hanging by my hands from the sill. I dug into the deep seam between the stone blocks with the edge of my boots. Leather soles aren't designed for climbing, and the slick bottom added to the problems.

Everything went haywire from the minute I turned loose. An explosion somewhere in the building startled me, causing my foot to slip when I shoved off. Twisting in the air, I hoped to straddle the ridgeline like the Lone Ranger dropping onto Silver.

I missed like a big dog.

I bet my midair twist looked more like a rag doll falling from the window. Landing hard on my chest, I folded over the frozen ridgeline like a sock over a bedstead. It sounded to me like somebody had dropped a calf on the roof.

The air was thick with snow crystals. My lungs burned, making me cough. The wind howled, and snow blew down my neck. I couldn't get any traction with my leather soles, and ran in place on the metal roof like a cartoon character.

Gripping with my arms and grunting and cussing, I gained enough purchase to swing one leg over the ridgeline.

I didn't have time to rest and congratulate myself on still being alive. I couldn't stay there much longer. The wind cut right through my shirt and khakis. My hands were numb, and my face prickled as the icy crystals hit bare skin. I regretted not remembering the gloves in the coat I'd left with Arturo. I scooted a few inches at a time toward the edge of the roof like a tenderfoot adjusting himself in a saddle. Holding all my weight like a gymnast on a pommel horse, I twisted, threw my leg over, and settled again to ooch and scooch along the ridgeline to its terminus.

The turret was as close as it was gonna get when I pulled myself into position. Freezing, I swung the off leg over and let go. The slide was short and fast. I hit the turret wall with both feet at the same time. I grunted upright and stood, bracing one boot on the icy roof and the other in the valley.

The sill on the turrets' double-hung window was

thick with snow. I started to knock the glass in with the butt of the telescoping stock but stopped when my old daddy's voice spoke up in my head.

Keep it simple, stupid. Check the obvious first.

When I rubbed the pane clean, I saw the window was unlocked. I thumped the frame with the heel of my hands a couple of times to break it loose. When I pushed upward, my right foot slipped and I fell, cussin' a blue streak.

I clawed back upright, heart pounding like the first time Kelly asked me to go out with her. Steady once again, I lodged the heels of my unfeeling hands against the top rail of the lower sash and pushed upward. Nothing moved but my feet on the slippery roof. I was afraid the window was painted shut from the inside. If that were the case, I'd have to break the window after all. I didn't want to do that because it would make too much noise.

Like I'd been quiet as a church mouse up until then.

Whimpering with frustration, I slapped the sash upward. Ice flaked away, but it moved about an eighth of an inch. I popped it again, planted my numb feet best I could, and pushed hard.

The window rose a couple of inches, giving me room to slip my fingers into the crack and heave upward. It resisted at first, but gave enough to crawl headfirst into the room full of HVAC equipment with barely enough space for maintenance workers to maneuver.

I pulled the window back down, shutting out the flood of cold air. I was in out of the weather, above and behind the Grand Jury room, where the terrorists were holding my family and the other hostages. I flexed my fingers to get the blood flowing again. Feeling returned with pins and needles, then an ache that made me clamp my jaw.

I checked my weapons to be sure they were clear. The cell phone in my back pocket vibrated. My brother's name appeared on the screen, but I didn't have time to talk. I figured he was calling to check on how we were doing in the storm. After serving as sheriff in a little New Mexico town named Rio Vista, he was used to snowstorms and probably wanted to make fun of us whining about a little weather.

It irritated me that he could get through from out of state, but I couldn't call across the street. I ignored the infernal thing and rested there on my knees until enough warmth seeped into my chilled body to clear my mind.

Chapter 34

While the blizzard raged in West Texas, the sky was overcast in Houston, six hundred miles away.

Marc Chavez sat at the granite bar dividing his gourmet kitchen from the spacious living room. Beside him, Lucille Banks, the woman of advanced age who'd worn diamonds to plan a terrorist attack, sipped Malbec from expensive crystal.

She placed the fragile Waterford glass onto the coaster to avoid chipping the delicate stem. "This doesn't seem to be working as well as you'd hoped."

Chavez pressed the earpiece of a wireless headset against his ear. He held up a finger and listened, concentrating hard not to reach out and move her glass to the exact middle of the round rest. He'd already moved the laptop on the bar half a dozen times, so that it rested square with the edge.

Adjusting the earphone and mouthpiece was an effort, heightened by the tension he felt about the takeover. The earpiece went in after three tries, but the mouthpiece was a problem from the outset. It didn't seem to be in the proper place at all, and no matter how many times he tilted it up or down, close to his mouth or farther away, it didn't feel right. He gave up and hurried into the bathroom to use the mirror. When he was satisfied with the microphone's position, he padded back to the counter in sock feet and made a neat note on the pad beside the laptop.

DO NOT TOUCH THE COMMUNCATIONS GEAR!

The pad also contained several rows of complicated numbers and letters ending in one row highlighted with an asterisk.

DeVaca's voice came through the earpiece. "There's still no response. We have all four entrances covered, but at this time I see no impending assault. We'll video the woman and email it to our friends in Washington within half an hour. They'll burn a disk and drop it off."

"Good. Let me know if anything changes."

Chavez released the talk button and picked up their conversation. "Lucille, this isn't television, and it sure isn't scripted. We had a plan, but changes are inevitable. You just need to get that into your head, your head, head."

"Well, I hoped it would go much smoother than I've seen."

Chavez burst out laughing. "Good God, woman, I have no control over the *weather*! Don't you remember the last time you were involved in forcing Change? Wasn't that in Dallas somewhere around November 22, 1963? I bet things didn't work out as your people planned."

She dabbed at her lips with a crisp napkin. "That day went as designed. This looks like a mess."

"You knew the risks two years ago. You can leave if you want."

"I have no intention of backing down. We have the same beliefs and the same goal in mind. The country needs to be rebuilt, and this is the next step. Don't underestimate me, Chavez, or I might not continue to do that thing you like so much." She smiled at his shocked expression. "I didn't say I *wouldn't*, I said *might* not."

He licked his lips, torn by the operation at hand, and the potential for momentary relief from the stresses of overthrowing an entire government.

Lucille stood. "I'm going to sit on the couch for a while. Would you care to join me?" Before he could answer, she strolled across the thick carpet in a skirt much too short for her age. She sat on the sofa, crossing her dancer's legs that were the envy of women decades younger. She patted the seat with a hand that revealed her true age.

He corrected the position of her wineglass, walked to the sink, and prepared to wash his hands three times. After all, they'd touched that filthy keyboard.

After Lucille Banks retired to the house's guest suite, Chavez dialed a number with a drop phone. The call was answered on the first ring.

"Yessir."

"It's a go."

"Do they have her yet?"

"Yes. She's separated from the group, somewhere

within the building. They'll contact me when they're ready to broadcast the video. I need to make sure you're ready to receive it immediately, immediately, imm—." He bit it off.

Team Five, three men Chavez had never laid eyes on, had been ready for weeks, but Chavez didn't trust anything to chance. His compulsive personality had propelled him to success, but it also drove others crazy as he checked and rechecked the same details again and again.

The man with a distinctive Middle Eastern accent waited until he was sure Chavez was finished talking. "We'll deliver a thumb drive to the congressman's office as soon as possible, along with the phone number you gave us. I'm sure he'll call after viewing the contents."

"Why don't you send it to him through email?"

"Despite what you see on television, those magic routers that change IP addresses can be traced by any tech-geek who knows what they're doing, and believe me, there are many of those people out there. A clean thumb drive is untraceable."

Chavez stared out the window at a live oak spreading outward, some limbs reaching the ground before climbing back toward the humid Houston sky.

"Fine." Chavez hung up and tapped a key on his laptop. A razor-sharp image of a smiling young woman stared at him, her eyes a startling shade of green. He circled her face three times with the cursor. "Miss Bright, you're not going to like what happens next."

No matter what DeVaca or the donors thought, Chavez's real target was U.S. Representative Donald Bright, Chairman of the Homeland Security Committee. The congressman was getting *wayyy* too close to Chavez's drug pipeline across the Mexican/U.S. border. With him gone, no one else had the power to force a shutdown of the border.

With less emphasis on border control, Chavez's men could wash over the Rio Grande with a tidal wave of cocaine that would bring millions of dollars, and he didn't care if the Mexican gangs followed.

Chavez was a firm believer in the Chaos Theory, as long as it didn't apply to him.

He pushed the disconnect button three times, though the icon disappeared at once. Even in this world of chaos, there were necessary protocols.

Chapter 35

Dorothy met DeVaca at the disabled elevator across from the County Extension office. Katie Bright was zip tied to a wooden chair in the back of the cubicle, her head covered with a cloth bag. She was panting as Dorothy double-checked the plastic ties binding Katie's wrists and ankles tight to the chair.

When Dorothy was finished, she raised an eyebrow at DeVaca and waited. With his nod, she whipped the bag from their captive's head and walked away.

The young woman blinked in the dimly lit enclosure and found DeVaca watching from a few feet away. She drew in several large breaths of fresh air before speaking. "Who are you? What's this all about?"

"I am Wicked." He angled his head in thought. "The *what* is politics, people, power. The usual. Mostly power."

"I can't help you with any of that."

"Yes, you can."

Dorothy returned, propped a newspaper in Katie's lap so the headline and date were visible. She bent to retrieve a cell phone from a miniature tripod and moved in close.

Katie recoiled. "What's this for?"

Dorothy checked the image on the screen. "Proof for your *padre* . . . daddy."

"This won't do any good. Dad can't do anything. You know as well as I do that the government doesn't negotiate with terrorists."

DeVaca ignored her comment. "Young lady, we would like for you to ask your father for your life. You don't have to say much. Tell him to do what we say. Once you do that, we'll take you upstairs and you can wait with the others."

"What do you want him to do?"

"Personally, I would have loved to see him blow his brains out on national television, but I was overruled. Instead, he will take the easy way out and follow the directions he received from my superior."

"But what—"

DeVaca's smile didn't include his eyes. "It really doesn't matter, does it? You are in no position to ask questions, only to do as I say."

Katie licked her dry lips. "If this is about ransom, he doesn't have much money."

The smile disappeared. "This is not a common kidnapping." He drew a razor-sharp knife from the sheath on his belt. "If you do not do as I say right now, I will remove one of your little fingers, then I will ask you again to make your plea."

He used the knife as an indicator. "This has recorded everything we've said. He has heard your heroic attempt to stall, but now the time is over. Tell him now. Say, Daddy, they're going to cut me to pieces if you don't do as they say."

"But—"

"I don't argue. Your stubbornness just cost you an appendage." DeVaca moved so his back was against the camera and knelt in front of Katie. He grabbed the little finger of her left hand, stretched it so hard it almost broke, and held the edge against the second knuckle, slicing just hard enough to break the skin.

Katie shrieked, not from the pain, but from the horror of losing a body part.

Standing just outside the open elevator, Dorothy stiffened and touched the bud in her ear. "We have a problem."

DeVaca kept his head averted, so his face wouldn't be recorded. "What's that?"

"No one can raise Scarecrow."

"What the hell is he doing up there?"

"I don't know."

"He *did* get the jammer in place, didn't he?" The device was an essential part of the plan, relying on the latest technology to block calls as far away as a quarter of a mile. He realized that the beeping desk phones had become merely unnoticed background noises.

She waved the cell phone. "No. I have full bars."

"That means cell phones are working near this building also. Do we have anyone else who can operate the jammer?"

"I can."

"Good. Scarecrow failed us. Kill him." DeVaca stared at the knife in his hand. He bit his lip, thinking. "This might present a problem."

DeVaca stood and backed out of the camera's view to think.

Katie wept, staring at the little finger she'd almost lost.

Chapter 36

I needed to see what was outside of my HVAC room. Still above the main roof, the way out was through another floor hatch inset like something out of a tree house.

I gave the knob a turn. To my relief, the mechanism was smooth as silk and the door lifted without a sound. I peeked through a thin crack.

Nothing but a gust of warm air rushed into my face. I shivered at the delicious sensation. Listening through the thin crack, I choked down the fear that threatened to overwhelm me. I'm not sure what I expected. Shouting? Cries? Bad guys talking about their plan so it would make things easier to figure out?

I raised the door to reveal a spiral staircase leading into a claustrophobic storage room half filled with boxes and files. I tiptoed down the skinny steps behind the MP5's muzzle, finding it easy to maneuver the ugly little machine pistol. I understood why those guys carried them.

A wide gap under the door leading to the conference room caught my attention. Dropping to the floor, I squinted underneath and saw nothing. I cracked the door and took a peek, hoping I wouldn't interrupt any invaders sitting around the table and having lunch. The office contained a sturdy conference table, two chairs, and a desk phone.

Letting out a long-held breath, I relaxed my tight shoulders. Half a dozen steps later, I was at still *another* door that led into the courtroom.

That's where I figured the hostages were. I decided I'd better text Ethan an update.

Chapter 37

Warm yellow light cut the gloom and stretched across the Posada hotel's rear patio. Dozens of footprints in the snow were startling against the deep, smooth accumulation on the metal outdoor table tops and chairs.

Herman had to park half a block from the Spanish arches leading into the Posada's wide plaza. He and Gabe hurried past the tall three-tiered fountain freezing into an ice sculpture. Snowflakes swirled in the protected area before piling up on every surface.

Herman yanked at the brass handle, and Gabe followed him into the warm, damp air of the noisy hotel lobby. Dozens of people huddled in groups under the heads of longhorn cattle, buffalo, and elk. Most were townspeople.

Scanning the room, Herman stomped his feet to dislodge the loose snow on his boots, noticing dirty puddles on the polished Mexican tile. That was unusual. Andy Clark, the owner of the hotel, always had his maintenance man nearby with a mop and bucket.

A gaggle of women in thick coats and bright red

hats caught sight of the ranchers and one pointed. "Oh. More cowboys."

"Probably Texas Rangers. That's who they need right now."

A stout woman under a hat full of feathers pressed her pearls and spoke in a Boston accent. "Does *everyone* in this town wear cowboy hats?"

Her friend patted a stray strand of hair back into place. "Most of 'em, if they were born and raised here."

A pure Texas voice answered. "Well, I swanny, those two aren't Rangers. Look at those boots and the cow mess on their jeans."

Hearing the conversation and knowing the ice would melt off his boots and jeans before long, filling the air with the smell of fresh cow manure, Herman thought about joining the women just so they could get a good whiff. His fun dissolved when he saw the concerned faces of the law-enforcement officers gathered in the banquet room.

They weren't there because of a snowstorm.

He stopped at the desk to catch Andy's attention and saw a Judge revolver on the counter. Herman smoothed his gray brush-pile mustache and studied on the pistol's implications.

The frazzled owner cradled the telephone receiver between his shoulder and his ear. He jerked his chin upward in acknowledgment and answered a question into the receiver. "No, I can't get anyone to talk with you right now. We're taking numbers and somebody'll call you back when they get the chance. Who? Bailey? CNN? What's that number?"

He jotted it down and hung up. The phone rang again, but he ignored it. "Herman. Y'all come to help?"

"We stopped to get a room 'cause the snow's so deep I won't make it to the house tonight." He nodded toward the pistol. "What'n hell is going on? What do you need help for?"

"You don't know?"

"No, I reckon that's the reason I'm asking. We just got to town."

"Well, you being a retired Ranger and all, I figured they needed you, and ever'thing."

"Might do. Why?"

As Andy explained, Herman watched Sheriff Ethan Armstrong through the glass. Faces glistening with sweat, Ethan and three townspeople were gathered around an impromptu command table covered with white butcher paper. Wearing a tactical vest, Deputy Frank Malone was drawing with a marker while the others pointed and talked. Men and women in civilian clothes filled in around them.

Knowing Andy's predisposition to trailing off, Herman left the desk while he was still talking and passed the fireplace and conversation pit. Gabe followed, unbuttoning his coat.

Sheriff Armstrong waved the retired Ranger in. Herman opened the glass door and heard Ethan's side of the conversation. "There aren't enough of us to do anything at all right now. This storm's locked us down, and nobody's getting in until it lets up. That leaves me with two deputies, four firemen who were on duty, and two highway patrol officers."

Standing in the open doorway, Gabe pulled at one ear. *"Algo está realmente mal, jefe."*

"This is bad all right." Herman surveyed the room, catching pieces of conversation.

"Hey, you think I don't know the proper response for this situation? Let me tell you something, buddy, we're outnumbered and outgunned here. An unknown number of people with automatic weapons have our courthouse. The only ace I have is—" Ethan held the phone from his ear and caught Deputy Malone's attention. "Do you have any reporters nearby?"

Busy with his own duties, the deputy glanced up and then back down. "Nope."

"Good. Major, my ace in the hole is your man, Sonny Hawke."

Ethan put his hand over the mouthpiece. "Sorry, Herman. Hang on. He's all right."

Herman took half a step back as if he'd been punched in the chest.

Gabe put a hand on Herman's shoulder to steady his boss. "Shit hell. *Fácil mi amigo. Se va a estar bien.*"

Easy my friend, it'll be all right.

Ethan met Herman's eyes. "He's trapped in there with them, but they haven't taken him hostage, yet." He spoke into the phone. "Of course, I tried to call. I may be sheriff in a one-horse town, but I've got *some* sense."

Pause.

"Don't know. He managed to get some info out to us, but we haven't heard from Sonny in a while. I'm not reading anything into it. He could be laying low, and that's what I'd do if *I* was inside of something like this. I'm waiting and hoping he'll call back to give me some more. Everything I have from the inside has come from him so far. The terrorists haven't contacted us yet."

Another pause as he listened.

"Yep, they have everyone who was at work, plus a teacher and a class of kids that was touring the court-house. That includes . . ." He read from a list in his hand. Herman listened, recognizing some of the names. Ethan dropped the list to the table when he finished. "That's if they all showed up for work this morning. We're trying to contact their homes to see if they made it in.

"I know for a fact there are other civilians in there, too. I don't have a count on them. Some of the kids got through to their parents, but the info I've gotten from *them* is cryptic at best. Now the phone lines are clogged and we haven't been able to get any more information. I'm surprised you got through. Are you getting the pic-ture?"

He listened. "No, I don't know how many kids, yet. This snow's slowing everything down. We're trying to get a head count from the school, but they're having their own problems with parents who heard what was going on and drove over *there*. When they couldn't get close, they left their cars right where they were, lock-ing up the streets and now *they're* all stranded in the school and jamming the phones even more. It's gettin' harder'n hell to get a call in or out." He scanned the crowd beyond the doors. "I'm-a tellin' you, Major, this is a damned blizzard here and no one is going any-where for a while."

Without a doubt, the Rangers would already be there if the roads weren't closed, along with every first responder within a hundred-mile radius.

The Posada's maintenance man tapped Herman on the shoulder. He held out a walkie-talkie. "Mr. Herman, I had an idea that y'all might be able to use these. I found out after we got 'em that they were on the same frequency as the high school. I charged 'em up and gave the school a holler. Somebody answered, and I told them where the command center is. They're sending someone over." He pressed the walkie-talkie into Herman's hand. "Here." Herman absently held the device as Ethan listened to a response from the other end.

It was obvious that Ethan was ready to hang up. "No. We haven't heard any more shots, so I think they're getting ready to make their demands. This has now moved from an active shooter scenario to a hostage situation. My men have the perimeter secure."

Deputy Malone snatched a vibrating phone off the table and answered. As he listened, he wrote a note on the white paper covering the table and caught Ethan's attention. He mouthed, "FBI. Said they've been dialing steady for an hour before getting in to us."

Ethan picked up a pencil and wrote: They'll just have to hang on.

He returned to the call. "No, they pushed us back, so I don't have any idea what's going on inside. Yep, I understand protocol, but you need to *listen*. This isn't one loony inside intending to shoot everyone, then himself. These people took the building with military maneuvers and now we're in the middle of a situation that's controlled from the inside."

Herman sat the walkie-talkie on the table and examined the drawing that sprawled over half of the white paper. Like everyone else in the country since the terrorist attacks in 2001, he expected another one some-where. But he never expected terrorists to take over a building in *Ballard*. The threat of violence from the drug cartels south of the nearby Rio Grande was the main concern.

"Meant to tell you, Major, I have someone here with me you might have heard of. A retired Ranger named Herman Hawke." He listened. "That's right, Sonny's dad." He met Herman's gaze. "Half his family's inside with *my* daughter."

Ethan's voice choked. "We're doing all we can for them, you see?"

Herman hadn't spoken to Sonny in several days. He leaned close to Gabe. "Evangelina have a class trip today?"

Gabe's eyes turned to flat, black pits. Herman had never seen that look, though he knew the man who'd worked with him for years had a dark side he'd never witnessed. The wrinkles in Gabe's forehead smoothed as his jaw tightened. "*Sí. Un viaje de campo,* with Kelly."

Wheels turned and the old Ranger evaluated the news. Evangelina was in the same class as the twins. Herman felt sick. "A field trip with Kelly means the twins are in there, too. That's what he meant by half my family."

"Yes."

"Go out to the truck and get my rifle, and yours. There's a box of shells for the .30-30 in the glove box, and one for the .243."

"Yes."

"Hey."

Gabe stopped.

Herman studied on the expression on his hired hand's face. "Get the pistol out from under the seat, too."

Gabe's eyes narrowed. He backslid into Spanish, a sure sign he was under stress. *"Crees que nos dejarán ayudamos?"*

You think they'll let us help?

"Yep. I 'magine Ethan's gonna need all the help he can get before long."

"Nos va en?" Gabe sounded hopeful.

We going in?

"We'll see."

Outside, a train whistle filled the air, muffled by the snow. The three engines and a hundred cars full of coal weren't the least bothered by the weather.

Recalling the look on his face, Herman hoped Gabe would come back with the guns instead of going after Evangelina alone.

Chapter 38

Lorenzo DeVaca watched as a dusty cylinder rose on the end of a rope through the hole in the floor. "You were right."

The elderly man who rode in with the American team stood to the side. He looked like a street person. One finger scratched under the wool cap pulled down over his ears. A sprig of gray hair sprouted from a hole in the side. His speech was juicy due to a lack of teeth. "Told you they were there."

DeVaca refused to look at the man's disgusting profile. "I wouldn't have believed it. No one would believe it unless they could see these containers. Who would have thought the U.S. government would store nerve gas under a *courthouse*?"

Fred Bailey, the former employee of a black company called GORS, Global Ordnance Retrieval and Storage, watched the squatty stainless steel cylinder rise on a rude pulley system. The covered valve bumped against the end of an exposed floor joist with a hard thump and he winced. "Hey! The cap on that thing ain't foolproof. It's damn near old as I am. Be careful with that stuff or we'll all drop dead in our tracks."

The terrorist handling the rope swallowed and tried not to look at DeVaca, who was just as deadly as the sixty-year-old Sarin nerve agent squirreled away by the government during the Cold War. The man whose face was obscured by a blue bandana took a firm grip on the dusty container and guided it to the floor.

DeVaca knelt and pulled a camouflaged handker-chief from the pocket of his pants. He rubbed the dust off the side, as if he were waxing the steel. Finding nothing but the letters GB stamped into the metal, he adjusted his horn-rimmed glasses. "You're sure this is Sarin?"

"That's what I heard when we upgraded the build-ing in 1956." Fred eyed the canister like it was a live snake. "I was part of the team that did the cellar. That was a long time ago."

"How old were you?"

"Twenty."

"And you haven't said anything since?"

"They paid me not to, and I had to sign a paper, but it's been too many years, and I don't care anymore."

"And there are other storage locations?"

"You bet. They're everywhere. They're even buried in junkyards in the middle of cities. 'Course they weren't in the city limits when we buried 'em, but some of these places have growed so much the towns have spread out and covered everything up. I 'magine the government's forgot where they put some of 'em, or them crooked bastards is keeping it quiet."

He scratched at his cap.

"Shoot. We buried some of that stuff straight in the ground in Mesquite. It's four or five stories deep in a pit right beside the LBJ loop around Dallas where they dug fill dirt for the highway. It sat empty for six or seven years, and people took to dumping trash down at the bottom. We went in one day and got rid of 'em by using a dozer to move the trash and dig a hole, then we planted 'em like daffydil bulbs and covered 'em up."

DeVaca felt an electric jolt at the thought of the chaos he could cause with that much gas.

"There's a hotel on top of that dump in Mesquite now, and it's all grown up around there with houses and gas stations and such. I'd hate to be diggin' in some of those other places that weren't as deep."

DeVaca rose, savoring a pleasant mental image of a cloud of Sarin gas engulfing an innocent driver on a bulldozer, then drifting toward a nearby town, no wait, even better, a school or hospital. He knew better, though. Sarin is invisible and left a trail of twitching bodies to prove it had been released. With a slight smile, he hit his transmit button. "How many more are down there?"

His earbud was silent before Tin Man came through. "More than we can use. Some large canisters, others that size."

"Send two more of these up. We're taking the rest out through the tunnel."

"What tunnel?"

"The one you're going to find. Look for anything out of the ordinary on the west wall. Differences in brick, if that's the foundation material. If not, variations in the rock they used for the walls. It has to exist, since the gas is there."

"Yes sir."

DeVaca watched Fred's face. "There *is* a tunnel, right?"

"That's what I heard. All 'at mess was brought in through a tunnel that comes up in a house across the street on the west side."

"You *heard*?"

"Yeah, the whole damn thang was so top-secret, one group didn't know for sure what th'others was doin'. I heard 'bout the gas when a buddy of mine got drunk one night and told me his part of the operation." Fred was hit with a realization. "You know, I never saw Duke after 'at night."

"Does anyone live in the house?"

Fred brought himself back. "No, that's the beauty of the whole thang. No one's lived there since the fifties. The gov'ment pays to keep ever'thang looking normal from the outside. If anybody goes snoopin' around the paperwork, they'll find out it's been part of a lawsuit that's dragged on for years. It'll be in the courts 'til hell freezes over because the gov'ment owns it and they want it to stay that way.

"I bet you didn't know they's houses in neighborhoods all across the country that looks like all the others, but when you go inside, they ain't nothing but shells for water pump stations. That's where they got the idea . . . from that house across over 'ere."

Fred hitched his baggy pants. "I've been wonderin'. Why didn't we just find out which house it is and sneak in 'ere and come up down there'n the basement? It'da been easier and made a lot less noise."

DeVaca turned on him with the dead gaze of a rattlesnake. No one on *his* teams knew all the parts of the operation. He kept his cards close to the vest. In fact, neither he nor Chavez trusted the other and for good reason. Chavez had no idea DeVaca's part of the operation involved nerve gas.

Once DeVaca learned their target was the Ballard courthouse, he investigated on his own. Despite the extensive file provided by Chavez, DeVaca didn't trust anything to chance. Always attentive to detail, DeVaca researched Ballard, the courthouse, and the surrounding area in the months leading to the takeover.

During his investigation, he came across stories of a basement beneath the courthouse. Most of the locals laughed it off as legend. One Internet story said the basement was constructed as a last-ditch retreat in the event of an Indian attack, with a tunnel leading to an escape point still hidden somewhere several hundred yards away and maybe now under one of the nearby houses.

The mythical basement was also rumored to contain the contents of the fabled Lost Dutchman Mine, documents dating back to the original Spanish land grant, survival supplies in the event of a governmental meltdown, gold and silver discovered from lost Spanish expeditions, and forgotten historical archives.

When he discovered the courthouse had been renovated and restored in 1956 and again in 2001, he found an unknown company that was selected over the job's low bidder and knew he was onto something.

He dug deeper into chat rooms full of stories about illegal payoffs giving a clandestine company the job. DeVaca wasn't interested in political maneuvering. He wanted one thing, the truth behind a mysterious offhand mention by an individual with the online name of Reddy Freddy. Finally descending into the Dark Net, he found obscure comments in antigovernment chat rooms, rumors of something called GORS, and Reddy Freddy, who told stories about his career in unnamed government organizations.

DeVaca tracked him down. Freddy, or Fred, was disenchanted with the government, which had subsidized the renovation. DeVaca offered Fred more money than he could spend for the rest of his life if he agreed to help the Cause. The sour-smelling old man agreed.

Standing in the middle of the busy rotunda, DeVaca's rattlesnake eyes held Freddy's gaze until the man dropped his eyes. The Demon swelled with pleasure at the small victory and the hair on DeVaca's neck rose, a delicious response that made him want even more. Unfortunately, he was running behind schedule and knew he had to check in. He'd been out of communication for too long. He pressed the dedicated transmit button to call Chavez. "Oz."

Chavez came back a second later. "Go ahead."

"We sent the video to Team Five. Any news on our progress?"

"The primary target has been contacted. Maintain your position. The talking heads are still reporting on outgoing phone calls. Is there a problem with the scrambler?"

DeVaca felt a flush of anger, both at Chavez's questioning of his performance and the failure of his soldiers. "I'll get back to you." For the first time that night, he felt uneasy. He hadn't heard a word about Scarecrow and the scrambler.

He activated the VOX radio to speak with the other team members. "Dorothy. Why isn't Scarecrow finished?"

"*No se*. I started to find him, but then something happened."

The edges of the operation were fraying. Gritting his teeth, he turned his back on Reddy Freddy. "Scarecrow, report."

His earpiece was silent.

"Scarecrow, report."

Still nothing.

"Lion."

"*Sí.*"

"Something is wrong. It might be Scarecrow's radio, or worse. This damned building isn't that big. Check it out."

"*Sí.*"

DeVaca peered into the basement. "Tin Man. I need that tunnel. Now."

"*Trabajando en ello.*"

"Of course, you're working on it. Dorothy?"

Her voice was quiet, as if he'd dressed her down for failing to follow orders. "Yes."

He thrilled at the fear in her tone. "What arose?"

"I was with the one whose photo we took."

"And."

"She tried to get loose. I had to restrain her. Scarecrow slipped my mind."

"After I left? You were the first to leave with the orders I gave."

"I had to go back. You were busy with the excavation, and I didn't want to bother you."

He wondered if she's seen the hunger in his eyes when he looked at Katie. The young secretary's fresh innocence beckoned him almost as much as Dorothy's eyes. Maybe Dorothy saw his desire and beat the woman in jealousy. It was a wonderful idea and his roller-coastering spirits rose. Either woman would help relieve his frustrations over Chavez's constant nagging. "Is she secure?"

"She is now."

He'd have to check that out just to be sure. Now he was doing the jobs that were the responsibility of others.

DeVaca studied the container at his feet. In a few days, he'd travel the highways with a load of Sarin, opening one canister after another in as many crowded locations as possible in Dallas, Atlanta, Washington, D.C., and where it would cause the most damage and panic, on Wall Street.

His Demon giggled as targets lined up in his mind. Times Square on New Year's Eve, the Super Bowl, a college graduation . . .

Chapter 39

The short terrorist thought he'd turned off the confiscated cell phones one by one before tossing them into the trash can. Those lifelines to the outside world had been silent ever since, but music filled the air with a sense of urgency. In addition to the ringtone, the missed phone buzzed against the metal side with an annoying rattle.

Every hostage snapped toward the sound, most wondering who was on the other end. America's insatiable need for instant information and socialization made Kelly want to scream. It was all she could do to sit there under guard, rubbing her face in frustration.

It fell silent.

In their corner beyond the judge's bench, the frightened kids had migrated toward their teacher like filings to a magnet. The guards ordered them to remain behind the fixed separation bar that Kelly once found pleasantly ornate, but the crotch-high pecan-wood spindles offered no protection from the men carrying automatic weapons.

Matt leaned against her, and the others slid closer. They were all touching in some way, seeking comfort as best they could, except for her twins.

They'd positioned themselves at the edge of the group to better see their captors. Neither had their heads raised, but she knew her kids well enough to tell they were watching the terrorists. That worried her most of all.

The tallest captor, Stretch, stepped out and hadn't returned for some time. The terrorist she thought of as Shorty sat against the opposite wall, submachine gun resting across his lap.

Kelly couldn't stand sitting any longer. "Hey, you."

He shifted the weapon. "No talking."

"Fine. I won't talk, but I have to stand up and stretch."

"No."

"Listen, buddy, none of us are as limber as them kids." Mr. Terrill's voice was stronger than Kelly expected. The weathered veteran was tough enough to spit nails. "Let us up for a minute."

The terrorist stood and raised his weapon. "I said no."

Kelly felt her ears redden and started to stand anyway, thinking she could appeal to the young man's sense of propriety. Jerry raised his head, glaring at the man, and she had second thoughts. If the situation accelerated, he'd be the first one to swell up at the guard. She didn't need that.

"Fine. Guys, move a little so I can unfold my legs. Give me some room. It's all right, Mr. Beck."

"No talking!" Shorty stalked halfway across the courtroom. He moved like a weight lifter. "I said no *talking*!"

Jerry tensed. The kids rustled, recoiling from the

angry young man looming over them. Kelly had to do as ordered to keep the students safe.

Matt's legendary stubbornness rose. "I need to go."

"We'll go pretty soon, baby."

"No, I need to *go*."

She understood. "Oh."

Shorty stepped closer and noticed Matt's shoes were on the wrong feet. "Are you stupid or something? What is he doing?"

"No. He's smart as a whip." Kelly clamped her jaw to regain control. "Listen, he needs to use the restroom."

"No one is leaving this room. You, pee your pants."

The annoying ringtone again cut through the tension and vibrated against the metal trashcan. In a rage, the terrorist rushed across the courtroom and swept the can full of phones to the floor. He crushed them underfoot like ants, stomping with hysterical gyrations. Plastic shards flew across the polished floor as his fury increased, then he found the right one and the music ended.

With a grunt, Shorty kicked an undamaged phone that skittered across the floor and stomped back to his position at the rear wall. He squatted, facing the judge's elevated bench, and stared at Kelly with an expression that made her shiver.

Matt's face twisted at the outburst. She pulled his head against her shoulder to whisper in his ear. "Don't think about it. Hold it as long as you can. If you have to, let go, it'll be all right."

"No, it won't."

She watched Jerry, praying he wouldn't do anything, and wondered where her husband was.

Chapter 40

A steady stream of anxious and frightened parents trickled into the Posada's lobby.

Instead of being underfoot in the Command Center, as the banquet room was now called, Herman chose to stay in the lobby with the people he'd known for years. He and Gabe took positions near the roaring fireplace, doing their best to calm the more hysterical moms and dads.

Herman's soft, steady voice worked, at least for a while. "Cool your jets. The sheriff is doing what he can. You have to let 'em figure this out."

Tall and slender, Dale Perkins, who ran the Conoco, held onto his short wife like an anchor. "So what is it they're doing?"

"I don't know for sure, but they have a plan, you can be sure of that."

"I need to know more than that. What's their *process*?"

Herman held back a growl. He hated people's demands for information. In his past experience, people didn't need to know *everything*. "What difference does it make? Just give 'em room."

"We heard those people have machine guns."

"That's what I heard, too." Herman gave them the rundown, omitting some details because he didn't think Ethan wanted them discussed.

Blair Rogers was white with either fear or fury. A move-in, Blair had arrived in Ballard ten years earlier and opened an art gallery. He had a son inside the courthouse. "They need to go on in there and get my boy out."

"I know, but you can't just walk up to the door. This is a nervous situation, and it's gonna take those boys in there some time to figure it out. They won't go in right now, because it's not an active shooting situation. That's good. Hostage situations give us time."

Herman stopped when the side door off the Posada's plaza slammed open. Two men bulled through like linemen taking the field in the state playoffs. Shaking snow from their worn gimme caps and coats, the Mayo brothers scanned the crowd. Seeing Herman standing inside a semicircle of worried parents, they came straight over.

The ring parted as they pushed through. Luke unzipped his Carhartt coat. "Who's running this outfit?" The look in the thirty-five-year-old rancher's eyes said he was sober as a judge.

One year younger, Danny shared his features, tousled hair, solid noses, laugh lines, and thick cowboy mustaches. "Tell us what to do, Herman."

"Guys, *I'm* not in charge. We're just here to support

them." Herman twisted in place toward the Command Center.

"Well, hell, Herman. You know more'n the rest of these city people. Let us help."

Dolores Hernandez, the owner of the Chat 'N Chew café, pushed through the patio doors with a pasteboard box full of coffee cups, creamer, and sugar. The generations-old Southern tradition of bringing food to any tragedy was ingrained in every Ballard resident.

Behind her, three café regulars hauled containers of hot coffee. She pointed to the Posada's registration counter for one of the tall containers. "Put that right there and plug it in." She continued on to the command center with the rest following like baby ducks.

Rogers ignored her and faced the Mayo brothers. "They're just talking in there, but we don't need some *cow*boys to start ordering people around."

Danny's eyes narrowed. "Buddy, I don't know you, and you don't know me, so I 'magine the safest thing for you is to not get in our business. You need to back out and let these guys do their job."

Herman held up a hand. "Easy boys, we don't need to go fighting among ourselves."

The noise level dropped off enough for Sheriff Armstrong's voice to filter through the open doors. He was back on the landline because cell phone service was still jammed from the number of calls coming from panicked citizens.

"We're blind here." The frustration in his voice was thick as he paced behind the table with a receiver against his ear. "We're trying to operate in a blizzard. No . . . you aren't getting it. *Drones?* It's a blizzard out there. The storm's paralyzed this whole town. I'm wearing the big hat until you get here, and I don't care if you *are* Homeland Security. You and the FBI and the CIA and any other son-of-a-bitch who works for three-letter outfits can all lock horns when y'all ski in, but I'm gonna hang up now. What? When do you think you're gonna get here?"

Silence.

"By that time it'll be too late, I'm afraid."

Ethan glanced up to see the faces through the glass-panel wall. They ran the gamut from hard, to furious, to blank, and frightened.

He pointed and Deputy Malone closed the glass and wood doors to block off the remainder of the conversation.

Chapter 41

Arturo found a flashlight on the maintenance man's worktable and flicked it on, probing the dark corners beyond the fluorescent lights' reach. The noise downstairs quieted, and he felt safe for the first time since he and Sonny Hawke heard the gunshots.

The skeletal structure of the attic revealed itself as he painted the darkness with the weak yellow beam. Crisscrossed supports, ductwork, dusty wires stapled to rafters, and dust-covered insulation stretched into the distance. He flicked it off and wondered what to do.

"Javier?"

The voice came through the attic door seconds before the lock rattled against the latch. A sharp, audible snap followed the metallic clatter. The lock thudded to the floor. Terrified, Arturo flicked off the overhead lights. The door opened, spilling feeble light into the pitch-black attic.

He backed around the chimney, keeping one hand on the rough bricks and feeling with his feet. Light footsteps on the boards made them creak, torturing him with the need to peek. The fluorescent shop lights suspended from the rafters buzzed back to life.

Arturo swallowed as loud as a horse drinking from a trough. Every instinct shouted for him to bolt. Instead, he placed the palm of one hand against the rough bricks to steady himself.

"Espantapájaros?" The strange voice cut through the attic. "Javier!"

The frightened kid wondered why he was calling for Scarecrow. Maybe the guy knew Arturo was there and calling him by that name was some version of *scaredy-cat* back where he came from.

Arturo was sure he hadn't been seen, but the guy probably knew he was hiding. He'd watched plenty of movies where people were discovered by the littlest thing like a footprint in the dust. One thing was sure. He wasn't going to answer the guy.

"Es León."

It's Lion?

Arturo decided that Javier was most likely the corpse on the antique canvas cot. Then he got it. Scarecrow and Lion, characters from the *Wizard of Oz*. What was up with that?

Switches clicked, the sound crisp. The man muttered as tools clanked in harmony with more clicks. An electronic whine came alive, followed by the hum of a computer booting up.

The sound of a hammer smashing metal made Arturo jump. He choked down a cry and forced himself to remain still.

The man quieted again and more clicks from an electronic device followed. He whistled an unidentifiable tune through his teeth. The man appeared to be enjoying his work, but then Arturo got it. The computer was slow in booting up and the guy was killing time.

Mouth open to breathe as quietly as possible, Arturo heard footsteps coming around the chimney. The acoustics made it sound as if the intruder was on both sides at the same time. Wanting to back away, but restricted to the platform, all the teenager could do was flatten against the bricks and hope the shadows would work to his benefit.

A flashlight beam probed the corners, following the crude walkway around the chimney. It found the cot and danced over the blanket, coming to rest on the legs sticking out. "Javier? *Usted vino aquí a dormir?*"

Arturo translated the question. *You came up here to sleep*?

Shaking, the boy squirreled around the chimney, keeping his face away from the probing beam. He heard the blanket rustle, and a quick intake of breath.

"*Madre de dios!*"

Arturo moved again. This time Sonny's oversize coat scraped on the rough bricks. He glanced downward and saw the beam of white light play along the dusty planks.

Two quick footsteps, and a sudden glare blinded him. Arturo squinted past the tactical light into the surprised eyes of a man wearing a bandana over the lower half of his face.

"Don't move!"

Arturo again did what any normal kid would do.

He ran.

"*Deténgase!*"

The teenager had no intention of stopping. Blinking the spots out of his eyes, Arturo ducked around the chimney and took the only escape route he had, and that was deeper into the attic. A thin walkway of weathered boards angled away, but Arturo ignored it, jumping from one rafter to the next, ducking under the trusses.

Lion followed and lost his balance on the narrow catwalk. Catching one of the collar ties, he swung the short machine pistol to bear, but the kid skipped across the rafters with the sure feet of a mountain goat.

"Stop!"

Instead, Arturo circled around toward the darkest part of the attic. The frustrated terrorist used the light mounted on his machine pistol to pick his way along still another narrow, dusty line of boards half-buried under drifts of dusty insulation. The kid risked a glance backward to see the man moving in a slow crouch to intercept him.

Arturo moved deeper into the attic, using both hands and feet to skitter over the rafters. His pursuer cracked his head on a truss and cursed. The chase slowed as the sloping roof pitch forced them both to a stop.

Thinking he had the boy trapped, the man crouched in an awkward, off-balance position and aimed his machine pistol. "*Stop!* Stop!" His accent was thick and heavy, one Arturo was familiar with. "*Paro o te pego un tiro dónde está parado!*"

I'll shoot you if you don't surrender!

Whining deep in his throat, Arturo froze and pointed the weak beam of his flashlight at the bad guy named Lion. Arturo again squinted into the bright tactical light on the weapon aimed at his chest. He felt he was being drawn into the dark man's eyes that were as paralyzing as those of a cobra. They surely belonged to a demon instead of a lion.

Arturo used his left hand to make a sign against *mal de ojo*, the evil eye, and saw the startled look on the Mexican's face. The man took one step to the side to dodge the curse from the left-handed witch and found nothing of substance underfoot.

Lion dropped between the two-by-ten joists and disappeared into a cloud of insulation as muffled gunfire rattled somewhere below. The ancient plaster and lath of the ceiling below gave under his weight with a soft crunch and he fell through.

Arturo was stunned when the man disappeared.

He *must* have been *El Diablo* himself. The *mal de ojo* had worked, just like his grandmother promised.

Chapter 42

Rural electricity is iffy at best, and the violent snow-storm played havoc with the power lines. It was only a matter of time before two lines blew together, or the accumulated weight of ice and snow caused one to snap.

Kelly gasped when Wilfred Bates, the County Extension agent, launched himself from beside Mr. Beck the instant the lights flickered and went out.

Like almost everyone in the room, Shorty and Stretch glanced upward at the large white pendant lights hanging overhead. Stretch turned to the window. Shorty reached for the doorknob and gave it a twist.

Despite his potbelly and out-of-shape physique, the middle-aged agent who worked with ranchers and farmers vaulted the bar and charged Shorty. Running light as a feather on the toes of his soft-soled shoes, the man was silent on the polished floor.

Had Wilfred Bates waited, things could have worked in his favor. Shorty might have opened the door to peer into the hallway, blocking his view of the hostages.

The lights flickered back on and steadied.

Bates was four steps away when Shorty saw him coming. He had just enough time to drop his hand to the grip, spin, and raise the muzzle.

The agent was another step closer when Shorty squeezed the trigger. The first round hit the floor inches from the man's foot.

"Kids!" Kelly's voice was sharp. "Look at me!"

A few listened. The rest turned toward the sound of gunfire

Two steps away, and the next round punched a hole just above Bate's kneecap, shattering the femur.

The muzzle swing was hard and fast, causing the third round to miss and punch a hole through the bar's railing and bury itself into a woman's chest.

Screams from the hostages followed the man's falling body as he crashed into the short terrorist, knocking him back against the wall. Stretch whirled in time to see half a dozen hostages stand, including Jerry and his buddy Stephen.

"Sit or I will shoot!" His eyes flicked to Shorty, kicking himself free of the stranger who moaned and grasped his leg with both hands. Blood poured from the wound and the county agent rolled onto his back in agony, away from Shorty, who rose.

Cowed by the rifle pointed in their direction, the hostages settled back to the floor, some raising their hands, many crying.

"Enough! Silence!" Stretch brought the rifle to his

shoulder, sighting on first one, then another of those who expected him to open fire. "Shoot the next one who moves."

"Yes!" Shorty joined him in sweeping the room. "I will shoot again."

Dorothy pushed into the room. "What is this?"

Stretch pointed. "He chose to fight back."

Dorothy watched the bleeding, moaning man writhing on the floor. "Kill him, as a lesson. The rest of you, watch and understand that we are in control." Throwing one last look at the hostages, she pivoted and disappeared through the door.

Time slowed for Kelly as Stretch let his rifle dangle from the strap with a grin. He drew a knife from the sheath attached to his vest. A terrifying grin split his face.

"Students!" Kelly's voice broke. "Look at me now and don't make a move. Matt honey, squeeze 'em shut like it's bright outside." She held his face against her chest and locked eyes with her son. "Do it!"

Shorty approached the weeping adult hostages, his finger on the trigger. "No! Watch and understand who is blessed by Allah!"

Stretch grabbed Bates's collar and dragged him across the smooth floor to the wall opposite the door. The man groaned and held up one hand in defense.

"My God," Mr. Beck said, as if the muzzle of an M4 wasn't mere feet away. "Not here. Not in this country."

Spittle flew. "Silence!"

Stretch dropped, one knee on the agent's head and the other on his chest. He lowered the blade.

Kelly met Mr. Beck's gaze. Both knew what was coming next.

The adult hostages' cries of horror drowned the sounds of the beheading. But the voices couldn't cover the coppery smell of pumping blood.

Chapter 43

Homeland Security was raising his blood pressure, and Sheriff Ethan Armstrong felt like the phone was growing to his ear. Another part of his mind registered the amount of food coming in the hotel from townspeople who wanted to help. Despite the storm's intensity, more people packed the lobby. His attention flicked from one to the other. "Yessir. I understand protocol."

He wondered how many times he'd have to repeat that phrase in one day.

"I'm sure, being Homeland Security and all that, you know the roads are already closed. There's no traffic moving in or out because visibility is zero. I'm operating blind. This is worse than the storm that popped up over Haystack Mountain in Alpine back in 1983. Back then rain came after a three-foot snow, and we were iced in for a week. I hope that don't happen again, but you never know. We're puttin' together a response, but I'm not going to tell you over an unsecured line."

Sheriff Armstrong watched Herman talking with a clot of concerned people in front of the fireplace. He thanked his lucky stars to have the retired Ranger turned rancher out there acting as a buffer between the command center and the growing throng.

"I could use the help. Frankly, I'd like nothing more than to turn all this over and let you guys handle the whole thing, but we're doing what we can, and you're taking me away from it."

In such situations involving several different agencies, the man with the biggest hat took charge. Ethan wore that hat, and he was done answering questions over the phone.

"Here's the deal. You're there and I'm here, so I'm handling it right now. We'll talk when you show up."

He hung up and pondered the drawing on the white butcher paper covering the table. The maintenance men from both the Posada and the courthouse had fleshed out most of the rooms and offices. The floor plan was as close as they could recall.

"They won't be here for hours. That's the last time I'm gonna explain what's going on. From now on, that's your job, Frank. Congratulations, you're my new communications specialist." He tapped the paper with his index finger. "Now is this the best we can do?"

"Yessir." Deputy Frank Malone adjusted a wooden twelve-inch ruler to draw another line in pencil. "We don't have a floor plan of the courthouse, so we've drawn this from memory. Sometimes there was a difference of opinion, but most of what we have here is right."

"How the hell can we not have a floor plan of that building? Answer me this, didn't the city put together a response plan after nine-eleven?"

"They did, Sheriff, and our copies are in our shot-to-pieces file cabinets, but there aren't any *floor* plans for the courthouse. We don't know what went with them."

"The stinkin' *Chamber* is through those doors. They don't have blueprints or something?" The Chamber of Commerce shared one commercial corner of the Posada with gift shops and a gallery.

"Nothing. There's a real nice layout of the hotel here on the Internet, but that's all we've found." Deputy Malone concentrated on his notes and drew another line.

"Fine." Sheriff Armstrong caught Herman's eye and waved him in. He left the Mayo brothers and joined them in the command center. "Herman's been around here for years and has more law experience than I do. I want him to see this before we decide which way to jump."

The sheriff shook his hand. "Sorry you found out about Sonny and your people the way you did, and thanks for talking to everyone out there. Most of 'em'll listen to you better'n anyone else I know. Now, I have more bad news."

"I already know. Kelly and the kids are in there, too. There ain't much that these folks don't know, or haven't made up, and that's the part that's growing like a weed. We're gonna have to move soon."

"We?"

"Hell, Ethan. You know as well as I do you don't have enough men to handle this. Half of those guys are ready to do whatever you say, and I suspect more are on the way. There's a lot of experience standing out there, too, military vets and a couple of ex-cops."

"I don't need a posse. This ain't the 1880s."

"No, but what you need ain't here. You can't wait

around, and you know it. If I's you, I'd do something pretty quick before someone acts the fool. Gather the *veterans* in here at least. They'll have calmer heads."

Ethan figured that in other parts of the country, the folks might not do much more than wail and cry. The people in his view appeared ready to go to war. Long guns were making an appearance in the lobby, and he was sure most everyone out there had quick access to a handgun. He'd already seen the revolver tucked into Herman's waistband.

It also worried the hell out of him because some of the hotheads might take it upon themselves to move on the courthouse. If they did, it would be a slaughter.

Ethan waved him around the table. "We're gonna do just that, but I ain't ready yet. We need to negotiate with these people inside and find out what they want." He pointed to the floor plan. "Y'all's plan, right?"

Herman joined him on the backside of the table. "Best I can tell. Who's trying to make contact with those people?"

Deputy Malone motioned toward the front desk. "Andy Clark's dialing every number we have for the courthouse. He'll transfer the call in here if anyone answers."

"Good." Ethan tapped the map with a forefinger. "I want my men in here right now. Can somebody go out and pull in the guys who're standing post?"

Herman waved Gabe through the door. He came in, the .243 hanging over his shoulder by the sling, muzzle toward the ceiling. "Hey, hoss, go out and gather up the lawmen that're watching the courthouse. Tell 'em the sheriff wants to talk."

"You want some men to take their places, to keep an eye on the *palacio de justicia?*"

"We better had." Herman leaned his Winchester in the corner. He and Ethan put their heads back together over the hand-drawn map as soon as Gabe left. They stopped when Ethan's cell rang and vibrated on the table.

Ethan spun it around to face Deputy Malone. They watched the phone as if it were alive. "Answer it."

Malone flicked the screen and listened. Lips tight across his teeth, he held the receiver out. "I believe you need to take this."

Ethan took his phone back. The men in the command center closed in. "This is Sheriff Armstrong. Can I ask who's talking?"

"You can ask, but it doesn't make any difference."

"How'd you get this number? How the hell'd you get through?"

"That doesn't make any difference, either." The man spoke in a German accent. "Ve hev our veys."

"Funny."

A soft, muffled crump vibrated the windows. Screams erupted from the lobby. A rush of men flowed through the glass doors and into the storm.

His face tight, the sheriff put the cell phone tight against his chest. "Frank! Find out what just happened. Tell those people not to do anything stupid!" The deputy charged out of the command center. Ethan watched him disappear into the storm and turned his attention back to the phone call. "I hope to hell you haven't blown part of the building up. What was that explosion?"

The man's voice was different. Weaker. "Nothing of consequence."

"Fine then. What can I do for you to let the hostages go?"

The man resumed the conversation with obvious self-confidence. "Well, for one, you can forget any plan you may have to free the detainees. We'll release them in our own good time."

"Good. Help me with that. When can we expect it to happen?"

"I'm talking on a drop phone, and I didn't load it with very many minutes." A dry, irritating snicker came through the line. "Your people are safe, as long as you stay out there, right there, right there . . ."

"You trying to be funny?"

The voice was sharp. "I'm *trying* to save the lives of those inside."

"Let the women and kids go. As a goodwill act."

"No." The answer crackled through the speaker. "I know how hostage negotiation works, and I'm not playing your game. *Capishe*?"

"What is it you want then?"

"I'm calling to tell you not to worry. They are fine, and I'll release them at the appropriate time."

"How do I know that? When's the right time?"

"When I say so. You'll have to trust me."

"I'd love to trust you, but I need something back. Release the kids as a goodwill gesture."

Another sharp laugh. "I'm not going to get entangled in pointless negotiations, and neither should you. I will call you back in half an hour. Please be patient."

"Pointless?"

The phone went dead.

Ethan calmed himself as a flood of questions washed over him. The guy on the phone didn't know about the explosion until Ethan made him aware, and he said "not to worry about those inside," meaning he wasn't in there with them.

And he didn't like the phrase "pointless negotiations."

Deputy Malone was back. Cold radiated off his snow-covered coat and hat. "I got as close as I thought I could without getting shot. The building is still standing, and there's no smoke or fire. I can't tell if anything is going on inside. The boys watching said they can't tell if anything happened. Ethan, those people out there are about to torque off. They want their kids."

"So do I."

A loud voice cut across the Posada lobby. "We've waited long enough! Ethan!"

The Mayo brothers pushed through the crowd. Luke Mayo rolled into the command post as if he belonged there. Danny followed. Luke leaned over the table. "They're blowing things up in there. Why haven't you gone in to get them people out?"

Armstrong felt the heat rise in his face. "Because we're outgunned and there's no good way in. Now, get out and let me—"

"Go in through the tunnel."

The activity around the table stalled.

"What tunnel?"

"Why hell, Ethan, the one from that house across over there on Bayless Street."

"I've heard that story. It's nothing but a myth."

Danny unbuttoned his coat. "Bullshit. My daddy said he'd been in it."

Armstrong reached a decision. "Somebody close the glass doors." His deputies pushed inside and gathered around the table as melting snow dripped off their clothes. "That call was from one of the men who said he was inside. He said to disregard the explosion and that everyone is all right." His gaze roamed over the grim-faced men around the table.

"Said he'd call back in half an hour. Well, he's a lyin' sonofabitch. He's no more in there than I am, so listen up. Things have changed." He addressed the Mayo brothers. "Now, boys, tell me about that tunnel."

Chapter 44

Marc Chavez paced through his luxurious house, worrying about the explosion the sheriff mentioned, while Lucille Banks stirred cream into her coffee. It wasn't the bold coffee-shop blend, but plain old Yuban. No one ever drifted completely away from their roots, and hers were anchored in the dry, rocky ground of Benjamin, Texas. "Dear, you said yourself there would be unanticipated events."

"There are too many, too many, too many. The storm has caused all kinds of problems. There's no television footage and I need those images. Now explosions, and DeVaca isn't updating me. What exploded? I need *information*!"

Taking a sip, Lucille smiled. "I understand, but it could have been anything, or nothing. Maybe the sheriff's smarter'n you think he is and he was trying to unsettle you. If that's the case, it worked."

"No, no, no. He thought I was calling from inside the courthouse."

"Well." Lucille flipped a page of the *Texas Monthly*

magazine on the counter before her, pausing on a Vera Wang advertisement.

A voice spoke in Chavez's ear. "Oz."

Chavez raised a hand to his earpiece and pressed three times. "You're not coming through."

His fingers flicked over the keyboard. "Are you there, Wicked?"

"Right here."

"About time you checked in. What happened?"

"We're maintaining control."

"I want to know about the explosion."

DeVaca's answer was immediate. "That issue has been rectified. There was an attempted breach."

"I haven't heard anything about that."

"Because I just now told you."

"I was on the phone with the sheriff when it happened. He asked *me* what blew up."

"You called early."

While planning the mission, they'd discussed the need for updates on the hour, but Chavez couldn't stand not knowing every detail in an ever-evolving situation.

"Yes. I hadn't heard from you, and then I hear an explosion in the background and the sheriff discussing it. I think it's something you should have told me."

"We're supposed to be on a *schedule*. You of all people understand the need to maintain a proper timetable."

Chavez didn't like being scolded, especially by someone under his command. He collected himself. "The schedule has been abandoned. I was able to call the sheriff's phone and was surprised when he answered. How did that happen? The scrambler should have been activated and *what blew up*?"

"Are you testing *me*?"

He knew the accusatory tone irritated DeVaca, but he didn't care. Calling Sheriff Armstrong's phone was another of Chavez's control techniques to make sure the plan was on track. "You know how I am." Chavez's tone was that of a petulant child.

"We've had issues with setting up the jammer and lost a man. There was a little uprising from some of the male hostages and one of our brave partisans used a grenade to . . . alleviate the situation, giving his own life for the Cause."

"Why didn't you say that in the *first* place?"

"I was trying to do my *job*. I can't call in and tell you every time we pull a trigger."

Chavez's face closed. He touched each finger of his right hand to the tip of his thumb, and repeated the process to calm himself, a throwback to when he was a child in bed with his mother, touching *her* fingertips with his own until he dropped off. He slept with her until he was twelve.

"The congressman has less than an hour to respond to our demands. I'm confident he'll comply, and when he does, you know what to do."

"Yes. I'm out."

Chavez figured that DeVaca would let the extremists make their own decisions. It would serve to satisfy DeVaca's ongoing needs, however defined. Sated, he'd be ready for the second part of Chavez's stratagem a month down the road.

Chavez didn't mind if everyone died. It would add even more horror to what he believed was a rapidly growing bubble of American vulnerability. "Out." He licked his lips. "Out, out, out."

Chavez rubbed his hands together, as if washing them clean, then gave Lucille a brilliant smile as he felt himself stir.

She sighed, closed the magazine, and left her coffee to get cold.

Chapter 45

The deputies and emergency responders who took turns watching the courthouse told Sheriff Ethan Armstrong that nothing moved on the streets except for groups and individuals struggling on foot toward the Posada Hotel and the high school.

Harp Webster brought his portable CB base unit to the command center and set it up on an empty table. They heard from other radio-heads that beyond the town limits, the highways for a hundred miles in all directions were impassable.

Half a dozen grim, snow-covered apparitions pushed through the hotel's eastern doors, bringing a wave of frigid air behind them. Every one of the hard-eyed men carried weapons ranging from bolt-action hunting rifles, to vintage World War II carbines, to more modern semi-automatic AR-15-style weapons.

He suspected they wore pistols under their heavy coats, because he knew for a fact that at least three of that group had their License to Carry permits. The others were a toss, but almost everyone he knew had a pistol. They were as common as water bottles in West

Texas. It wasn't the right time to start asking questions, and besides, licensed Texans had every right to carry both concealed and in the open.

Sheriff Armstrong drew a deep breath when he saw the anxious men. He knew most by name, and had gone to school with many of them. They stopped to take stock of the busy lobby.

Armstrong picked out Ernie O'Neal as the leader when he cast around, located the command center, and pointed. Quick to anger and just as quick to cool off, Ernie was an impatient city councilman who never liked to wait on anything. He pushed through the anxious crowd, followed by Clay Burke, Dale Haskins, Concepción Cuevas, Blair Rogers, and Rafael Hernandez.

As the last name ticked off in Armstrong's head, he realized they all had children in the courthouse. The sheriff left the floor plan and met them in the lobby, keeping the lounge area clear to maintain his "no-man's-land."

"Keep them long guns pointed up, boys."

Not one of them shifted the weapons they carried.

Ernie O'Neal planted himself like a tree in front of the fireplace, a location of power. His face was boiled red as a lobster. "What are you doing about getting our kids out of there?"

One part of Ethan's mind wondered if the raw, cold wind had reddened Ernie's face, or the hypertension he'd been fighting for years. From the tone of the councilman's voice, he decided it came from pure anger. "We're working on it."

"We need to know what you're gonna do to get our children out." Concepción seldom spoke more than two or three soft words at a time. Thirteen words strung together was a speech for him.

Ethan crossed his arms and held his ground. He angled his head to address Concepción, the most restrained of the group. His words were calm. "Guys, right now we're getting the layout of the building down to try and figure out where they have your kids. Once that's done, we'll see what it'll take to get in if we can't talk to the people who have the courthouse."

"You don't need a floor plan." Ernie swept the room with an arm. "We've all been inside."

"Do you know where all the offices are, or the conference rooms?"

"Well, no, but most of them."

"That's not enough. We need to know where every closet is."

"Why don't you call 'em and ask 'em to let our kids go?"

The last man to speak was Clay Burke. Maintaining his composure, Ethan met his moist eyes and knew Clay's impaired son, Matt, was heavy on the man's mind.

"Don't you think we've already thought of that, Clay? They haven't answered any of the phones in there."

Rafael Hernandez jerked his chin toward the courthouse. "Send somebody over."

Ethan understood their frustration and choked down a sharp response. "Boys, my guys and a civilian who were too close to the courthouse got shot down like dogs. Right now, y'all need to be patient and let us work this out."

Ernie O'Neal took half a step forward. "We're going to help you."

"I appreciate the offer, but right now I don't need a posse." That archaic word had surfaced twice in the last hour.

"You need help. Look around, Ethan. You're outgunned both in here and out there, from what I've heard. They have our *kids*. If you don't do something pretty soon, we're going to have enough men to do the job ourselves."

"You'll do nothing of the kind!" Armstrong's voice was flat. "You'll get yourselves and everybody else killed. You might have *one* child in there, but right now they're *all* mine and *I'm* the one responsible." He pointed his finger at one after another to make it personal. "Not you, not you, not you, and not you! This takes planning."

Hearing the authority in his voice, the line of men went wobbly. Indecisive. For the first time, Ethan took note of the crowd around them. Women filled in the voids among the taller males. The smell of fear and wet clothing was rank.

They're scared, and scared people can be dangerous.

Ethan was surprised to feel sweat droplets the size of BBs roll down his cheeks.

All tensed and bunched up in the lobby, the faces of friends, neighbors, and family members reflected the strain of the day. These were people Ethan grew up with, who knew one another, had been married-in relatives, then cut adrift to become parts of other families who sometimes argued, fought, and talked bad about one another. But in light of what was happening down the block, they moved and reacted as one to protect their own. He expected nothing different.

"We have one thing in our favor. Sonny Hawke's inside and giving us the information we need, but it's coming out in bits and pieces."

Ernie ran his fingers up and down the rifle strap over his shoulder. "How're they letting one hostage talk to you and not the others?"

"He's not a hostage. The last time I talked to him, he was in the attic."

"He's hiding in an attic while somebody points a gun at my kid?" Ernie feigned surprise to incite those around him. "We got a lawman, a Texas *Ranger* hiding out instead of doing something?"

Ethan's face flushed. "Those are your words, not mine. Sonny will do what he has to, when he can." His eyes narrowed. "How about I call him over when he gets out? Then you can call him a coward to his face."

Ernie seemed relieved when a dark-haired, athletic woman pushed to the front. Ethan remembered seeing her in BDUs several times on the street after she returned from a tour of duty overseas. This time she was dressed in jeans and a heavy coat.

"Is there any way we can sneak anyone in there with him?" Her accent was soft, the kind most men like to hear from a woman of Spanish descent. Her sun-darkened skin was the color of oiled mahogany.

"No. We believe they have people watching every side of the building." He studied her. "You've been overseas."

"Yes."

"I can't recall your name."

"Yolanda Rodriguez. I'd like to help."

Ethan waved toward the command center. "Go on back there if you want. We might can use you."

She plucked at the sleeve of a tough-looking man Ethan didn't recognize. "Perry's someone you want, too."

The stocky man who hadn't shaved in several days oozed confidence. Like Yolanda, he moved with a military bearing. Both wore sidearms and carried AR carbines.

Ethan flicked a hand. "Go on back." He stopped sharp at still another idiotic comment.

"I say we go in and make a citizen's arrest."

Ethan raised his head to identify the voice. It came from another move-in who he recognized but didn't know. "Citizen's *arrest*?"

The man found somewhere else to look, but it was too little, too late.

"Citizen's arrest?"

He felt a hand on his shoulder and shrugged it off. Herman moved up and addressed the speaker. "Buddy, if I were you, I'd get myself shed of this place and let these men do their jobs. Ernie, you better go with him before you open your head again."

The men faded to the rear as Clay Burke leaned in, his voice full of emotion. "Ethan, Matt's in there. You know how he needs his routine. I can't imagine what he's going through right now . . . hell, I don't even know how he'd react to shootin' and strangers with guns. I'm afraid he's gonna do something to make those people mad, and they'll hurt 'im." His voice broke. "I couldn't live with myself if someone hurt my sweet son while he was in there, calling for me while I stand here and do nothin'."

Ethan's chest ached. "I know that, Clay. We're all scared. Me too. Y'all, my daughter's in there, and

Gabe's girl, and Phil's boy, and Sonny's twins and his wife." His voice was hoarse and forced from his chest.

"And my wife." Carlita's husband spoke up, his expression a combination of dread and immense sadness.

"That's right." Ethan gathered himself. "There's lots more. I have to do this slow and make decisions that might cost lives. I don't know if there's a right or wrong answer. There's never been anything like this in the whole United States. Ever."

He jerked a thumb over his shoulder. "If that phone rings and we get a conversation started with those people, I may say the wrong thing, so don't think I don't understand."

He didn't want to tell them that the terrorists probably planned to kill the hostages if their demands weren't met, if those came at all. For all he knew, this was a murder raid that had already proven successful.

He swallowed. *Good lord. That's a phrase that should have died out at the end of the Indian wars.*

"Y'all give me a little while longer to work on this. We're putting something together right now, but it isn't concrete."

The phone in his pocket vibrated with a text from Sonny.

Chapter 46

Texting is a young person's way of communicating, but I did the best I could do. Keeping an eye on the door, I finished and pushed send. The skinny blue bar at the top of the screen grew longer.

Perplexed held in missing Norge
3 Ed fleur courts loo

The instant before the message went I saw the misspellings and the damn autocorrection. I typed again.

Hot Dogs.

Dammit!

Hostages

I tried again and hit send.

on 3

Send.

Dammit!

The battery icon in the upper-right corner showed it had dropped below twenty percent. I hoped Ethan would figure the rest out, but there was no time to retype the whole thing. What I wanted was to call and talk to him in detail about what I'd found. I wasn't sure, but I remembered one of the kids saying that texting took less juice.

How the hell can it keep going down? I haven't made any calls.

I reached for the doorknob as the phone on the conference table blared with that annoying business ring that's supposed to be less jangling. I was coiled as tight as a mainspring, and unwound the same way. I bet my feet lifted three inches off the floor. I yanked the cord from the wall, cutting off the next ring in the middle of the tone.

Two steps back. I cocked my hat and put my ear against the door. Hearing nothing, I reached for the knob the exact second it twisted from the other side. The sight scared the pee-waddlin' out of me. I stepped inside the swing with my back to the wall. Lady Luck was still with me because there was two feet of space behind the door with nothing back there but a hat tree wearing a dusty gimme cap.

Whoever was on the other side didn't enter the room like I would in the same situation. Any lawman is trained to first check between the jamb and door to see if anyone is hiding back there. Instead he pushed it open and followed his nasty little MP5 inside. I backed up until the door hit the wall, leaving me standing in that small triangle of space.

The guy pulled up sharp at the sight of the ripped-out phone cord.

I stepped out at the same time the ceiling collapsed. Something big and heavy landed on the conference table with a wallop in a cloud of dust and wood. The startled guy snapped an MP5 to his shoulder and froze, processing the sight of a fellow terrorist groaning and covered with plaster, dirt, and insulation.

He recognized his buddy and laughed loud and sharp while the swan diver groaned and thumped his heel against the table, struggling to suck air back into his lungs.

"*Que idiota!* You fell through the *techo*!"

I never did like a smartass.

I took two steps, reached around under his chin with my right hand, and jerked his head up and to the right as hard as I could. At the same time I dropped my weight yanking downward. I wasn't sure twisting his neck up and back down would do what I wanted, but it worked better than I imagined.

His neck broke with a crack. Arms stiffened at his sides, the Mexican seized up and dropped like a pole-axed steer.

The room was full of dust as more insulation trickled thought the opening. The dead guy's friend on the table rolled onto his side to get up. I untangled from the first body and lunged forward, grabbing the Fall Guy from behind.

He recovered faster than I expected and caught me by surprise when he shoved backward with both feet. We flew back from the table and slammed into the wall. I needed to get him off balance, and fast, but all the crap on the floor from the ceiling kept tripping me up.

He grunted and did his best to twist in my arms. We spun halfway around, but I wrapped my right arm around his thick bull neck and squeezed as hard as I could with the sleep hold banned by police departments all across the country.

I didn't think anyone would care at this point, other than the guy who still had the gas to get both feet against the heavy table and push backward a second time.

We hit the floor beside the corpse with the Fall Guy on top. Had he not still been out of breath and hurt, I couldn't have taken him. The guy was made of spring steel and saddle leather and he damn-near got away from me. If he had, it would have all been over but the cryin'.

I wrapped both legs around his and used my wrist against his throat to compress his carotid artery. Grunting, he elbowed me in the ribs. I couldn't believe how tough he was after dropping ten feet and knocking the breath out of his lungs. His hands flailed at my arms and fluttered about, trying to find something, anything to use against me.

Gagging and coughing, I squeezed harder like a boa constrictor, tightening my bizarre embrace every time I got the chance. It seemed like an hour before he weakened, and when he did, I increased the pressure on his carotids to finish him off.

His legs twitched, feet drumming on the floor. I felt him quiver as he died, and it was one of the most personal things that had ever happened to me. My body went numb, and I gasped in horror at what I was doing, but I didn't let go.

I couldn't.

He trembled again and his arms fell limp. I kept up the pressure as long as I dared, all the while expecting someone to blow into the room with guns firing.

Exhausted, I turned loose and lay there limp as a dishrag, thankful there hadn't been more fight in the guy. He was a stud hoss. Throwing an arm across my nose and mouth, I laid on the floor coughing and gagging. When I could open my eyes, I saw Arturo staring down through the hole in the ceiling.

I closed my eyes again, and rested for another second.

Chapter 47

DeVaca's frustration grew in direct proportion to the information *not* coming into his ear. The faint voice of the Demon whispered louder, urging him to lose control and do what he did best to satisfy his hunger.

Ignoring what his grandmother called *El pequeño monstruo Lorenzo*, the little Lorenzo monster, he leaned over the hole to see Tin Man staring upward. "You're telling me you can't find that tunnel out of there?"

Tin Man shook his head. "*No, señor.*"

"How can it be that hard? The damned basement can't be any bigger than this building's footprint."

"This place is packed solid with *mierda* stacked against the walls, including *perdirdas cilindros llenos de muerte*. We have to move them *very carefully*, then inspect the areas behind them. We're tiptoeing on *cascaras de huevos* down here."

The corner of DeVaca's mouth twitched at *lost cylinders of death*. He liked the sound of the phrase.

Despite his frustration, DeVaca understood how the basement had been kept secret and almost forgotten.

His research showed the plumbing was installed in the 1920s. The extensive renovation in the 1950s was most likely part of the government's need to store chemical weapons with as little knowledge and fanfare as possible, funded out of a black budget.

"Sir."

DeVaca tore his mind from the problems in the basement to find Dorothy beside him, still wearing the hijab. Her blue eyes, though, were expressive.

The Demon made DeVaca wonder how those soft orbs would taste if he had the opportunity to roll them around in his mouth like peeled grapes. He thought they'd taste of blueberries. The Demon squirmed in hunger.

"Go ahead."

She blinked, long lashes catching the harsh lights. "There's a problem. We have no connection with Scarecrow or Lion."

"For how long?"

"When we still hadn't heard from Scarecrow on your last check, I sent Lion to check on him. He isn't back yet."

"Well that means they're probably together or with the hostages." He scanned the rotunda overhead, then double-checked the four doors at the end of the short intersecting hallways on the ground floor. They were secure. "Go find them. Start with the communications and electrical panels."

She narrowed her eyes, and he remained fascinated by them. "They'll be organizing a response soon. We need to be ready."

"They're waiting for *us*. Oz will radio back in"—he checked his watch—"fifteen minutes. That's when he will draw them into negotiations, and that will buy us more time."

She shot a cuff, checked her own watch, and wrote the time on her slim forearm with a ballpoint pen. "What do we do about the hostages when they send people in?" Dorothy jerked her head upward. "We'll need everyone to repel, and it's snowing so hard outside they'll be on us before we see them."

"All right. Pull everyone down to this floor except those guarding the hostages. Leave one post on the second floor, just in case."

"Done." She hefted her weapon. "Anything else?"

He'd been chewing the inside of his lip until it bled, anything to keep his hands off the woman who was drawing him like a magnet. DeVaca savored the metallic flavor. "If an assault materializes and they get in before we're ready, I want *you* to kill the hostages if our men up there are incapable of doing it. That will free them up to pull back here." He pointed toward the southern door. "If we're breached and can't get out through that tunnel"—he leaned over and spoke into the hole—"and they better *find* the sonofabitch!"—he lowered his voice again—"then we'll deploy gas in here and use the van, if we can get through the snow with it."

"It won't hold everyone."

"It won't need to." He tapped the dusty cylinder with his shoe. "Alternate plan. That's why the gas masks and bio suits are in the van."

She smiled with her eyes, and he tasted blueberries.

Chapter 48

It took me a while to recover from the fight. Struggling to my knees, I hoped no one else was coming, because I was worn out. I decided to just shoot the next guy because it'd take a whole lot less effort.

I squinted up at Arturo straddling two rough-hewn joists. I held up a hand, telling him to be quiet and wait. "Are you all right?" My voice was soft, just loud enough for the youngster to hear.

Instead of answering, Arturo gave a thumbs-up.

"Good. Stay out of sight." I swung the MP5 back into position and checked the weapon to be sure it was ready. I glanced back up, but Arturo was already gone.

Even though I had a good idea no one was in the Grand Jury room, I was careful just the same. Hand on the grip and finger in line along the trigger guard, I opened the door and slipped inside, my sight line following the muzzle. The dark, cavernous room was almost empty, with nothing but a backpack on a table that belonged to the guy with the broken neck.

Chapter 49

The text from Sonny was all boogered up.

Ethan held the cell out. "What does this mean?"

Despite the situation, Deputy Frank Malone grinned. "It's autocorrect. He's telling us where the hostages are, but it keeps changing the words on him. He says some of them are in the third-floor courtroom." He used a marker to place an X on the floor plan. "Sonny says they're right here."

The command center filled with people's questions and comments. Silent and watchful, Yolanda Rodriguez and Perry Hale leaned in to see where he was pointing.

"That's the Grand Jury room." Herman fiddled with his mustache, thinking. "The third floor is a long way up."

Sheriff Armstrong chewed his lip. "Yeah, and the only way to get up there is the stairs or elevator."

Charles Irwin jerked a thumb upward. "Can we get a helicopter over the roof?"

Others chimed in with so many questions that they ran together.

"I say we send somebody out to negotiate."

"Who's in there with them?"

"All y'all shut up and listen." Ethan's voice wasn't loud, but it held the power to make them stop talking. "Let me think a little while."

Chapter 50

Keeping an eye on the double doors leading into the hallway, I scanned the Grand Jury room, making sure no one was hiding behind the judge's bench. That's where I'd be if I was laying for someone who'd just killed two of my friends. Then again, it wouldn't offer much cover if anyone opened up with a rifle. Keeping the telescoping H&K's butt snug against the hollow of my shoulder, I sidestepped away from the conference room.

Despite two walls of twenty-foot windows reaching to the ceiling, the snow-filtered light was dim, making the room dark and gloomy. I kept an eye on the rows of wooden seats bolted to the floor, half expecting someone to rise up from the gallery and start shooting.

I'd trained with SWAT teams in the past, but had never cleared a room alone. With a team, each man has a specific assignment, and that's where they concentrate, knowing the other guys are doing their jobs. Alone, I was like an owl, twisting my head in circles.

A plastic folding table leaned against the crotch-high bar, made of lathe-turned spindles between the attorneys' tables and the gallery seats. The guy who designed the building must have liked spindles as much as he liked trapdoors, because they were everywhere.

Knees bent, heart thumping, and chest tight, I was ready to turn the folded table into a cheese grater if that's what it took. No one was waiting to ambush me when I reached the see-through barrier. I stepped over the bar, keeping the weapon trained on the judge's bench. The damn thing reminded me of a jack-in-the-box. If some clown jumped up, I was gonna slap him right back down. I dodged an empty table to find the elevated platform and nothing but a worn chair.

A large barrister bookcase blocked what I figured was the door to the Judge's chamber on the other side. It had been there for a long time, as evidenced by dust collected around the base. No one was coming through there any time soon. That left the double doors leading to the hall as the only way in or out.

I sat in the chair for a second to calm my nerves. My heart was beating ninety to nothing, and in Texas lingo, that's pretty damn fast.

Well, hell.

I'd sent a text telling Ethan where the hostages were, and now here I was, in that same courtroom that was as empty as my head. The battery was down to fifteen percent when I slipped the phone from my pocket. I thumbed another text and hit send.

Wrong room. More to follow.

The little indicator started to show something was happening, but it stalled. I waited, staring at the screen like a kid watching cartoons.

I couldn't hang around all day rewriting texts and waiting for the technology to cooperate. I didn't have the time, knowledge, or inclination to root around in the phone's mysterious nether regions to find out how to turn off that stinkin' autocorrect, either. I made a mental note to have the kids show me a few things after this was all over.

A red balloon popped up on the screen saying the text failed.

Great.

I put the phone back in my pocket. The double-stacked windows vibrated with a sudden blast of north wind and leaked icy air. A soft squeak from the conference room drove my blood pressure right back up.

I slid out of the chair behind the bench. *I'd* become the clown in the jack-in-the-box. I knelt on one knee, waiting to see which one of my "dead" terrorists refused to stay down.

The door opened with glacial speed. I cursed myself for not anchoring those two by cutting their throats. I tucked my cheek into the stock.

Instead of a zombie in a ski mask peeking around the edge of the doorframe, Arturo came in wearing my hat. He slipped inside, walking toward the double doors leading into the hallway.

I lowered the weapon. "I wouldn't do that."

He jumped and saw me rise beside the bench. He offered a sheepish smile, matching the volume of my voice. "There was a lariat rope in that pile of dried-up harness. Besides, that dead guy on the cot *farted*, man. I couldn't stay up there with *that*."

"I'm gonna strangle you, kid."

Chapter 51

"I need to check on my kids, Ethan."

The soft voice full of concern cut through the steady buzz around him. The crush of people inside the CP quieted. Frustrated, Sheriff Armstrong tightened his jaw and snapped his head upward. "Everybody's concerned about their kids."

He recognized the lined face of school superintendent Damon Cartwright. Beside Damon was Victor Hernandez, the principal of Big Bend High.

Both men were covered in snow, and Ethan expected they'd walked to the Posada from the high school, where the administration offices were housed. Armstrong's gaze slipped past them toward the crowded lobby.

His face softened. "I've been expecting y'all. Come on in, guys. I wish I could tell you something, Damon, but all we know is they're inside with Kelly Hawke."

The building principal loosened his tie. "No demands? No offer to trade hostages?"

"Nothing like that yet, Victor." Armstrong didn't want to discuss the earlier phone call. "I know you're getting beat up by those parents out there who want answers, but I can't help you right now."

Victor Hernandez unbuttoned his overcoat. "I'll go in for the kids. Tell them they can have me in exchange."

Damon raised his hand as if asking permission to speak. "It'd be better if it was me."

"It don't make any difference at this point, guys. I'm not kidding. The terrorists aren't answering the phone. They'll talk when they're ready, and that's been once."

"I thought you said you hadn't heard from them."

Sheriff Armstrong stared at the floor plan without seeing it. "It wasn't much of a call."

"You're sure they're terrorists? Maybe it's just one or two crazy people."

"It's more than a lone-wolf takeover. Those people in there are trained and organized. Guys, hang close, but give me some room. What I need from y'all is to keep those parents out there as calm as you can while we work. They're my biggest distraction right now, and I'm half-afraid one of 'em'll do something stupid."

"That wouldn't surprise me none," Hernandez said.

A shrill voice cut across the lobby. A gaggle of snow-covered women came through the plaza door and rushed toward the command center. The same men who'd been in earlier fell in behind.

A blonde with East Texas teeth led the way. She slammed the French doors open, pushing Herman out of the way. "They're going to tell me something *right now*! Sheriff Armstrong! We want our children out of there this minute! What are you doing waiting in here and talking—"

Ethan saw red. "That is *enough!* Y'all stop right

there and listen! We're doing all we can with what we have to work with, but I can't do a *goddamned* thing about it when I'm standing here listening to you yell!" He jabbed a thumb at the superintendent and principal. "You talk to *them*, but do it out there or so help me God I'm fixin' to cuff the next loudmouth and stuff 'em in a bathroom."

The woman's charge was broken, but she wouldn't quit. "We want something done."

"So do *I*!"

Ethan saw half a dozen people holding their phones aloft, filming the chaotic scene. He ignored the angry woman, who wilted and spread her hands. "I'm just scared."

"So is everyone else. Now get out of my sight."

Superintendent Cartwright took the woman's arm. "Mrs. Stevens, y'all come outside with us."

Hernandez spread his arms wide and waved the others back toward the lobby. "Please, let's see what we can do, *together*."

On his last nerve, Ethan took Deputy Malone's arm and leaned in. "The whole world's a news crew now. They're recording everything going on in here. It won't be long before they have this whole cluster posted on the Internet. We can't take their phones away, but don't let 'em in close where they can hear us."

A black-haired woman of medium build caught his eye. Kathryn Boswell was the editor of *The Ballard News*. She listened to a man bending her ear and took notes on a stenographer's pad.

"Frank, tell Kathryn we'll let her in here to get the whole story as long as she stays quiet, don't get in our way, and holds up on tweets and web reports until we get to the end of this. If she does that, we'll give her exclusive information."

"Is that a good idea?"

"Hell-if-I-know, but if we give her the truth, she might override whatever nonsense those people are peddling."

Ethan noted the heavy sag in the pockets of Herman's and Gabe's ranch coat pockets that suggested they were carrying extra ammo. "Herman, close those doors, but stay in here. I'm damned tired of people running in and out. Gabe can stay, too. Come over here."

Sheriff Armstrong returned to his map. "If it's so bad out there on the roads, how are all these people getting here?"

Herman followed. "Walking, for the most part, those who live close enough. I heard some drove as far as they could, then got out and hoofed it the rest of the way."

The retired Ranger studied the hand-drawn plan. "Ever'body's scared, Ethan. The roads are a mess. Your boys pulled a bunch of cars across the streets to block the courthouse, and when folks came up against 'em, they just got out and walked. It's gridlocked all around us now."

Gabe spoke for the first time. "I hear the highways are the same, with people in ditches everywhere. The *padres* . . . parents with kids are either here or over at the school, but there's more drifting in ever' time I look up."

Ethan smoothed his mustache. "Well, by God, we'll have bodies froze all over this county if they don't quit it."

Deputy Malone came back into the command center, followed by the newspaper editor. She took up a position as far away as possible and placed an electronic recorder on the table.

Ethan ignored her, squinting at the static-filled picture on television. The crawl bar on the bottom of the screen showed the temperature was deep into the twenties and looked to stay there for the next few days. "Frank, do we have people out there freezing to death while they watch the courthouse?"

"Nope, just had a change to pull them out for coffee and a warm-up."

"Who'd you send to replace 'em?"

"Some of the vets." Malone held up a hand. "It won't be but for a few minutes, and I didn't do a complete shift change. They're out there in two-man teams, each with an officer. We'll switch 'em as soon as the boys defrost a little."

Ethan tilted his hat back. "Herman, this could fall apart any second now."

"I know." Sonny's dad mimicked Ethan and smoothed his own mustache. "They have people at all the entrances?"

"Yep." Ethan pointed at the rough map. "We're sure there're people here and here, at the north and south doors. We've taken fire from both, including me." He stabbed a finger at the east entrance. "We've seen men here through the storm. I don't have eyewitness reports, but I 'magine the west entrance is covered, too. There's no way in."

The exchange helped them sort their thoughts while at the same time giving the editor the information she needed. Despite the recorder, she scribbled in her notepad.

"You're not thinking of trying to go in right now?"

Ethan massaged his aching neck. "I don't plan to. This isn't an active shooting scenario, so we have some breathing room. No one can get here. Homeland Security, the FBI, and your Rangers are all telling me to dig in and wait, so that's what I'm doing. But if something happens to change this stalemate, I want to be ready. They're all gonna ask for what we're pulling together here anyway."

Herman tapped his fingers on the table in thought. "I believe you're right. I don't think we need to do anything right this minute. They're hunkered down for a while." He picked up a yellow pencil and drew a series of lines and dashes on the paper. "But if you *do* have to go in. Here's what *I* think." He was outlining his thoughts when the lights flickered and winked out.

Beeps came from a variety of electronics deprived of power, and everyone stopped talking.

The moaning wind filled the void until the high, thin voice of Andy Clark, the owner of the Posada, carried over the lobby with crystal clarity. "The generator should kick on in a second . . . and ever'thing."

It stayed dark, and the wind shrieked.

Gabe summed up what everyone was thinking. "Well, butt . . . ass."

Chapter 52

Tugging Arturo against the wall, I put a finger to my lips. "Shhh."

"What are we doing in *here*?"

Keeping my voice low, I spoke into his ear. "We're being quiet, for one thing." The boy was shivering again. "I told you to wait."

"You held your palm up to me."

"Yeah, that meant *wait*."

"Oh. I get it now. You want your hat back?"

"Naw, hang on to it for a while. Tell me what happened up there."

The kid told me what led to the terrorist's fall through the ceiling. He pointed upward. "I seen a loop of rope up there beside that harness, so I doubled it up and put some knots in it like we have in gym class. I tied it to a rafter, and came down. That's a lot easier than going up."

"That's using your noggin." I felt a grudging admiration for the little knothead. "How'd you hold on? That would have cut my hands to pieces."

He reached into the pockets of my coat and held out the leather work gloves. "You left these."

"I could have used those outside a little while ago."

"You were *outside*?"

"It's a long story we don't have time for right now. Can you climb back up?"

"I don't think so, and besides, I'm afraid to stay up there. That guy got in as easy as pie."

"There ain't nowhere that's safe. Get back in the conference room and hide."

"Uh uh. Not with these *dead* guys."

"I can drag them out." The kid looked like he might puke. "All right. Come with me. Maybe you can slip back up to the lantern room and stay there while I go downstairs."

"I'm afraid to be alone."

"You can't stay with me."

"You done said there was no place safe."

"All right. Curl up like a dog under the Judge's bench. I don't care. *I* still have to move, and I can't do it with you hanging onto my back pockets."

Arturo set his jaw. "You got two of them with my help, and the other guy, too, if you'll admit it."

The kid was exasperating. "It wasn't *planned*. None of this is planned. All I'm doing is reacting, and my luck's gonna run out sooner or later. Right now, I have to get down to the next floor where I think they're keeping your class . . ."

And my kids.

". . . and you can't tag along. Now that's *it*!"

"Fine. I'll stay here." He pulled up. "Can I have a gun?" He flicked his eyes toward the conference room. "We have plenty now."

"Hell no. You'll shoot yourself, or me."

"You can't carry 'em *all*."

"I'll take and carry what I need, now, get over there in that hidey-hole like I told you."

"Fine."

"Fine."

Here I was in a fight for our lives and playing mind games with a high schooler moving at teenage speed just to get my goat. My stomach tightened once again at the thought of going through those doors to find Kelly and the kids.

That's when the power failed.

I wouldn't have known it, because the overhead lights weren't on. The HVAC's sudden silence made me realize what had happened. It's strange how we get used to noise. The blowers had been a constant, unnoticed backdrop.

Three pops sounded like gunfire.

The hair rose on my neck, and I started to charge into the rotunda.

Arturo surprised the hell out of me when he dropped to the floor.

"What are you doing?"

He shushed me with a finger to his lips. He sat up. "They're right below us."

"The kids? You can *hear* 'em?"

"Yeah, they screamed and some guy's bitching at 'em now."

His hearing was a helluva lot better'n mine. I remembered Kelly telling me that some of the kids used a ringtone called the Mosquito that was so high only *young* people can register the tone. They used it in class without her knowing it until somebody spilled the beans and she shut 'em down.

Icy wind moaned under the eaves.

"All right. You still need to get over there and hide."

An engine rattled to life somewhere in the building. A dim glow filled the gap below the courtroom's double doors. "Fine then. I can't hear anything else over that *máquina* anyway." He rose and slouched behind the judge's bench. Like a scolded dog sent outside, he found something else to do before he stopped. "Hey, it's even darker outside than before. I think the power's out all over town."

I hurried to one of the tall windows. He was right, from what I could tell through the thick snow. The houses across the street were dark as well, and when I glanced up, the glow from the turret lights was gone.

"I don't know if that's good or bad." I waved a hand. "Now, stay there." I gave the knob a gentle turn and peeked through the crack.

A man with a Spanish accent barked orders over the steady clatter of a generator. I was glad they bought cheap, instead of a quieter Honda. I eased out and blended into the shadows.

Our floor was empty. I stepped light on the wooden boards, staying well away from the circular banister and skulking along the edge of the wall past the glowing rotunda. The generators running the lights down there made me think of a construction site.

They were already accustomed to the bright lights, and anyone looking up would be unable to see me in the shadows above. I had a vague plan to work my way along the northeast quadrant of the long, rectangular building, clearing each floor.

I was as nervous as a cat in a doghouse. The first door was unlocked. Twisting the brass knob, I pushed it open just enough to squeeze through, and entered a dim office that had long been empty. Gun to my shoulder, I passed the muzzle over every corner and possible hiding place as I swept the room.

No frightened secretaries jumped up asking to be saved, but no terrorists popped up, either. I took a few deep breaths and stepped back into the open, sliding along the wall like a rat. The janitor's closet was empty, the door shattered inward.

Tension was one big knot in my neck. I clamped my jaw and cleared the empty tower office on the corner. Back in the open hall, I paused to listen. Something new was happening.

It sounded like a team of furniture movers down below. For some reason, they were dragging desks and file cabinets from the offices. I peeked through the spindles and figured out they were stacking the heavy furniture in the short east/west halls to block the entrances. By the time they were through, it would take a tank to force the doors.

Ethan needed that information. I backed into the corner office and dug out my phone. The icon on top said the battery was down to 13 percent. I thumbed in a quick text.

East west entrances blocked

Once again it looked as if it failed to send. I stuck the phone back in my pocket and gave up. Back in the open, I passed two tall windows, gray from the storm. The temperature inside was falling, and I wondered if my shivering was from the cold or nerves.

It didn't matter, I still had the other side to clear.

Chapter 53

Never indecisive, Congressman Don Bright raised the volume on the television. Willa Mae Dalyrumple waited beside the door, ignoring the phone ringing at her desk. "Don . . ."

"Listen." He held both arms out. The gesture was odd, because Don had never hugged her. She stepped forward and they embraced.

He whispered in her ear. "Stay close, like you're comforting me."

She got it. The office might be bugged. There might have been listening devices or a camera in the room, but the contact was as comforting as a warm blanket. Willa Mae pulled him close and rubbed his back as if he were a child.

He whispered. "There was something on the History Channel a few months ago, and I have an idea."

"What?"

"Shhh. Leave the building. Give me your phone and then beg, borrow, steal, or buy another one in the next ten minutes and call my friend Jess McDowell. You have him in your Rolodex." She knew him as one of

Bright's oldest friends. "His son is an FBI agent here in D.C. His name's Landon. Tell him to come by in an hour and announce he has an appointment. Make it appear normal, and that we forgot."

She patted his back.

"This is the weird part, but don't argue or talk. Bring back a bottle of ketchup. Don't let him in until it's time."

Willa Mae stiffened. "How will we know?"

"Don't worry. I'll be waiting in the bathroom. Get Daniella's phone and bring it with you, but don't tell her why."

Daniella Gibson was their young intern, a social butterfly who lived with a cell phone in her hand despite Don's warnings to put it down or find someplace else to work. Now he was glad that she was as stubborn as Katie.

His stomach clenched for the thousandth time at the thought of his baby in the hands of terrorists.

"Now go." The congressman grasped her arms and tried to disengage.

She refused to turn him loose. "Don't do anything. Let the professionals handle this."

"I can't. These people know I can't tell the authorities."

She pushed back and looked him in the eye. "Oh, Don. No."

"I'm sorry. I allowed some people to trap me into doing some things I shouldn't have done. At first it was gifts that led to favors, which wound up putting me in chains."

"But—"

"But nothing. I screwed up, and I have to pay. We don't have time for this. Go."

She pulled away and left.

The congressman opened his personal laptop and keyed in his offshore account code, then tapped a long series of numbers, letters, and symbols to send the six million dollars to the terrorist. To save his daughter, he'd have sent the entire amount of dirty money Desi Arnaz asked for.

When the notification popped up saying the transfer was successful, he opened the upper right-hand drawer and took out the .38 revolver that was illegal in Washington D.C. He checked the loads and thought about what he'd have to do next.

Chapter 54

Three quick pops following the power failure irritated DeVaca. He pressed the transmit button on his chest. "Kahn!"

"Yes."

"I heard gunfire. Check the hostages."

"Yes."

He'd been expecting the power to go off, either by design from the locals or from the storm. Either way, it didn't matter. Flashlights flicked on at the same time the security lights snapped to life high up on the walls. They flickered, dimmed, and died.

One of his men yanked the cord on a generator. Half a dozen portable halogen work lights came alive, flooding the room and making it seem like nighttime beyond the courthouse doors.

Someone passed the open elevator seconds after the building went dark. Katie Bright heard the rustle and rattle of gear in the tiny enclosure. She'd managed to get one foot free of the zip tie binding her leg to the wooden chair and planted her feet.

A flashlight snapped on as one of the terrorists stepped close to check her bindings. Katie launched her head at where she hoped the man's chin was in an effort to head-butt the terrorist. The move had worked hundreds of times on television.

She missed, held back by the weight of the chair, and her head grazed the terrorist's cheek. Katie heard the intake of breath as she used her free leg as leverage, throwing herself to the side and knocking her enemy to the ground.

She twisted her face into the terrorist's neck, doing her best to find flesh with her teeth. She wanted a nose, an ear, an artery! Growling like an animal, the slender girl burrowed into the scarf covering his neck.

The flashlight went skittering across the floor, and Katie squirmed even harder, hoping another of the bindings would come loose. Hands grabbed her long hair and pushed her away. She bit and snapped like a mad dog until a blinding light sparked in her head. Another blow felt like her skull was cracked.

The next landed with even more power as the terrorist gained leverage.

The elevator's dim overhead security light flickered, revealing the furious face of the female terrorist.

That was the last Katie Bright saw as the woman attacked.

Kahn rapped the door and pushed inside to find short and skinny Muhammad Qambrani guarding the hostages and Usman Muhammed Al-Zahwi holding Wilfred Bates's severed head by the hair.

He stopped, startled at the bloody sight and the county agent's body. "Why did you kill this man?"

Al-Zahwi answered in their native language. "He fought us."

Quambrani pointed a shaking finger at the adults cowering in the corner. "It is true. He attacked and I shot him."

Kahn didn't bother to turn. Instead, he met Al-Zahwi's dead stare. "Why was he beheaded?"

"To serve as a message to these infidels."

Kahn answered, "Good. Behead *two* of them the next time, because they won't see the sunset anyway, but drag this pig into a closet. DeVaca might not like it."

He spun on one heel and left.

DeVaca waited at the edge of the hole in the glare of the halogen lights. "We're running out of time."

Tin Man appeared below the opening and raised his voice over the hammering. "Found it. Give me a few minutes."

The leader allowed the corner of his mouth to tilt. "Make it quick."

Things were looking up. The storm's intensity and the loss of power worked in DeVaca's favor. Even though the trailer wasn't in position, they now had a good chance of escaping with the canisters. With that many potential weapons, they could open one to cover their retreat. It would be nothing to steal two or three cars or trucks and disperse.

Amped up now that they had a way out, DeVaca needed to burn off some energy. He left the central rotunda floor to check on the men posted at the north entrance. Cold air met him at the door they'd propped open with a box full of printer paper.

"I'm coming out." He spoke loudly so the American team would know he was behind them. Outside for the first time since they took the courthouse, he was taken aback by the severity of the storm. Driven by the wind, snow obscured the buildings across the street. It piled up in deepening drifts against every stationary object in sight. Nothing moved in his frosted field of vision.

"Report."

Huddled behind unopened cases of paper, Billy Koval turned his attention from the snowfield. The bulky winter clothes over his battle gear made him round as a bear. "All's quiet. After we shot everyone in the sheriff's office, we've seen no one. They're afraid to come close."

Milton Jordan shifted into a more comfortable position. "We've seen a few shadows of people in the distance. I thought some of 'em were gonna come into range, but they've stayed away. I wish we had more targets."

"You'll have plenty before this is over."

"How long before we load up in the trailer and get out of here?"

"Less than an hour."

"Good. This weather is killing me."

DeVaca's eyes flashed. "I'll send replacements out soon. I don't want you to get so cold you slow your responses."

"Yessir." Koval turned his attention back to the wintry landscape. "We'll be in directly."

DeVaca scanned the area. Seeing no movement, he went back inside and crossed the length of the long, rectangular building. "Kahn, report."

"All quiet."

He stopped in front of the open elevator guarded by Dorothy. She ignored him, concentrating on the activity in the rotunda.

Puzzled at her actions, DeVaca turned his attention to their prisoner sitting in the shadows. "Katie Bright."

"Yes." Her voice was thick and watery.

He flicked on a tactical light and played the beam across Katie's swollen and bruised face. Without expression, he studied the young woman's black, closed eye, puffy lip, and the twin streams of blood running from her nose.

"This is all your fault."

Katie's voice was incredulous. "What?"

"The fault of you and your father."

"I don't know what you're talking about." She spoke around swollen lips. "I haven't done anything."

She sounded like a child, and that pleased him. "Your father cares nothing of people in other countries. He doesn't care if they die of disease, guns, or starvation."

"That's not true."

"It *is* true. He wants to seal the borders to protect all you fat, lazy Americans from the real world. You're all soft, and that will soon work against you."

Tears ran down her bloody and swollen cheeks. "I don't know what you're talking about."

"You will! The atrocities you've brought to this world will soon be revealed. Blood will run in American streets. There won't be enough body bags to bury you all."

He was pleased with the effect the speech was having on his own spirit. The Demon was feeding on the woman's fear. The shell game he was playing with everyone from the teams to Chavez was as exciting as sex, and even more fulfilling.

The jihadists with him wanted a holy war, and thought it would start here.

The Mexican team dreamed of the long-awaited restoration of Texas to Mexico.

The American team, tired of governmental interference, didn't much like the Mexicans, either.

DeVaca no more believed in their causes than the man in the moon. To enhance the fear of terrorism from both inside and out of the nations' borders, he'd assembled homegrown teams to operate alongside the other feared entities. Each group despised the others, but agreed cooperation was necessary to further their cause. His heart swelled at the memory of convincing each team that the others were pawns to be sacrificed as the mission's goal was fulfilled.

"We are here because of what your country has done to others. The importance of this comes from the fear we will instill. Call it the 'what if' factor. What if they take another more important facility or building? What if they kill even more hostages?" The back of his neck tingled when he saw Katie's reaction. "What if they take over a school next or a mall? If they can do this, *they* can do that. What we've done here today will shake this country to its very foundation."

Katie leaned forward against her bonds, her fear replaced by anger. She snorted a clot of blood from one nostril. "Oh, please! You're an asshole if you think this little attack is going to do anything other than piss off an entire country."

He smiled. "No matter. You've done your part, and for that, you can die happy."

He ignored Katie's one-eyed glare and took Dorothy's arm, pulling her to the side and out of earshot from the others. "What happened to her face?"

"Like I said earlier. She attempted to escape and tried to bite me when I restrained her."

"So you beat her? Like this?" He was angry that Katie's face was so swollen. It took away from her innocence, and his desire for the young secretary withered.

Dorothy met his gaze. "I was angry."

DeVaca leaned in. From a distance it looked as if he were about to kiss her through the *hajib*. "That's the last time. If you strike her again, I'll bite your lips off and swallow them. I decide who is punished, and who dies. Is that clear?"

Dorothy held her ground. She put both hands on DeVaca's hips and pulled him closer. Tilting her face, she whispered. "You gave me a job. The beating showed her that any attempt to escape will not be tolerated. I had that man executed upstairs. You don't care if I made that decision alone, do you?"

A long-buried desire awoke, nudging the Demon away. "We might still need her if her father lags in any way. I want her conscious and able to function. Leave her alone."

Dorothy ground her hips into him before stepping back, smiling with her blue eyes. "As you say." She strolled back to the pit without looking back.

DeVaca thought of blueberries again as he walked with a light step to the California team's position behind the van. He needed to calm the Demon before it could fully awaken and take over. Frosty air nipped his ears as soon as he stepped outside the southern entrance. The terrorist standing at the rear of the van backed against the single step glanced over his shoulder. Much of the wind's force was blocked by the building's 4-by-4-foot entry enclave. There was barely a shoulder's width between the van's open back doors and the two brick walls on either side.

Despite the *shemagh* covering his face, DeVaca recognized him as the one who chainsawed the hole in the floor. "Anything, Mslam?"

He spoke over his shoulder. "No. Other than those out there under the snow, we've seen nothing."

"You'll have the opportunity to kill more soon."

"I look forward to it."

DeVaca took one last look into the storm and spun on his heel. "I bet you do."

Chapter 55

Sheriff Ethan Armstrong's phone dinged. He thumbed it open and read the message from Sonny.

East west entrances blocked.

"What the hell?" Those around him craned their necks to read the screen. "It's Sonny, He's telling us they've blocked the east and west doors."

Deputy Malone picked up a marker and drew two big Xs over those doors on their floor plan. "This' gonna be harder now that we're down to two points of access."

Ethan tilted his hat back. "There's no easy way in, not covered the way they are." He was torn between the gut-wrenching need to rescue his daughter and the professionalism and responsibility that required him to wait. "Well, it's still quiet inside, so we wait until something happens and hope the phone rings."

He wished he had some Maalox and that Sonny would call instead of trying to text.

Chapter 56

I was back at my starting point outside the Grand Jury room.

Standing there against the wall, I realized that if I'd waited for a while, I wouldn't have needed to climb out the window and make that dangerous crawl across the roof. I could have crept down the stairs when they all gathered in the rotunda. The whole stupid episode was the result of being impulsive, a problem I'd had all my life.

But now I needed to check the second floor, and that scared me worse than a rattler because I'd bet a dollar to a donut lots of those creeps were down there. The only way to reach that floor was the twin north/south staircases. Then I had an idea. I opened the door into the Grand Jury room and stepped back inside.

In the next instant, stars and little bluebirds circled my head.

I staggered to one knee and realized it was the kid who'd conked me. "*Goddlemighty*!"

"Oh, shit! Sorry, Mr. Hawke!"

Arturo's soft voice cut through the pain and anger. "Watch your language!" I yanked the wooden spindle from his hand. Instead of hiding, he'd worked one loose from the dividing bar. Pretty resourceful, but aggravating just the same.

I closed the door and put my hand to the back of my head to feel for blood. My fingers came back red and sticky. Figures. Dead terrorists were scattered like marbles both above and behind me, and one of the kids I was trying to save came close to knocking my head off. "Damn, boy!"

"I thought you were one of *them*. Did you find anyone?"

"Haven't you noticed *they* don't look like me?"

"I was scared."

"Not scared enough to run."

Despite what I'd said, he'd gone back into the conference room to arm himself with an MP5 slung over his shoulder and covered by my oversize coat. I didn't say anything, but it made me kinda proud that he'd taken some initiative. It halfway pissed me off, too.

"Stay here."

I rubbed the knot on my head and returned to the conference room. The bodies were still in the same place, and I waited for a surge of remorse or regret. Counting the man I shot weeks earlier on the highway, and the three dead terrorists, I was all out of repentance. I felt nothing for the men I'd killed and for those who would follow.

They brought a war to my town, and I wasn't going to stand for it.

Coughing again from the dust still hanging in the air, and gagging from the foul odor of voided bowels, I unwrapped a scarf from the one with the broken neck. I took his black knit cap and wrestled him out of his tactical vest. Breathing hard from the effort, I thought about putting them both on in there, but didn't want to walk back into the courtroom and provoke another attack from the kid. As an afterthought, I picked up the remaining machine pistol and left, trying not to cough.

Arturo was waiting beside the door. He saw the long scarf and vest in my hand. "What are you going to do with *that*?"

"Blend in, I hope. Do you know how to use that thing?"

He held up the firearm. "Yessir. I've used it in Assault."

I raised an eyebrow.

"A game, you know?"

Kids were becoming proficient with war through video games. "Well, I'm glad you didn't use *that* on me when I came in."

"I was trying to be quiet."

"Um hum." I unpinned my badge and slipped it into a pocket, shrugged into the vest and took inventory of the pouches. Magazines, at least six of them, a smoke canister, a flashbang, glow sticks wrapped with a bungee cord, LED flashlight, a package of peanut butter and crackers, long zip ties, a tourniquet and compression kit, and assorted personal items. The most surprising was a rosary.

I opened the backpack on the table and found it contained MREs, more ammo, and faded clothes. "All right. Keep your finger off the trigger and don't use it unless you have to."

I pulled the dark cap farther down over my aching

head and tied the blue scarf over my mouth and nose like an Old West outlaw. I didn't think I'd pass close inspection, but then again, I didn't plan on letting the sonsabitches get that close, either. "It might be me again, and I don't want to get killed by you. Got it?"

A dimple formed in his cheek. "Got it. You want your hat back now?"

"I don't believe it'd fit over this cap, and besides, my head's all swole where you hit me." I slapped the little guy on the shoulder to let him know I was kidding, sort of. I didn't want a pack on my back, so I distributed most of the magazines and gear in the tactical vest's pockets. "Close the door when I'm gone."

The rag was suffocating, and I wondered how people wore those things for hours at a time. It smelled of sweat, cigarette smoke, and other things unimagined. I tried not to think about the former owner's bad breath I was inhaling.

I wondered if he had tuberculosis, or some other horrific disease a happy terrorist might pick up while skipping around the world murdering people. I forced the thought from my mind.

A thin stream of warm blood trickled down the back of my neck. The stink and the blow to my head made my stomach roll, and all that took some of the spirit out of me.

The mechanism clicked behind me as I slipped back into the walkway around the rotunda. I'd have liked nothing better than to lay down for a little bit, but that wasn't happening.

I hoped the bad guys were busy enough with whatever they were doing down there not to notice my clothes. None of 'em were wearing khakis and blue shirts, but in the dim light, I expected the tactical vest and face covering to be enough of a disguise for anyone seeing me at a distance.

What I took for the commander's voice became louder and clearer as I neared the staircase. People were moving with a purpose down there. Two men passed below, both carrying weapons battle-slung across their chests.

My first inclination was to lean over the rail and pour it on those guys, but I'd been studying on it long enough to decide against suicide. I needed to find the kids before I could take any action, but I had no idea what that would be.

With no other options, I went hunting.

Chapter 57

Willa Mae entered Don Bright's outer office as if she didn't have a care in the world. She'd called the number he gave her. Jess McDowell agreed to call his FBI son, Landon, and ask him to drop by the congressman's office.

Willa Mae carried a bag from the local Subway sandwich shop. "Congressman? Lunch is here and your appointment will be here in a minute." She knocked again, louder. "Don?"

Spine tingling, but forewarned, she peeked inside.

Chapter 58

Halogens on the ground floor of the rotunda lit the detailed tin ceiling far overhead. The lights intensified the contrast between the shadows on the upper floors and the balustrade, working in my favor. If those guys were staring into the brightness, they'd have trouble making out any distinct features on the upper floors.

I peeked at the southern staircase to find out what they were doing. Cases and boxes lay scattered like someone was cleaning out an attic. With nothing to block the noise, the generators were louder, and I knew why they hadn't heard the fight upstairs.

A hole had been sawed in the floor. The glow from its opening was like something from a Stephen Spielberg movie. Three dusty metal canisters sat beside the opening.

I'd heard rumors all my life of a basement below the courthouse, but I also heard tell of Santa Claus, the Easter Bunny, and the boogeyman. Still, I recalled that worn wooden floor always had a lot more give under my feet than it should have.

I backed away and let my eyes readjust to the

gloomy light. The generators covered the sound of my footsteps as I worked around the perimeter, listening at doors. Several had been kicked in. The shelter in place didn't work. The terrorists hadn't behaved like we'd all been taught. That's the problem with radical Islamic terrorists or jihadists or lunatics, they don't think like normal people.

Go figure.

These weren't random shooters after targets of opportunity. They had a specific plan and followed it, rootin' out anyone trying to hide. In one of the offices I found a man and woman who'd been murdered. They'd absorbed more than half a dozen shots each and lay in coagulating pools of blood. I recognized their faces, though I couldn't recall either of their names.

I wondered why they'd been killed when others were taken alive and figured they did it for pure-dee meanness. That thought fueled the rising anger I kept tamping down. It wouldn't do to lose my temper, because it scared me to death when I lost control.

I'd about decided there weren't any terrorists up there on the third floor until I found another rat in the second-to-last tower on the west side. He'd left the office door cracked open and a soft smoker's cough let me know he was inside. I walked in like one of the boys.

He was staring into the storm, down what would have been South Charles Street if he could have seen it. Like I feared when *I'd* earlier passed the upstairs windows, he was silhouetted against the glass.

The office was full of desks, chairs, and file cabinets with no clear aisle leading toward the guy. Dreading that he might turn around, I ran the maze, zigzagging on my toes through the obstructions. It's a wonder I didn't kick a trashcan on the way.

The generator wasn't as loud in there, but the wind moaning past the building covered my charge. I didn't want to shoot, but then again, I didn't want to fight him, either. I was too damned tired and scared. So I did the next-best thing and rammed him like a linebacker, noting at the last second that he was a redhead. He heard or felt me coming. It could have been the change in the air pressure between us or the rustle of clothing as I neared.

He pivoted in my direction, his right hand dropping toward an M4's pistol grip. I hit him with all my weight, high in the chest and hard enough to rattle his mama's teeth.

He crashed through the window and flipped over the sill in a splinter of glass as the brittle wooden frame gave way. The guy vanished into the river of cold air pouring into the room.

I had so much momentum that I barely got a hand on the sill to stop. Regaining my balance, I covered him with my pistol in case he started to get up, but he was spraddled out and twisted up, half-buried in the snow and as still as road kill.

Four down.

The idea that I'd killed still another human being should have had an impact, but I was numb to the violence I'd been part of since the terrorists took over.

Good God, killin's coming easy now, and I'm getting good at it.

I didn't dally long, because I wasn't sure if someone looking out a window below saw the body fall. Once back in the hallway, I closed the door, just in case one of his buddies came along to check on him and felt the draft.

I was still fuzzy, and my head ached from the knock Arturo gave me. The whole nerve-wracking thing was stretching into next week, and I figured my luck and time were running out. Ethan and his men were sure to try and make entry soon, or those guys below were going to realize something was up and come to find their buddies.

I had to be ready.

Chapter 59

Congressman Don Bright didn't waste any time. He was standing in the doorway of his attached bathroom when Willa Mae returned. "Come in here. Did you bring the ketchup?"

She followed him inside. He stopped beside the shower stall. Searching with her eyes for an explanation, Willa Mae withdrew the plastic bottle from the sandwich sack and handed it over. She noted the pistol stuck in her boss's waistband. "What are you doing? I hope that's legal. You realize it's a federal offense to possess a handgun in D.C. without a permit."

Bright ignored the obvious and tried to squirt the ketchup on the tile wall. Nothing came out. "Did you call McDowell?"

She flapped a hand. "You told me to."

The congressman unscrewed the cap and peeled off the foil seal. "Keep your voice down.

"What the hell is going on?"

Voices rose in her outer office and both knew time was ticking away. She watched him screw the cap back on and flick the bottle at the shower's wall opposite the fixtures. Satisfied with the spray, he splattered it again and again.

"I don't understand what *you're* doing."

Bright flicked the bottle again, adding more spray as the thick red fluid splattered against the tiles. "We don't have much time. Did you get another cell phone?"

She repeated her usual answer as if were an everyday question. "You told me to. Look, I'm sure we have other options."

"No. We don't. This'll be better. The guy on the phone gave me the idea, and I think it's the only one that'll buy Katie some time. I'm going to give them my body. That should be enough to make them release her or delay whatever else they're planning, since I'll be out of the picture."

Willa Mae watched Bright shake ketchup into his hand and smear it on the side of his head. "*This* won't work."

"I think it will. The ATF did the same thing several years ago."

"What are you talking about?"

"Operation Black Biscuit. An undercover agent, Jay Dobyns, posed as a gunrunner for the Hells Angels. He earned his 'patch' by faking the murder of a rival Mongols gang member. They took a picture of another officer dressed in the Mongols colors and covered in an animal's blood and brains in a shallow grave. The undercover agents delivered the blood-covered vest, a videotape, and a photo to the Hells Angels leadership. They bought the story and made Dobyns a full-patched member of the club."

Willa Mae looked unconvinced. "That beats all I've ever heard. That was a long time ago, Don, and things weren't as sophisticated then. Now with reality television, people recognize fake photos and videos pretty damn quick. You're playing with Katie's life. They'll kill her when they find out."

"The man I talked to is insane. He'll kill her anyway and this might gain her some time, enough time for a SWAT team to get her and the others out." He added more ketchup to his hair and sat down in the walk-in shower. Laying the snub-nose revolver to the side, he leaned back and went limp. "Shoot a picture."

Willa Mae held the borrowed phone up and snapped a quick photo. "This is stupid."

"It's my call. Desi said at first that he wanted me dead, so I'm gonna give it to him. How does it look?"

"Almost real, but the image is way too sharp." She squinted at the phone. "Let me try again."

Willa Mae pushed the button again before the device had time to focus. This time it looked more like someone had snapped a quick photo, hoping not to get caught. She studied the screen. "I have to admit, this came out better than what I thought."

Bright rose to his feet and took the phone. He checked the image. "That's what I wanted."

"Look, Don. Don't do this. Let *someone else* handle it."

He picked up the pistol, aimed at a high corner of the shower, and pulled the trigger.

Willa Mae screamed. "What are you doing? That may have gone through the wall and hit someone."

The congressman grunted. "Check the angle if it'll make you feel any better. I imagine the bullet lodged somewhere in the outside wall, and I doubt the hollow point went through the brick."

He pushed her toward the door. The odds were that someone'd already called 911 and police units were rolling. "Meet McDowell out there and have him come in. Tell him I'm already dead and to check on me. I'll do the rest."

The red-eyed secretary backed into the outer office and spun to find a growing crowd gathered at her desk, frightened and curious. She straightened her shoulders. "Everyone into the hallway, please."

Eyes full of genuine tears, she shooed them back. "It's bad in there. The worst." She wasn't lying to that point. "The congressman shot himself."

Gasps and moans filled the air. Willa Mae held up her hands. "Please, let's handle this with decorum."

Agent Landon McDowell pushed through the crowd with a stricken look on his face. "What happened?"

Without a word, Willa Mae took his arm and led the FBI agent into Bright's office.

At the same time, cell phones in the hands of the crowd vibrated with a tweet sent from Daniella's borrowed phone.

Chapter 60

DeVaca glanced up to see one of their men watching over the rail's edge. Something was strange about his clothing, but Wicked's attention was elsewhere.

Chavez was once again speaking into his ear. "Status?"

The annoying interruption frustrated DeVaca. He took several calming breaths to satisfy the Demon and pressed his comm button. "All is fine. They're doing what we expected, just waiting. Any news from Washington?"

"I haven't seen anything on television yet. I may have to call him a second time. He doesn't want me to do that. Is his relative close? Is she secure?"

"Of course."

"Fine then. Once I have confirmation that the congressman has stepped down, do what is necessary."

"It will be slower than expected. I am sure you are aware of the blizzard outside."

"I'm watching it on the news, of course. Do you think I'm just sitting here, twiddling and twiddling and twiddling my thumbs?"

DeVaca thought of Chavez's malady. *Washing them to excess, no, wait, probably letting Lucille diddle something for you.*

"No. Just making sure you are aware of all the factors in play. Our primary extraction is a no go. We will use the alternative method, but even that is questionable with the snow." He checked his watch.

"Do what you have to do. I don't care about them." His voice rose in excitement "Wait . . . all right. CNN just broke in with a special report. The congressman is going to make his statement in ten minutes. I'll be back in fifteen."

Chapter 61

Hugging the wall, I slipped down the staircase to the second floor in a gut-wrenching repeat of what I'd done upstairs. Slide along the walls, creep through the doors with my stomach fluttering, then on to the next office.

I had reached the municipal courtroom and put my ear against the door when the cell phone in my back pocket vibrated.

The caller ID identified Ethan Armstrong. I let the phone vibrate until I could duck into the office beside the courtroom. I answered by swiping the screen without speaking, continuing through Judge Dollins's main office and into his conference room. I'd already cleared it.

Closing the door, I pressed the phone against my covered ear.

Ethan's voice was near panic. "Sonny! Sonny! Can you hear me? Hello? Hello?"

The static was bad, frustrating me to no end. I was wired tight as a mainspring. I tilted my head and moved the phone, hoping to get a better signal. "I said never to call me at this number."

"Uh, Sonny? Can you hear me?"

Keeping my voice low, I kept talking and hoping I was coming through. "Yes. I was in a meeting and couldn't answer."

The signal wavered and Ethan missed the funniest thing I'd said all day. He plowed ahead. "We've been trying to get through for a while, but everybody with a damn phone's clogging up the cells."

"Sorry. I'm on the second floor. Everything's clear from the third up, and most of this floor is, too."

"What?"

"Don't talk. Just listen. My text was wrong. There's four less bad guys than they started with . . . oh, while I'm thinking of it, there's a kid on the third floor with a little machine gun. Try not to shoot him when the time comes, he's one of Kelly's students and he's wearing my coat and hat."

"A kid with a—!"

"It's Arturo, the kid we were talking about at breakfast this morning. I'll tell you all about it later. I think I've found the hostages on the second floor, but I 'magine there's guards in there with 'em."

"Where are they?"

"They're in—"

The phone beeped in my ear as the connection was lost. When I checked the screen I saw the CALL FAILED message. To make matters worse, the phone was down to 11 percent power. I couldn't believe how fast the battery was going, then I remembered something the twins had taught me two weeks earlier.

I doubled-clicked the button and saw that same end-less stream of open windows again, draining what was left of my battery. Swiping my finger across the bottom, an even longer line of apps appeared; Google, Photos, Notes, Maps, Health, App Store, Game Center, Settings, and more.

I don't know what all this is.

I flicked them closed, wasting precious time before stuffing the phone back in my pocket. I hoped it would have enough juice left for at least one more call if Ethan could get through again. In order to save the battery as long as possible, I wouldn't be dialing out.

I stopped when a stupid idea popped into my head.

Nope. Not going to do it.

It's stupid.

It won't work.

It's straight out of television.

But I couldn't open the door and sashay into the courtroom without knowing how many people were guarding the hostages or where they were in the room. It would guarantee a firefight that I'd lose, and if by some miracle I didn't get killed, the shooting would draw the rest of the bad guys like bees to an orange blossom.

So, you're going back up to the Grand Jury room, try not to get shot by Arturo this time, then get that rope he knotted to get down through the ceiling, tie it off, and go back outside in the storm to climb down to this floor and into the window behind them.

I couldn't think of anything else, until . . .

What's that noise?

I'd been hearing a soft knocking that was part of the

background sound of the growling generators, the constant moaning wind outside, and the noises coming from the rotunda floor.

Someone was tapping on the other side of the wall.

I put my ear against the cracked plaster beside an interior pecan-wood door. The noise was louder.

The kids were inches away. I put my hand on the smooth plaster, feeling the slight vibration as something bumped the opposite side.

This is the door behind Judge Dollins's bench. When the judge is ready to call the court to order, he walks right through here and into the courtroom. My kids and Kelly are right there!

They were all the turn of a knob away, if there wasn't a bookcase in the way like upstairs.

A violent shiver took over and I vibrated like I was having a rigor. Everything I'd been doing since the first shot was to get down and find my kids. After what seemed like hours, I'd arrived. The feeling was almost overwhelming.

I checked my phone and saw the battery indicator hadn't gone down after I cleared all the apps. I needed to let Ethan know what I'd found.

I pushed the screen to text, recalling the kids saying that a text sometimes goes through when a phone call wouldn't.

Hostages in second floor courtroom.

I mashed the send key and watched the little line on top move halfway across before stopping.

Seconds ticked by while I chewed my lip, cussing

technology, those who developed cell phones, and just to make myself feel better, everyone I'd gotten cross-ways with for the past five years.

I cooled off and pushed the button to put the phone to sleep, hoping the text would go through at some point. Knowing I couldn't stay there all day, I gave the knob a slight turn. It wasn't locked.

Now all I needed to do was get inside, without getting killed right off the bat, and take out an unknown number of terrorists.

Right.

Chapter 62

Kelly gave up trying to keep her students quiet. They were kids, and no amount of shouting or begging was going to keep them silent once the initial shock had worn off.

The terrorists understood the futility of threatening the class. The only recourse was to beat or kill them all, and the beheading seemed to have taken some of the fire out of them.

They retreated as far as possible and sat with their backs against the rear wall under the tall windows. Now and then one would glance over, as if expecting the door to open.

Kelly wondered if they were waiting for someone to relieve them, and she hoped that wasn't the case. The next set of guards might not be so lenient about letting the kids talk, but then again, maybe the new guys wouldn't leer at her like Stretch. His steady stare made her feel creepy.

The terrorists had separated the adults from the kids when they brought them in, putting the office workers and patrons against the courtroom's inside wall to the left of the judge's bench.

Still stunned by the brutal murder, they followed the rules and were silent, though one gray-haired woman had ooched across the floor until she was within arm's reach of a female student. Smiling at the rest of them, she patted the girl's back, more for human contact than anything else. The youngster didn't seem to pay any attention to the strange interaction.

Matt sprawled on the floor with his head in Kelly's lap. Twisted like a pretzel, with one foot beside the tall baseboard, he tapped the edge of his shoe against the wall.

Kelly rubbed his forehead with her fingertips. "Honey, you don't need to do that."

He didn't stop tapping. "I'm hungry. I want pizza. Cheese pizza."

"We'll get something later."

He tapped harder.

Jerry caught her eye. Her son tilted his head toward the terrorists and raised an eyebrow. Kelly knew what he meant. The guards were whispering together, paying little attention to their hostages, and he wanted to do something.

Jerry shared a look with one of the larger boys in the room. Stephen Haskins was a big kid, a lineman on the varsity team. His eyes flicked toward the guards, then back to Jerry.

She read her son's lips. *You ready?*

She saw the shift in their body tension. Horrified to realize they were going to charge the armed men, she coughed loud and long to get their attention.

Shorty and Stretch glanced up, and the boys froze. The other kids caught the change in the room and their low buzz ceased. Kelly drew more attention to herself by shifting her position. Jerry and Stephen found something interesting to study in their laps.

The tension bled off. Matt's rhythmic tapping against the wall continued, and the kids resumed their murmuring.

The guards went back to whispering. Kelly caught Jerry's eye and put on her mom face. At a soft knock, Stretch rose from where he squatted, cracked one of the double doors, and spoke to someone in the hallway. The room fell silent as the hostages watched the exchange.

Matt rose to his knees to see what was happening. He spoke in a normal tone. "Can we go now?"

"Shhh, honey. Inside voices so we don't make those guys mad."

"I need to use the ba'room." His pronunciation was blurred, but clear to those who knew him.

Kelly pulled him back down and whispered in his ear. "I'll see what I can do. But *please* use your quiet voice."

Stretch closed the door and relayed a message to his partner. They whispered together, casting glances at the hostages. The silence seemed to agitate Matt, who struggled to find a comfortable position. "I wand my daddy."

"I know you do."

"And Mama, too."

"Right, right." Kelly spoke to Sheriff Ethan Armstrong's daughter, Gillian, in the softest voice imaginable. "Honey, I want y'all to keep talking just like you were—low, very low."

"Why."

"Because the noise helps Matt. Isn't that right, baby?"

"I'm tired of being quiet."

"I know. That's why we're going to use our inside voices, but very, very low."

She hoped her husband hadn't been killed in the takeover and was trying to find a way to rescue them all.

Matt tapped again, with the wrong shoe on his right foot.

Chapter 63

I turned the knob on the door leading from the judge's chambers. Unlike the courtroom directly above, this one was still in use, and there wasn't a bookcase blocking the way. The voices stalled and I tensed, thinking that slight movement had been noticed. Something else was going on, and Matt's voice came through loud and clear.

Good boy. Give 'em hell.

But why are the guards letting 'em talk?

It came to me. The terrorists had learned what teachers had been battling for generations.

I lay on the floor, drew the Colt from my holster, and used one finger to pull the door open a fraction of an inch, hoping that even if the guards were watching it, they wouldn't notice the movement. The hinges didn't make a sound, thanks to the building's maintenance man.

I vowed to kiss the guy on the lips if I ever met him.

When I peeked through the crack, I found myself looking into the familiar blue eye of a young girl lying on her side less than six inches away.

"Shhhhh. Angie. It's me. Sonny Hawke." My whisper to Evangelina Nakai was nothing more than mouth noises.

I don't know if she was numb, terrified, or savvy beyond words, but Angie didn't move a muscle.

"Take it easy, sweetheart. How many guards?"

She mouthed *two* and I wanted to reach through and hug her neck.

"Close or far?"

She lipped, far.

"Are they close to the main door?"

A very slight nod.

"Together?"

She raised an eyebrow. The expression revealed more than a long conversation.

It meant she wasn't sure.

"Where's Kelly?"

She rolled her eyes upward, my left.

I thought long and hard about my next statement. "Pass the word for everyone to stay on the floor, no matter what. Stay low. Five minutes."

A slight nod was all I needed. I pushed the door back against the latch without engaging the mechanism, and stood, thinking hard. A wooden cane made of what looked like mesquite hung on the coat rack and caught my attention. I had an idea.

I dug the Old Timer lockback knife out of my pocket and went to work with the razor-sharp blade, shaping the seasoned wood into a rough point. When I was finished, I had something like a thick spear.

A spear. Jeez.

Moving as quiet as possible before I could change my mind, I slipped back into the hallway. The noise continued below as I sidled against the wall to the courtroom's double doors.

Chapter 64

Congressman Don Bright's outer office was full of people—paramedics, local police, the FBI. Though he didn't wear a big hat like Sheriff Ethan Armstrong, FBI Special Agent Landon McDowell commanded everyone's attention and wouldn't let anyone into the bathroom.

A paramedic squared off with him. "We need to get in there to make sure he's not still alive."

McDowell favored the paramedic with expressionless eyes. "The back of his head's gone."

"Still, we have—"

"I'm in charge of this scene until my supervisor arrives. This is a special case. We're going to go as slow as possible to make sure no one makes a mistake."

His longtime friend FBI Agent Nathan Witherspoon leaned in close. "I think you've already made one. This isn't how we handle suicides. What's going *on*?"

McDowell's phone saved him from answering.

"Quiet, people." He swiped the screen. "McDowell." He listened without speaking. "I'll check it out."

McDowell ended the call and punched another icon on his cell phone.

After examining the screen, he spoke to everyone within hearing distance. "I want to know who got in there and tweeted a photo of Congressman Bright's body, and I want that person right now! No one will leave this room until I get some answers."

He hid his relief. The congressman's plan was working. Now all he had to do was wait for his superior so he could pass off the responsibility for this weird event. He met Agent Witherspoon's gaze and wondered how he'd earn a living, starting tomorrow.

McDowell played the scene like a pro.

Still in the bathroom, Bright heard the comment and built a wry grin. His hair was stiff and his skin pulled against dried ketchup. He touched the borrowed phone in his coat pocket.

Told you it would work.

He made a mental note to clear Daniella Gibson's name once things settled down. At worst the intern would have to find a new job. He hoped he could do the same for the poor FBI agent holding everyone up in the other room.

It was a real suicide. I've killed my career. It's all my fault. All of it. I'm too far away to save my baby, and I had to do something, anything, to make it right.

Chapter 65

Marc Chavez pumped a fist in the air, three times of course. "I don't believe it!"

Lucille crossed her legs and rested an elbow on one knee, being careful not to spill wine onto her white skirt. "What is it?" She'd never seen Chavez so animated.

"Bright didn't announce he was stepping down. He panicked and shot himself." He pumped three more times. "He *shot* himself. He *shot* himself. He *shot* himself. That's *beautiful*! I never thought he'd do anything so drastic and permanent. He shot himself. He shot himself. He shot himself!"

"How can you be sure?" Lucille swirled the wine and watched the legs run downward inside the crystal glass. She thought about switching to gin. She needed something to fortify herself.

Chavez snatched the RF television remote off the bar and cranked up the volume. The female host of the current newscast read from the teleprompter.

"We have breaking news that a tweet identified as coming from an intern in the office of Congressman

Don Bright, Chairman of the Homeland Security Committee, moments ago broke the news that the congressman has taken his own life this afternoon in a bathroom off his office suite." A snapshot of the tweet appeared over the woman's shoulder.

> @Danni84ABC OMG, authorities investigating the suicide of Congressman Don Bright. Grieving. #suicide #congress

"This trending tweet is shocking the world, along with an accompanying graphic photograph that we won't be showing here. It appears that the congressman was overwhelmed by the thought that his daughter, Katie Bright, is in the hands of the terrorists who have the town of Ballard, Texas, hostage."

Chavez lowered the volume and took his phone off the charger. He thumbed the screen. "Here it is. Check this out. He shot himself in the head." He held the cell phone out so she could see.

Lucille peered through her trifocal glasses. "How do you know it's real?"

"This is something that the authorities won't fake. You can't do something like this and send it throughout the world. It would ruin careers. He's opened the gates for us."

"I'm not sure."

He grinned like a kid at Christmas. "I am." He hurried to the communications unit and pressed a button. "Wicked!"

The answer came back faster than Chavez expected. "Go ahead."

"Bright is dead."

"Did you say dead?"

"Yes. He killed himself."

"But the video hasn't been delivered."

"No matter. He took my phone call to heart and killed himself to save his child." Chavez marveled at the action of a man who loved his daughter enough to take his own life, even without guarantees. "Your work there is finished."

"Not quite. I think we need to stay. This is the perfect opportunity to put the screws to them."

"Do you see any evidence of a response?"

"Nothing. The fools are waiting for us to contact them for negotiations. They're doing everything by the book. We've been lucky because the blizzard has shut the town down."

"You need to leave while you can. I'm calling the sheriff now for the last time with the demands. That'll keep them busy while you escape. Those left behind should make it as bloody as possible."

Chavez quit talking when the newscaster reported from a snowy street devoid of automobiles. She was so bundled up that she looked to be in a deep freeze. He pressed the volume button again.

"The terrorist takeover of the Ballard courthouse couldn't have come at a worse time for authorities. The heavy snow here in El Paso has grounded all aircraft, and the response vehicles can't use the highways. Now . . ." She put one hand to her ear in the hood, listening. "This just in, we've just received confirmation that the tweet reporting the suicide of Congressman Don Bright is true. Congressman Bright, the father of one of the Ballard hostages, is dead of an apparent suicide. Before taking his own life, Congressman Bright issued a statement saying that he had taken bribes to fund his push for border security, while at the same time diverting funds that would have sent hundreds of personnel to the Texas/Mexico border to stop this kind of terrorist attack. In the statement, he admitted the linked terrorist takeover in Ballard is his fault. At this time, we can't confirm the condition of his daughter or the hostages or if they'll soon be released."

Chavez hurried to his laptop and keyed in a long series of letters and numbers. At the prompt, he tapped in more numbers and a password. A page opened with his account number at the top. He clicked on an icon to find another page of columns to find a new seven-figure deposit.

Ecstatic, Chavez clicked out of the report and raised a fist toward the ceiling. "Yes, yes, yes!"

Lucille watched him approach the couch, glad she'd been drinking.

Chapter 66

Kelly sat upright with her eyes closed and her head against the wall. She was still rubbing Matt's brow when she noticed a shift in the room. The kids' soft noise level dropped off and bodies shuffled.

She cracked her lids and watched Angie put her lips to Gillian Armstrong's ear. Gillian listened, checked to make sure their captors weren't watching, then leaned over and whispered into Chuck Marshall's ear. He repeated the process. Their version of the telephone game ran its course, passing a message through the class.

Olivia O'Neal was sitting beside Kelly when Maddy Rogers heard the message. She leaned in and spoke in a voice almost too low to hear. "Miss Hawke. Someone's coming in. Stay on the floor."

A chill skittered down Kelly's spine. She wondered how the kids knew if it were true or if it was one of those rumors that often swept through a school like wildfire.

The adult hostages on the opposite side of the court-room also noticed the change. Heads swiveled toward the class.

The captors realized something was going on. They rose, alert.

Stretch walked around the fixed seats and down the center aisle to stand at the bar, beside the swinging gate. "What are they doing?"

The students fell silent, all except for Matt. The terrorist's tone and forceful question disturbed the boy who sat up, annoyed. "I need to go to the bat'room." His diction was muddy, and the guard missed the statement that Kelly understood.

"What's wrong with him?"

She flushed. "There's nothing *wrong* with him. He was quiet until you came over here. They were all being good."

He jerked the muzzle toward the other students. "Why did they quit talking?"

Kelly rubbed her forehead, feeling the oily sweat from fear and tension. Words she knew she should bite back flowed as if a dam had burst.

"For the love of God! You've been complaining they won't be quiet, and now that they are, you're bitching about *that*. What do you want them to do? Tell me, and I'll make it happen!"

The look in his eyes was like flies bumping against a window. "Stand!"

She rose.

"Come!"

Resisting or arguing would make matters worse.

Kelly picked her way through the students and stood before Stretch. Something inside the man changed as if a switch had been thrown. He slapped her. The sharp crack staggered her.

"You don't *speak* of God to me, you infidel! Your God is not mine, *woman*! The only God is *Allah*!"

Stunned, the students recoiled. Kelly gathered herself, shocked into immobility and expecting another blow.

Stretch's hot breath in her face stank of something she couldn't identify. His eyes were glassy. "You come with me."

Her mouth went dry. "Why?"

He swiveled the muzzle of his rifle toward her stomach. His Middle Eastern accent thickened. "Because I *said* to."

"No."

He pointed at Evangelina Nakai. "Then *she* comes with me."

Kelly watched his eyes rove over the students. He licked his lips and flicked his fingers upward. "You, stand."

Trembling, the girl rose, and Kelly shifted to block his view. "Leave her alone."

"The girl comes with me."

"You'll have to kill me first." Kelly's mind raced. Without looking, she knew her son was preparing to launch at the man pointing a gun at his mother.

Stretch slapped her again with the sound that cracked off the walls. "I am in charge. I take *who* I want, *when* I want, you *whore*!"

Kelly closed her eyes. "You want me. Not a child. I'll go because I want to, Jerry, so relax."

Stretch's hand slipped down to her chest, cupped her breast, and slid down her flat stomach. "Jerry? Why do you call me Jerry?" The rifle barrel rose up her inner thigh. "Are you making fun of me, *woman*?"

Kelly gasped. "Sorry. I don't know why that came out. I'm scared."

His voice softened. "Yes. You should be scared. You come to me."

Kelly needed to maintain his attention so Evangelina could settle back into the crowd. Any further argument would escalate, bringing her son off the floor in a rush. To keep him from being beaten, or worse, she made sure to catch the eyes of both Jerry and Stephen.

She was right. Jerry's face was red with rage.

Matt crawled through the crowd of students faster than she could have imagined and reached up to grab her blouse. He pulled, trying to keep her with him but tightening the material across her breasts and revealing her bra. "No. Stay with me."

Stretch licked his lips again as she urged the boy to release his grip. "It's all right, honey. Stay right here with Gillian and Evangelina, who needs to turn her back on this room." She hoped the girl got the message. "Keep them company for me. I'll be right back."

Matt didn't let go until Gillian put her arm around his shoulders and hugged him. Kelly saw from Gillian's stricken expression that she knew what was coming. Gillian laid her cheek against Matt's and closed her eyes. "Will you stay with us until she gets back?"

Matt rubbed her cheek with a soft hand. "Okay, but I want to go, too." Evangelina pulled him down beside her and they faced the back wall.

Kelly pushed the gate. Stretch's hand shot out and held it closed. "Climb over."

Doing her best not to anger him further, she raised up on her toes and straddled the rail. His hand darted out like the strike of a rattlesnake and grabbed a handful of hair. Stretch yanked her close, folding her over the railing. Her eyes filled with pain.

"Who is in charge here?"

Tears welled and she tried not to cry. "You!"

"Who is in *charge* here?" He tangled his fingers even deeper into her hair, giving her head a violent shake.

She closed her ears to the anguished screams and groans coming from behind her. "You!"

"That is right. Over!" He jerked hard and she fumbled over the rail. The wool skirt she wore rode up, her modesty protected only by the tights she wore against the cold. Stretch's face glistened and he licked his lips. "Yes. You come with me."

Jerry rose and started toward his mother.

Holding the pistol grip of the M4 with one hand, Stretch aimed at him. "Sit down or I will take your head after you watch me take hers!"

Kelly blinked the tears away and found her balance. She held a hand. "You kids stay there!"

Bodies rustled as Mr. Beck Terrill rose to his feet, along with three others. Shorty shouldered his weapon. "Down! Everyone down!" He charged forward and threatened the room with shouts and curses in a language none of them understood before reverting back to English. "Sit *down*!"

Jerry bent his knees, whether to lunge forward or to sit down, Kelly couldn't be sure.

Stretch swung the muzzle toward the high school junior. "Sit you!" He yanked hard at Kelly's hair.

She groaned, tears rolling down her cheeks. "*Ahhh!* Everyone sit!*"

Jerry settled back down without releasing Stretch's glare. Tension crackled in the air. Kelly feared what might happen after Stretch was finished with her. What was coming had been inevitable since she saw him staring at her.

Kelly gave in to the fire in her head as Stretch used her hair as a leash, leading her between the fixed chairs toward the conference room in the corner tower. Neck bent and twisted from the pain, she stifled a moan and walked faster to gain some relief.

He spoke to Shorty in their language and pushed her into the empty room. Shorty's eyes glinted at the high school girls huddled together.

Mr. Terrill remained upright, glaring at the guard. Those people were in *his* courthouse, *his* country.

The conference room door slammed as loud as a shot.

Shorty turned his attention from the girls and jabbed the M4 at Mr. Terrill. "Sit or die!"

The old veteran remembered the North Korean soldiers who did their best to kill him during that bitter

December back in 1950. A long-buried rage boiled up, but from the corner of his eyes he saw Jerry and Stephen tensed and ready to launch themselves at their guard and realized that if he did anything at all, it would spark the boys to action.

Mr. Terrill was tough as a hickory knot, but right then wasn't the time. He didn't want the deaths of those kids on his hands.

He bent his creaky knees. "It'll be me and you before long, bub."

"Sit!"

"I'm a-doin' it, but it won't be fast. Boys, y'all settle down, and I mean it."

As Mr. Terrill made his way back to the floor, Stretch pushed Kelly inside the conference room and slammed the door behind them. The sounds of a slap came through to those outside.

Jerry and Stephen turned their attention to the terrorist beside the door. Jerry mouthed. "We go when I say."

Stephen's response was a nod.

Mary shifted onto one knee. Jerry saw the motion. "Y'all stay down."

Her voice rose, and the air became thick with tension. "Shut up. He has Mom!"

The short terrorist swung to face the new threat. Before they could move, a soft "shave and a haircut" knock captured the man's interest. The room fell quiet. Jerry shifted into a modified stance with his hands on the floor, ready to launch himself over the rail.

Stephen followed suit. "I'm hittin' him high."

Keeping the room covered, Shorty backed to the door and grasped the knob. When he pulled it open, the suction caused the door behind the judge's bench to click shut.

The noise startled the terrorist.

"Hey!" The voice came from outside the door.

Out of position, Shorty whipped back around as what appeared to be a spear lanced through the narrow opening, piercing his eye and going deep into the jihadist's brain. Letting the M4 drop, he gasped and grabbed the thick spear with both hands. A second thrust was so powerful Shorty's head snapped back and his feet flew into the air.

A collective keening rose from the hostages when the recoiling terrorist slammed into the floor. A man dressed similar to their captors followed the spear into the courtroom and pushed harder, driving the end deeper into Shorty's brain. It appeared that he was trying to force the end through the other side of the dying man's skull as his contorting body slid on the hardwoods.

Moans and soft cries from the hostages filled the room as Shorty's feet drummed the floor, hands grasping at nothing as his brain shorted out.

The newcomer released the spear and swept the room with a handgun as the hostages recoiled. With one finger, he pulled the scarf down, revealing his face.

"Dad!" Mary's voice was firm but not loud.

Jerry's voice came from the back of his throat, low and full of anguish. "Dad, hurry! He has Mom in there."

He and Stephen vaulted the bar and charged toward the conference room like linemen off the snap.

Sonny rushed forward to block the boys and snatched a handful of Jerry's sleeve to halt his charge. "No! I'll take care of it."

Chapter 67

I couldn't believe how easy it was to kill the man at the door. The sharp end of the cane slid through his eye and into his brain as smooth as butter. Putting all my weight behind the curved handle, I jammed it forward, and he fell with a thud.

I shouldered the door open while maintaining pressure on the polished handle, making sure he wasn't going to get up again. I'd had enough trouble from those sonsabitches who died hard.

Somehow the Colt 1911 appeared in my hand and I swept it across the room, looking for targets, but all I could see was terrified hostages. The body kept twitching as I stepped over it, and most everyone in the room recoiled. Jerry and Stephen Haskins were about to rush me, and I realized the nasty rag around my face kept them from seeing who I was.

I pulled it down, and Mary recognized me. "Dad!"

The fear in my daughter's voice cut right through my heart, but I motioned to keep her voice down.

Jerry and Stephen leaped the rail and charged

toward the conference room. They were talking loud enough to be heard on the bottom floor despite the generator. "Dad, hurry! He has Mom in there!"

I snagged a handful of Jerry's shirt to slow him down. "Boys, no!" I shouldered them out of the way. "I'll take care of it."

The MP5 hung on my chest on the sling, but the .45 led at high ready. I was through sneaking around. I'd already taken all I was gonna take.

I hit the door hard with my shoulder. It flew open and I and saw Kelly, blood pouring from her nose and sprawled on the conference table, half-hidden by a man with his back to me. A heavy weight sank in my chest.

The air thickened and our motions slowed as her hand disappeared under the man's *shemagh* to rake his face with her nails. He snarled and jerked his head back and struck her with the sound of a steak hitting the floor. I saw him standing between her legs with his pants around his knees. My wife's tights were torn and hanging off one leg while the other bare leg raised and bent in an effort to get between his.

My son shot around me. The guy caught the movement in his peripheral vision and jerked an elbow back to catch Jerry full in the face. The blow knocked my son off his feet. He fell back hard.

Kelly got her knee against the guy's chest and pushed him off balance. As he stumbled back, I could see that her face was a mask of blood. He caught a glimpse of me rushing forward and grabbed for the weapon slung around on his back.

I stepped forward, pushed the muzzle of the .45 against the back of his head, and pulled the trigger.

His skull acted as a spongy silencer to muffle the detonation and his brains sprayed over the wall beyond the table and he dropped. I registered that my wife's ripped underwear was dangling around one knee . . . and I saw red.

Chapter 68

Feeling antsy, DeVaca knelt beside the maintenance man's ladder jutting from the hole in the floor. He stopped when Chavez's voice crackled in his head.

Angry at the interruption, he felt the Demon rage in the back of his mind. "Go ahead."

"It's confirmed. Bright has killed himself."

DeVaca ground his teeth. Chavez's OCD was distracting him from his duties. He cupped a hand over the earpiece to muffle the generator noise. "You've already *told* me that."

"I'm *confirming*. It blew up on Twitter when someone snapped a photo of his body."

DeVaca's spine tingled. He rolled his head to relieve the tension in his neck and forced his hands to relax. "This isn't an accurate source of news."

"I believe it. The buzz I'm hearing says it's true. Television picked it up and now it's all over the news. Every channel."

"Well done, then, and thanks for letting me know, *again*."

"We're way ahead of schedule. Are your people ready?"

"I said we were. *Yes*."

DeVaca glanced up to see Kahn standing inches from Dorothy. He felt a jolt of jealousy as they talked. Though he couldn't hear them over the generators, he knew they were planning something against him. The canisters of nerve agent at their feet looked menacing, and he wondered if they intended to use them against *him*.

Chavez's tinny voice cleared up, the static gone. "Like we've said, these situations are fluid. It's time to extract yourself and those you want to preserve."

DeVaca watched Dorothy's blue eyes, thinking that her eyebrows weren't thick like some of the other women he'd worked with. She agreed with something Kahn said and tilted her head in a way that meant more than business. She glanced up and met DeVaca's gaze.

Once again he wondered if her skin would be smooth under his tongue, then firm between his teeth as he bit hard and the former prostitute urged him on with that soft, warm accent telling him to consume her living body bite by bite.

He drew himself back. "Do you have any further use for the Bright girl?" DeVaca was afraid that Chavez might have discovered another use for the girl. He'd promised DeVaca that he could have her once the congressman announced that he was stepping down.

"No."

DeVaca became excited. His mood swings were shorter, and the one kind of relief that would stabilize him was long overdue. He licked his lips and watched Dorothy's rear end twitch as she turned to disappear into an office.

"I will extract now."

"Good. You know what to do. I want this to be talked about into the next century, the next cen—."

"Out." DeVaca pressed the comm button. "Tin Man."

"Yes?"

"Is the tunnel cleared to leave?"

"No."

DeVaca's Demon railed in frustration. He felt the power of that silent shriek in his eyes and eardrums and choked down a real scream of his own. He regained control of the madman squirming in his brain and spoke over the din only he could hear. "Why not?"

"There was a partial collapse. We're moving some of the debris, but there's a danger of the walls collapsing even more. I'm looking at a hole big enough to crawl through, but it will be one person at a time. Then we'll have to pass the canisters through and load them into packs on the other side—and that's if there's not another cave-in farther down."

"Will you be successful?"

"I don't think so. Should we give up down here and try to shoot our way out while we still have the storm for cover?"

"I'll have to decide."

"Give me five more minutes."

Dorothy returned. DeVaca took her arm and leaned in to speak. "Change in plans. Take two men with you and pull those idiots Qambrani and Al-Zahwi away from the hostages. They've had it too soft and warm in there for far too long. Have them relieve Mslam on the south entrance. Let's see how they like it outside."

Fear flickered in her eyes, and he realized she'd made a mistake somewhere. He squeezed her arm. "What? I fear you have not performed all the duties I required."

Her eyes flashed, and he was sure her brow furrowed behind the *hajib*. "I've done everything you asked."

The obvious lie raised DeVaca's ire. "Then tell me, where are Scarecrow and Lion? I haven't seen them in far too long."

"You keep pulling me away to manage other problems."

DeVaca's mouth twitched. He changed his mind and fell back on a secondary plan to leave Dorothy with the rest. "Check on them now. You better hope everything is quiet up there."

"I know what you want." She waved at Fuentes and Torres, who were finished with their technical duties. "Come with me. I'll take care of it right now, in a way you'll approve."

She led, taking the stairs two at a time, light as a feather, while the Mexican team members followed with footsteps heavy as anvils.

DeVaca watched her hips swivel and promised himself that he'd make time to roll those blue eyes of hers in his mouth before they left the building.

Chapter 69

I came back to the real world with a long, bloody knife in my hand, not knowing where it came from until I saw the corpse at my feet and the empty sheath at the belt around his knees.

I let it go and the knife fell point first, sticking into the wooden floor.

Choking back her sobs, Kelly rose from the table and removed her tights and torn underwear. In a strange move, she picked up my dropped Colt and put it back in the holster like she was tidying up. I saw Jerry holding his bloody nose by the door and pushing Stephen back out.

"Go with him, son."

"Did he—"

"No. Out!"

He followed Stephen without looking back.

Kelly leaned into my arms. Trembling, we clung to each other in the middle of hell, almost on top of the body at our feet. She held my head against her cheek and I held her with my eyes closed, not wanting to see the bruises again. Not yet.

"I'm not going to ask if you're okay."

"It didn't happen."

I had to grit my teeth to bite back another storm. "You weren't––?"

"No. Hush. You got here in time. Are *you* okay?"

My breath hitched in my chest. In the midst of all that, she was worried about me. I wiped my tears and collected myself. We'd already wasted too much time.

"We need to move."

She used a thumb to collect a tear on my cheek in a sweet, ridiculous gesture, because I figured we looked like we worked in a slaughterhouse. All was silent on the opposite side of the half-closed door.

I got a good look at the split across the bridge of her nose. Blood was clotting in her hair from a scalp wound. Both eyes were turning black.

I waved a hand toward a headless body at the back of the room. "Who is that?"

She refused to look in that direction. "Wilfred Bates. They did that when he tried to fight back."

We opened the door to find shell-shocked teenagers and adults watching us with big eyes. Mary spoke through the hand over her mouth. "Dad, are you all right?"

I didn't need to look down to know what she was thinking. "Fine."

She hovered on the edge of a sob. "Are you sure? Dad, you're covered in blood."

I saw the looks on their faces and wished I could kill the bastard again.

I held out my arms and the twins rushed forward. "All right, y'all. Easy. If more of those guys come in, we're gonna feel pretty stupid standing here hugging one another."

Jerry stepped back and I saw an MP4 slung over one shoulder. It belonged to the terrorist I'd killed with the cane. "Did you figure out how it works?"

"Yessir."

"Safety on till you need it."

"But Dad, he didn't have the safety on."

"He was an idiot. That's why he's laying there. Remember what I've taught you."

"Yessir."

I wondered what kind of damage was being done to the kids in that room.

Stephen stood near Mr. Beck, who held a Glock. From the expression on his face, he was ready to use it. He scratched at a hairy ear. "Good to see you made it, son."

I was glad to see Mr. Beck was alive and kicking. I'd been afraid one of those shots at the outset had taken the old warrior down. "Mr. Beck. You all right with that pistol?"

He straightened a couple of inches. "Sure 'nough. This ain't no .45, though. Where's the safety?"

"There ain't one."

He gave me a look like I'd grown another head. "No safety? How come people don't shoot themselves?"

"Sometimes they do. Point it and pull the trigger."

"Don't you worry about that part."

Stephen couldn't take his eyes off my blood-splattered clothes, and when I moved in his direction, he backed up a step. I reckon I'd have felt the same if I'd seen my best friend's dad go berserk.

The terrorists were causing more damage than they'd hoped for.

I hoofed it back to the conference room for more hardware. I handed the second M4 to Kelly and gave a pistol to Mary. My family got the weapons because I knew they could handle 'em.

I took stock of the adults in the room. I knew most of them, except for two women who were complete strangers.

I saw trouble with Maribelle Baird, who stood there stiff and prim with her eyes loose, looking the kids over and voicing a disapproving grunt each time I armed one of them.

Maribelle stalked up to Mary and stuck out her hand. "Give me that gun. Give it here. You children have no business with those things."

My daughter's eyes flashed. She twisted away from the stout woman to keep her body between the pistol and Maribelle. "No ma'am!"

Maribelle wagged her finger first at Mary then the kids. "Those things are dangerous. You'll hurt some-one with them."

Mr. Beck put himself between us. "Maribelle, I've heard you holler for fifty years about things that ain't none of your business, but this is the *last* time. You let them kids alone and shut up!"

Her voice sounded like a sore-tailed tomcat. "Aren't you afraid they might shoot one another with those guns, or me?"

I couldn't *stand* that cranky woman, even when I was a kid. "If those people come back in here, what difference does it make? You're all gonna die anyway.

They can at least have a chance to protect themselves, and maybe you, if one of 'em don't take a notion to shoot you first for being so aggravatin'."

Mr. Beck spoke up. "That's liable to be me."

I handed the pistol I'd taken from the first guy to Stephen, who was a good shot. I knew, because he'd gone into the desert with us to practice many times. He took it, keeping his finger off the trigger.

"Y'all listen. We're far from out of the woods here. Sooner or later, someone's gonna come up to relieve these guys, or to find out why they aren't answering their radios, so I doubt we're going to be lucky much longer."

"Mr. Hawke?" Evangelina Nakai put her hand on his arm. "My phone isn't working."

If we'd been out of trouble, I'd have laughed. Most of the devices looked as if they'd been through the wringer. No matter whether they worked or not, a couple of the kids held onto 'em as if they were lifelines.

"Hon, you can try, but Ethan says the cells are clogged with so many people trying to call."

They stared at the hunks of plastic in their hands, as if the technology had betrayed them.

Mr. Beck raised an eyebrow. "You've talked to the sheriff?"

"For a second. They know a little bit about what's going on."

"Why haven't they come in to get us?"

"Firepower."

A soft, round man stood beside Mr. Beck. Neal Hampton worked at home, and we didn't often see him out of the house except for church on Sundays. "You have any more guns?"

I handed him a well-used Russian Makarov pistol I took off the man in the conference room. He'd been armed for bear.

"This isn't much, but it'll do." I looked at the frightened faces around me. "Bet y'all wished you'd stayed home today."

Hampton shrugged. "Came in to pay my taxes." The corners of his mouth twitched. "Think I'll mail them in next time."

Chapter 70

Dorothy knew she should have already checked on Al-Zahwi and Qambrani, the two Syrians guarding the hostages, but the floor was so quiet she assumed they were doing their jobs. The truth was she couldn't stand the way Al-Zahwi kept staring at her. He licked his lips so much the material over his mouth was always wet.

She'd been overwhelmed with the additional duties DeVaca had assigned after he saw how efficient she was, even though there were more than enough men to carry out his orders.

Now she'd failed him and a ball of fear lay heavy in her stomach. She hadn't been in contact with either Lion since he left to destroy the communications system or Scarecrow after he went to find him.

She pointed at the courtroom's closed doors when they reached the second floor, directing Fuentes and Torres as if they'd been her immediate team members. "Relieve those two in there and send them out to Mslam. I'll be back soon."

Dorothy took the stairs two at a time. She needed to find those two *right now* and give them a dressing-down before solidifying their story and taking them down to Wicked.

Fuentes and Torres headed for the door. They'd been friends for over two years and were excited about their successful first operation in *los Estados Unidos*.

Both were glad they hadn't been assigned as lookouts in the snow. Down in the basement would have been just as bad, so watching the hostages was easy duty.

Gerardo Torres liked to clown around, trying to get a laugh out of his friend Rafael.

Torres opened the door, bent at the waist, and waved Fuentes through with a flourish. "*Después, mi amigo. Edad antes de belleza, ya que estos norteamericanos dicen.*"

After you, my friend. Age before beauty, as the North Americans say.

The man who'd only that morning cut a tweaker's throat and left her dying in the snow laughed when he stepped through the door.

Dorothy was on the third floor when the sharp report of a gunshot stopped her. She knew Fuentes and Torres had stepped into something unexpected.

Chapter 71

"Here's the deal, guys."

There wasn't a person in the room who wasn't scared, including me, but most of them were determined. Behind their mama, my redheads Mary and Jerry waited with their shoulders touching, weapons pointed downward.

"I know y'all want to go charging out of this place, but that ain't gonna happen. There's an ass-load of killers one floor down, and I'm pretty sure they all know how to hit what they aim at. If they knew what was going on up here right now, they'd swarm us. They're trained and you're not—shut up, Jerry."

He'd opened his mouth to say something, but I wasn't going to allow any discussion. I gave him a wink to soften the order and he clammed up.

"All y'all are fixin' to sit in the same places you were when I came in. Put your weapons down beside you and *wait*. If any of those guys come to check on their friends, they'll just walk in, because they're overconfident right now.

"If you're standing up and ready, they'll shoot you. It's that simple. You won't win in a fight. This isn't television. You will die. What you'll do is wait until they're in the room, point at the office there, and when their attention is directed that way, then you shoot them. In the back if you get the chance. Pour it on 'em, then you real quick reload and barricade the door with everything you can move, kick these chairs loose from the floor if you have to, and wait some more."

"Where will you be?"

"Mr. Beck, I've got a couple of half-baked ideas, but they involve *me* and no one else."

A girl I didn't recognize pointed at the window. "We can get out that way."

"Hon, it's a long drop to the ground. We don't have anything to lower you guys, and most everyone here couldn't get down even if we had a rope. Climbing down like that is harder than it looks in the movies."

Kelly stiffened. "Sonny. Where's Arturo?"

I loved that woman even more right then. In spite of all that had happened to her, she remembered one of her kids was still out of the nest.

"He's hid out the next floor up." I pointed to the ceiling.

"I still say we can get out the window." That came from Maribelle Baird.

I felt my face redden. "Go ahead on. Jump. I won't stop you, but this isn't a democracy. The rules went out the window the minute they hit the courthouse."

"But—"

"Go, then, if you want to!"

She wouldn't quit. "*Fine*. But I think we need to do

something besides wait. What if we wrote help on something and hung it out the window so they can see where we are?"

Mr. Beck's face hardened. "I don't see anything in here bigger'n a sheet of typing paper, and with that blowing snow, no one can read it anyway. Why don't you sit down somewheres and think some more?"

The whole room fell silent as the rest of 'em tried not to catch my attention.

"Y'all need to get quiet now." Mr. Beck gave me a pat on the shoulder. "Sonny, go ahead on with what you're gonna do. I'll take care of things in here, and I don't want to hear another word about it. They caught me by surprise, once. It ain't-a-gonna happen again. Good luck, son."

That instant revealed the young man inside that wrinkled face who'd seen more than I could imagine.

Kelly touched my arm. "What are you going to do?"

"I don't have a clue."

Chapter 72

Arturo couldn't take it any longer. He fidgeted behind the judge's bench, shifting back and forth to bleed off nervous energy.

His attention wandered to the snow blowing against the windows, then he scanned the room. A folding table leaned against the railing. Beyond that were two heavy oak tables for the lawyers and their clients, an easel, a portable rack of electronic gear with a giant tube television strapped to the top, and a long orange extension cord on the floor.

Arturo picked up the cord that was rolled in an odd, chainlike series of loops. He tugged at one end, expecting it to knot. Instead, the loop pulled free of the next link. Another tug and still another loop came free. In no time, he had a hundred-foot extension cord in his hands.

"Hijo de puta!"

Son of a bitch!

Arturo rushed to the window. Expecting the window to be painted shut, he put both hands under the lower rail and pushed upward. It didn't budge. He checked the frame and, feeling like a dummy, flipped the lock and pushed again. This time the window slid open. Icy wind poured inside, cutting through his jeans like they were made of tissue. Despite the falling snow, he saw a deep drift piled against the courthouse two stories below. It didn't seem to be that far. The snow looked soft and inviting.

Excited that he was about to escape, he tied one end of the cord into a slipknot and secured the loop around the armrest of the chair nearest the window, figuring that since it was bolted down, the iron and wood should hold his weight. Dropping the free end out the window, Arturo stuck his head out, pleased to see that the cord reached the snowy ground with plenty to spare. Wind snatched Sonny Hawke's hat from his head and sent it spinning into the storm.

The extension cord felt stiff when he grabbed it with both hands and threw one leg over the sill. He pulled on Sonny's gloves.

With the courage of a teenager, he leaned outward and almost fell when his grip slipped on the thin plastic covering. He yelped in fear and struggled back inside. Heart thudding, he glanced at the door, all the while expecting another terrorist to come in. He well-roped the cord back inside.

Let's say sixty feet to the ground. Half of a hundred is fifty, and that snow's deep and soft enough that I can drop the last few feet and won't get hurt.

Pleased with his estimations and problem-solving abilities, Arturo doubled the extension cord and tied a series of knots at intervals, just like he did with the rope in the attic, though that seemed like days earlier.

Finished, he threw it back outside. It dangled short of the ground, but close enough for a safe drop.

Taking a deep breath, he once again straddled the windowsill and gripped the first double knot with both hands. It felt smaller than he expected, but he couldn't stay there. The youngster slung the MP5 out of the way and wiggled out on his stomach, feetfirst. With a terrified gulp, he pushed off with his elbows, dangling in the wind. The drop stretched twice as far away and the entire idea seemed stupid.

Snow blew down his neck. Gasping, he snagged the skinny cord between his feet and slid down to the next knot. Hanging on like a monkey, he slithered downward another foot at the same instant the wind slammed him into the side of the building. Dangling free, Arturo knew he'd made a serious mistake when he found it impossible to climb back up.

No matter how hard he tried, the slick cord defied his attempts and he slid downward several more inches. The wind gusted again, twisting him on the doubled cord that seemed hair thin. The next knot shot through his hands. Despite giving it everything he had, Arturo lost his grip and fell with alarming speed.

The sickening drop was a blur. The earth rushed upward and he expected to slam into the ground and crack his head open. Instead, the youngster was yanked to a violent stop when one leg slipped through the doubled loop at the end, catching him with a painful snap in the groin.

He flipped upside down. The H&K slapped the side of his head with a loud crack. He came up short, and the extension cord pulled tight against his leg, jerking him to an abrupt stop.

Folded in half by the sling caught under his arms, he dangled like a parachutist tangled in a tree. The strap dug into his shoulder, and the only thing keeping him from strangling was the bulk of Sonny's coat and the shirt bunched up under his arms, leaving his midriff bare to the blowing snow.

Adding insult to injury, the wind slammed Arturo against the side of the building, once again knocking the breath out of him in a harsh bark of pain. He swung like a pendulum against the rough pink stucco.

Helpless, and fighting for air, he dangled in the blizzard and realized his calculations were wrong.

Chapter 73

The two guys who came stumbling into the second-floor courtroom broke the whole thing wide open. I guess they'd all gotten a little lazy, what with no trouble from anyone after they'd taken the courthouse and raked everything outside with gunfire. With the blizzard raging, no one was giving 'em any grief and they must have felt pretty secure.

I'd seen a lot of things happen pretty fast within the last few hours, but the speed with which our fragile sense of security evaporated was breathtaking.

The door opened and a terrorist with tattoos up his neck came *dancing* in, shuffling his feet in that cocky way young people have to show that they're cool.

The bad guy hadn't taken but two steps inside when he saw the body I'd speared. You could see him process the information at the same time he caught sight of us standing around like a bunch of idiots. I'll give it to him, the man was quick when he recognized what had hit the fan, but he wasn't as fast as the Korean War veteran standing a few feet away.

The guy shouted something unintelligible and pivoted at the same time Mr. Beck brought his unfamiliar pistol up with fluid ease. Aiming with one hand like he was at a pistol range, he shot the guy square in the chest two quick times.

The terrorist collapsed in a heap at the same time the other guy outside the courtroom doors threw himself backward and disappeared from sight. The barrage that followed filled my ears with cotton. The weapons I'd distributed to everyone chewed the doors and frame to bits, and accomplished nothing but a lot of noise.

"That's enough!" I didn't need to be quiet anymore, and I was afraid they were going to empty their magazines. "Enough!" I waved my arm to catch their attention.

The gunfire ended with the rattle of expended brass clinking at our feet. The first guy moved an arm and Mr. Beck anchored him with another bullet to the head.

"Cover! Now!" The unarmed children and adults screamed and scattered to hide.

Maribelle shouted from behind the judge's bench. "Beck Terrill! You shot that man in the head and he was already down!"

The pistol still extended in one hand, Mr. Beck covered the door with his shoulder pressed against the inside wall. "I sure as hell did. I didn't want the sonofabitch to get up."

I wasn't much in the mood to hide and bring gunfire on the hostages. We were in no position for a firefight. "Stay here, Mr. Beck. You're in charge."

Without taking his attention off the door, he kept the

muzzle of his Glock aimed at the opening. "Yessir, but I need to ask you something."

"What's that?"

"Can I trade you this plastic gun for that .45 you're a-carryin'? I'm more used to it, and I know I can hit with a Colt from a distance. This toy, I ain't so sure."

"You didn't miss much a minute ago."

"He was close." His eyes flicked to the Sweetheart grips. "I knew your grandmamma. I'll take care of her."

It felt a little weird to think about giving up my familiar sidearm, but his accuracy would improve the chances for everyone in the room while I was gone. We traded guns and I handed the Glock to Colleen Brooks, secretary to the game warden. Her boss was lucky enough to be somewhere else.

"Can you shoot?"

Eyes wide with fear, she nodded. "It's been a while, but yeah."

"Good." I unsnapped the two spare magazines from the other side of my gun belt and gave them to Mr. Beck. "Hope you don't need these."

He glanced at the clear left grip to check the rounds stacked there. "Me too."

"Here I go." Weapon ready, I swallowed a knot of fear and eased through the door, expecting to find our acrobatic terrorist waiting in the hallway that proved to be empty.

Chapter 74

Snow flew against Arturo's bare midriff, prickling like needles against his skin.

He reached up and grabbed the doubled extension cord, trying to free himself, but the tangled machine pistol's strap held him as secure as an animal in a snare. The loop tightened even more, but one hand caught the last knot.

They say adrenaline performs miracles when frightened people enact superhuman feats of strength. Grunting and scraping against the wall with every gust of wind, the youngster used that burst of hysterical strength to pull himself upward, hand over hand, gaining enough slack to wriggle his trapped leg free.

He didn't have time to yell before falling the final ten feet, arms pinwheeling. The deep snowdrift that looked as soft and comforting as a stack of mattresses did little to break his fall. Arturo dropped through the fluff and his head slammed into the frozen ground.

One second later, the MP5 pulled free of the extension cord and fell, striking him in the stomach with the force of a solid punch. He thrashed in the drift, desperate for air as his brain demanded that the nerves in his diaphragm release. Rolling over in an effort to find relief, he thought he was going to pass out. Sparkles flashed in front of his eyes.

To make matters worse, ice crystals filled his throat when he inhaled, making him cough like he had the croup. After what seemed like an eternity, they melted and he laid still, drawing great whoops of air.

The snow was like razor blades against his bare skin. Collecting himself, he pulled the shirt and coat down, and raised his aching head to peer across the white lawn.

A yellow glow muted by the falling snow signaled a large fire behind the houses on the west side of the courthouse. It almost seemed normal in light of what had happened so far.

Expecting to get shot to pieces, Arturo gained his feet and loped across the barren west lawn toward a snow-covered truck and horse trailer parked across the street. The run warmed him, and he was feeling loose by the time he reached the end of the trailer and spun around to put it between him and the courthouse.

The building was as serene as a monastery. There were no shouts. No gunfire.

He was free and out of danger.

Grinning wide enough to split his head, Arturo jogged down the street, heading toward the sheriff's office.

Chapter 75

I hadn't taken three steps out the door before the bad guys poured enough firepower up the open staircase and rotunda to shred everything in sight. Maybe they thought I was with a team of commandos or wanted to make sure no one was coming down after them.

The military calls it suppressive fire, and it suppressed the hell out of *me*. I dropped to the floor while rounds buzzed overhead, splintering the paneling and punching holes in the windows. They were yelling at one another and shooting into the shadows, but some of that lead came pretty damned close. I knew they were getting ready to come charging up pretty soon.

I ignored the screaming from the courtroom off to my right and waited for a lull. When it came, I squinted through the red dot sight on the MP5 and poured return fire down below to keep everyone where they were.

The little machine pistol ripped off thirty rounds in a hurry. I slapped in a fresh magazine and caught a glimpse of someone coming up the southern stairs. I cut loose again with the little automatic, and he dropped to roll back to the bottom.

The shooting stopped like someone threw a switch, and we were back to rattling generators and the wind moaning under the eaves. I wondered how long the battery was going to last on the H&K's red dot. There were no iron sights, and if the battery gave up the ghost, I could do nothing but point and shoot.

Chapter 76

DeVaca ducked when gunfire erupted one floor above. "What was that?"

Dorothy's tinny voice spoke in his ear. "It wasn't me. Hold please."

Another crack appeared in DeVaca's demeanor at the trite response. *Hold please.* He hadn't asked her to find a goddamn phone number. He waved two fingers toward the staircase. "Cover fire, now!"

Enrique Rivas hesitated. "We have people up—"

"Now, I said!"

The rotunda vibrated with the thunder of gunfire. DeVaca swiveled in place and pointed to the opposite set of stairs. "Move!" Morales charged in that direction.

DeVaca knelt and shouted into the hole. "How much longer?"

The voice was dim over the thundering gunfire. "We might be able to make it."

"*Prisa!*" A second burst of fire came from above. A round whanged off metal, skipping through the hallway and burying itself into a wall inches from De-Vaca.

Alfonso Morales made it halfway up before return fire brought him down. The MP5's butt to his shoulder and aimed upward, Kahn backed toward DeVaca, searching the darkness above and ignoring the body rolling back to the bottom. "Who is up there with automatic weapons?"

From his demeanor, DeVaca appeared as calm as if he were standing in a cocktail party. "Go find out for yourself."

Kahn refused. "That's why we have others."

With grudging admiration for his willingness to sacrifice his men, DeVaca hit the comm button. "Dorothy, if we're being breached, tell me now."

Dorothy's panting voice crackled in his ear. "Can't tell yet, but those *idiotas* down there almost shot me."

Silence confirmed his suspicions. "All right. Can you see anything?"

"Not sure yet. I think Fuentes is down. Torres is somewhere on the floor with me, I think. Hold your fire."

"Where are *you*?"

"Third floor. They must have infiltrated a team and gained control of the second floor."

DeVaca bit his lip, wondering if someone they'd missed had gotten his hands on a weapon. But it might be SWAT or a Special Forces team who somehow found a way into the building. He'd been expecting something like that, but the maneuver had been delayed by the weather. It didn't matter.

"Fine. Force them down." He backed farther from

the open area above. "Kahn, have your men hold this floor as long as possible."

"Allah's will be done."

"Whatever."

Someone below saw movement above and opened fire again, followed by long, continuous volley.

Chapter 77

Dorothy listened to the infiltrators' return fire coming from below her feet. Staying in the shadows, she angled for a clear shot, working around the rotunda the way Sonny had done earlier, hoping to gain a clear line of sight toward the shooter on the floor below.

A triple tap answered from the shadows. Bullets destroyed the rails and pecan panels on the walls. She stayed well back from the danger zone. Instead of finding SWAT or Special Forces, she was stunned to see what appeared to be one of her own people shooting toward the first floor from a prone position. She crouched and crept closer, knowing his attention was directed downward.

The lower half of his face was wrapped in a *shemagh*, and he wore a familiar combat vest. She wondered if one of her own people had snapped, or worse, was an undercover agent. It didn't matter. She had the angle.

Dorothy pushed her transmit button. "Stop shooting. I see him."

The shooting trickled off. She moved out of the

shadows, dropped to one knee, and leaned on the railing to steady the shot. She acquired the red dot through her CompM2 sight, and used the splintered rail as a bench rest.

In an effort to steady the dancing red dot, she adjusted her position and put more pressure on the spindles. The damaged 130-year-old pecan wood cracked and gave just enough to jar her aim.

She knew she'd failed when the man's head jerked toward the dot that skittered across the floor. He rolled and sent a wild stream of 9mm rounds in her direction. Dorothy recoiled and twisted away to throw herself back so the shooter couldn't see her.

Those below opened up again. The last thing she saw was the railing and spindles shattering into splinters, but four well-placed .45 rounds closed her blue eyes forever.

Chapter 78

I couldn't believe how much firepower they poured in my direction. I returned the favor just enough to keep those people scrambling for cover.

Motion on the other side of the rotunda caught my attention when another guy charged up the opposite staircase. I sent three rounds in his direction to discourage that kind of thinking, and he went down. I moved my elbow to find a new position and the firing fell off.

That's when a bright red dot jumped into view and skittered along the floor like something a cat'd chase. I knew the dot had been on some part of my body a second before, and it came from above.

It had to have been the gymnast who'd gotten away. I rolled, holding the trigger down to send as many rounds as possible toward where I thought he would be, in the hope that he'd duck back long enough for me to scramble away.

A roar of automatic weapons filled the air again. I was impressed at how fast he'd scurried up to the next floor, but I guess that somebody throwing lead at you can spark a little extra effort when you're running the stairs. The Old Man called it "running a dog up on the porch." A yard dog might run, but when he gets somewhere that he can watch his back, he'll turn and fight.

I was doing the same thing, so I understood the guy's motives.

I think he and I were both surprised when I held the trigger down and blew up the railing around him. Empty hulls danced on the hardwood floor and my weapon ran dry. I was fumbling to change magazines when four heavy shots came from my right.

I rolled again, fearing another terrorist was behind me, but Mr. Beck Terrill was far more accurate with the handgun than I was with an automatic weapon.

The terrorist didn't see the elderly man standing just outside the courtroom, shooting the way he was taught many years ago. Mr. Beck squeezed the trigger of my .45 slow and steady, as if he were on the range. The terrorist collapsed and came to rest against the railing that bowed outward from his weight. I saw the head covering slip free, revealing a mass of black hair.

Mr. Beck quit firing at the same time as a woman's slim hand fell between the spindles.

Chapter 79

Arturo jogged through the heavy, blowing snow for a dozen yards before angling off the sidewalk and across the street toward the sheriff's office. The icy wind jabbed his lungs like an icepick and he pulled Sonny's coat tighter around his neck. Halfway there he saw the empty building was shot to pieces, the door standing wide open.

Half a second later, bullets whizzed and snapped past Arturo's head. With a yelp, the youngster threw himself onto the ground, sliding under the snow, and crawled like a turtle swimming underwater.

The pounding machine-gun fire coming from the courthouse plucked at the thick blanket with deadly fingers, but visibility was so bad the terrorists did nothing more than spray lead. Gasping from the icy crystals that again tortured his lungs, Arturo scuttled like a crab toward the abandoned sheriff's office.

He hoped they wouldn't see him move, but after trying to crawl even farther in the fluff, he gave it up when he couldn't breathe. Desperate, he rolled, pointed the machine pistol at the courthouse, and squeezed off a burst.

The automatic weapon's report was deafening, and the recoil scared him to death. The muzzle rose, stitching the building at an acute angle. He knew he'd made a serious mistake when the terrorists opened up again, this time closer than before. He wished he had time to say a rosary, because he was sure he was going to die. The terrified boy was ready to make a break for it when a weapon opened up overhead, firing fast and steady.

A second rifle joined in and Arturo screamed at the concussions that felt like slaps against his head and ears. Instead of feeling the impact of bullets, more sonic hammers from still another gun made his ears ache. Shocked into immobility, Arturo screamed again when a hand plunged through the snow, grabbed him by the collar, and jerked him upright.

"C'mon kid. Run!"

An automatic weapon overhead hammered hard and steady as the stranger in insulated Carhartt overalls slung Arturo toward the sheriff's office. His feet lifted off the ground as he flew through the door. He crunched across shattered glass, scrambling through the dark, frigid building with a man yelling in his damaged ear.

"Move move move!"

Bullets saturated the area, shattering everything they touched. Covered in snow, stunned, and disoriented, the boy passed a uniformed deputy pouring fire into the north entrance of the courthouse, and he wondered if everyone in the world had machine guns.

"Go, go!" The deputy shifted his aim and fired again. "You boys get him out of here!"

A man who looked like a carbon copy of the first popped up out of nowhere and grabbed a handful of coat. "I got him, Luke. Haul ass!"

The Mayo brothers hit the back door running with the boy between them. The deputy caught up just as they lifted him off the ground, and they all ran like bastards.

Chapter 80

Sonny's text came through.

Hostages in second floor courtroom.

Ethan pounded the table with a fist in satisfaction. "Hot-damn! Sonny found 'em and they're in the second-floor courtroom."

The brief moment of elation disappeared when automatic gunfire punctuated the howling wind. The shooting stopped, started, and stopped again. The lobby went silent. The stunned crowd waited, some making eye contact with others, hoping to find an answer that eluded them.

More guns opened up with a different report, popping and crackling a block away in a long, sustained volley that rose in intensity. Ethan watched the crowd in the lobby stiffen then undulate in indecision.

He addressed the men and women in the CP. "All right. We've outlined this mess the best we can and if y'all do what you're supposed to do, we might be able to get everyone out. It's time to go to work."

Low murmurs rose, and those Ethan had deputized

started for the street. Seconds later, even more sustained gunfire rose over the storm. Ethan saw his response plan dissolve as those in the lobby who hadn't been selected for the ad hoc SWAT team reacted to the increasing gunfire.

"Oh, hell."

The crowd moved as one, and had it not been so terrifying, Sheriff Ethan Armstrong would have thought it wonderful. The instinctual response of the armed men and women fearing for the safety of their families would have swelled the heart of any military commander or Texas pioneer.

With a head full of doubt and chest aching with fear, Ethan followed the stream of people flowing through the doors. They hit South Charles Street, leaving trails in the deep snow that led straight to the Ballard courthouse.

Some might have called them vigilantes, but Ethan saw citizens protecting their town and their families, as Texans have done since Stephen F. Austin placed his settlers between the Comanches and Mexico City way back in 1821.

He followed the horde into the howling wind, hoping the vets who'd been around the command table remembered their duties and could control those who wanted to rush the building and charge in shooting. The deputies and highway patrol officers shouted at the others to fall back, but their words were lost in the wind.

They were out of Ethan's control.

The storm hadn't lessened one iota, and the courthouse didn't come into clear view until they reached West Washington Street, which directed traffic into a one-way, counterclockwise circle around the building.

The stream made of parents and citizens wavered in indecision. Ethan felt momentary hope. "My squad! North entrance! Everyone, remember what you're supposed to do! The rest of you fall back!"

The wind snatched his words away, and the citizens of Ballard were absorbed by the storm.

He was surprised that none of the continuing gunfire sought the barely controlled mob. Sonny's information about the east and west doors being blocked popped back into his head.

But why weren't they shooting from the windows facing South Charles?

The volunteers separated without casualties in front of the Palace Theater. Ethan's group split to the right, toward the sheriff's office. Others veered in the opposite direction toward the southern entrance. Herman and Gabe stuck to the plan and circled through the nearest alley.

Ethan thought they'd reach the building without encountering resistance when automatic weapons from the north and south ends of the courthouse opened the ball in a long, unbroken roll of thunder.

A dozen individuals charged the eastern side of the building. A ground-floor window exploded outward, and gunfire shattered the charge. A sickening number of bodies dropped into the knee-deep snow, some limp, others to take cover. The assault broke and those still on their feet retreated to cover and return fire.

Ethan slid to a stop, thunderstruck at the volume of fire poured on by the enraged citizens of Ballard. It seemed that half of the townspeople carried AR-15s or similar weapons. Those with experience were conservative in their responses, keeping their fire restricted to short, accurate bursts.

For the most part, they threw lead toward the vague muzzle flashes as they ran, hoping some would connect. The rounds smacked into the building like smoking hot hail, pulverizing the stucco exterior.

Muzzle flashes from first-floor windows strafed those fanning out around the courthouse. The citizens sought shelter behind cars parked around the building. Deer rifles cracked and the hunting calibers joined 5.56, .223 rounds, and .22s that spat lead at the terrorists who dared to invade the West Texas town.

Ethan led a mixed team in a sweep toward the sheriff's office. They ducked behind the Palace and into the alley as bullets followed, shattering glass and blowing out chunks of brick.

He slid to a stop beside the theater as two figures half-carried a much shorter person from the alley. He recognized the snow-covered Mayo brothers when they emerged from the white veil. "Who's hit? Is she bad?"

"It ain't a she." Luke Mayo pushed the figure forward.

Arturo stumbled forward and stopped in front of the sheriff. "Naw, I ain't hurt, and I ain't a she, neither, *vato.*"

"Jesus! Where'd you get that gun? Who are you, kid, and where'd you come from?"

"I was inside with Sonny Hawke."

Ethan recognized the boy. "Arturo. Sonny said you were with him. How'd you get out? Is he still alive?"

"He was when he left me. He's whittling them down, but I don't know what's going on in there now. I climbed out a window."

"As quick as you can, tell us what you know, son."

Chapter 81

Gabe, one of the first out of the Posada, spun up tight at the thought of his Evangelina inside with the other children in her class. He wanted more than anything else to make entry on his own, but the death pouring from the courthouse proved he'd made the right decision in following the sheriff's plan. He'd have been shot down long before reaching the building.

He clung to the hope that Evangelina was safe with Sonny.

Gabe held back so Herman could keep pace as Ethan and his team split off and raced across the street toward the alley beside the Palace. Gabe slowed and ducked behind an abandoned, snow-covered car when he reached a point across from the theater. A stitch of exploding snow erupted to their right, and the men dove behind his questionable shelter.

Herman slipped and fell hard. "Goddamn it!"

"Puta madre," Gabe muttered.

"We need to keep moving, and that's the best you've cussed since we met." Herman pointed. "This way."

"Damn yeah. I'm better in *Español*." Gabe led them around the corner to duck behind another drift-covered car.

Big Bend School Superintendent, Damon Cartwright and High School Principal Victor Hernandez joined Sheriff Armstrong beside the Palace. Principal Hernandez recognized Arturo before he could answer the sheriff's question about what he'd seen inside. Hernandez grabbed the young man in a bear hug. Shocked, Arturo hugged him back.

"Are you all right, son?"

Arturo looked at the men surrounding him. His eyes welled as he ran fingers over the back of his head. "Bumped my head, but I'm okay."

Superintendent Cartwright squeezed his shoulder. "How are the rest of the kids?"

"They're still inside."

"Have you seen them?"

Arturo wiped at the tears rolling down his cheeks. "No, but I think Mr. Hawke has."

Hernandez noticed the little weapon hanging over the boy's shoulder. He reached for the strap. "Where'd you get a gun? You better give that to me."

"Nossir." Arturo stepped back. "Not right now."

Both unarmed school administrators ducked when a round shattered the glass on the movie placard around the corner.

The day was so bizarre Sheriff Armstrong had to laugh. "Let him keep it." He squinted at the Mayo brothers. "I thought you guys were looking for a tunnel out of the courthouse."

Danny wiped ice from his thin mustache. Snow covered his hat and shoulders. "Yessir. We found it."

Leave it to the Mayo brothers. Ethan had lived there his whole life and didn't believe the rumors were true. "I don't think it'll do us much good. We've lost the element of surprise." He pointed to the west. "What'd I see on fire over there?"

"The house where the tunnel comes up."

"How'd it catch fire?"

"Danny set it."

"What the hell?"

"We couldn't figure out any way to make sure they didn't get out through there, and there aren't enough of us with the experience to cover it. Hell, they might have pitched grenades out the door for all we knew." Danny grinned like a kid who'd made the honor roll. "So we lit it."

Luke chimed in. "We figured the smoke'll drift down the tunnel and into the courthouse to smoke 'em out."

"There's folks living close by."

"We checked. They skinned out through the back doors."

"What I mean is their houses are gonna catch fire."

"Don't think so." Luke pulled his collar higher. "There's so much snow and ice, and it's settin' there on that big corner lot. I believe they'll be all right."

Ethan pulled his hat down lower to keep the blowing snow out of his eyes. "You two beat all I've ever seen. Did y'all think what might happen if the smoke did fill the courthouse? There's hostages in there, you know."

The impulsive Mayo brothers exchanged surprised looks. They hadn't thought of that twist.

Deputy Don Nelson, who'd provided covering fire while the brothers dug Arturo out of the snow, spoke up. "Once things simmer down a little more, we can get the fire truck in. It really was the best thing to do."

The roar of gunfire rose and fell. "They're killing us." Ethan felt sick knowing bodies were falling into the snow, neighbors, men and women he'd grown up with. "We need a miracle now. I wish we had some grenades or a rocket launcher or something to hit that south door while we go in the north."

Danny and Luke exchanged grins and the mischievous glint sparked into something more dangerous. "Y'all hang on." Luke led off with Danny falling in behind. They disappeared into the storm.

Chapter 82

The terrorists surrounding DeVaca sprayed the dark floors above, their muzzle flashes painting parts of the second floor with sparkling light. Others rushed to the ground-floor offices, responding to a crush of charging townspeople.

It provided the perfect opportunity for DeVaca to use the nerve gas. A hail of hot brass rattled through the overhead spindles and jangled on the rotunda floor. "Kahn."

"Yes."

"Where are you?"

His voice over the comm unit competed with the staccato of automatic weapons. "Tax office."

"Get back here."

Kahn left the shattered window after emptying one more magazine and raced into the rotunda. DeVaca pointed at a dusty tank. "Wire that one." He checked his watch. "And put one of the smaller canisters in a pack."

He again moved the pea in the great shell game of the day. The canister of Sarin going into the pack wasn't much bigger than the Boston bombers' homemade pressure-cooker IEDs. DeVaca hit the radio again. "Tin Man. Where are you?"

"In the basement!" His voice was muffled by the SCBA mask.

The burst from an M4 close to his ear made DeVaca wince. He spoke in the midst of the cacophony as if they were sitting on a porch. "How many more of this size are down there?"

"Four."

"Good. Help Kahn load them into backpacks. Each man takes one as he leaves to use when the time comes." DeVaca rubbed his hands together. He didn't expect any of the others to escape, but the idea was so delicious he couldn't help himself.

"I have some bad news." Tin Man's voice was muffled and he'd reverted to Spanish. "The tunnel is out of the question. Smoke is pouring through, and I'm the last one down here."

DeVaca ground his teeth. "How many big containers can we get out in the van?"

"Half a dozen. But do you think we can get away in the *van*?"

He didn't think so, but there was always a chance. "There's no choice. We need to *move*. Get them in and ready. We'll disperse as we escape."

The firing upstairs fell off.

Reddy Freddy, aka Fred Richardson, left the safety of an alcove that once held a pay phone. He picked up an empty backpack as if he were going to load it with gas. "I did my part. I get the rest of my money when we get out, right?"

DeVaca drew his pistol and shot the old man in the forehead. "Sure. Thanks."

He holstered the weapon as Tin Man popped up through the hole with an oversize blue daypack over his shoulder. "This one is yours."

"Bring another." DeVaca keyed his mike. "Dorothy!"

Kahn pointed. "She is right above you. Dead."

Instead of answering the Syrian terrorist, DeVaca crept forward and glanced upward to see a slim hand dangling through the spindles. The Demon gave a strangled laugh of regret and fell silent.

Kahn pushed his comm button. "My men. Delay them as long as you can, with as much damage as possible, and give your lives to Allah!"

The enthusiastic Syrians almost made DeVaca laugh. Zealots, either religious or political, would do as their leader said to further their cause.

The gun emplacements at both ends of the building opened up again with a roar. Bullets snapped through the windows and doors, searching for flesh.

DeVaca felt a calm fall over him. "Time to go."

Chapter 83

Gabe and Herman slipped through the alley protected by a line of tired houses.

"This one! It'll give us position to see the doors and east side."

Gabe saw Herman point to a stucco house facing the southeast corner of the courthouse. Instead of trying to help the old Ranger climb over a ragged patchwork wood and metal fence separating the yard from the unpaved alley, Gabe kicked a rotting plywood panel out of the way. It dropped into the ill-maintained back yard that would have looked harsh and dry in the summer heat. The blanket of snow softened the landscape, but despite the cover, clumps of tall grass shivered in the wind.

Herman jogged through the knee-high snow to the rear of the house with two lit windows. Fragrant piñon smoke scented the Arctic air. Inside, a yapping dog tuned up when Gabe tripped over a buried wheelbarrow.

"Damn and hell!"

Frightened by the battle across the street, a middle-aged Hispanic man peeked out the back door, revolver in hand. "*Quien es?* What are you doing out there? What's going on?"

Gunfire snapped and crackled. Gabe stepped close to the house, making sure the muzzle of his .243 was pointed away from the frightened homeowner. "*Estás solo?*"

The man's pistol came up. "*Por qué?* Why do you want to know if I'm alone?"

Herman held up the wallet from his back pocket containing his retirement badge. "Easy, hoss. Texas Rangers."

Gabe spoke in rapid Spanish. "Because there's a lot of shooting across the street and no one needs to be in your front rooms. This man really is a Ranger. He's the law."

"I am alone. My wife is on the other side of town. She was cleaning a woman's house when all this started. Are you really the law, too?"

"I am now. You don't have any idea what's going on?"

"No."

"Well, stay back here. *Mala gente* have taken over the courthouse."

Herman grunted, thinking "bad people" wasn't strong enough for those in the courthouse. "We're gonna move around the side here and see if we can get an angle."

An automatic weapon rattled. Glass broke in the front of the house. Without another word, the overweight man scooped up his yapping dog and rushed out the back door to follow their tracks out of his yard.

Gabe eased around the house, the stock of the deer rifle against his shoulder.

"Easy, hoss, don't stick nothing out there you don't want shot off."

He took Herman's advice and took a quick peek around the corner. Even if the snow hadn't been falling, his line of sight toward the southern entrance was still blocked by a bull pine and a granite slab monument. Four trucks were parallel parked in front of the house and offered the only protective cover in sight. Gabe rounded the corner and ran forward in a crouch against the front fender of the nearest pickup.

Return fire from behind a white van backed up against the courthouse door kept the pressure on. Herman joined Gabe behind the truck. "I can't see a thing."

"*Vamos a tener que estar más cerca.*"

"Slow down, hoss. My Spanish ain't near what you think it is."

"We'll have to get closer."

Gabe's ears rang from the din. His heart was beating hard, and he grimaced as needles of ice pricked at his face. Bullets pinged and ricochets whined into the streets. The concentrated fire was near constant. He never expected to hear anything like it in the Estados Unidos, let alone *his* town. The gunfire was muffled by the thick, icy baffling that covered the entire town.

"I can't see a thing through this *alcance*."

"Scopes ain't made for this weather. That's a fact."

Gabe sensed movement over his shoulder. The Mayo brothers followed their tracks around the house, trailed by the bearded veteran from the command center. He ran with fluid ease, with the attractive, self-assured woman bringing up the rear.

Gabe remembered her name. Yolanda Rodriguez. She stopped at the corner of the house and squeezed off a short burst with an automatic carbine. The name Perry Hale snapped into his mind. The stocky man was also carrying an M4 with the familiar ease.

Two men materialized in the thick snow behind Herman and darted for cover, throwing rounds toward the building. He saw them wave the vets forward. They slid to a stop on either end of the truck, one using the engine for cover, the other, the rear axle.

Reverting to Spanish again, Gabe's attention locked on what Danny Mayo had in his hand. "*Que es eso*?"

Danny grinned and set an orange five-gallon bucket from the local hardware store at their feet. Most of the upper third was covered in duct tape. "The key to that door."

Herman hunkered down behind the truck's front wheel. He saw the white plastic lid duct-taped to the top.

"What is it?"

"Tannerite."

"That stuff from the hardware store?" Herman had seen young people shoot the mixture out in the country. Once he saw a rancher detonate a container of Tannerite in the middle of a pack of wild hogs with devastating results.

Luke grinned. "We mixed it day before yesterday and didn't get to use it."

Danny smiled. "Got picked up, but it's a good thing. We figure twenty-three packed pounds'll do the job."

Herman saw they knew what they were doing. "What'll it take?"

"One of us needs to get close enough to throw it under their van, or in that alcove if we can."

Gabe squinted at the distance. "It'll take some doing."

"Then what?" Herman couldn't imagine how the powder was going to help.

Luke jerked his head toward his brother. "Then dead-eye here needs to shoot it."

Herman raised an eyebrow. "That's all?"

Danny nodded. "You can only set it off with a high-velocity bullet."

"Think that bucket will be enough?"

Luke peeked over the truck. "Mr. Herman, it's liable to blow that van to pieces."

Gabe studied the building and the car parked between them. "I'll throw."

Herman held his arm. "We're gonna have to get their heads down first."

"Then shoot straight, *jefe*."

"This'll be something like you've never seen. We're about to shoot men and them that don't get shot'll blow plumb up."

"*Amigo*, I've killed before."

For the second time that day, Herman saw something in his hired hand he'd never seen before. "People?"

"*Sí*. It's a hard trip into this country, full of bad men. As bad as these, I think."

The man with a three-day beard tapped Gabe's leg. "Name's Perry Hale. I've been in the shit before. I was supposed to be with another group, but they're shot up. Me'n Yolanda'll get you close enough to the door, but you need to move fast."

Before Gabe could ask questions, Perry Hale pointed two fingers to the right. Yolanda raised the M4 and squeezed off two three-round bursts. She crouched and rushed to the granite monument, taking cover and waiting for Perry Hale.

Confident in the maneuver, he rose in crouch. "You guys grab my ass and let's go. Stay with me!"

He darted through the deep snow on the lawn, firing short bursts. Return fire erupted from behind the van. Bullets cracked past with the sound of snapping fingers. Luke and Danny spread out and rushed the courthouse.

"Well shit, shit from a cow!" Gabe traded Herman the bolt-action rifle for the handgun in his belt and snatched the orange bucket's handle. He ran toward the van.

Herman rose to one knee. "Pour it on 'em!" His .30-30 barked with a steady message as he jacked the lever.

It became a full-scale war when their fusillade pushed the terrorists down. One popped up to take a shot but dropped in an instant. Perry Hale and Yolanda kept up the pressure as they worked to set up firing positions, moving in the way they'd been taught. At least two rounds found their target and a terrorist fell back, still moving and shooting, but slower. Another darted out the door and took his place, stepping into a swarm of bullets that pocked the stucco around him.

Perry Hale managed to get the van between himself and the defending terrorists and angled for another shot from the opposite side. Luke and Danny kept up a constant barrage. Caught in a crossfire, those at the doors fell back. Luke took a knee and fired, covering his brother, who set himself up for the shot needed to

detonate the Tannerite. Hale slapped in a fresh magazine and kept pressure on the rear of the van to discourage any more defenders who wanted to be heroes.

Herman's .30-30 clicked dry and he reloaded from
the loose rounds in his coat pocket, watching Gabe's
advance. Their covering fire didn't decline. The others
picked up the slack, allowing Gabe to get close enough
to throw. He grabbed the handle with both hands and
spun like an Olympian to gain momentum and released
the bucket. It bounced and skittered across the snow,
coming to rest under the van's rear end.

Danny angled for position with the .223 in his hands.
He stood erect, lined the iron sights up on the bucket,
and squeezed the trigger.

And missed.

Herman groaned, knowing they'd been lucky so far,
but someone was going to get shot pretty soon. Bullets
snapped through the air, and Danny snugged the stock
into his shoulder and squeezed the trigger again. The
semiautomatic rifle chattered, setting off twenty-five
pounds of Tannerite.

Herman watched with openmouthed amazement as
the rear of the van vaporized in a cloud of smoke.

Chapter 84

Mr. Beck and the armed hostages were behind the locked courtroom doors, and I had all the bad guys hemmed up below, though I bet they didn't see it that way. I was making progress.

From all the shooting, it sounded like SWAT or a Delta team was assaulting the building. The sentries down below turned their attention outside, giving me some relief. I knew better than to get up, and at that point, I was pretty happy with the situation, what there was of it.

All I had to do was keep the staircases covered in case someone tried to come up and take the hostages back again. Acrid smoke boiling from the hole in the rotunda floor burned my eyes as I locked a fresh mag into place. I waited, figurin' I'd just take up space until the response team took control of the building.

A massive kick in my back made me holler right out loud.

I scuttled across the floor like a crab, trying to dig in on the slick floor with my boot heels. Somebody on the landing above shot again and missed. I caught sight of a figure with a rag tied around his head and rattled him some with a short burst. That damned little machine pistol shot *fast,* and I was afraid I'd emptied the mag already.

My lower back lit up with electric bolts of blue pain as I crawled away. The adage kept playing in my head. If you're not shooting, you're reloading, if you're not reloading, you're moving. If you're not moving, you're dead.

I couldn't move fast with the wind half-knocked out of me. The Old Man always said that what gives wild game away is movement. That's how I knew where the shooter was. I scooted back against the wall and out of his line of sight. It had to be Mr. Acrobat, the one who'd flipped out of the way and disappeared from the courtroom door.

I'd made a mistake thinking the female terrorist was the one we'd missed.

A glimpse showed me he was angling for another shot, and he might have had me if good ol' Mr. Beck hadn't showed up again. He slipped through the shadows to find a position that was better'n mine. With the shooter's attention on me, Mr. Beck had time to aim. He fired twice.

The bad guy collapsed like someone cut the strings on a puppet. The man's head came to rest against the spindles and Mr. Beck shot twice more. He damn sure believed in anchoring a threat.

Not paying any attention to the open stairway, he hurried over. "You hurt bad, son?"

"Don't know. Get back inside."

He ignored me, ejected the magazine and reloaded. "Told you I could hit with this old girl."

I rolled onto my side to check the wound. My back and left leg ached like a mule'd kicked me. Instead of finding blood, my fingers found a hole in the fabric of the tactical vest. There'd be a mother of a bruise come tomorrow.

If I lived that long.

Mr. Beck knelt, knees popping. "You're one lucky son of a gun."

"Not that lucky the way my back's screaming."

"You'll feel better when it quits hurtin'." He grabbed my arm and we struggled upright. "Let's get *you* inside."

My cell phone buzzed as I regained my feet, but I figured the caller on the other end could wait.

Chapter 85

The snowstorm provided DeVaca with a glorious opportunity to succeed, but at the same time it caused a disruption in the schedule he was banking on.

He checked his watch and shouted over the firestorm. "We need to go, now!" He pointed toward a dusty canister between the rotunda and the south door. "Kahn, set that timer to detonate in ten minutes."

The explosion and resulting release of the nerve gas would take most of the responders out. He wasn't concerned with his remaining men. They were chaff.

"Kahn, you're in change. You're now my right hand."

The jihadist fell back into familiar rote. *"Allahu akbar!"*

DeVaca spoke to himself. "Tell him in person."

Richard Carver'd had enough. The firepower concentrated on the north entrance convinced him the dance was over. "Let's go."

Shot twice and bleeding from his mouth, Tom Jordan emptied half a magazine at two figures moving through the snow. The remainder of the team were dead. "Where to?"

"The van. I think that bastard DeVaca's gonna leave, and we're going with him."

The homegrown terrorists crawled through the open doors. Once inside and out of sight as the doors blew shut behind them, they stood. Jordan threw his arm over Carver's shoulder. They stumbled down the hallway and past the ravaged rotunda. Smoke was boiling from the ragged hole in the floor. DeVaca knelt beside a backpack, zipping it closed. Neither Kahn nor those beside him looked up.

The southern doors were open and taking fire, but the open van beckoned.

Carver pointed, relieved that DeVaca had his back to them. Something cool dripped from above and landed on Carver's ear. He rubbed it to find blood on his fingers. "C'mon! When we're in, I'll climb through and drive. You shoot!"

"What about the others?"

"I don't care about those wetbacks and ragheads!"

"Are we gonna make it?"

Carver knew they'd screwed the pooch. He threw a glance into the dark elevator where the Bright girl was tied up. "We have to."

They emerged onto the enclave and a hail of bullets.

Jordan's ballistic vest didn't help in the face of so many incoming rounds. He yelped and dropped as round after round of ball ammo punched through flesh and bone.

A bullet punched into the hollow of Carver's throat, just above his ballistic vest.

* * *

A rifle appeared around the edge of an open door at the unguarded north entrance and the owner emptied a full magazine with the semiautomatic. The terrorists returned the favor on full automatic and the rifle withdrew.

Unfazed, DeVaca glanced down at the canisters that were in the direct line of fire, wondering how the shots had missed. He pushed the comm button. "Oz."

The response came a beat later. "Here."

"Our mission is fulfilled. We're under assault. It won't be long now."

"Excellent job. Good luck, and I'll see you in a couple of days."

DeVaca pointed at the remaining canisters. "Get those ready to take with us! Now."

He remembered Katie Bright was still tied to a chair in the disabled elevator. His plans for her were no longer possible, and it disappointed him. He'd already lost Dorothy and those delicious blue eyes.

It would have been fun to throw the Bright girl's trussed body into the van for a little fun on the road, a delicious payment for a job well done. But she was nothing but baggage that would slow his alternate escape, if that came to pass. He crossed the hallway and studied the frightened young woman who stared at him with one swollen eye.

Gunfire rose and fell in a great roll of thunder. Bullets rattled against the walls like sleet. Katie Bright glared through her one good eye at the little piece of hallway in front of the elevator, hoping a rescue team would arrive. The other eye was swollen shut from the beating. She'd ridden up and down on a roller coaster of pain and terror for the past few hours and hadn't found a place in her mind that would take her away.

Katie's myopic view of the hallway hadn't revealed much after that. Her head cleared after a while, and she watched men move back and forth with a purpose. They occasionally stopped to look at her. Tied with both hands behind her back, and strapped to the chair, she had no option but to glare back.

That defiance had already earned her extra slaps from the animals who liked to prey on the weak. She refused to stare at the floor and ignore what was going on around her. Katie did her best to memorize their faces, so that she might identify them at some point in the future, if she survived.

The men were an odd mix. Some were Middle Eastern, she was sure of that. The one named Kahn seemed angry, and she figured he was mad because her head wasn't covered. Katie was sharp enough to realize that's why Dorothy wore a hijab, to keep from raising the jihadist's ire. She couldn't figure out the other men. One group was American, and they had ignored her, except for one sad look from their leader as he passed earlier, supporting a wounded man.

After thinking about it and connecting the dots, she understood why the last group was Mexican. With a sick feeling in the pit of her stomach, she knew they were trying to get rid of her dad and his stance on border security by using her as leverage.

Her dad was the toughest man she'd ever known. He wasn't about to back down or make deals with terrorists. They'd made a huge mistake that rested on her shoulders.

Gunfire swelled again, and her spirits rose, hoping a Delta team had arrived to slaughter everyone who'd taken over the building. The odor of wood smoke reached the elevator, and she hoped that some of the terrorists were burning alive.

Instead of a rescue team, a single figure blocked the elevator door. She squinted through her good eye and recognized Wicked by his glasses. Her stomach fell.

There would be no help for her, because the muzzle of a pistol gaped wide and deep in her limited view. His lips moved, but she didn't understand over the noise of gunfire.

It didn't make any difference because she said what she needed to tell him anyway.

"You can kiss my ass."

"Katie, time is up."

She was answering when DeVaca caught Juan Salas from the corner of his eye. He opened the exterior southern door, pulling an Arctic blast of air down the hall as DeVaca pulled the trigger on his pistol.

Katie's hair flew, and blood splattered against the back wall.

Behind the van, one of the terrorists absorbed round after round and dropped into a heap inside the pink stucco inset pockmarked by bullets and awash in freezing blood.

Salas rolled back inside and kicked the doorstop, propping it open.

"We're almost out of time!"

DeVaca waved. "We're loading!"

Salas shouted. "I need more cover fire!"

Kahn rushed past DeVaca and down the hallway to add his own weapon to their defense. Kahn's appearance gave Salas the courage to lean out into the space between the brick wall and the van. He emptied an entire magazine and was answered by a fusillade from across the street. A bullet missed his tactical vest, striking him in the unprotected area under his arm. He died before his body hit the ground.

Kahn paused when a large orange container slid against the van's left rear tire. He frowned at the out-of-place item.

Concentrated fire ventilated the van and slapped out chunks of the stucco until a stream of bullets struck the mixed Tannerite. The rear of the vehicle disappeared in an orange-and-yellow fireball, and the explosion blew parts of Kahn and the van back into the building. The pressure wave rolled down the hallway, leveling everything in its path.

Chapter 86

The bloodbath was softened by the falling veil of white gauze. Heavier clouds promised to dump even more snow on the already-frozen landscape.

Despite the chaotic attack, Ethan's plan caught the terrorists at the northern entrance under sustained triangulated fire. Men with no military training fell into a loose formation behind the veterans, adding sheer numbers to the assault.

Confusing orders from different locations slowed the advance until Deputy Frank Malone took control. He grabbed three men huddled at the mouth of the alley behind the theater. "Stay with me!" He motioned at another group. "You guys angle in from the corner! See the deputies?"

They followed his point and saw two teams emerge from the sheriff's office.

"Move up beside us and cover them! Shoot 'til you run dry!"

With Frank taking charge on one flank, Ethan led the men with him in from a different angle. They focused their fire on the barricaded doors.

Swarmed by overwhelming numbers and a concentrated barrage, the defenders fell or fled, but not before Ethan saw half a dozen citizens drop into the snow. The townspeople charged forward with the apparent intention of rushing through the doors to engage those inside, but the sheriff waved them back.

"Stay back!" He crouched behind his shot-to-pieces sheriff's car. With more than half a dozen automatic and semi-automatic rifles pouring it on the barricaded door, the terrorists' response slowed, then fell silent. The door opened behind the barricade and closed as the defenders crawled inside.

One by one, the guns on their side of the courthouse fell silent while the volume rose in intensity at the south entrance. Armstrong and his men rushed the barricade, anticipating the worst, but found nothing but bodies.

Completely out of character, Concepción Cuevas yanked one of the double doors open, jammed the muzzle of his semiautomatic deer rifle inside, and pulled the trigger until it ran empty.

"Get back!" Armstrong grabbed his coat and yanked him away from the entrance. "Wait until we can get set! Y'all get away from the doors until I tell you!"

A massive explosion at the opposite end of the building rocked the square. The doors on the north entrance blew off their hinges. One of the men beside Sheriff Armstrong screamed like a woman and the rest fell back. They huddled in stunned silence in the swirling snow and wind.

Malone tapped Armstrong's arm. "I don't guess we're going in right this second?"

"We will in a little bit."

*   *   *

At the other end of the building, Herman and Gabe stood upright, mouths gaping in awe. The Tannerite did everything the Mayo brothers said it would and more.

The residents of Ballard breached the courthouse as a plume of yellow/orange smoke boiled out into the snow.

Chapter 87

The explosion was a heart-stopping thunderclap. The pressure wave hit us like a sledgehammer and dampened my ears even more. Already damaged by all the gunfire, my head *really* felt like I'd packed it full of cotton.

I wondered if someone brought in a tank or an RPG.

Icy air poured into the rotunda from dozens of broken windows. I figured that anything made of glass had shattered. The explosion knocked down or destroyed almost all of the lights running off the terrorists' generators, leaving one to illuminate the bodies littering the floor.

"What'n hell was that?" Mr. Beck looked like he'd been slapped. "If my hearing wasn't so bad, that woulda hurt."

The volume of muffled gunfire from outside escalated enough to get through the cotton in my head. After a couple of seconds, it fell off and a thick, dark smoke rose from the basement. Frigid wind blew through the north entrance, creating a venturi effect, sucking the cloud through the south doors.

I kept an eye on the staircase. A guy on the floor down there kept flexing one leg, but he was doing it in a sleepy way that reminded me of a kid trying to stay awake.

"Anybody? Sonny, can you hear me?"

I didn't answer the voice from below, waiting to see what would happen next. It sounded like Ethan, but I couldn't be sure. I stayed prone with the MP5 aimed downward. Mr. Beck knelt beside me, the .45 pointed toward the staircase.

I angled my head like a puppy listening to a new sound and felt the scarf around the lower half of my face shift. Those boys coming in downstairs were *hoping* for targets, and they'd ventilate the rag as soon as they saw me. I took it and the cap off and pitched them away.

The north wind howled through the gaping entrance, blowing snow and papers across the ground floor. I had started to answer when a guy wearing a gas mask popped up out of the hole in the floor.

There's something downright *creepy* about people crawling out of the ground. I shivered at the sight of him slithering out through the cloud of smoke that roiled up into the slipstream.

I wondered what he was up to when I saw a canister against the wall. I had no idea what was in the silver container, but the way that guy seemed determined to reach it proved to me it wasn't full of Dr Pepper.

One part of my brain screamed, *Gas!*

"I'll get 'im." Mr. Beck raised the Colt and I pushed it downward.

"Easy. You might hit that tank. Let me."

I snugged the stock against my shoulder and lined

up on a dead guy. When I squeezed the trigger, nothing happened. The magazine was empty. Terrified at what might happen, I fumbled for another in the empty muslin bag, wanting to scream in frustration.

Despite my warning, Mr. Beck cranked off a round, then another while I limped around the rotunda's banister to grab the female terrorist's weapon that proved to be another MP5. Those guys just *insisted* on inferior weapons.

Taking a knee, I saw the crawling guy reach the cylinder and wrap himself around it like a drowning man with a life preserver. He threw his head back and that's when I saw something in his hand and realized he was praying.

The man was on the verge of a classic terrorist suicide, using something even more horrific than explosives, if I was right about the containers.

I leaned over the rail and put the red dot on the guy's chest and squeezed the trigger like the Old Man had taught me. The weapon bucked and I raked it away from the canister. The sound was unusual, muffled because my eardrums hadn't recovered from the explosion.

The jihadist's body recoiled with the impacts, and he went limp.

The dusty cylinder rolled once and stopped.

Snow-covered men advanced though the smoky hallway. I recognized they were the ones who'd blown the door and they had no idea what they were getting into. "Gas! All y'all get back from the door!"

Chapter 88

Ears ringing, DeVaca adjusted his glasses and stepped out of the elevator where he'd taken shelter. Using the smoke as cover, he darted out and grabbed the blue daypack containing one of the squatty canisters of nerve gas. His eyes fell on the remaining containers of the deadly toxin.

Tin Man crawled out of the basement and wrapped his arms around the wired canister. DeVaca saw that he was about to detonate the charge. He dove into a ground-floor office beside the elevator and kicked the door shut. A single burst of gunfire echoed in the court-house, originating from the second floor. The charge didn't detonate, and DeVaca knew Tin Man had failed.

A brown canvas carry-on case was waiting for him, dropped there by Dorothy when they first entered the building. A matching case was hers, but she wouldn't be needing it.

He shucked off the tactical clothing he wore over his Pendleton shirt and yanked down his 5.11 pants to reveal a pair of Wrangler jeans. Knowing he didn't have much time, DeVaca opened the case and pulled on a ranch coat.

He tucked the Scorpion out of sight under his arm, slapped a battered Stetson on his head, and threw a chair through the window. Frigid air met him with an icy blast. "Somebody! Help!"

A barrel of a man emerged from the falling snow and hurried forward with a vintage World War II M-1 carbine at port arms. He waved at the man in a cowboy hat and eyeglasses. "Come on! Hurry!"

"Thank God you're here!" DeVaca lowered the blue daypack and rolled out the window, landing in a snow-drift. Pulling himself up, he slung the heavy pack over one shoulder and ran toward the civilian responder. "They're all dying in there. People are shooting!"

"Go!" Keeping the vintage rifle ready for use, the man kept an eye on the courthouse. "Get behind the cars back there."

"Thanks!" DeVaca ran past, wishing he could cut the idiot's throat, but it wasn't the time for self-indulgence. Shrugging both of the pack's straps into place over the bulky coat, he checked his watch.

Time to get gone.

Chapter 89

Arturo ran down the alley through knee-deep snow, following the weaving trails of footprints made by men determined to set their friends and children free. The youngster ducked behind the sheriff's office to the sounds of gunfire.

"Hey kid, get your ass outta here!" Deputy Don Nelson was the one who'd provided cover when the Mayo brothers pulled him through the shot-up station.

Arturo started forward. "Hey, I got something to tell you!"

Nelson turned back toward the courthouse.

The boy dodged through the alley and stopped behind a wide-eyed civilian who racked the bolt on a deer rifle, aimed at the courthouse, and pulled the trigger on an empty chamber. He racked the bolt again and did the same thing twice more, never realizing in the heat of the moment that he was "firing" an empty rifle.

The youngster followed the alley until it dead-ended into the road running along the west side of the courthouse. The position gave him a clear line of sight to the window that was still open where he had climbed out.

Pete Williams, an off-duty highway patrol officer, was behind a snow-covered car.

"Hey! Don't shoot me, Pete!" Arturo rounded the corner.

"Kid, get the hell out of here!"

Tired of hearing the same phrase, he pointed. "The hostages are in that courtroom on the second floor."

"How do you know that?"

"See that window? I climbed out of it."

Williams squinted through the snow. "Say you climbed out of there?"

"Yep. I was inside with Sonny Hawke."

The name stopped any further argument. "Say they're in *there*?"

"Yessir."

Williams keyed the radio and related what he'd heard.

The sheriff's tinny voice cut was full of frustration. "I already know that. What the hell is that kid doing there? He's supposed to be in the Posada."

"Guess he didn't listen."

"Keep him there."

Arturo saw a man in a cowboy hat hurrying down the sidewalk in the opposite direction. Forgetting he'd lost Sonny's hat and thinking it might be the Ranger, the youngster followed, using the parked cars for cover between him and the courthouse.

Chapter 90

We headed back to the courtroom. Mr. Beck held my Colt down at his side. He gave a knock and the door cracked. Jerry stuck his head out. "Dad?"

I pushed inside. "Close it now. Gas!"

Mr. Beck slammed the door behind us.

Jerry stepped back, not understanding. "Gas?"

Kelly rushed forward to check me out for herself. "Are you all right? What kind of gas?"

"I'm fine. I saw the containers and that's all they *could* be." The window-lights in the room were still intact, and I figured they stayed that way because the doors were closed when the explosion went off downstairs. Even so, the air was full of dust. "All y'all stuff whatever you can under the doors."

The less shell-shocked kids packed the gap full of hoodies and sweaters. They'd already been through a lot, but I was proud of them for hanging in there. Some were sniffling and more than one had tear-tracked cheeks, but they were focused on surviving, and that's all that counted.

Kelly watched them follow my orders. "What next?"

I pointed at the windows. "Open them, or knock 'em out. Now."

Some opened without a problem. Those that were stuck or painted closed gave as the kids and other hostages attacked them with anything not nailed down. The glass exploded outward and cold air poured in.

"Stay close to the windows."

"We'll freeze without our coats."

"It's better than dying from the gas."

Chapter 91

DeVaca's frustration increased as he waited behind Burt Bowden's snow-covered truck and trailer. The gunfire tapered off, and the people he left inside hadn't set off the Sarin. He ground his teeth and wished for ten men just like himself to get the job done, but then he almost smiled.

He wouldn't be able to trust a one of them.

The five minutes he made himself wait were up.

"Hey buddy, you're gonna get your ass shot off!"

DeVaca jumped. The voice wasn't aggressive. The guy with the big belly was still trying to help. He pushed the horn-rimmed glasses back into place. "I'm scared."

"I don't blame you, but right now, you need to get under cover. I don't think those guys are finished."

We're not, DeVaca thought. "I just need to get out of here." He checked his watch. "Cover me."

The Good Samaritan clamped his jaw and again faced the courthouse, proud to assist someone who had no stomach for a gunfight. "I've got you. Go!"

Angry and frustrated that he'd lost all the nerve gas except for the tank in his backpack, the Demon in De-Vaca's head screamed until he felt his control slipping away. He trotted a few steps, then stopped.

What the hell?

In two steps, DeVaca was behind him. Resting his left hand on the Good Samaritan's shoulder, he spoke in his ear. "Thanks for your help."

Without turning, the guy squinted into the falling snow. "You're welcome."

DeVaca shoved the blade of a long, slender knife into the base of the man's skull and worked it hard, severing the spine. The Good Samaritan convulsed and dropped into the deep drift. With one arm, DeVaca swept snow from the hood and onto the body, kicked more over the corpse, and without a backward glance, ducked his head and jogged south through the storm toward the railroad tracks.

Escape Plan A was out. On to Plan B.

On its way to Laredo and the Mexican border, a train shrieked its arrival, the whistle cutting through the storm.

Chapter 92

An occasional shot rang from outside, but it sounded like the firefight was over.

We were still string-haltered, though, forced to wait. I kept expecting to hear another explosion or shrieks as the gas destroyed people's nervous systems.

Other than the wind blowing through the open windows, the shot-to-pieces courthouse was silent except for the sounds of chattering teeth and moans and the sounds of crying. Squinting into the ocean of white, I saw dark shapes moving toward our end of the courthouse.

"Mr. Beck, y'all be ready for anything." I leaned into the window and cupped my hands. "Outside! Here on the second floor! Sonny Hawke!" I waved, wishing for my Stetson. "I'm here with the hostages!"

"Sonny!"

A half a dozen men carrying long guns appeared as dark smudges in the storm and sharpened as they rushed the building.

I leaned into the gale and saw them huddled against the outside wall. "Don't shoot! Ethan, is that you?

There may be one left on this floor. Can't tell you much else, except we thinned them out some."

He used his hat to shield his face. "You have everyone?"

"Kelly and her class, and a few more folks. I doubt it's all. Remember, one kid's holed up one floor above."

"Y'all safe enough?"

"We have weapons, but be careful. They have containers down there that might be some kind of nerve or mustard gas."

"Well, we have to do something. We're coming in."

The Fire Chief cupped both hands around his mouth. "What's on fire?"

"A hole in the floor. That's all I can tell you, but I don't think the building's on fire. I'm more worried about the gas, if that's what it is."

All I could see were their hats as three, then four of those down below huddled in to talk. The next thing I knew, Chief Jack Barker turned and jogged away into the storm.

"Ethan, tell your men to come in from this side. If the gas is leaking, the wind'll blow it out the other end." We waited for what seemed like a week before a shout came from below. I leaned out to see better and my skin burned in the wind.

"We had an idea." He checked over his shoulder. "No one's coming in the ground floor."

Two volunteer firefighters materialized in the snow, carrying a long extension ladder from the firehouse three blocks away. It slapped against the sill moments later.

Deputy Malone was the first up. He crawled through the open window to find himself in the middle of a crowd of people who wanted out. "Y'all get down that ladder quick, but be careful."

A hard-looking stocky guy in a three-day beard and carrying enough firepower to start his own country came in next and slapped me on the shoulder. He gave the armed kids a glance and placed himself between the room's double doors and us.

"Good job. Now y'all get out while you can."

A Hispanic woman who looked like she could take care of herself came in next. She took up a position a few feet away without a word.

I caught Malone's eye. "Who're they?"

"Name's Perry Hale. She's Yolanda Rodriguez."

"They know their business."

"They're a couple of booger-bears." Malone's voice was full of respect and sadness. "People step up when they need to."

Two more armed men scrambled through in a gust of frozen air. I wanted to get people *out* of the building, and instead, they were streaming in like a bus had pulled up outside. I was tickled to death to see them.

Fire chief Jack Barker came through the window. "This ladder isn't the best way, but it'll do." He raised an eyebrow at the crowd of former hostages. "We got the engine out, but all the roads are clogged with abandoned cars. The snow is so deep my driver stuck it when he cut through a yard. Some of the boys are trying to dig it out." He looked embarrassed. "Y'all don't need to know all that. We need to move, fast." He pointed to Evangelina Nakai. "Let's go."

No one could get out though, because School Superintendent Cartwright and Principal Hernandez struggled inside, shaking snow from their clothes. They moved through the crowd, touching every student in some way, as if a hug or pat might help.

Matt rushed Hernandez and wrapped both arms around his waist, a tear trailing down his cheek. Hernandez hugged him back. Matt turned loose and the principal looked down. He grinned. "Matt, you have your shoes on the wrong feet again."

The boy bent at the waist to look. "People keep telling me that."

Always the mom, Kelly helped her charges over the sill. The rest of the kids drifted to the window without crowding or shoving. The superintendent and principal helped her organize the evacuation.

Mr. Beck still covered the doors with my .45, despite the new company. From where I stood, he, Perry Hale, and Yolanda Rodriguez looked like warriors from different times, standing shoulder to shoulder to protect their people and their country.

My emotions worn thin by the day rose, bringing a lump to my throat. Eyes burning, I let the others take over security detail.

Chapter 93

I kept expecting the snow to let up, but it fell hard and heavy as the first kids reached the bottom of the ladder. As soon as the students stepped off, armed townspeople rushed them across the street and through the sheriff's office, where they disappeared from my view.

Chief Jack Barker let Kelly sort things out and it all worked well until Matt's time came. The familiar Down syndrome stubbornness rose when my daughter urged him toward the window. "C'mon, buddy. It's your turn."

He pulled his arm free. "No. I want to ride the elevator."

Gillian Armstrong joined Mary once again to double-team him. "We can't ride it right now. My dad's waiting outside. Let's go talk to him about being a sheriff and stuff."

"It's cold out there."

She glanced toward Kelly, who leaned into the boy and whispered in his ear.

Matt gave her a pat on the cheek. "Thank you. You are very kind." He worked his chubby behind around on the sill and backed down the ladder between the arms of the fire chief.

I leaned in. "What did you tell him?"

"I said he could go to the bathroom when he got to the bottom."

Slinging the weapons across their backs, Mary and Jerry ignored the conflict and zipped down the ladders. I wondered what the guys down below would say about the armed kids, but after the day's events, they probably figured it had become the norm.

The evacuation came to a halt. Maribelle Baird seemed to swell even larger with stubbornness. "I'm afraid of heights."

Chief Barker took her arm. "It'll be all right. Just straddle the sill there, turn around, and get your feet on the ladder."

She rolled her eyes like a frightened horse. "I'm not going."

"Maribelle, you have to go."

"Find another way."

The Chief looked at me for help. I wished I had a lead rope to drag her to the window. "There's no other way. You're putting the rest of us in danger."

"I'll wait 'til I can go out the door."

Kelly flashed and I knew she'd reached the end of her rope. My little wife stepped between the chief and the horsey woman. "Listen up honey-child, here's what's fixin' to happen. Those twins that just left are my kids, and Matt's already down, and it's still dangerous up here, but I won't leave until my husband does, and I'm tired and out of patience."

Kelly glanced down to see the ladder was clear. She stepped close to the woman who'd set her jaw, determined not to move. "On second thought, my husband got shot to save you." She reached out, grabbed Maribelle's blouse, and yanked her forward. All semblance of a schoolteacher was gone. "Climb out, now!"

The big woman pulled away. "I can't!"

Yolanda Rodriguez had had all she could take. She charged across the courtroom and grabbed the woman by her thick shoulder. "I've heard enough of this shit." She dug in with her fingers and the woman bent to the pain. "They have to be nice to you, but I don't. Get on the damned ladder or I'll throw your ass out this window myself."

Maribelle deflated. "I'm afraid."

"You better be afraid of *me*!"

She took one last look at the woman warrior and swung one leg over the frozen sill, yelping at the frozen rungs. With Chief Barker's assistance, she turned around and backed out of sight as nimble as a teenager.

Still growling, Yolanda touched knuckles with Kelly. "Motivation."

Kelly gave the room one last glance to make sure all the kids were gone before following.

I touched Mr. Beck on the shoulder. "You're next."

He handed the .45 back to me. "Told you I'd take care of your grandmamma. Y'all don't dawdle up here, son."

I glanced through the clear handle to see a thick line of stacked rounds and dropped it back into my empty holster. The weight was reassuring. "We won't."

The school administrators went next. The rest of the responding team took turns, leaving Perry Hale and Yolanda, who remained fixed on the door.

Perry Hale backed in my direction. "You next."

"I'll take you up on that."

"What I've always heard about you guys is true. Good job, Ranger."

That was the only acknowledgment I needed.

Instead of answering, I slapped Perry Hale on the shoulder, caught Yolanda's wink, and left.

Chapter 94

The armed, snow-covered adults were trying to sort things out, sending the students to the Posada while others kept watch. They worked to clear the street so the fire truck could get to the burning house.

A couple of the kids didn't have anyone to meet them. The chances were some of their folks lay still under the snow. The courthouse, which had been the center of so much attention, sat silent and full of death.

Ethan held Gillian close with one arm, issuing orders while cautioning everyone that the situation was far from over.

Deputy Malone appeared at my elbow with a hat in his hand. "You're standing kinda funny."

"Got hit in the back. The vest stopped it, but it aches like the devil."

"My daddy always said it'll feel good when it quits hurting."

"Mr. Beck's already told me that one, and it wasn't that funny then."

"Um hum. Well, since you're still alive, you might

need this. One of the boys kicked this hat out of the snow over there under the window. Your name's in it."

The dented and stained hat was cold when it slid down over my wet hair. The crowd parted and I was shocked to see Arturo talking to his principal. He should have still been in the attic, safely stowed away until I went back to get him, or sent others to bring him back.

"Come over here, knothead. You should have been under this instead of it layin' out there."

Arturo rubbed his frosty hair. "I lost it."

"How'd you get out?"

He seemed embarrassed. "I used an extension cord."

I couldn't help myself. I gave him a hug, intending to ask him later for a detailed explanation. He pushed himself back. "I need to tell you something."

"Can it wait?" I saw Kelly and the twins in the flow of former hostages headed to the Posada.

"No." Arturo grabbed my shirtsleeve and pulled me back inside what was left of the station. When we were out of earshot, he pointed toward the west. "Something's up."

"And what's that?"

"I saw a guy get away."

"From where?"

"Out of the courthouse."

I could tell the kid was worried. "Go ahead on."

"He crawled out of one of the downstairs windows."

"Probably just someone else who was hiding." I chewed a lip, weighing his statement. "How was he dressed? Did he have his face covered or anything?"

"No. He looked like a rancher. He hung around that truck over there and headed off that way."

A connection snapped awake in my mind. I recognized the long drift of snow as the truck and cattle trailer that belonged to Burt Bowden, and remembered seeing him drive past that morning as I talked to Andy Clark in front of the Posada. He had no business parking a trailer beside the courthouse.

It dawned on me how so many terrorists had arrived at the same time. "How long ago?"

"Just before y'all started down the ladder. I thought it was you, but I changed my mind when I saw his hat was one of those cheap truck-stop felts."

Arturo's story was odd enough to raise the hair on the back of my neck. There *could* have been a citizen hiding inside while the terrorists had control of the ground floor. He *could* have stayed out of sight until he figured it was safe enough to slip out of a window and escape. Was it the chaos and shoot-out that rooted him from whatever hole he'd crawled into, or was it something else?

I wondered if one of the last terrorists decided dying for his cause wasn't the way to go after all. The idea of a murderer on the loose in my town was too much for me to quit right then.

"Gimme my coat and stay here." He handed it over. I saw Kelly and the twins peel off and head my way. "Better yet, run your little self to the Posada with Kelly where it's warm and safe."

I slid my arms through the sleeves, feeling the boy's delicious heat push at my cold, damp shirt.

He hunched his shoulders and shrank without the oversize coat. "Yessir."

I gripped his shoulder. "You did good, kid."

He grew a couple of inches as Kelly stepped close for a hug. One of her eyes was swollen shut, and she still had dried blood in her hairline and one ear. I gathered the kids in close and held them while the heavy snow gathered on our heads and shoulders.

"Y'all get to the hotel where it's warm and get that eye looked at. Arturo's going with you. I have something to check out."

The expression on her face hurt my heart. "Can't you let someone else go? You've done enough."

"Ethan and the guys need to make sure everything's buttoned down here. They'll have their hands full."

"Take someone with you."

I glanced around, but saw no one I could trust, or a life I could risk, other than my own. "I'll be all right."

She kissed me on the cheek. "They say your daddy was in the middle of all this. He was in the fighting on the other end of the building."

I looked in that direction like I could see through the snow. "Well, it don't surprise me. Is he all right?"

"Ethan said he was. Him and Gabe and the Mayo brothers were the ones who blew the doors in."

I wanted to laugh, but my back was hurting too much. "I'll be back pretty quick."

She put her arms around the twins. "Come on, Arturo. Let's go."

Jerry shrugged her arm off. "I want to go with you, Dad."

I stopped him. "Hold your horses. Give that gun up to one of the deputies and stay close to your mother. I'll be back soon."

"I need to do my part."

"You've done it."

"No, Dad, you know what they did up there."

"I know, but you're not." I gave him the look reserved for when I was pissed, and it worked. His shoulders slumped.

Kelly kissed my cheek and took a measure of my bloody, dirty clothes. "Do what you need to do, but be careful, cowboy."

Mary hugged my neck and took her brother's hand. They followed Kelly toward the Posada with Arturo in tow.

I trotted across the street and down the sidewalk toward the dually pickup and trailer. Tracks crisscrossed the street. A fresh line of footprints cut south past the truck and came back, overstepping the first. A distinctive third line trailed away.

Then I found a body in front of the truck.

Chapter 95

It may have been a mistake to come back and kill the man. Nonetheless, DeVaca was pleased with how easily the knife had severed his spine. It helped make up for the lost containers of gas and sated the Demon for a while.

A dull roar followed by the shriek of a train whistle filled the air. He broke a path through the undisturbed snow, hurrying down the sidewalk past houses and a brick church. The surprising weight of the canister slapping his back with every step slowed his progress. Worried that he was leaving a distinctive trail, he increased his pace to a slow jog.

The silent houses ended at the practice field behind the high school. His footing felt different as he reached a wire fence, telling him that a secondary road led around the schoolyard and behind a neighborhood. He picked up his pace, circling the campus in near-whiteout conditions, and threaded his way through side streets clotted with abandoned cars.

His chest swelled with excitement at how much terror their takeover had inflicted on the town and ultimately the nation. He knew it was spreading in ripples like a stone thrown into a still pond.

He slowed and stopped, sucking frozen air and considering the idea of cutting across the practice field to the school. On a normal day, it would be full of parents concerned about their kids.

His heart fluttered at the thought of slipping in one of the back or side doors and opening the gas. The attraction of still another attack was as exciting as the lost prospect of Dorothy in his arms.

If I had a little more time, he thought. But his time was up. The shriek of an approaching train whistle said he needed to hurry.

With another earsplitting whistle, an eight-thousand-foot coal train materialized through the snow. The heavy storm hadn't impacted its speed as much as DeVaca expected.

Ducking his head, he fought the knee-deep snow as the rumble of steel wheels on the tracks roared louder. DeVaca passed the last of the houses and broke into an open field. Though the wind swept the open area, the snow was still deep enough to slow his progress.

Gasping, he forced his aching legs higher to fight the snow's resistance, relieved to see the rails were level with the surrounding landscape and not on a higher grade.

It would be easy to swing aboard.

Chapter 96

One thing about snow, you can't go anywhere without leaving a trail.

You don't need a lot of skill to follow fresh tracks neither, which was right up my alley. I could tell right quick which ones were his. The deeper, sharper prints led southwest, toward the edge of town. I wondered if the guy had it in his head to try and get away in the wide-open ranch country that bordered our town. It would have been idiotic. A man would freeze to death in no time out there.

I wasn't afraid I'd lose him, but there was a good chance he intended to hole up somewhere 'til the storm cleared. I doubt he knew anyone was after him, but a guy like that would watch his rear to be sure.

Seeing him wouldn't be easy through the storm. He could be anywhere, behind a parked car, or around the corner of a house. I caught the distant whistle of a train and stopped, looking at the trail leading toward the tracks.

"Son of a bitch."

He had an escape plan after all, and that was to hop the train as it slowed down through the city limits. It became obvious that I was following the head of that snake I'd been fighting all day.

Chapter 97

Sheriff Ethan Armstrong barely registered the train whistle.

Fire Chief Jack Barker joined him at the door of the shot-to-pieces sheriff's office that was fast becoming a frigid secondary CP. "Ethan, we have more than two dozen people hurt or dead out here."

"I was afraid of that. How many civilians?"

"I don't have an accurate count yet."

"Any of my men?"

"Yessir. Deputy Malone told us about Eric Goodlett getting shot down at the outset. We have his body. Todd Calvert's, too. Two more wounded, one critical. We found Ben Carerra dead not far from Burt Bowden's truck."

Ethan knew the heavyset man with a thick girth. "Ben's the owner of Big Bend Pizza."

"That's him." Barker's eyes filled. "He was a good friend, and someone stuck a knife in the back of his neck." Gathering himself, the chief cleared his throat. "There's more bad news. Burt's behind the wheel with his throat cut. Lots of tracks around there, and two sets leading away."

Ethan's heart sank with understanding. "All right. Get a couple of badges to follow those tracks." He shot a glance toward the filtered glow over the Fire Chief's shoulder. "Y'all gonna get that fire under control?"

A hundred yards away down West Charles Street, the house was fully engulfed, but visibility was so bad neither could see those fighting the blaze.

Barker slipped both hands into his coat. "It's far enough away from the others that we don't have to worry about it spreading."

Once again, the sheriff relied on the deputy who'd been at his elbow throughout the entire ordeal. "Frank, see if you can find half a dozen men to go in the court-house. I want to make sure it's secure before we do anything else. There may still be civilians inside." The unflappable deputy hadn't slowed one whit. "These boys are still charged up, so that shouldn't be too hard."

"You don't have to go if you don't want to. This one's volunteer."

"I'm in."

Wish I wasn't, Ethan thought.

Chapter 98

DeVaca felt light as a feather when he drew close enough to the tracks to see the train through the whiteout, but his sprits sank at the sight of nothing but a mix of boxcars and flatbed container cars. The weather had impacted the schedule up and down the track, stalling the car haulers he was expecting.

His composure slipped as he stared at the passing rail cars with an unfamiliar sense of failure. The Demon screamed in fury. DeVaca stopped himself from clawing his face in frustration.

A car hauler would have provided the perfect escape. It would have been easy to hop aboard, break into a vehicle to hot-wire the ignition, and ride in warm luxury to El Paso.

The mixed cargo train was heading south at a much higher rate of speed than he'd anticipated. He rushed forward and ran alongside, hoping to swing aboard. The thundering steel wheels filled the air with a cloud of ice crystals that blended with the falling snow, making it even harder to see. DeVaca soon slowed, realizing that even if he'd found something to grab onto, the velocity would have jerked his arms out of their sockets.

He stopped, panting great clouds of white vapor. True to form, the terrorist studied the passing train without expression. *"Puta tu madre."*

Chapter 99

Footprints through the deepening snow led past scattered houses at the edge of town. Drifts caught in the branches of the bare cottonwood trees. In the summer, the houses and trees looked lonesome and dispirited, but with thick snow, yellow kerosene, and candlelights in the windows, they were living Thomas Kinkade paintings.

I followed the trail around a tall yucca and past a snow-covered pickup. At first it looked like I was mistaken about the train and thought the guy was headed for the house beside it. My neck prickled at the thought of still another hostage situation, but the prints followed a pipe fence that disappeared into the falling clouds and wound back toward the tracks.

The familiar area off Oak Street was a gravel road, and I knew it dead-ended at a corner fence post on the edge of an open lot. I was close enough to see the vague shape of Ballard's defunct feed mill and its four tall steel silos connected by the long, angled transfer augers. A train growled past in a long blur in front of the silos.

I stopped to study on it.

That was his escape plan!

I plucked the cell phone from my back pocket and thumbed it to life. A warning popped up.

Low Battery
10% Remaining

Hoping that infernal device had enough juice to send at least one more text, I thumbed a message to Ethan.

Terrorist on south bound train.

Eight percent left.

No more time.

I had a train to catch.

Chapter 100

Deputy Malone and Mr. Beck Terrill described what they'd seen inside, including Sonny's report of what he believed to be nerve gas. Ethan sent one deputy and three war veterans in Hazmat gear to the south entrance of the courthouse with strict instructions to enter only if they heard from him. He planned to lead the final squad through the north doors.

"Boys, we're not going to touch those containers. Whoever gets here first'll take care of that. We're clearing the building and gathering up any other hostages. That's all."

Since there hadn't been any action from the east and west entrances, he placed two-man teams at a distance to act as sentries.

Ethan studied the faces of the men and women around him—people who worked hard every day to get to heaven but found themselves in a situation where they might have to take even more lives. Others had seen war in Vietnam, Iraq, and Afghanistan, but something about fighting on home soil put a different look in their eye, one that was full of white heat.

Chapter 101

DeVaca stood in two storms, one delivered by nature, the other blown upward by the passing cars. He was rooted to the frozen gravel ballast, feeling the weight of the gas container on his back and a deep vibration in his chest.

He studied the flashing cars through foggy glasses. His attention focused on a flickering image between them, reminding him of a black-and-white silent film.

Another train idled on the shoofly.

As the image solidified in his mind, the last rear-facing locomotive passed in a bright blur. The noise receded and he beheld the glorious sight stretching in both directions.

A coal train was sidelined for the other to pass. The unseen engine far to his right changed pitch as the engineer prepared to pull back on the track as soon as the computerized rail command office in Omaha threw the switch.

DeVaca spread his arms and laughed.

Chapter 102

"Sheriff, I'm your Number One."

Ethan Armstrong raised an eyebrow at the stocky man with hard gray eyes standing in front of him. "How so?"

"I did a couple of tours in Afghanistan. I'm still a little more fresh than you. I doubt you've cleared a building in a while."

"I'm good to go, too." Short black hair highlighted the woman's fine features.

Ethan could have told them he hadn't cleared a building in longer than that, even though he'd had plenty of tactical training. "Well, I'm not going to argue. Guys, I don't recall your names. It's been kinda busy around here."

"Perry Hale." The veteran gave a wry grin and dimples formed under his short beard. "Folks who know me call me Perry Hale."

"Yolanda Rodriguez, we met inside."

"I know. I'd hug y'all's necks if we didn't have all these guns between us."

"I'm in, too, but don't you touch me." Deputy Malone stepped forward. "I need to see this thing finished."

"Fine." Ethan watched a mix of deputies, civilians, and military veterans step into line behind them. Though they all looked ready to handle whatever was necessary, he swallowed the fear that they were going into a hostile building without any tactical training as a team.

With a dry swallow, he jerked his head toward the door. Perry Hale put his left hand on Ethan's shoulder and pulled him back. "You're Number Two."

Yolanda squeezed in between them. "Nope. You're three."

Deputy Malone opened his mouth and Ethan shook his head. "*I'm* Three. Fall in." Malone put his hand on Ethan's shoulder and he knew the others were doing the same up and down the line.

With Perry Hale leading, they entered the dark building.

Chapter 103

In addition to carrying snow, the north wind brought the odor of wood smoke from the burning house back in town. I shifted gears to a slow jog when the guy I'd been following appeared in the whiteout.

My heart skipped a beat at the sight of him just standing there with his back to me, staring at the passenger train. I thanked God he couldn't get on board and slid to a stop, bringing the MP5 to my shoulder. My ongoing frustration mounted when I found the red dot wouldn't penetrate the falling snow.

The Old Man's voice spoke in my ear. *You can buy a cheap drill to bore one hole, but a smart man'll spend the money to buy a good one that'll last a lifetime and drill many holes.*

Inferior weapon, inferior sight. To top it off, there were no iron sights. I had one option and that was to point it and hope for the best.

The trailing locomotive thundered by and I barely heard my own voice. "Put your hands up! Your hands! Show me your hands!"

He kinda sorta did by extending both arms out to his sides. I couldn't tell if he was surrendering or wanting me to walk up closer.

You talking to Allah right here at the end, before you take us both out?

"I said show me your hands!"

He tightened up and pivoted just enough to put his backpack between us. I suspected one of those little canisters I'd seen in the courthouse was in there and he was planning something ungodly with it. His hands were still extended as I angled for a better position, but he swiveled like a kid playing a game.

He turned his head in my direction and I got a look at him. It didn't seem right that a terrorist wore horn-rimmed glasses. He looked more like a storekeeper than a bad guy. "Get on the ground! Get on the ground!"

He reached his right hand to the pack's shoulder strap to slip it off. The way his left arm bent brought back the conversation with Arturo that morning about left-handers.

I dropped to one knee half a second before the guy twisted sideways like an eighteenth-century dualist and opened up with a pistol in his left hand. A bullet cracked past, and I cranked off a three-round burst.

I couldn't chance staying upright. Hitting the ground gave him what he wanted. He made a break for it, running fast and low toward the train. Through the veil of snow, I caught a glimpse of him crabbing underneath a car and out the other side.

Chapter 104

The wind brought a faint shout to DeVaca. Someone had trailed him through the snow after all. He heard his mother's voice as he turned to keep the backpack between them, and a corner of his mouth rose as he lifted his right hand toward the shoulder strap.

"Don't ever let anyone know that you are mano izquierda. *Learn to use your right as well as your left. Our people feel that it is* muy malo.*"*

"But I am not a bad boy."

"Then use your right and be mama's good boy."

DeVaca drew a pistol with his left and whirled. The snow that collected on his frosted glasses obstructed his view, preventing him from acquiring both the target and his sights. The Glock bucked in his palm again and again, but the man with the hat wasn't there. He'd dropped to one knee.

DeVaca angled his head to see through a less-obstructed section of one lens, adjusted his aim, and fired again at the flashes coming from the snow-covered ground. A bee stung the little finger on his gun hand and he dropped the weapon. Only when he snatched it up did he see a red splash on the snow and realize his little finger was gone, despite the Demon's voice in his head that said Wicked couldn't be hurt.

Shocked that he was wounded, he fled. The train whistle shrieked and the couplings tightened as the unseen locomotive started forward. DeVaca crawled under one of the cars and paused, fascinated by the sight of blood. He resisted the urge to lick the stub like a dog, forcing himself to concentrate on finding a safe place on the train that was groaning forward at a snail's pace.

Getting more than a hundred rail cars full of coal up to speed was a slow process. He considered running in the direction the train was heading to catch the locomotive before it picked up enough speed to move away. It was manned by the conductor and engineer. It would be easy to kill them and ride in comfort until the train reached its next stop.

The train, however, stretched in both directions, disappearing in a swirl of white, and he had no idea how far away the engine might be. He trotted alongside until he realized the futility of looking at the exact same kind of hopper cars. Each was draped in ribbons of snow caught against the vertical supports.

He dismissed the possibility of trying to survive the trip under either the sloping front or rear overhang of the cars that funneled the coal downward to the dump doors. It offered a shelter of sorts, but the tracks ran east and west. The north wind sucked underneath the cars and piled snow against everything that jutted out. Staying there would be suicide by freezing to death.

A burst of fire slapped the steel wheels on the opposite side. Several rounds clipped the rails and more than a few buzzed past DeVaca's legs. With the realization that he could actually be wounded or killed, he decided he had to escape the incoming fire and gain some distance between himself and his pursuer.

An icy metal ladder offered the opportunity to swing aboard. He scrambled upward with the intention of riding for a short distance away from his pursuer. It would also give him the opportunity to clear the snow collecting on his glasses.

Though the stub of his finger ached, he ignored the pain and climbed higher, intending to roll onto the load of coal with the new idea of jumping from car to car until he reached the engine.

He peeked over the top to survey a scene as barren as a sand dune, with just as many opportunities for shelter. The wind cut across the drifted surface with gale force. No one could stay up there for any length of time and survive.

He considered his options at the same time his well-tuned sixth sense kicked in telling him someone was behind him. The Demon cried in frustration as DeVaca twisted toward the following car, at the same time bringing the little Scorpion level with his wounded hand. He held the trigger down, sweeping it in a semicircle.

The berm in front of DeVaca's pursuer spurted black dust. The man squeezed off his own burst. The mounded snow beyond the terrorist erupted into gouts of black scars as bullets whizzed past his head. One struck DeVaca with the impact of a sledgehammer, almost knocking him off the ladder. He grunted, and fired again, stitching the snow around the man who fell back, disappearing from view.

The pain was incredible, and DeVaca knew he couldn't hang on any longer. He descended as quickly as he could and stepped off the moving train, slipping and falling hard on the rock ballast. The canister in his backpack took most of the fall and ribs cracked on his wounded side with a breathtaking lance of pain.

Gasping for breath, he scuttled away from the dangerous wheels and groaned into the deep snow he hated so much. He raised the Scorpion toward the following car and realized the red dot wouldn't work through billions of falling flakes. He pointed the muzzle upward and emptied the magazine anyway.

The man who no longer thought of himself as Wicked rose and did the unexpected. He lumbered alongside the train in the direction of travel, hoping for one more chance at the stubborn Texan who wouldn't leave well enough alone. Teeth clenched in pain, DeVaca watched the cars and offered the Demon anything he wanted as long as he could get one last shot at the guy.

The Demon laughed, screamed in rage, and urged him on.

Chapter 105

A newscaster on the flat-panel television frowned at her audience. "Information from a trusted source tells this station that despite earlier reports of his death, Congressman Don Bright is alive and well, at the same time calls and texts from the West Texas town of Ballard bring us news that a highly trained team, most likely Delta, has ended the hostage takeover in the courthouse.

"The congressman's daughter was one of those held by what we've learned were Pakistani and Iranian terrorists. This connection between the two is coming to light as reports of shots fired in the congressman's office earlier in the day seem to have some significance. Again, the terrorist attack in Ballard, Texas, is over."

Chavez's voice rose as his fingers flew over the keyboard. "What's happening? Wicked! Report! Report! Report!"

His radio remained silent.

Lucille finished her wine and slipped into the bedroom to collect her purse and the pink vintage Samsonite overnight bag she called her train case. A little vacation from Chavez and his plans was just the ticket.

Florida.

No, Hawaii.

When she returned, Chavez was muttering to himself and washing his hands in the downstairs bathroom. She settled onto the bar stool and opened a new window on his laptop. Logging in, she accessed Chavez's offshore account and typed in a complicated series of numbers and letters. At the prompt, she keyed in more numbers and symbols she'd copied months before.

His voice came down the hall over the sound of running water. "Those damned people in Ballard didn't surrender. They didn't panic. They didn't run. They fought back. How could they, how could this generation rise up?"

Lucille spoke to the empty room. "Honey, it probably wasn't *this* generation that just whipped your ass." She ignored his repetition as the authorization went through, clearing Chavez's secret account of the ransom money and then some, and transferring the easiest fifteen million she'd ever made into her own account in the Cayman Islands. Lucille spun the computer back around, aligning the corners with certain irregularities in the granite just as he did every time he used it.

She walked straight to the front door and left without a word.

Chavez returned and picked up the remote control to flick from one news station to another.

"New information now tells us that the takeover in the Ballard courthouse has ended . . ."

Click.

". . . just got word that the terrorists are dead . . .

Click.

". . . breaking news. The standoff between terrorists

and local authorities in Ballard is over. It is an historic moment in U.S. history, showing the true American spirit and Texans' willingness to . . ."

Click.

". . . Congressman Don Bright has been instrumental in bringing the Ballard siege to a halt and telling NBC news that he will work harder to ensure that our southern border is secure . . ."

Chapter 106

I didn't charge forward after our duel beside the tracks because I was afraid he was laying for me. The train was moving steady by the time I decided he was gone. I fired a burst in his direction, to be sure he stayed down, and crept to where I'd seen him last. The snow was stained red. I'd hit him somewhere, and that made me feel a helluva lot better, but any hunter knows that wounded game can be dangerous.

His footprints stopped at the tracks. I could see he'd crawled under, and knew without a shadow of a doubt he'd caught one of the cars. The train moved at a fast walk. I swung aboard and shinnied up the icy rungs to peek over the rim. The load mounded higher than I expected, but from my vantage point it looked like they were hauling snow instead of coal.

Everything in sight was trackless. The soughing wind cut like a knife. I crawled onto the snow-covered load at the same instant a dim shadow popped up at the rear of the car ahead. The falling flakes softened his shape.

I figured he'd be a lot farther ahead, but I guess his wound slowed him down. I rose to my knees, snugged the German machine pistol to my shoulder, and that's when everything went to hell.

The guy must've had eyes in the back of his head. He spun, sweeping a burst of lead toward me. I thought the MP5 I had was fast, but that machine in his hands threw a swarm of rounds in my direction before I could blink. The mound of coal between us absorbed most of them.

Any other time I could have made the shot, but without a sight, it was damn near impossible to hit the indistinct target in an icy cloud. I showered down on him, but I was fast becoming hypothermic and not thinking clearly. I had no reason to believe I hit a thing but the train and air.

He dropped out of sight between the cars.

I stayed down for a good long minute, then swung my legs over the edge. My boots slipped on the ladder's icy rungs. I strained to catch myself with nearly frozen hands that didn't react as quick as I wanted. My chin cracked on the top rung. I bit my tongue and tasted blood.

Automatic fire ripped the quiet to shreds, and rounds rang off the steel car. For the second time that day, my feet pedaled like a cartoon character to gain some traction.

Goddammit!

I got a better grip and hung there like a monkey until the wave of pain passed.

The guy was maddening! He was pacing the train, hunting *me*, instead of running like the wounded striped-ass baboon I thought he was. I grabbed the pistol grip of my own piece-of-crap machine gun and pointed it down under my left arm at where I figured he'd pop out again between the cars.

My left hand was freezing on the metal rung, but I hung tight. There was nothing but thick blowing snow between the ground and me. I was just about to give up and turn loose to drop off the opposite side when he popped up farther out than I expected. I pressed the trigger to squeeze out six fast shots.

He rolled once and regained his feet to shoot *again*! The rounds missed and whanged the steel close enough for fragments of metal to sting my face.

I become my old man when I get angry, and let me tell you, when he got mad, us boys always hunted a hole. "By God, that is *enough*!"

I was out of patience and time, because I didn't want to ride that coal car all the way to El Paso. Spitting blood, I turned loose and hit the ground with the moving train between us, surprised at how fast we were going.

My feet went out from under me like the first time I stood up on roller skates. I hit like a rag doll, plowing a deep furrow in the snow. My head slammed hard enough on the frozen ground to see stars *again*.

Somebody wearing my coat yelled, and I was pretty sure it was me, but I couldn't just lay there thinking about how I'd bitten my tongue *again*, or that my back was on fire, *again*.

I dropped the mag, reloaded, and tucked the MP5's collapsible stock against my shoulder like I'd practiced it every day of my life. When I stuck my numb index finger alongside the snow-covered trigger guard, I remembered I had gloves in my pocket.

Chapter 107

Dressed in HAZMAT gear from head to toe and equipped with SCBA breathing apparatus from the volunteer fire department, Sheriff Ethan Armstrong's volunteers met in the destroyed rotunda. The smoke billowing from the floor, the bloody bodies, body parts, dusty canisters, boxes and crates, weapons, scattered equipment, and shell casings all served to illustrate an image of war.

Ethan settled the wide straps on his shoulders and surveyed the wreckage through the full-face mask, surrounded by a forest of weapons aimed at the silent upper floors. "My God."

He edged close and peered into the hole chainsawed in the oak floors. Thick smoke boiled up, slipping through the building and out the south entrance.

"Here's what I want to do. Frank, take and put some guys here to keep an eye on the upper floors while we clear those offices on the southern entrance. Herman, I guess it won't do no good to tell you and the Mayos to leave and take Gabe with you."

They'd arrived and put on SCBA gear after Ethan pulled them from the destroyed south entrance. "Nope."

"All right. Just hold what we have here. When we come back, we're going up. Masks tight, boys."

They froze at the sound of a soft cough coming from the smoky southern hallway. As if choreographed, the deputies and experienced tactical veterans kept their rifles pointed upward. The Mayo brothers, Herman, and Gabe reacted, covering the direction of the cough. Ethan slapped Perry Hale on the shoulder. "Perry, on me."

The other veterans and lawmen in his team lined up and stepped into the smoke.

Chapter 108

I'd freeze to death if I stayed where I was, and I hoped and prayed that's exactly what would happen to that sonofabitch I was chasing. Close to hypothermia, I'd traveled way too far from the feed mill to walk back in a storm that didn't show any signs of slacking off.

I needed to get somewhere warm and safe, fast. I had one remaining option, and that was watch for the rear-facing locomotive on the end and the shelter it would provide from the storm, if I could get inside the crew's cabin.

The train was moving at a pretty good clip and that worried me. There was a good chance I'd slip on the slick rungs, and at that speed a slip could prove fatal.

It's funny how your mind works. While I waited, I remembered a conversation I overheard up at the little wooden community store in northeast Texas. I hung around there a lot before we moved to Ballard, listening to the old men talk. One day the conversation drifted around to hobos and trains. A retired railroad engineer said that you never grab the ladder on the back end of a passing car, because if you miss, it'll sling you around and under the wheels of the next one.

I heard him as clear as a bell in my mind. He spat a stream of tobacco juice and nodded as if explain some mystery of life. "Miss the leading end of a car, you'll fall, but at least you'll have the distance between the front and back wheels to roll out of the way."

The coal train had picked up considerable speed by the time the rear of the bright yellow Union Pacific locomotive loomed like a giant ship. Finally wearing the gloves that were in my pocket, I grabbed the handrail on the approaching end and used the momentum to swing aboard the metal steps, praying that old man was right.

Chapter 109

The man in the hat was faster than DeVaca expected. He twisted and fired at the same instant DeVaca tripped over something buried in the snow and landed hard. A hot lance of pain almost made him pass out. He swept the muzzle of his weapon toward the coal car and held the trigger down until the magazine ran empty. Frightened that he might miss his final chance, he cursed at the shooting pain in his chest and side.

A voice that didn't belong to his Demon kept demanding information. His head cleared enough to realize Chavez had no idea their once-successful terrorist attack was over. He'd had it with the obsessive little bastard. DeVaca ripped the earpiece away and flung it into a thicket of snow-covered prickly pear.

The world was blurry when he regained his feet. His glasses were lost under the snow somewhere in the vast, high desert. Shot, broken, in shock, and bordering on hypothermia, DeVaca grasped at thoughts that were fuzzy and disjointed. His breath was hot in his chest and throat despite the Arctic air.

The ever-present rumbling train was still there, appearing out of the swirling snow before fading from sight in a cloud of gauze. Despite the crushing pain, he broke into a trot and came within arm's reach of the passing cars. The gravel underneath the snow played hell with his footing. Stumbling alongside, he struggled to focus on any handhold he could find.

A ladder passed and he made a lunge for it. His fingers slipped off the icy metal, and he grabbed again. The hand missing a finger was numb and didn't cooperate when he seized another frozen ladder on the rear of a passing car.

The speed was too much. DeVaca's feet flew off the ground. Flailing for balance, he hit and rolled. The Scorpion slammed into his face, breaking his nose and cutting a long slash in his forehead.

He cursed at a sharp pain in his right hand. He came back to his feet in a desperate run in the direction of the train's travel. Snow crystals sprayed his face. Wheels clacked. He ran harder to match the train's speed, determined to survive.

Throwing a frantic glance over his shoulder, DeVaca saw his last chance was the oncoming engine. A handrail and short stairway appeared. He lunged forward and missed. One more chance, and that was the steps on the nose of the rear-facing locomotive. He made a frantic grab and caught it with his left. The other refused to cooperate. With superhuman strength born of desperation, DeVaca jumped and pulled himself up with one arm until his feet found the icy rungs that were as easy to climb as stairs.

He reached for the other handrail and the stunned terrorist found his right hand was no longer attached to the wrist. His mind reeled as he gaped at the horrendous wound.

Chapter 110

I was surprised that swinging aboard was that easy. But there I was, climbing the engine's icy steel steps. Despite another jolt of sharp pain in my damaged back, I whooped with joy, something I'd never done in my life. I was on the back end of the lifesaving locomotive that was moving in reverse. My muscles twitched and jerked from the effort and tension and I crouched on the landing until I could catch my breath and calm down.

In pretty good shape for the shape I was in, I rose and picked my way down the snow- and ice-covered steel walkway to the door at the locomotive's nose. When I got there, disturbed snow and bright splashes of blood on the walkway proved my friend had been just as successful.

I was so mad I could spit nails. I had no choice but to root him out.

Chapter 111

DeVaca had no idea how he lost the hand.

He staggered around the nose of the engine. Blood stained the pure white snow. He wiped blood away from one eye and blinked it clear as he reached the steel door. Without hesitation, he turned the handle and found it unlocked. Unfamiliar with trains, he didn't know if an engineer rode in the rear-facing locomotive. Unable to easily change magazines in the Scorpion with only one hand, he fumbled the pistol free with his damaged left hand and entered the dim interior.

The were no lights in the cab, but enough of a diffused glow revealed the elevated seats behind the control panel five feet above the entrance were empty. He was alone. He had to attend to the bleeding stump as fast as possible. The first door on the right opened into a disagreeable bathroom. He hit the light switch with his elbow, sending another howl of pain through his arm.

A stack of dingy hand towels on a shelf was what he needed. Wrapping one around the end of his stump, DeVaca used his belt both as a tourniquet and to secure the makeshift compression bandage in place. He dropped to the floor beside the metal toilet. Blowing bloody snot from his nose, he leaned back against the tiny room's steel wall. The Demon fell silent, giving him peace for the first time in hours.

The pain from his grievous injuries was mind numbing. As his remaining hand warmed, the raw wound of his missing finger sent electric bursts of fire to his elbow. At the same time, the stump of his amputated hand fired white-hot flames of agony up his other arm.

Desperate for relief, DeVaca lowered one shoulder to slip the backpack off. He dug in an outside pocket until his remaining fingers closed on a bottle of painkillers. Thumbing the lid off, he shook half a dozen into his mouth and dry-swallowed them. He closed his eyes as the train rushed through the high West Texas desert. The pills hadn't yet taken effect when Demon awoke and squirmed, giving him an idea.

At least he could take out a few more people if they boarded. Using two fingers, he unzipped the pack and rolled the steel canister of nerve agent onto the floor.

He cast the pack aside and heard the exterior door creak.

DeVaca snatched the pistol from the floor and waited.

It was't long before the steel bathroom door cracked open.

Blood again filled one eye, but the other worked well enough to see where to aim. He fired twice at the crack and the door slammed shut. The train rocked along for several seconds before the door cracked open again and slammed before he could shoot again.

In the sudden quiet, a dark object rattled to a stop on the grimy floor between his legs. A hammer-blow concussion and bright explosion short-circuited all of DeVaca's senses and silenced the Demon forever.

Chapter 112

The SCBA's facemask was aggravating, but Ethan soon got used to it. He led the way down the hall past the rotunda and into the first opening on his right, which he remembered was the elevator.

The door was open.

He stopped, swung his rifle's muzzle toward the interior, and saw a female body slumped sideways in a chair. He reached in and tilted her chin upward. Blood matted her hair on one side where a bullet ripped a long furrow, exposing her white skull underneath.

He recognized Katie Bright, and his heart sank. The phone vibrated in his pocket. Without thinking, he put his hand over her chest and was shocked to feel a strong heartbeat.

Then she coughed again.

His phone vibrated again with a message alert.

Ethan spoke over his shoulder. "Got a live hostage here! Katie Bright, but she's hurt bad."

The hard, flat report of a gunshot rang out behind him, then others joined in, banging fast and loud.

Ethan whirled around. "Who's shooting?"

Herman's voice came back through the smoke. "Y'all keep an eye on that hole. Damn bad guy in a gas mask popped up like a jack-in-the-box. Gabe there was watching and put him down. I bet no more come up. He didn't look like he felt good anyway."

While Ethan's team kept their rifles ready, Perry Hale and Deputy Frank Malone rushed the unconscious form of Katie Bright past the smoking hole and out of the building's north entrance. Yolanda Rodriguez followed, watching for other dangers, covering for them as if she and Perry Hale had been a team for years.

Ethan watched them leave. "Y'all keep men posted here. The fire and smoke took the rest of them out, I 'magine, but there's no tellin'. Good shootin', Gabe."

Herman slapped his friend on the back as Gabe grinned. He'd done something about one of the men who'd kidnapped his daughter. "Damn yeah."

"Boy, you have *got* to learn how to cuss."

Chapter 113

The terrorist was inside the locomotive. Streaks of blood froze on the deck, and a smear showed where he'd opened the door.

Railroad employees could be in there with him. No matter. I had to do something because I couldn't stay outside.

Tensing for the bullet that would miss the ballistic vest and tear through my shirt, I squirted through the door, the .45 in my hand. A wave of delicious warm air smelling of diesel, oil, and grease wrapped around me as I swept the dark interior.

A set of steep metal steps led up to the empty driver and engineer seats. A groan from behind a door on my right caught my attention.

Nothing moved in the cabin, so I slipped the cell phone from my pack pocket and punched it alive. The glow illuminated fresh blood on the floor, the wall, and the door handles.

A clatter behind a metal door told me where the terrorist was hiding. Heart once again pounding like a jackhammer, I knelt and slowly cracked the door to peek inside. It was surprisingly light in what I realized was a tiny bathroom. He was alone, lying on his back with a pistol aimed at where my head should have been. The guy opened up on me. At least one round missed me by a hair and whanged off a steel wall behind me. I slammed the door.

"Sonofabitch!" I remembered a little gift from the previous owner of my ballistic vest. I slipped the flashbang out of the pocket. The primary ring was already gone. I pulled the secondary pin, pushed down hard on the lever to crack the door.

Pitching the flashbang inside, I slammed it back before he could shoot again. The explosion inside the steel box made my already damaged ears ring again.

The compressed detonation must have been enormous. I yanked the door open, feeling a quick gust of air sucking into the room. The terrorist sprawled on the floor beside a stained toilet. Despite the confined explosion in a four-by-four room, what was left of the guy *still* wasn't dead.

He lay propped against the peeling wall, bloody bubbles popping on his lips. The flashbang must have landed right between his legs, because the insides of both thighs were cored out and blackened. His eyes and ears were bleeding, and he juked for breath. One hand was gone, the stump covered by a dingy towel. The other was whittled down to four fingers.

Even with all that, he had the muzzle of a Glock against a canister of gas and was trying to pull the trigger with what was left of his hand.

I followed my own advice and used enough gun, double-tapping the aggravatin' son-of-a-bitch with the big .45. The hollow-points shelled out his skull, blowing brain matter all over the wall behind him.

The thing was over.

I latched the door and climbed the steps to one of the cracked leather seats on the platform above. The weak glow from the instrument panel was all I had to see by. A bottle of water vibrated in a holder attached to what looked to me like a dashboard. I cracked the seal and drained the whole thing in three long gulps. Feeling a little better, I took out my cell phone and it woke up to show one bar.

2% Power
Dismiss?

I typed one final message.

On train w drt bad gy. El P

I hit send even though the message was somewhat mangled. They'd figure out what train and where it was going by the shortened El Paso, and law-enforcement personnel across the state knew that DRT was short for "dead right there." The blue bar shot across the top, and my phone died.

The train plowed through the gloom as snow swirled outside the thick window and the receding tracks disappeared into the gloom. At least Kelly wouldn't be putting crepe on the door at our house, but it had been close.

The longer I sat there, the tireder I got. My eyes grew heavy.

I slapped my stained and dented hat on the dash and settled back in the seat. My adrenaline dump spent, I twitched a couple of times and drifted into a deep sleep as the locomotive traveled backward through the frozen desert.

Chapter 114

"My God." No stranger to violence, Herman Hawke stopped at the top of the second-floor landing.

Ethan, Perry Hale, and the rest of the impromptu SWAT team looked around in awe. The devastation on the ground floor was stunning, but the destruction on the second level recounted the story of a desperate fire-fight. Spent shell casings littered the floor along with empty magazines. The paneled walls were splintered and full of bullet holes.

Perry Hale whistled. "Mr. Terrill said that him and Hawke held them from here 'til we blew the south end."

Yolanda covered her end of the floor, never taking the AR from her shoulder. "This is unbelievable."

"This whole day is unbelievable."

Herman swallowed. "It don't do to piss my boy off."

Bodies sprawled beyond the landing, and another leaned against the railings. Herman made sure they were out of action and glanced downward. Keeping an eye on the next level above, his energy drained as if someone had pulled the plug on a bathtub.

He lowered his rifle and squeezed Gabe's arm. "You know, if it's all the same to y'all, I'd just as soon stay right here. I don't need to see no more." He made his slow way down the stairs.

Sheriff Ethan Armstrong took a breather two hours later at the Posada's command post and checked his messages. The building was cleared and the living were safe. With one arm around his daughter, Gillian, he thumbed the screen to find Sonny's texts.

A train whistle sounded at the same time Ethan reached for a landline and called El Paso.

Two hours later, a heavily armed SWAT team raced off an Amtrak passenger train at the Ballard depot to find they were late to the dance.

Chapter 115

I woke up when the train slowed, then stopped. The clouds were still heavy and dark, but we'd traveled out of the storm. I glanced out the window when we came to a stop to see an army of law-enforcement officers and Border Patrol agents waiting on both sides of the track.

Ethan had gotten my last message.

I took off my coat, pinned the badge back on my shirt so it would show, slid the window open, and stuck both hands outside toward the nearest hard-eyed officer dressed in combat gear. "Good to see you, boys."

His rifle snapped to his shoulder and the men around him followed suit. They reacted as if I were aiming a pistol. "Don't move! Don't move!"

Footsteps thundered up the outside steps and the door slammed open. The cab filled with shouting, combat-ready young men aiming automatic weapons. "Don't move! Don't move! Hands! Hands! Hands!"

I remained still and gave them a grin. "Wouldn't think of it. Name's Sonny Hawke. Texas Ranger."

ACKNOWLEDGMENTS

Though I've been writing novels for the past five years, this first Sonny Hawke adventure came about due to a chance meeting with bestselling author John Gilstrap, who has become a great friend and mentor. Without John's friendship, guidance, and wisdom, Sonny Hawke would never have been born, and my writing career wouldn't be where it is today. He also provided the answer to the mystery in the basement. Thank you, my good friend.

I'd also like to thank the good people of Marfa, Texas, who will realize their town and wonderful courthouse are the foundation for my fictional Ballard.

Sincere thanks go to my college buddy Captain Landon McDowell, UP Railroad (Ret.), who provided valuable advice on trains, railroads, and schedules.

Chief Channel 5 meteorologist in Dallas, David Finfrock, opened his home to me while a thunderstorm raged outside and we pored over Texas and North American maps to create the super-snowstorm that covers the town of Ballard in this volume.

Dr. Curtis Culwell helped create the character Congressman Don Bright and his committee charged with border security. You're right, Cap'n: Life's one big adventure!

I always appreciate my sister-in-law Sharon Reynolds, Mike Miller, Buddy Minett, Steve Brigman, and my best friend of forty years, Steve Knagg. All caught issues and offered excellent suggestions.

Ranger Brad Oliver, Company B, took time from his busy schedule to answer dozens of questions about modern Texas Rangers. Thank you, sir, for your service.

Jorge Rodriguez, *muchas gracias* for the *mal de ojo* and *mano izquierda* twist!

Thanks to Jeffery Deaver, C. J. Box, Craig Johnson, Sandra Brannan, Hank Philippi Ryan, T. Jefferson Parker, Jamie Freveletti, Marc Cameron, and especially my East Texas buddy Joe Lansdale for your support and advice. You guys are great!

Thanks to my family, daughter Chelsea Hamilton and her husband Jason, daughter Megan Bidelman for the conversations and suggestions about plot.

My outstanding agent Anne Hawkins believed in me the first time she read one of my earlier novels and never gave up as I struggled to reach this point in my career. Thanks, Miss Anne!

I sincerely appreciate Kensington Executive Editor Michaela Hamilton for bringing me into the Kensington family and taking a chance on this series. Your enthusiasm is infectious and boundless.

None of this would have happened if the love of my life, my wife Shana, didn't believe in me. She even offered many years ago to support the family so I could quit my full-time job and write. Sure glad we didn't do that, babe. As she always says, things happen in their own time and when they're supposed to.

And to you readers who've followed my magazine and newspaper columns for years, or those who made the Red River series a success, and everyone new to my work, as we say in East Texas, much obliged!

Don't miss the next exciting Sonny Hawke thriller

by Reavis Z. Wortham . . .

HAWKE'S WAR

Coming soon from Kensington Publishing Corp.

Keep reading to enjoy a sample excerpt . . .

Chapter 1

Thunderheads boiled over the peaks of the high-desert county in Big Bend National Park as four hikers stretched out along the winding Chisos Spring Trail. The experienced thirty-somethings filled the dry, cool morning air with comments and good-natured ribbing.

Trailing last as usual in the group's fifteen-year relationship, Harmony Cartwright stopped to tighten the faded Texas state flag bandana she used to keep her blond hair under control. She adjusted the pack straps on her shoulders and seeing that she wasn't falling too far behind, bent to pick up a 520-million-year-old-stone from the trail.

She scratched away a few grains of sand with a chewed, unpainted thumbnail and angled it toward the sun. After a short examination, Harmony blessed it with a quick smile and tucked the rock into the pocket of her cargo shorts, where it clacked against half a dozen similar stones. The others maintained a steady pace and she hurried to catch up with her husband, Blue. He trailed behind Chloe Hutchins, who followed *her* husband and the troop's leader Vince.

The veteran Marine stopped to take a long, deep sip of water from his bright yellow Camelbak pack. Solid as the hardpan under their feet, Vince had been an adventurer all his life. He came home from the Marine Corps after two tours in Afghanistan and settled down to sell real estate, but the months of inactivity were almost too much. He'd been looking forward to leading their foursome into the remote Big Bend backcountry for a little adventure.

He swiveled to see Chloe hoofing along at the same pace that was as quick as her wit. "Hey, Spousal Unit, how about you walk point? That way I can watch your transmission twitch."

Chloe gave Vince a wink and pinched the blue nylon shirt from her damp skin, pumping it like a bellows. Both wore wide-brimmed straw hats they'd purchased from the general store in Terlingua. "You wouldn't be able to concentrate then, Sergeant Hutchins. You'd probably trip on something and break a leg, and none of us can carry you out of here, so mind your business."

Blue caught up with the cheerful couple and tilted his Tilley hat upward. Built like a fireplug, he wore khaki shorts that revealed thick legs built for walking. "Y'all drinking enough water? This dry air's suckin' it out as fast as I can pour it in."

Chloe rolled her eyes in fun. "Not as much as Big Guy here, but he's working harder than I am."

"I'm still fresh enough out of the Sandbox to think this is chilly." Vince frowned in mock anger. "You're right though, make sure you drink enough, Little Bit."

"You should be sweating out all that beer y'all

poured down last night." Chloe poked him in his stomach with a finger.

He raised an eyebrow at the petite brown-haired woman who weighed less than a hundred pounds. "Twelve little ol' cans ain't that much, besides, I run a bigger machine, so I can handle it."

Blue watched the clouds in the distance. "I wish I had one of those yellow-bellies right now."

The quartet had formed in college, and Blue was used to the same good-natured sparring matches he'd been hearing in the years since. He stopped a few feet away. "Couldn't you guys find somewhere in the shade to stop?"

Vince spread both hands at the yucca, prickly pear, honey mesquite, and creosote bushes scattered around them. "We're a little short on trees around here."

Blue scanned the sun-blasted high-desert landscape. The only sign of active life was a buzzard floating on the thermals high overhead. "Yeah, which is why we should be hiking in Colorado, where there's trees, instead of this godforsaken desert." He kicked a rock the size of a softball. "I get to pick next year, and it's gonna be a hike in Hawaii . . . from the condo to the beach."

Harmony caught up with them and tugged a bottle of water from her pack. "This is beautiful! I love all this space! Look." She knelt to pick up a twisted piece of mesquite. "This will look good in a flower arrangement." She brightened. "You know, I'm gonna use it to make one for Kelly Hawke. I tried to get them to come with us, but she said Sonny couldn't get loose this week."

"Honey, that'll just add weight to your pack." Blue

watched the love of his life tuck the wood into a side pocket. "I've already seen you put three pounds of rocks in your pocket, and besides, it's *illegal* to take anything from a national park."

Harmony winked at Chloe. "They have plenty of rocks around here. I doubt they'll miss a handful."

Chloe tore open a packet of powdered electrolytes and was pouring the contents into her high-tech water bottle when Vince grunted, staggered, and folded in half. The sharp whip-crack report of a rifle shot reached them half a second later. Shocked, her hand moved and the remainder of the powder drifted on the slight breeze in an orange cloud.

Unable to grasp what was happening, Chloe sat the bottle on the ground and knelt beside her husband as he dropped to one knee. "Vince. Vince?"

The look in his eyes from under his hat brim was one of pain and confusion. "Oh hell. I've been shot."

Blue's head whipped toward the ridge high above. "Some idiot isn't paying attention to where he's shooting! Y'all, get . . ."

A second shot hit Vince above his left ear. The soft-nosed round expanded, blowing out the side of his head. His gore-splattered hat flipped off to land in a clump of skeletonweed. The man who'd survived two tours of duty in Afghanistan dropped without a sound onto the American soil he'd sworn to protect.

Recovering faster than he would have ever imagined, Blue slammed Harmony onto the dry trail in a full-body tackle. They hit the hard ground at the same instant a third round punched through Blue's pack. Digging in with his hiking boots, he yanked his wife against the rising terrace of the rocky canyon wall. "Chloe! Get down!! Get over here with us."

She grabbed the straps on Vince's pack to drag him out of the line of fire coming from above. His dead weight and the heavy pack proved too much for her slight frame. She grunted, and jerked back on her heels. Vince's body moved an inch.

The shooter's next round plucked at the top of her shoulder. The material fluttered and blood wet the nylon. Chloe lost her grip and fell, catching herself with one hand.

Blue and Harmony squeezed against the shoulder-high rise between them and the shooter on the ridge. Keeping one eye on Chloe's struggle with her husband's body, Blue slipped out of his backpack and dug into its contents. "Get under cover!"

Harmony crouched low, her shoulder against the bank of rocks, dirt, and scrub. "What are you doing?"

"That's no accident. Somebody's shooting at us on purpose!" Elbow deep in the pack's contents, Blue fished around and pulled out a Glock 19. He would have left the heavy weapon home had they not planned on camping overnight in the backcountry.

Vince had a pistol tucked under his shirt, but neither expected a sniper attack in the middle of a national park. The conversation the night before centered on their concern over illegal aliens who often crossed into the U.S. from Mexico. Though most came looking for a better life, there were always a few with bad intentions.

The guy above seemed to be something completely different. Blue jerked the slide back to chamber a round.

* * *

Feeling a little better now that he could shoot back, Blue took several deep breaths to settle his nerves. Another chunk of lead slapped into a rock near Chloe and whirred away with a low, vibrating buzz.

Assuming the shooter was using a bolt-action rifle for accuracy, Blue figured it would take a few seconds for the sniper to rack the bolt and reacquire a new target. He peeked through a scrubby honey mesquite and squinted upward to locate the shooter. The ground exploded inches away, spraying the side of his face with sand and pebbles.

"*Shit!*" Skin hot and stinging, Blue fell hard onto the trail and gasped when he realized he was fully exposed. A round punched through his left shoulder and his arm went numb.

Grunting, he flipped onto his good shoulder and squirmed back to the sheltering rise, far enough away from Harmony to draw the fire and keep her safe. She screamed at the sight of blood welling from his wound. "Stay there!" He held out the hand with the Glock, muzzle toward the sky. "No! I said stay down!"

Mere yards away, Chloe gave up on pulling Vince out of the line of fire. She sat against the rocks. Blood soaked the front of her shirt, but the shocked woman's soft voice floated over the bare ground with the inflection of a worried child. "Blue, Vince's been shot!"

"So have I!" He groaned and used his feet to push away and gain more distance from the women. "Stay down!"

Another round hit Vince in the chest. His shirt fluttered from the impact, but he was already beyond hurting or responding. Chloe shrieked, palms against the sides of her head. "They shot him again!"

Blue reached the rise's downward slope that tapered to a dangerously low level, ending his cover. He wondered why the sniper was shooting at the motionless body. Then the realization struck him. "Stay down, Chloe! They're trying to draw you out! Harmony, don't move, baby!"

"Why are they *shooting* at us?"

Blue ignored Chloe's question that didn't need an answer. It didn't matter why they were under fire. Someone was trying to kill them, and that was the hard, simple truth.

The numbness of the shot was already wearing off. His arm hung limp and useless. He'd never felt such pain before and was swimmy-headed. Afraid he'd pass out, he ground his teeth to keep from puking and focused on a piece of quartz to get hold of himself.

Harmony stripped the pack from her shoulders and crawled toward Chloe at the same time Blue rose just enough to peek through a cluster of honey mesquite. Movement from above caught his eye and he saw the upper half of a man's body.

"There you are." Drawing on hours on the shooting range back home in Dallas, he aimed and adjusted for the elevation. He cranked off six fast shots from the fifteen-round magazine, thinking the sounds of the empty brass tinkling off the rocks was odd in such an intense situation.

The rounds fell short, most of them impacting rocky soil with ineffective explosions. Still, the man's hands flew into the air and a rifle flipped end over end.

"Got you, you son-of-a-bitch!" Blue started to rise, but the shots drew a stunning fusillade from above.

The world erupted in noise as fully automatic weapons hosed the area below the ridge.

The geysers of dirt and rock exploding around Blue looked like hailstones falling onto still water. Rounds shredded the leaves off his covering brush and punched through to find flesh. He went down hard.

Harmony screamed over the rolling man-made thunder. Reversing her direction, she belly-crawled as fast as possible toward her husband.

Startled by the sudden continuous gunfire, Chloe became the next target as she straightened into view. The rifle spoke again. Chloe's hair flew from the round's impact. Dead before she landed, she fell across Vince's legs and stilled.

Harmony's tan shirt and shorts blended well with the landscape. She kept her head low, grabbed a handful of Blue's shirt, and rolled him out of sight from the rifle above.

He was already gone. A single tear ran from the corner of his eye. The sight of that clear drop of liquid defined the moment. Harmony cradled her husband's body and wept.

The high desert grew silent. The buzzard tightened its spiral, waiting.

The day's heat rose as the sun reached its peak. Thunderheads built in the west. Flies buzzed the corpses and clotted pools of blood. Beyond those insects, nothing moved but the half dozen buzzards circling in an airborne funeral procession.

No one came down to inspect the carnage. Throughout the day, Harmony had expected the shooters to come check on their victims. She worried that other hikers would stumble onto the massacre and become victims themselves, but she remained the only living human on the sun-blasted trail. The buzzards dropped lower, but wouldn't approach with one of the figures still moving. Dusk arrived, bringing relief from the blazing springtime sun.

Stiff and dehydrated, she released her husband's body and risked a quick peek at the empty ridge above. She kissed Blue's cold forehead and ran a finger along the thin white line of the dried tear.

With a deep, shuddering sigh, she hooked two fingers through her backpack, and swung it over one shoulder. Hesitating for a second, she picked up the Glock. Still cautious, she belly-crawled along the edge of the low rise. Rocks gouged every part of her body that scraped along the trail.

Her elbows, thighs, and knees took the brunt of the abuse. After a hundred yards, her clothes were cut and torn in a half a dozen places. She stopped to dig the rock samples from her pockets. Her crawl resumed, and when her bare legs couldn't take any more cuts and scrapes, she decided she'd had enough.

Hoping she was out of range, Harmony rose and ran in a crouch for another hundred yards without drawing gunfire. The sun winked out over a ragged line of mountains, and she straightened, slipped into the second pack strap, and with the pistol in hand, the only survivor of the attack jogged through the dusk to get help.

* * *

From above, the sniper wearing a *shemagh* head scarf watched through the scope. It would have been an easy shot to bring her down, but then there wouldn't be anyone left alive to tell the story.

Chapter 2

The Devil was beatin' his wife several days after the triple homicide in Big Bend National Park. Chilly raindrops fell despite the bright sun casting my shadow on the rocky ground.

The hikers' bodies had been airlifted by helicopters and the responding law-enforcement agencies were long gone. The .308 Win, 5.56, and 9mm brass followed in route to Washington, along with the plaster casts of footprints and the tire tracks from three four-wheelers.

Since the murders occurred in a national park, the FBI was still in charge of the case. I wanted some time alone to study on what might have happened without the input from them, the park rangers, Border Patrol, or the highway patrol. There are sixteen Texas Rangers in Company E. I told the boys to come on out if they wanted, but they knew what that meant and said they'd be there if I needed 'em.

My wife Kelly and I had a personal stake in the murders. She and Chloe had been good friends since they were in the third grade. Blue and I had gotten to know one another after my bride and I married and we became hunting buddies. Vince was a good enough guy, but we only saw each other when he was home from the service.

Because I knew the victims so well, I stayed back out of the way to let the other agencies complete their jobs. My boyhood friend Sheriff Ethan Armstrong and I visited with Harmony in the hospital to take her statement after the FBI guys finished, but what I wanted was to be on my own.

Major Chase Parker changed my position in the Texas Rangers with a new title after what had become known as the Ballard Incident a few months earlier. My recent Shadow Response Designation was a new concept in Rangering, one that adapted modern techniques with those used by the rough old men who'd protected the Lone Star State a hundred and fifty years ago.

I was no longer attached to one particular district, but now moved about the state, supporting the district Rangers, but operating at my own discretion along the shadowy edge of right and wrong. I knew it'd be a dangerous balancing act, but changing times dictated a new approach.

My horse snorted and I rubbed his nose. Red tolerated it like he always did. Horseback sure wasn't the way I wanted to travel, but the rugged country in the Big Bend region of Texas sometimes required that we use the tried-and-true methods that worked for generations.

I knew why the victims wanted to hike that spring day, even though I'm color-blind. The landscape that disappeared into the distance was the same as what I'd ridden through to the ridge. The hardpan was alive with color in the unusually wet spring. Cactus flamed with yellow blooms. Other flowers that I'd grown up with but couldn't identify to save my life carpeted the rocky country.

Jagged ridges at the higher elevations bristled with piñon and junipers, depending on the elevation, and spread in all directions. Bare ridges in the distance were devoid of timber and reminded me of older men losing their hair. The canyons below were already starting to shadow, worming dark and mysterious with the promise of pitch-black nights if the clouds continued to build.

I tilted the straw O'Farrell's hat up on my forehead and turned away from the murder scene below to scan the area. Black clouds stacked behind the craggy ridge promised another afternoon of pop-up traveling thunderstorms that arced torrents of rain onto the hard ground until they cried themselves out.

The sudden out-of-place echo of automatic weapons bouncing off the mountains sparked a jolt of dread. The hair on the back of my neck prickled, and I shivered as if it were cold. I angled my head, using my good ear to find the source of the sound. Like many hunters and gun enthusiasts, I suffered from "Hunter's Notch," a slight hearing loss on the side opposite the shooter's gun hand.

The firefight I'd been involved in a few months earlier hadn't done my hearing any favors, either, and now I had tinnitus to deal with. The steady ringing didn't block sound, but it remained a constant annoyance.

The best I could tell, the shots came from far away, back toward where I left the truck and trailer. I checked the phone in my back pocket, and as usual, I didn't have a signal. I wondered why I ever toted the damned thing around.

Red pointed his ears toward the west. I trusted his hearing more than mine. "That's what I thought, too."

He snorted what sounded like an agreement. I stuck a boot in the stirrup and swung into the saddle. Red knew where we needed to go and took off toward the pops like I'd reined him that way. I kicked him into a lope and settled back in the saddle as his rhythmic clatter of shod hooves ate up the ground.

We were halfway back to the trailer when I heard the shots again, hard and fast. The echoes bounced off the broken land, and Red prickled his ears each time. I resisted the urge to kick him into a run.

After a while, I realized it wasn't a firefight, unless the guys were in a running gun battle.

The truck was just as I left it, and I had Red loaded up before the shots came again. They weren't any closer than when I first heard them, despite the distance I'd traveled. A single report sounded heavier, sharper. Lighter rounds followed, almost drowned out by thunder from the clouds dumping a curved curtain of gray rain in the distance. I slid behind the wheel and snatched the microphone off the dash.

"Ethan, you there?"

We were supposed to use the codes I learned as a highway patrol officer, but Ethan and I had slipped out of that habit long ago. He came back, but the storms were causing so much havoc I couldn't make out what he said.

"Ethan, I'm at the Lost Mine trailhead. I'm hearing automatic gunfire."

His response was even worse. I pitched the mike on

the seat in disgust and rolled the window down. There still weren't any bars on my cell phone and I tucked it back into my shirt pocket and buttoned the flap.

I pulled onto the gravel road, driving over the rough ground toward the general direction of the gunfire. Two single pops came again, and the sound was stronger.

I got to thinking I was hearing a gun battle between drug dealers. I had no doubt that smugglers called mules hoofed their crap through the desert in primitive packs. Maybe two groups from different cartels found themselves on the same trail.

I really didn't care if they shot one another across the river, but this was my country, and I didn't want their troubles to deal with. I shouldn't have run toward the fight. Most the time, those guys were armed to the teeth, but there was one thing a Ranger didn't do, and that was run away from a fight.

I came upon a two-lane dirt track splitting off the road and stopped to stick my ear out the window. Thunder rumbled again, and I sat there long enough to think the shooting was over until they another flurry came again from closer to the Rio Grande and rose to a crescendo before trailing off. It sounded like *two* automatic weapons this time, followed by reports from the heavier rifle.

My imagination said some poor sucker was holed up and shooting it out with several some*ones*. The recent murders and distinctive sounds of two rifle calibers made me think it might be a second ambush of innocent hikers. Maybe another armed civilian like Blue was fighting back.

Clear tread marks in the rocky soil revealed that someone had recently driven an ATV down the trail. I steered off the gravel road and followed the bumpy two-lane track with the trailer rattling along behind me. "Sorry Red! Hang on back there."

The gunfire came again, but I still wasn't gaining.

It must be a running gun battle.

The phone still said **No Service**, so I checked the radio again. "Ethan!"

Static.

It seemed like I'd been driving for miles before the trail petered out for my Dodge dually at the foot of a steep, rocky ridge. I killed the engine and studied the tire tracks of at least two ATVs heading toward the west.

Dammit. I need to get help and come back.

Not happy about having to back the trailer to some kind of turnaround, I glanced out the window and saw enough open space to make a circle.

One shot.

Then another.

Two more.

Once again my impulses won. Knowing better, I killed the engine and backed Red out of the trailer. Thunder rolled across the Chihuahuan Desert as I stuffed my Winchester into the saddle scabbard and swung aboard. I rationalized that at least he would get me across the rough landscape until I could get a peek at what was ahead. It might be something I could handle alone, or at the very least, I might get high enough for that damned cell phone to work.

If somebody got after me, Red was the perfect way to cut through the country and get away. We took off at a lope as a cool breeze washed over me from the collapsing thunderstorm ahead. Red pricked his ears forward. I let him have his head, and we went to see what was going on.

It seemed like an hour later before I came to the edge of a steep, high-desert canyon. There hadn't been any gunshots for a good, long while, and I wondered if everyone was dead and all I'd have to do was count the bodies.

A well-worn, bright orange ball cap surrounded by several dozen bright brass hulls lay on the ground beside a thick clump of cactus. I reined in and stayed in the saddle, checking the area. Nothing but the cooing of a white-wing dove broke the silence. I figured no one else was around, so I swung to the ground.

Ears flicking, Red sniffed at a trumpet flower shrub, unconcerned. I'd learned long ago to trust the horse's instincts, so I relaxed.

Holding the reins in one hand, I studied the empty brass at my feet. I didn't see any blood, but that didn't mean anything. Footprints in a clear sandy spot pointed toward the edge of the canyon. Stepping close, I peeked over the edge, thinking the cap's owner might be down there.

I tensed at a sudden movement far below, but relaxed when I saw a saw a whitetail deer working its way along the canyon floor. The sun disappeared behind another approaching thunderstorm, and I realized it'd be dark soon and I'd have to ride back without the aid of the stars or moon.

I turned and glanced up at still another ridge high above my position at the exact moment a white-wing dove floating past caught the bullet meant for me. The bird vaporized in an explosion of feathers about twenty yards from where I stood. The impact with the tiny body diverted the projectile enough that it wasn't the center shot that would have blown out my chest. It still punched a hole through the big latissimus muscle under my left arm.

A number of things happened at the same time the rifle's crack reached my ears. Red yanked the reins out of my hand. He spun and took off like a striped-ass baboon at the same time I took a step back to catch my balance.

My foot came down on nothing but air.

I screamed like a girl for the first time in my adult life. Anyone would, knowing they were plummeting over the edge of a canyon rim. The breath caught in my chest and I fell back in time past the strata of millions of years.

Images both blurred then came sharp as a tack as I fell. An upside-down glimpse of the rocky wall included my boots flashing past the heavy clouds off to the southwest. The next time I saw them, they were defined against the blue sky in the opposite direction.

A strobelike image of the sun peeking between clouds and a sweeping gray curtain of falling rain became rocks flashing by. A crisp crack inside my skull hurt worse than the bullet wound when I slammed against the hard surface of the canyon wall's acute slope. Despite all that, I was lucky I wasn't on the virtually straight drop of the nearby Santa Elena Canyon.

I cut a flip and my shoulder smashed hard on the rocks, reversing the spin so that my hip took the next hard blow. I still had the presence of mind to try and stop my accelerating fall. I spread my arms and legs to gain traction on the steep slope. The bottom of the canyon was still a long way down, and I sure didn't want o roll like a meat cannonball, knocking chunks and pieces of myself off on every rock and boulder all the way to the bottom.

It seemed like a month of Sundays before I managed to grab a tough bush with one hand and slide to a stop. *Thank God, I might just make it.*

Rocks jarred loose by my fall continued to rattle within earshot. I waited until everything was quiet before taking a deep breath of relief. Gunshot wound. Check, but nothing felt broken. I wiggled all ten fingers and toes to make sure. Stuff ached, but all was still good.

One foot hung over a big rock and I dug my other heel in. Stable for the time being, with a heart pounding like a jackhammer, I turned loose of the brush.

The scree stretching in all directions broke free and I slid again with the terrible realization my foot wasn't hanging over a rock, but another drop. I grabbed at the bush again, but missed. The dry ground melted away as the dusty flow took me over the sheer edge like a leaf slipping over a waterfall.

"Well, hell."

I dropped again. Nothing but luck kept me upright, and I fell feetfirst.

Kids love the feeling of stepping off a high diving board, but there wasn't anything fun about looking down past the slope and seeing the long dark shadows stretching across most of the canyonland still far below.

I landed in the soft river of fine dirt and rocks that poured into the tops of my boots. I went down again on the steep angle, this time on my rear for another wild ride through the gathering dusk.

Control was impossible, and I dug my heels into the

loose ground, grabbing at everything grabbable. Material tore and my funny bone banged on a boulder and my arm went hot and numb.

I was upside down again before thumping off what felt like a rock big as a hall closet, then it was freefall city. The thought that a storm was coming, but not the one in the distance, was the last thing I remembered.